My Woman
His Wife Saga

My Woman
His Wife Saga

Anna J.

www.urbanbooks.net

Urban Books, LLC
97 N18th Street
Wyandanch, NY 11798

ISBN 13: 978-1-62286-919-0
ISBN 10: 1-62286-919-2

First Trade Paperback Printing November 2015
Printed in the United States of America

10 9 8 7 6 5 4 3 2 1

Distributed by Kensington Publishing Corp.
Submit Orders to:
Customer Service
400 Hahn Road
Westminster, MD 21157-4627
Phone: 1-800-733-3000
Fax: 1-800-659-2436

In the Beginning . . .

Table For Three

Imagine that, imagine that, imagine that, imagine . . .

At five foot two, 136 pounds, dark chocolate skin, and almond eyes, sexy Monica was standing over me topless, in a red thong, and giving me one hell of a show. My girl was popping it like she was trying to get rent money and only had two days left to scrape it up. You would think there was a pole in the center of the bed the way she was rotating and grinding her body to the beat of the music.

My eyes were fixed on hers as she did a sensual butterfly all the way down until the lips of her tunnel kissed my stomach, leaving a wet spot where they landed. She bent over and a tattoo spelling her name in neat cursive peeked out over the band of her thong. She took her right nipple into her mouth and caressed the other as she continued to move to the beat of the music. Her body seemed to shimmer as light from outside landed on her skin.

Stepping off the bed, she bent over to remove her thong, afterward hooking it onto my foot. A dildo magically appeared as she crawled toward me. My legs spread invitingly when her lips made contact with the space behind my right knee. I heard R. Kelly hyping it up with the guitar, making the love of my life sweat just a little.

Well, the second love of my life. While I was laying there, legs spread eagle and playing with my clit, I can't even get into it because I knew I should be at home with my husband and two kids. I could just get up and go, but I didn't feel like the drama and tears I had to see every time I was ready to leave. I knew in my heart that I had no damn business being there in the first place, but I was thinking with my pussy in anticipation of all the wonderful orgasms I would have. Shit at home died down a long time ago, but it wasn't until I found myself lying there looking up at another woman's breasts did the guilt set in.

It wasn't supposed to be like this. I knew I should be at home making love to my husband, but he wasn't producing multiple orgasms like Monica. She does things with her tongue no one has written about yet. She has ways of making me explode that my husband has no idea on how to find that spot, and I can forget about him lasting all night. The five minutes he gives me I can do myself. I need satisfaction that my own hands don't produce, and Monica gives me what I need without any questions.

I don't want to have to tell my partner what I want. After all these years, he should already know what makes me cum. If you're going to hit it from the back, put a finger in my asshole or leave a handprint on my ass cheek. Take it with one of my legs on your shoulder while you use your thumb to play with my clit. While I'm riding, take both of my nipples into your mouth at the same time. Do something besides pound me all hard for five minutes then roll over and fall asleep.

Then, if that wasn't enough, this fool wanted to invite company into our bed. And that's why I'm in this mess now.

It all started about two months before the twins' fourth birthday. It had already been eight months since my husband and I had so much as fondled each other, let alone had any actual sexual contact. He had been on my last nerve about having a threesome with some hoochie he'd met, and I was about tired of hearing it. All I got was five minutes. What was he gonna do? Break it down to two and a half minutes between the both of us? He must have been suffering from too much radiation from sitting up in that news station all day or something. And what the hell was this girl and I supposed to do? She could munch all the carpet she wanted to, but I don't get down like that!!!

Back in the day, my husband and I made love constantly. It was nothing to be bent over the kitchen counter getting served from behind. He would be stroking me from the back with one finger playing with my clit and the other in my asshole, while kissing my neck and talking dirty to me all at the same time. I would ride him in the dining room chair until my legs hurt, and he would then pick me up and lay me on the table, devouring me from feet to head, and not necessarily in that order. He liked for me to hold my lips open so my clit stood right out as he simultaneously sucked on it and fingered me with three fingers the way I liked it.

All of that stopped for one reason or another. It got to the point where this fool started leaving notes around the house, practically begging me to jump on board. One night he tried to show me a picture of the girl, and I just snapped. What part of "no" didn't he understand, the "n" or the "o"?

"Babe, just hear me out," he said, pleading on his knees at my side of the bed. "You won't even listen to what I have to say."

I remembered the days when he would be on his knees on my side of the bed, only my legs would be thrown over his shoulders as his lips and tongue would have me squirming and begging for mercy. But right then, the sight of him was contributing to my already pounding headache.

"James, I done told you fifty thousand damn times that I'm not doing it, so why do you keep asking me?"

He didn't even realize that I was ready to bust him in the head with the alarm clock. Why wouldn't he just go to sleep?

"Because you're not keeping an open mind."

"Would you want me to bring another dick into the bedroom?" I asked.

He looked at me like I was crazy and got up to go lay on his side of the bed.

That shut his ass right up, if only for a second. I was so damn tired of hearing about this Monica chick, I was ready to just go ahead and get it over with. This entire scenario was making me sick to my stomach. What his dumb ass didn't realize is I might have gone along with it just to please him, but I'd be damned if I would be pressured into doing anything I wasn't down for.

"So, is doing it in the bedroom the problem?" he asked in a desperate voice.

"What? Didn't I just tell you I didn't want to talk about it?"

"I'm just saying that if your concern is bringing her into our home I could easily get us a room over at the Hyatt or the Marriott."

"James, how do you even know this girl? What kind of shit are y'all into over at T.U.N.N.?"

I'm guessing this fool couldn't see the big-ass pile of salt on my shoulders. If we were in a cartoon, steam would've been coming out of my ears at that point.

"My buddy Damon hooked it up for me. It's his wife's sister or something like that. They do it all the time."

That only made me wonder what kind of freaky shit her family was into. I don't know too many people just putting their own flesh and blood out there like that.

"What do you know about her, James? This chick could be HIV positive for all we know. There is no cure for that!"

"We would all be using protection," he said as if he was offended. Shit, I was offended he wouldn't let it go.

"Will she be putting a condom around her mouth?" I asked. "Semen and saliva can carry the same shit."

"Here you go taking the conversation to another level. Why can't you just relax and enjoy life for once? It's only this one time."

"What I'm about to do is enjoy this six hours of sleep. Good night!" And with that, I turned my behind over and went to sleep.

Of course it wasn't over. When I woke up, James was in the shower. As much as I hated to go in the bathroom while he was in there, I figured if I could at least brush my teeth, I could shower real quick and be out the house before he had a chance to come at me with some bullshit. I was hoping he wouldn't bring this Monica shit up at 6:37 in the morning because I would hurt him.

By the time I was done brushing my teeth and cleansing my face, James was stepping out of the shower. Through the mirror I peeked at his toned body and semi-erect penis. At the age of thirty-two, standing at least six feet three inches, he still had the body of a college football player. He's definitely well endowed, but what difference did it make if he was only good for five minutes? He caught my eye as he was drying off and a sly smile spread across his face as he covered his midsection with the towel and went into the bedroom. I hopped in the shower and lingered a little longer because it was his morning to get the kids ready.

When I stepped out of the streaming water and into our room, I could still smell his Cool Water cologne. That made me wet instantly, but he'd never know. I'd just as soon please myself than waste my shower on a few minutes with him. After putting my outfit together and plugging in the electric curling iron, I was finally able to sit on the bed and moisturize my skin. Out of the corner of my eye I noticed a single yellow rose on my pillow and a piece of heart-shaped chocolate with "I Love You" printed on the foil resting next to it. I smiled but continued to rub my Happy by Clinque body lotion into my skin.

I loved my husband, and maybe we could talk about this entire threesome thing later.

Surprisingly, he had nothing to say at breakfast. He smiled a lot, and that just pissed me off. Not that I had any conversation for him, but his being quiet made me nervous. At least if he was talking I'd know how to vibe off him. He just sat there smiling the entire time, and that just made me suspicious.

When I started gathering my stuff up to leave for work, he already had my briefcase and files along with my lunch stacked all nice and neat in the passenger seat of my 2003 Blazer. I got a kiss on the cheek, and he even offered to take the kids to childcare for me. Something was definitely up, and I wasn't at work for five minutes before I figured it out. I was looking through the files that I was supposed to be working on over the weekend when a hot pink folder that I didn't remember having before caught my eye. When I opened it, a 5x7 photo of Monica was pasted to the left, and a three-page printout about her was on the opposite side. I was too shocked to be offended.

The pages included her date of birth, zodiac sign, likes and dislikes, a copy of her dental records, last HIV test results, and the results of her gynecologist exam, which I was glad to see were all negative. Her address and phone number were also included, along with directions on how to get to her house from my job off Map Quest. I had to laugh to keep from being pissed because I was sure my husband was going crazy.

If that wasn't enough, further inspection produced a key card from the Hyatt and an invite to meet him and Monica at the hotel restaurant for dinner. A note, handwritten by James, said the kids would be at his mother's house, and I should be at the hotel by seven. I put everything back in the folder and went to my first meeting of the day. I didn't even want to think about that right now, and I had a few choice words for James later on.

When I returned to my office for lunch, I opened my door to at least three hundred yellow tulips crowding my space. On my desk sat a bouquet of tulips and white roses mixed in a beautiful Waterford crystal vase. My secretary informed me that they were delivered only ten minutes before I got there, and the card could be found next to the vase on my desk. I was too overwhelmed to think clearly and mechanically walked over to my desk to retrieve the card. It was in a cute yellow and white envelope to match the flowers, and was written with a gold pen. It read:

> Jasmine,
> You must know that you're the love of my life, and there is nothing in this world I wouldn't do to make you happy. This one time I want us to be happy together. Please reconsider . . .
> Love Forever,
> James

In that instant, I knew I would be at the hotel later. I figured this one time wouldn't kill me, and it might spice up our love life so that it would be like it used to. I hoped I wasn't making the biggest mistake of my life. After gathering my thoughts, I went on with the rest of my day, trying not to think about what I would be getting into later. I had a trial at two o'clock that I had to go to, and on my way there I mentally checked my schedule to make sure I would be out of the office by five and chillin' in the suite by five thirty. That way I could freshen up and put on something sexy for dinner.

I got out of court at four thirty, having had my client's charges dismissed. That made me feel great, and I planned to take the next two days off to celebrate. When I got back to the office, my secretary was smiling at me and holding a vase with at least two-dozen powder pink roses accompanied by another card. She gave them to me and offered to open my office door because my arms were full. When I walked in I almost dropped the bouquet I was holding because I was totally surprised. As if all the yellow tulips weren't enough, my office was now crowded with just as many powder pink and white roses.

"Someone is either madly in love with you or is apologizing. Whatever it is, let me know your secret," my secretary said as if she really wanted an answer. I just turned to her with a smile on my face, stepped to the side, and closed my door. Me and her weren't cool like that, and then wasn't the time to start.

I set the bouquet on my desk next to the one I received earlier. There was nowhere for me to sit, so I walked over to the picture window so I could gather my thoughts while I looked down onto the city from the twenty-third floor. The envelope holding the card smelled like Ralph by Ralph Lauren. That puzzled me for a second because I didn't own that particular scent. When I opened the envelope and pulled the card out, little gold hearts and stars fell from it. The card was from Monica requesting my presence at the hotel later. I was flattered and speechless. Maybe she wasn't that bad after all.

Deciding to head on over, I left my secretary with directions to have all of the ladies in our department come get a bouquet to put on their desks. I wanted my office cleaned out except for the two bouquets on my desk. On my way to my Blazer I called to check up on the kids before stopping at Victoria's Secret for something sexy.

I decided on a cranberry spaghetti strap one-piece with matching thong. The gown was ankle length with thigh high splits on both sides, and the front dipped down all the way to my navel. The back opened to the middle of my back, showing off my curvaceous size ten, even after a set of twins. I purchased a bottle of Breathless perfume and a pair of sandals to match, and then made my way to the hotel.

When I got to the suite, pink and white rose petals decorated every inch of every room and floated in the Jacuzzi on top of rose-colored water. Yellow tulips sat in crystal vases around the living room and bedroom, and Maxwell's *Urban Hang*

Suite played softly in the background from invisible surround sound speakers. A mixture of pink and white rose petals and yellow tulip petals covered the California king-sized bed. A bottle of Alizé Red Passion sat in a crystal ice bucket accompanied by three wine glasses on the end table closest to the bathroom door. On the other table was a glass bowl filled with condoms.

A note was tucked into the mirror in the bathroom with instructions to meet my dinner guests in the dining room at seven o'clock sharp. It was already six thirty judging by the clock on the bedroom wall, so I stepped up the game as I showered, dressed, and did my hair in record time, all while not disturbing the romantic setup. I was walking into the dining room at five of seven. The waiter sat me in a cozy booth away from the other guests with a glass of Moet, a yellow tulip, and a powder pink rose courtesy of my husband and Monica. At exactly seven, my dinner guests walked in.

James was sharp, dressed in cream linen slacks with dark chocolate gator shoes that perfectly matched the button-down shirt with different shades of browns and tans swirled through it, compliments of Sean John fashions. His wedding band glistened and shined from the door, and the light bounced off it from all the way across the room. I could smell his Cool Water way before he reached the table.

Monica was equally impressive in a short, champagne-colored one piece that showed off perky breasts and fell just above her knee. The bottom of her dress had that tattered look and it accented her long, chocolate legs. Her toes peeked out of champagne stiletto sandals, and her soft, jetblack curls framed her face. Her makeup was flawless, and she smelled sweet.

I stood up as they made their way to the booth and couldn't stop staring at them. When my husband and Monica reached the table, he gave me a soft, lingering kiss on my lips that made me wet instantly. He hadn't kissed me like that in months. Monica gave me a soft kiss on my cheek, and James made sure we were both seated before he took his seat.

Before we could start conversing, the waiter was at our table with appetizers. We were served stuffed mushrooms and

Caesar salad with glasses of Moet to wash it down. I glanced over at my husband periodically and couldn't believe the thoughts I was having. For the first time in months, I wanted my husband the way a woman wants her man, and I couldn't wait to get upstairs.

"Did you get the roses I sent you?" Monica asked between small bites of the crab-stuffed mushroom she was eating. She had the cutest heart-shaped mouth that made you want to kiss her. Her tongue darted out every so often to the corners of her mouth to remove whatever food or drink was there. That turned me on and made me wonder how her tongue would feel on my skin.

"Yes, thank you. They were nice."

"Did you enjoy the tulips?" my husband asked, his eyes never leaving me. "I know yellow is your favorite color."

Tonight, he looked different, kind of like he was in love with me all over again. His eyes twinkled with mischief, and his lips begged for me to kiss him. I wanted to so badly.

"Yes, baby, I did. Thank you."

"You're welcome, baby. How'd your day go?"

Me, Monica, and James made conversation over the smoked salmon, wild rice, and mixed vegetables we were served for dinner. Before dessert was served, James and I slow danced to "Reunion" by Maxwell as I watched Monica from the dance floor. She swayed from side to side in her seat, never taking her eyes off me. I don't know what she did when I wasn't facing her, but when I did she looked me right in the eye, her facial expressions telling me what I had to look forward to.

As we danced, my husband held me close, his mouth on my ear singing the words to the song. His warm hands felt good on my bare back as he made small circles, massaging me. I truly felt like this was indeed our reunion because it had been a long time since we'd been like this. I closed my eyes and tightened my arms around his neck, enjoying the feel of him in my arms and me in his.

Slices of double chocolate cake waited for us when we got back to the table. I couldn't touch mine because I was ready to go upstairs. James fed me and Monica his cake off the same fork, and that only made me more excited. I wanted to get this party started, but I went with the flow because I didn't know what they had planned.

"Are you ready for ecstasy, baby?" my husband asked me after we finished dessert. Instead of answering, I grabbed both of them by the hand and led them out of the dining room.

Anything Goes

Once we got into the elevator, James pulled us into a group hug, our heads resting on each of his shoulders. We looked at each other curiously, probably thinking about how far the other would go. Before I could react, Monica leaned over and kissed me, and it wasn't a peck on the lips, either. She slid her tongue into my mouth, allowing my taste buds to sample the chocolate cake left on it from dessert. Her lips felt soft as she sucked on my bottom lip, then my top, causing a tingling sensation to shoot down my back, straight to my toes, and finally resting warmly on my clitoris.

I could taste a hint of her cherry lip gloss when my tongue touched the corner of her mouth. A moan escaped my lips when her hand made contact with the left side of my neck, pulling my face closer to hers. I opened my eyes to look at her facial expressions while she kissed me, and to my surprise, she was already watching me. I blushed, a little embarrassed at being caught, but she let me know it was cool by kissing my eyelids. She kissed the tip of my nose and went back to my lips while my husband made small circles on my back with his fingertips. Her kiss was slow and sensual, and thankfully not wet and sloppy like most men do. She allowed me to lead, then I allowed her to teach me what she knew.

My right hand found my husband's erect penis just as we were approaching the fourteenth floor. When I stepped back to adjust my hand around his shaft, the elevator suddenly stopped and the lights went out. We were all stuck on stupid for about thirty seconds. We were on our way to erotica beyond our wildest dreams and the damn elevator stopped. You talking about pissed! I finally got up the nerve to go through with this wild night and there I was stuck in a hot-ass elevator. Oh, how I was *so* not in the mood for that.

"James, do something," I said while slightly hyperventilating. We were stuck between the thirteenth and fourteenth floors, and I wanted out.

"Baby, just calm down. I'll call the service desk to see what they can do."

While James was on the phone, I sat down in the corner to slow my heart rate and collect my thoughts. I didn't know how long we were going to be stuck, and that was not the place to pass out from lack of oxygen. I was hoping to still be in the mood when we got out, because at that moment I wanted to be off the elevator and in my bed.

Just as I leaned my head back against the wall, I felt a pair of warm hands parting my legs. I still heard James on the phone, and my body tensed up because I couldn't believe Monica was trying to sex me at a time like this. Cumming was the last thing on my mind, and I was almost certain everyone else felt the same way. Before I could protest, Monica had my thong pulled to the side, and her was tongue stroking my clit. Her tongue felt hot on my panic button, and the way she used her fingers made my knees touch the elevator walls instantly.

She took her time moving two fingers in and out of me while she sucked, licked, kissed, and played havoc with my clit trapped between her lips. My body shook involuntarily because I was trying not to explode. I didn't want to moan aloud while James was on the phone, but it was killing me trying to hold it in. She held the lips of my cave open and her tongue snaked around inside me, my walls depositing my sweet honey on her tongue. For a second, it felt like we were the only two people trapped in that hot box.

"Okay ladies, the attendant said we'd only be in here for a—damn," when James hung up the phone and looked over at our silhouettes in the dark, he was speechless. I guess the sight of his wife being pleased by another woman shocked him.

His back was to us the entire time, so it had to have been a pleasant surprise to see Monica and me the way we were. James never could do more than one thing at a time, so it didn't surprise me that he didn't pay us any mind until he was done with his call.

He stood back and watched for a while, taking in the sights and sounds of what was happening.

With the little bit of light coming from the call box, I could see James massaging his strength through his pants. He squatted down behind Monica, lifting her dress up over her hips, exposing her heart-shaped ass. My eyes had adjusted to the dark, and even though I couldn't clearly see what was happening, his outline said it all. Monica was in the doggie style position with her head buried between my legs. James had inserted his fingers into her walls just as Monica did to me only moments earlier. I could see James maneuvering his body so that he could taste her. In the meantime, Monica was pulling another orgasm out of me.

She moaned against my clit from my husband pleasing her. The more James pushed and pulled on her, the more intense her pleasing me became. I scooted forward so that I could lay flat on the floor. Monica stood up and positioned herself over me. She pulled her French-cut panties to the side and placed her pussy lips on my mouth. I just imitated what she did to me, switching back and forth from kissing and sucking her clit and sticking my tongue inside her. James was inside of me, stretching my walls to fit him.

He stroked me slow, teasing me with just the head before sliding it all in. His thumb created friction on my clit and before we could stop it, I exploded on his length and Monica exploded in my mouth. We were about to switch positions when the lights came on and the elevator started moving. James pulled out of me still rock-hard, making it a little difficult to pull up the zipper on his pants.

When the elevator door opened, the attendant and the security guard were waiting on the other side. They tried to apologize, but we just rushed past them and scrambled down the hall to our suite so we could finish what we started. We didn't think about the fact that they could probably smell sex in the air, and I don't think we really cared.

Upon entry to the room, Monica went to run hot water into the Jacuzzi because the water that was in there had gone cold. I sat on the side of the bed, anxiety covering me like a blanket. I couldn't believe what I'd just done and what I was about to do. I was excited and scared at the same time. I was excited because I was finally letting go of my inhibitions and stepping outside the box, but scared because I didn't want to disappoint my husband.

I'll never do this again, I thought, but I did want him to enjoy this night of pleasure.

Monica came out of the bathroom in her bra and panties. I was hesitant about looking her in the eye because I knew my cheeks were red from blushing. We were all silent, not wanting to be the one to say something first. James changed the CD in the stereo to a slow-jams mix he put together. When R. Kelly started crooning, "Come to Daddy," Monica started doing an erotic dance in front of the full-length mirror. James leaned back on the dresser to watch the show, and I just sat there with a shocked expression on my face. She danced like she'd had ballet lessons, but with just enough eroticism to make you think she might have been wrapped around a pole in a strip club once or twice.

As she got closer to me, I scooted back on the bed to keep her at arm's length. What we did in the dark elevator was cool because I couldn't see it, but now we were in a well-lit room with my husband able to see everything. I wasn't sure if I wanted to go through with it, but when I looked over at James stroking his length and gazing at us I couldn't stop. Just the fact that he'd been hard for more than five minutes was amazing.

The look on my face screamed, "help" as I looked from James to Monica. Monica advanced toward me slowly, and James smiled as he watched us work. I was now up against the headboard with my legs up to my chest. When Monica reached me, she took my feet into her hands and started to massage them one at a time. I was as stiff as a virgin on her first night, and Monica did her thing to help me relax.

She took my toes into her mouth, one at a time. My moans escaped involuntarily. Her soft lips traveled up my thighs until they rested against my pelvis. Her tongue dipped in and out of my honey pot. She held my lips open with both hands, exposing my now wet pearl to my husband.

"James, can I taste it?" Monica asked my husband in a husky voice. I looked over at him to read his face. It showed nothing but excitement.

"Go ahead and make her cum," he responded in a deep, passionate voice. His hand moved at a slow, lazy pace up and down his erect shaft. A hint of pre-cum rested on the tip of his penis, and I motioned him over to the bed so I could taste it.

He disrobed on his way over, his body looking like he should be on the cover of *GQ* magazine. Monica had her full lips pressed against my clit, causing me to squirm and breathe heavily. James stood beside the bed with his chocolate penis standing straight out. I didn't hesitate to wrap my lips around him, taking as much in as I could without choking.

James fondled our breasts simultaneously while trying to maintain his balance as I gave him head. Monica held my legs up and kept her face buried in my treasure chest. Our moans were bouncing off the walls, drowning out the music that was playing. If there were people in the suite next to us, I was sure they heard everything.

Monica moved back off the bed and pulled me with her. James lay down in the middle of the bed on his back, his erection pointing at the ceiling. I straddled his thickness like a pro, dipping all the way down until my clit touched his pelvis then coming back up until just the head was in. James leaned up on his elbows and took my nipples into his mouth one at a time. Monica had my ass cheeks spread so that her tongue could make acquaintance with my asshole. I was having orgasms back to back like I used to when me and James first met. I was damn near about to pass out from exploding so much.

We switched positions in order to relax a little more. Monica put on a strap-on vibrator with clitoral stimulators around the base. I looked at her like who did she think she was using that on. She took James's place in the center of the bed and motioned for me to get on top of her. I looked at her and my husband like they were crazy.

"James, I am not getting on her like that. She done . . ." the mood was changing quickly, and Monica was looking frustrated. Ask me did I give a damn. Some shit just ain't meant to be tried, and this was one of them.

"Baby, it's okay. It'll feel just like the real thing. Trust me on this one," James said to me in a calm, soothing voice. I wasn't buying it.

"And what are you going to do with that?" I asked, referring to his erect penis.

"You'll see, and you'll enjoy it. Just trust me."

He gave me a reassuring look as he led me to the bed. I closed my eyes and got on top of Monica, doing to her what I did to my husband. It was feeling good, and I really got into it. When I bent over to kiss Monica, I felt a warm liquid oozing down the crack of my ass. My husband held my back so that I couldn't move, and I could feel him inserting a finger into my forbidden place. I tensed up automatically, and he whispered to me to try to relax.

I don't do back shots, and my husband knew that. I wanted to get an attitude, but what they were doing felt good. I reminded myself that it was only one night, and I tried to relax myself so that my husband could join in the fun. I wondered how he was going to fit it in because he was definitely blessed in the dick department. He's long and thick, with a big mushroom-shaped head that I knew was way bigger than the hole he would try to get it into. Ten inches in the ass was something to scream about.

"James, I don't think I'll be able to take it back there, baby," I whispered. "You're too big."

I was hoping he would have second thoughts when he heard how scared I was, but that wasn't the case.

"Jasmine, I won't hurt you, baby. I'll take my time, and I'm using this so you'll be okay." He held out a bottle of KY Warming Liquid for me to view.

"Won't it get too hot back there?"

"You'll be fine, just relax," Monica responded before taking my nipples into her mouth. A moan escaped from my lips, totally catching me off guard.

I tried to relax as James eased himself into my back door. Lord knows it was killing me, but I stuck in there. He slowly pushed the head in, which was the most painful part. It felt like he was ripping me a new asshole, and tears gathered at the corners of my eyes, threatening to fall and land on Monica's forehead. Once he got in as much as he could comfortably, he began pleasing me with long, slow strokes. In combination with Monica pushing and pulling on the bottom, I was going crazy from the new feelings I was having. When James pulled out, Monica pushed in, causing me to lose my breath on more than one occasion. James reached around my waist and teased my clit while Monica held my lips open for him. His other hand fondled my right nipple while Monica's mouth warmed the other one.

I didn't know whether I was coming or going. Some time during the mix, the pace quickened and we were going at it like animals. Monica sat on the lounge chair with vibrator in hand, watching me and James become one. He held me by my ankles, pushing my legs all the way back, my knees touching my ears easily. He was driving his penis deep in me with slow strokes, and I never wanted him to stop.

"I'm cumming, baby," I said to my husband between inhaling and exhaling. "Cum with me."

James slowed it down, and we looked each other as our orgasms played out. My legs wrapped around him tightly until our rapture subsided. Monica looked spent as she too was exploding along with us. James pulled out of me and rested with his head between my breasts while we caught our breath. The session we just had was the best thing since sliced bread.

"I'll meet y'all in the Jacuzzi," Monica replied as we reluctantly untangled ourselves from each other. At that moment, I wanted Monica to leave so James and I could enjoy our weekend alone, but I didn't want to be rude. I later found out that was mistake number one. The red light was practically blinking right in front of my face, but for reasons beyond even me, I went with the flow instead of stating my wishes. She served her purpose, and it was time for her ass to go.

We joined Monica in the Jacuzzi a little while later. James popped open one of the Alizé bottles, and we sat back and chilled. *Friday After Next* was playing in the DVD player, but I paid it no mind. I wanted some more of my husband, but with Monica there, I knew it would be a group thing. We relaxed a little longer, and before the movie was over we scrubbed each other clean and dried ourselves off.

James had another movie playing in the room while we fell back on the huge bed. He told us of our plans for the next day. Monica would only be with us for tonight. After breakfast, she would be heading home, leaving me and James to enjoy the rest of our mini-vacation, which was cool with me because I was ready for her to leave anyway. I didn't see why she had to stay the entire night. I mean, he could have easily put her in a cab and sent her on her merry way. I started to suggest that to James, but I didn't want to spoil the mood. He also made mention of a shopping spree and a couple's spa treatment we would be attending at the hotel.

I half watched the movie, and half played back what went down earlier. Out of the corner of my eye, I took in Monica. She was definitely a cutie, and I could see why James thought her to be the perfect candidate for our evening of adventure. She had skills and knew what she was doing, but I couldn't help but wonder how much it took for her to be here. *Had she and James hooked up before?* I tried not to entertain the thought, but it was bugging me. Then, on top of all that, I was wondering if I could maybe hook up with her at a later date. She was phenomenal, and I wanted to see exactly what she could do. Maybe it was just the liquor talking, but I was definitely thinking about meeting up with her soon.

We gave each other full body massages and orally pleased each other until we drifted off to sleep. The next morning we showered together and had breakfast over conversation of our activities the previous evening. When James got up to use the restroom, Monica just kind of stared at me. For some reason I felt a little uncomfortable.

"So, Jasmine, did you enjoy yourself last night?" she asked as if she really wanted to know. I answered after watching her tie the stem of a cherry into a knot with her tongue.

"Yeah, it was different. I had fun," I said nonchalantly. I did not want to have this conversation with her. I was still thinking about having her one on one, but I wouldn't dare approach the subject.

"Well, if you want us to hook up under more private circumstances, you know how to contact me."

"I'll do that."

Just then, James joined us at the table. He thanked Monica for a wonderful evening and put her in a cab to go home. I saw the envelope he slipped her but decided not to comment on it. We went back to our suite to change, and then we went on the shopping spree. We only had three hours to shop because James scheduled our spa time for early afternoon.

We made it back to the hotel with ten minutes to spare before we had to go and get pampered. Instead of shopping, we ended up going to a miniature golf course. After that we had lunch at the Hibachi, a five-star Asian bar located on Delaware Avenue.

All too soon our weekend was over and it was time to go back to work. We had a good time just hanging out and being stress-free, and we got into some hellified sex sessions that left me speechless and smiling every time. No more of the five-minute poundings going on. We made love for hours. Sometimes it was slow, sometimes it was heart-pounding fast, but it was more than five minutes, and that's what mattered.

Before we left I made sure everything was packed and we weren't forgetting anything. I sat on the lounge chair to catch my breath and enjoy the room for a second longer. James was in the restroom making sure he packed all of our toiletries. When he came back in the room, he kneeled in front of me and put his head in my lap.

"Jasmine, I am so happy you are my wife. This weekend was wonderful, and I appreciate you going through with our plans. You have made me very happy," James said while rubbing the backs of my legs.

"I'm glad you enjoyed yourself. We needed to get away for a second," I responded while fondling the wavy texture of his hair.

Instead of responding, he reached under my skirt and pulled my panties to the side. I couldn't protest because he was already tasting me. We went at it for another hour and were late checking out. We had to pay a fee, but it was well worth it.

Mistake Number One

Once James and I got home, things were better than ever. For the first time in months, we made love on a daily basis, and sometimes three or four times a day. In the past two months, we've met up for quick sessions during lunch, and we'd sneak off into the garage late at night while the kids were sleeping to add a little spice to our lovemaking. James sent me tulips at least twice a week, and we made it a must-do to have dinner out on Saturday nights just so we could have our time together. We made acquaintance with the kitchen table on more occasions than I can remember, and life was good.

I didn't think much about Monica, and for me that night was a distant memory—a thing we never spoke about once we left the hotel. I never let on to how much I really enjoyed myself and that I was seriously contemplating doing it again. Monica made my skin feel like it was on fire. I love a nice stiff one, but her soft lips could be a wonderful replacement.

The only thing that kept me from going through with it was my job. I didn't want anyone at the firm thinking I was a "swinger" or anything like that, and a scandal of that caliber could ruin everything James and I worked so hard for. We had our children to think about, and the high-priced vehicles that we were pushing around town. We were used to living ghetto fabulous, and I couldn't see anything that petty taking it all away, no matter how wet my pussy got thinking about her.

I pushed that thought out of my head almost as soon as I thought of it and tried to refocus on my most troublesome case. After a few hours in the office trying to wrap up my long, tiring day, my secretary buzzed me to let me know I had a delivery. I didn't think anything of it as I circled around my desk to pick up what I assumed to be a package. When I opened my office door, a beautiful bouquet of powder pink roses was waiting for me.

Speaking of the devil, I thought to myself.

I thanked my secretary and picked up the bouquet to take it to my office. Before I could close the door, my secretary called out to me.

"Mrs. Cinque, I have to say I admire you," she commented with a straight face. I was puzzled as to what brought that about.

"Why is that?"

"Because you bust your behind around here day in and day out, and to me it seems to go unnoticed. Then your husband does little things like send flowers to let you know he's thinking about you, and it all seems to be okay. My son's father would never do that."

I didn't know what to say, and my face must have said it all. The funny thing is she's been my secretary for the past two years and I can't even think of her name at this moment. I wanted to say something positive, but my mind drew a blank. I could smell Monica's perfume coming from the card in the bouquet, and I wanted to hurry and open it.

"You'll know when you've found the right one. Believe me," and with that said I closed my door and went to inspect my card.

Monica has beautiful, curvy handwriting that matches her perfectly. The way you write says a lot about you, and her script is just as sassy as she. She wrote a short para-graph inviting me to have dinner with her in her home, without my husband. She said that the night we spent together had been on her mind, and she wanted to show me pleasures I could only dream about. I was shocked, but pleased at the same time. That night we shared was nice, the girl had skills; I had to give it her.

Now my dilemma was this: we shared that one night on some threesome type stuff, but wouldn't me and her one-on-one make me a cheater. If she could make me feel like I felt that night, I thought I may just have to see her again.

At the end of the note she included her address and phone number, and asked that I confirm our meeting by five thirty this evening. I looked at my watch and it was already 5:20. I didn't know what to do, but curiosity got the best of me, and I decided to go for it. We were only having dinner, but my walls were already contracting. Monica can turn you into Spider Woman in no time, and I was ready to go there. Now, what do I tell James?

Before I had my story together, I was already dialing the number to the studio, and hoping I could come up with something by the time he answered the phone. I already decided to call my brother so that he could watch the kids until James got home, and I promised myself that I would not stay over there too late. As soon as I exploded, I would leave.

"Thank you for calling The Urban News Network. This is Cindy, how may I direct your call?"

Cindy is the overly polite receptionist over at the station.

"Hi Cindy, can you connect me to James, please?"

"Sure, Mrs. Cinque. Hold for a second." She put me on hold and Anita Baker crooning about being in sweet love flowed through my receiver. I felt bad for a second because I loved James, and even though Monica is the same sex as me, it was still cheating. I started to back out and just go make love to him instead until he answered the phone.

"Thanks for calling The Urban News Network, who am I speaking with?" James answered with his deep voice. It sounded like things were a little hectic over there, and he was a little agitated.

"Hey, sweetheart. How's your day going?"

"Hey, baby. I was just about to call you. Our system shut down unexpectedly and we've been trying to get it together for the past hour. I might be here all night."

"Baby, just relax. You're the best they have over there, and whatever the problem is, you can fix it. That's why you're the Director of Engineering."

"Thanks babe, but I know we had plans to dip off later, and I don't want to disappoint you."

"Sweetie, it's okay. I was calling to tell you I would be running late because I'm trying to finish up with the paperwork from the Campbell case, and Trish just made partner, so we were going to get a few drinks afterward to celebrate." I felt like shit. Those lies rolled off too easily. Well, they weren't total lies. Trish did make partner, but that was like last week and technically I was working on a case, but I was putting it to the side to go bump coochies with Monica. If James even thought I was still seeing Monica, he'd probably die. I know I would be pissed if he were stepping out.

"Tell Trish I said congrats. I'm sorry about tonight, and I'll make it up to you tomorrow, okay?"

"Okay, baby. Don't stress too much. It'll be fine."

"I know, boo, I know. I love you. Be safe."

"I will, and I love you too. Talk to you later."

We blew each other a kiss then hung up. I called Monica next to confirm, and she told me that dinner was almost done, and that I could come on through. I straightened up my desk and put everything in order so that I could bust it out when I came in tomorrow morning. I hate clutter, and never left my desk a mess. Afterward, I freshened up in my private bathroom and made my way down to Monica's to enjoy dinner . . . and whatever dessert came with it.

I was having all kinds of doubts on my drive over to Monica's house. I knew we would sleep together; that went without saying. My only problem was if James ever found out there would be some serious explaining to do. He would have questions, and I knew I couldn't possibly give him an honest answer. How do you tell your husband his sex is the bomb, but you prefer the feel of another woman's lips to his? That wouldn't go over too nicely.

When I pulled up to her house I wasn't the least bit surprised. She lived in a cute, two-story, Victorian-style home that sat way back off the street. Her house had a beautiful wrap-around porch set off by a well-manicured lawn. There was a wooden swing off to the left that was perfect for cool summer nights. Her windows sported pastel pink shutters to match the trim on her white house. She had several rose bushes sprinkled around her yard, and her address hung from a powder pink mailbox on a black address hanger. It was written in script with little roses around the border. Monica definitely loved pink flowers.

By the time I parked my car and began to walk up the path to her door, she was already standing there. Monica was a lot shorter than I remembered. A cute little petite something. She had on a halter dress that stopped just under her ass and showed off her perfect legs. Her hair was done in one of those spiky styles like Halle Berry would wear that showed more of her pretty face and bright eyes.

She greeted me with a tight hug like she really missed me and invited me into her home. The inside was just as breathtaking. She had a sunken living room decorated in pastel yellows, pinks, and blues. The fireplace was to die for, and I could almost picture us lying in front of it on a cold winter night touching and tasting each other.

There was a spiral staircase with steps made of clear marble with rose petals embedded in them. The railing was gold plated with a vine design wrapped around it with crystal roses appearing to bud from it. She had pictures of couples making love in various positions on top of pink rose petals with gold leaves. The flowers really stood out because the couples were sketched in black and white. It wasn't until I took a closer look that I realized that Monica was the woman in the pictures. That left me speechless.

Through the back door I could see her swimming pool, and I had to get a closer look. When I looked in, a portrait of Monica in a pink teddy could be seen painted on the bottom. I wanted to hate, but I was living good so there was no reason to complain. I just wanted to know what she did for a living to be able to afford all of this. I wanted to see the upstairs, but she suggested we eat dinner before it got cold. I mean, hell, we would be up there later anyway.

We had polite conversation while we enjoyed our meal. I was a little nervous and resisted the urge to jet several times. I felt so bad about being there while James was stressing at work, and the fact that I lied to him about where I was made me feel even worse. Monica kind of picked up on my mood and suggested we continue our conversation on the couch. I'm sure she was thinking it was something she did, but that was far from the case.

Once we got comfortable on her sofa, we resumed conversation while she rubbed my feet. It felt so good I could hardly talk. Before I knew it, my head was resting on the arm of the sofa and I was almost asleep. For a second I thought I was at home. I felt James massaging my feet turn into him moving his soft hands up my leg. Then I'm like *How did his hands get so soft all of a sudden?* When I opened my eyes, Monica's hands were high on my thighs, my prize not far away. Surprisingly, I didn't flinch or pull back. I almost wanted her to hurry up because I knew it was going to be good.

She stood up, I assumed, to take her clothes off. She walked toward the stairs, leaving pieces of clothing along the way. It wasn't a lot because she didn't have much on to begin with. By the time she got to the third step, she was standing in nothing but a thong, and I was like *damn*. She looked even better than the last time. Her chocolate skin made you want to kiss her all over, and her nipples were just a shade darker than the rest of her body, putting you in mind of a Hershey's kiss. I was hesitant at first, but I followed her up the stairs and into the master bedroom.

I stood inside the doorway, taking it all in.

Monica turned on the stereo, and I felt like I was listening to a late night smooth grooves session on the radio. She walked over to me and took my hand, leading me to the bed. No words were needed as she slowly undressed me, kissing the body parts she revealed on the way down. My head was screaming, "get the hell out of here", but the rest of my body was whispering, "girl, you about to explode, so chill."

She walked me up to her bed and told me to lay flat on my stomach. I did what I was told and closed my eyes, listening to the melody in the background. She straddled me, her warmth and wetness seeping into my pores, and causing a puddle of my own nectar to form under me. The oil she poured onto my back was cool on my already hot skin, but her hands warmed it up in no time. The room smelled like chocolate instantly. Monica was good at what she did, causing all of the tension in my body to leave almost instantly. James became a distant memory as I moaned under the hands of this woman.

She kissed the center of my back as she massaged me, her juice caressing my skin from her pressing her clit against me. She ran her hands down between my thighs, her thumb entering my tunnel then pulling out quickly. She traced the outside of my lips with her well-oiled finger, and I moaned like she done put something in me. I didn't even remember turning over, but Monica was kneeling on my right side massaging the front of me, her tongue feeling hot on my sensitive nipples. I tried to stay cool, but my back arched to meet her lips. I was about to cum, and we hadn't done anything yet.

Monica tied a silk scarf around both of my wrists and attached both arms to the headboard. Now, I was like *hold the hell up.* I don't even let James tie me down, but Monica didn't give me time to protest. She was between my legs and on my clit before I could say anything. It was a good thing my hands were tied because otherwise they would have been holding her head while I glazed her face completely.

She took her time "inspecting" me. Monica held both lips open, leaving room for her tongue to explore all of me. My legs were spread into a perfect V while she sucked and licked on me. She put her tongue so far up in me you couldn't have told me she didn't touch my cervix. I moaned like crazy and tried to catch my breath because she was pulling orgasms out of me left and right.

I felt something cold slide inside of me, and almost lost it completely. On the side of the bed I noticed amongst the bottles of oils and body butters sat two long and thick dildos made of ice. She must have had three, because one was inside of me driving me crazy. I was exploding all over it, almost ashamed because I was messing up her bedspread. She sucked on my clit and worked the ice in and out of me until there was only a small piece left. Silly me thought she would just toss it out. Monica put the ice in her mouth and pushed it into my cave using her tongue. She would push it up and suck it out, causing a whole 'nother explosion until it was gone.

The fact that my thighs had her in a serious headlock didn't seem to bother her or mess up her rhythm. She continued to push and pull on my clit until I was screaming for mercy, opening my legs wide so she could move her head. She leaned up to look at me, her wild hairstyle still in place. She licked my essence off her lips seductively while her middle and forefinger still played around my insides. My walls were gripping her like she had a penis and soon I found myself exploding again.

"Now, I'm going to let you go," Monica said in a soft sexy voice, "but only if you're ready to go there."

"Go where?" I asked already knowing the answer. She just gave me one of those "stop playing with me" looks before leaning over to the table next to the bed.

"If you don't know I guess I need to use another one of these," she said referring to the ice shaped penises she had sitting on the side. I knew for sure I couldn't take any more of that.

"No, I got you. You can untie me now."

She motioned for me to scoot down to the middle of the bed. I did as I was told with my arms still stretched out. She stood over me with her legs on either side of my head. Slowly she bent her knees until her lips rested on mine. My tongue found her opening instantly. She untied one hand and undid the other one once I captured her clit between my lips. I could see Monica's hands on the wall helping her to keep her balance over top of me.

I was barely able to reach the table, but managed to snag one of the ice pieces without missing a beat. I continued to stimulate her clit while teasing her with the ice just at the opening of her tunnel. She moaned in appreciation as I teased her with just the head before sliding it all in. I positioned the ice-cold sculpture on my chin and she rode my face like she was riding a real dick with me capturing her clit in my mouth when she came down, and her pulling it out on the way up. The ice melted quickly from her warmth. Her juices flowed effortlessly. I stuck my index finger in her asshole for good measure, and my girl went wild.

She stood up off my face and placed herself softly on my stomach, her explosion running down my sides and forming puddles on both sides of me. She rotated on me with her eyes closed, moaning until it was over. I rubbed her clit with my thumb until her shaking subsided and she was able to open her eyes and look at me. I blushed a little at what just went down, partly because I didn't think I had it in me to please another woman. The bullshit orgies I had in college never got this intense, and I never had to use so much of my imagination. I never wanted to. I was always on the receiving end and never had to put much into a performance, so this was something new.

Don't ask what made me do it, but for some reason I looked across the room toward the dresser and the clock caught my eye. I thought my eyes were playing tricks on me until I sat up in the bed.

"Does that clock say ten thirty?" I needed her to tell me because I didn't want to believe it.

"Yes. Why, are you in a rush?"

"Hell yeah! I didn't tell James I would be out this long. He's going to kill me."

"It's still early. Don't you want to finish up in the shower? I have some treats in there waiting, and . . ."

"Did I not just tell you I had to roll? I ain't got no business being here in the first place. My husband is going to kill me."

In the midst of me running around the room trying to find the damn light switch and a washrag, I thought I heard Monica sniffling. In the middle of my panic performance, I stopped to look at her. She was curled up in the middle of the bed crying. Even though the room was semi-dark, I could see her shoulders move up and down with every sob. I started to just leave her like that, but my heart wouldn't let me do it. I guess, for some odd reason, I cared about her. Dropping my head in defeat, I walked over to the bed to see what was wrong with her.

"Monica," I called out to her softly as I made my way up the steps to her bed, "sweetie, what's wrong?" I sat and listened to her, but on the real I wanted her to hurry the hell up. I had to get to the west side in twenty-three minutes and four seconds.

"Nothing . . . I don't want you to go."

"I have to go sweetie, but I'm sure there will be other times."

"You promise?" she asked as she sat up on the bed and wiped her nose with the sheet.

"I promise, but right now I need to get washed so I can go home and tend to my family. Can you help me do that?" I asked, hoping my gentleness would get her ass out the bed and some light in this room.

She got out of the bed looking like a helpless little girl, and I tried not to give a damn. I just wanted to hurry up and get home. She finally turned the light on and allowed me to see what was what. While she ran the shower, I gathered my clothes from the floor and tried to press the wrinkles out the best I could with my hands.

Without saying anything, she pulled me into the bathroom and into the shower, washing me quickly but thoroughly. She tried to go down on me in the shower, but I gently reminded her I didn't have time. Once we were done, she dried me off and gave me a cotton sweat suit she'd purchased for me to put on along with a new pair of sneakers to match. She said she figured I would need them since my clothes were a mess now.

I thanked her as I got dressed in record time. I practically ran to the door after I put my belongings into the bag my new outfit came in, but for some reason I couldn't find my panties. I told her if she found them to hold them for me, and I rolled out. When I got in my car, I could see Monica standing in the window waiting for me to pull off. I got home before James, and was in the bed a half hour before he came in. I tried to play like I was just waking up when he came into the room.

"Hey babe," he said to me after kissing my cheek, "how was the celebration?"

"It was cool. I only had a few wine coolers then I came on home," I lied to my husband with a straight face. I felt horrible because he looked like he'd had a rough day at work while I was out busting nuts with Monica across town.

"That's good, baby. Can we talk in the morning? Right now I need to close my eyes for a second and get some sleep."

I turned over on my side so he could lie in my arms. He was asleep almost instantly. I was awake thinking about what happened with Monica for hours. The sex was off the chain, but the entire scene at the end threw me off completely. I didn't really know what to make of it, but decided it wasn't worth the effort as I finally drifted off to sleep.

No More, No Less

For the next two months, I tried to avoid Monica. I felt absolutely horrible about how things went down on that night, and even worse when James woke up the next morning wanting to make love. I felt like he was getting sloppy seconds, and the night before did indeed get sloppy. The entire time James was in me I kept thinking about the ice sculptures and Monica's warm hands. A few times I almost slipped up and called her name out when James thought he was making me cum. I mean, I came, but it was because I was thinking about Monica's tongue roaming all over me. Not because he was banging my back out.

I received flowers and Thinking of You cards constantly from Monica and James, and it began to get a bit overwhelming. James would just pop up at the office unexpectedly, and I would have to hide the numerous cards Monica sent me and make up excuses as to where I was getting all the roses from. He hinted that maybe he knew Monica was sending them to me, but he never came right out and said it. The two of them competing for my time was exhausting, and I needed to get away from both of them for a while. I was seriously considering packing up me and my kid's stuff and going to Mexico. The two of them together were nerve-racking.

One day at the office, Monica and James must have been playing tag-team on the phones because no soon as I hung up from one the other would call, and vice versa. I'm like, *What the hell? I'm trying to get some work done, and these two are acting like fools.* It was like they knew what was up, and were trying to outdo each other. But in actuality, all they were doing was giving me a damn headache. During one conversation with Monica, shit got tense real quick and I had to hang up on her.

"Why don't you ever tell me you love me back? I show affection toward you twenty-four seven, even when you're at home playing house with James and the crew. Are you saying you don't care about me?" Monica asked like she honestly expected me to give her an answer.

Monica had been crying in my ear for the past twenty minutes about my so-called "lack of affection." How much affection did she want? I went down on her more than I did the person I was married to. She didn't even have to ask for it; it was a given. James had to damn near beg me to suck his dick, and even then it was only until he got it up enough to slide it in me.

"Monica, we have been over this so many times already. I don't love you, I'm not in love with you, and *James and the crew* are my family. They come first, and you act like you don't know that," I said after taking a deep breath. I hated when she got like that.

"That's stuff I already know, but . . ."

"Then why do you keep asking me do I love you if you already know the answer?"

"Because I know you have to care about me a little bit or else you wouldn't keep coming here," she said through her tears. I hated to hear her cry, and I was trying my best to console her so that I could get off the phone. I had a court date in a half hour, and I did not have time to be dealing with this emotional-ass Virgo.

"Monica, look," I said through clenched teeth as calmly as possible, "I care about you baby, okay? You know that already! I just don't understand why I have to constantly remind you of my feelings. It's too much at one time to deal with, and honestly you're starting to push me away." I tried to sound stern as if I was talking to one of my kids. She needed to understand the situation she was in. She was the sidekick in this play—no more, no less.

"Jazz, I'm not trying to push you away. I just need to know that you care about me. I need to hear you say it every once in a while."

"I care about you, Monica. I really do. Do you believe me?"

"Yes, I believe you," she said between sniffles as she tried to get herself together.

"Okay, now dry those tears and straighten up that pretty face. I'll make it up to you later on tonight." I figured if I knocked her off real quick, she would chill for a bit.

"Will you stay the entire night?"

"Monica . . ."

"Okay, okay. I'm sorry, I know you can't stay. Can you at least stay until eight?"

"Sure, I'll leave work at six and come chill with you until eight, okay?"

"Eight thirty," she pleaded from the other end.

"I'm about to change my mind," I warned her over the phone line.

"Okay, eight it is. I love you."

Instead of replying, I just hung up. This girl was going to drive me into a white jacket by the time all of this was finished. I gathered up my documents for court and threw on my leather jacket so I could head out. Just as I was reaching my hand out to turn the knob the phone rang again. I started not to answer it because I thought it was Monica again, but I went on and took the call anyway. My secretary was on lunch, so I had no way of intercepting the call.

"Jasmine Cinque's office," I said into the phone, praying it wasn't some bullshit on the other end.

"Hey baby, how's your day going?" my husband inquired. I wanted to tell him I had a lovesick stalker calling me every five minutes to make sure I didn't stop caring about her, and the reason why she was acting that way was because I was face to face with her clit damn near every night. Then I'd come home and tongue kiss him after giving my children a kiss on the cheek. Instead, I opted for the logical answer.

"It's going okay. Right now I'm on my way out the door to the Campbell trial. What's good?"

"Me and you, dinner at the Hibachi at six tonight."

"Tonight? Can we do it tomorrow?" I panicked a little because I just told Monica I would chill with her, and I knew if I didn't go I would be on the phone another three hours tomorrow trying to explain to her that my husband came first no matter how much sex we had.

"Baby, I already made the reservations," James responded sounding kind of down.

"Okay, baby. I'll meet you there." That gave me enough time to talk to Monica after I got out of court because I knew I would need at least an hour to calm her down.

"Well, actually you're scheduled to take the rest of the day off. Your boss cleared your schedule for the rest of the afternoon after your trial. I have a couple's spa set up for us, so I will be at the courthouse waiting for you. See you there. I love you."

He hung up before I could say anything. I didn't have time to call Monica because I would be late for my trial for sure messing around with her. I ran out to my jeep, and once I got into the flow of traffic I tried to call her. Her answering machine kept picking up, and I didn't want to be inconsiderate and just leave a message. I tried calling all the way until I got into the courthouse, and once I walked into the courtroom I had to turn my cell phone off. After concluding my meeting with the judge, I left out to meet James.

I was not prepared to see what I saw when I walked out of the courthouse. Upon leaving the building and trying to find my cell phone, I looked up to see Monica and James talking by his car. I knew why James was there, but why did Monica show up? I approached them cautiously because I didn't know who would cut the hell up first.

"Baby, you remember Monica, don't you?" he asked me after he embraced me in a bear hug. Monica was shooting me dirty looks over his shoulder, and I pleaded with my eyes for her to keep cool.

"Yeah, how have you been?" I asked reaching out to shake her outstretched hand.

"I've been good. Thanks for asking," she offered, leaving my hand dangling in mid air. I pulled my hand back, a little hurt by her actions.

"Baby, she was just telling me about a young lady she's been dealing with that has her head over heels. I ran into her out here on my way to get you. She was on her way to buy her flowers for their date tonight."

"Really?" I replied with a dry throat. I didn't know what type of shit Monica was trying to pull, but today I swear she would get her ass whipped.

"Yeah, she's a lawyer, too. You might know her," she replied trying to sound innocent. I wanted to black her eye on the spot.

"I might," I replied trying to change the subject. "James, don't we have reservations?"

"Yeah, we do. Monica, it was nice running into you. Be safe and I hope to see you soon."

"Yeah, both of you do the same," she replied after shaking James hand again. Maybe it was just me, but that sounded a little like a threat. I wanted to call her on it, but I didn't want to draw attention to our situation.

James walked around the car to open the door for me, and I moved to put my belongings in the back before I got in. When I looked up at her, I could see a single tear drop down her cheek before she turned and walked away. I felt like shit, but what could I do? Again, she was the sidekick in this play—no more, no less.

I was distracted during dinner and couldn't really enjoy the massage treatment at the spa because thoughts of Monica were weighing heavily on my brain. Every time James asked me what was on my mind, I told him I was thinking about the Campbell case so he wouldn't have too many questions.

Monica was just wearing me down. It's not like I was in a relationship with her, and I tried to reason with myself for treating her the way I did. Who thought a couple hundred orgasms would turn into stalker-mania? I should have known she had a screw loose when she cried that first night, but my dumb ass kept going back.

The girl was like a drug, though. She had a warm bath ready most evenings when I got there.

Whether I got in or not depended on how she acted when I walked in. Yes, I said walked in, because she gave me a key to her place. I know I shouldn't have taken it, but she started crying then, too. She would often have a meal cooked, or would feed me grapes or strawberries. She treated me like a queen, something James didn't do.

Now, don't get it twisted. James was doing well in the dick-Jasmine-down department. He was keeping up his stamina, and it seemed as though the days of the five-minute brother never existed. He was good to me. We went out often, and he surprised me with little gifts here and there. James gave me all the material possessions I could hold and more.

Monica, on the other hand, spoiled me. She catered to my every sexual need without me having to instruct her on what I wanted done. She always had a different way of pleasing me that amazed me every time. She gave me backrubs after my many long work hours, and made sure I was fresh and clean before I left her home. All of that came with a price, of course. Some days she would cry and holler at the top of her lungs because she wanted me to stay. I guess going with her to Vegas for the weekend that one time made her think I could stay like that on a regular basis.

A few times she got on the floor and wrapped herself around my legs so I wouldn't go. I had to practically drag her across the floor before she let go, and when she did she would lay right where I left her and cry. The next day I would go over and kiss her rug burns left from me having to drag her across the carpet the day before, and we would be right back to square one.

Emotionally, she was way too much for me to handle. I wanted out, but I also wanted to stay in. It's hard to explain, and every time I thought she would act right, she would start to cut up again.

I think her seeing me with James that day might have made her snap. She was truly in love with me, and it was a shame because I wouldn't allow myself to love her back. It wasn't fair to my husband or our children, and I just wasn't having it. I just hoped she wouldn't start leaving dead rabbits on my doorstep or playing on my phone or whatever it is stalkers do to get back at their mates. I wasn't in the mood, and I had to find a way to end it . . . for a little while, at least.

After dinner, James and I went to the movies and only ended up seeing half of it before I started riding him in the back of the nearly empty theater. We were into the film, or at least I was. James kept kissing me behind my ear and fondling my breasts through my shirt. At one point he reached between my legs and stroked my clit until he had to kiss me to keep me from moaning too loud. There were only about twelve of us in the theater, but we were the only ones sitting in the back.

To make up for my stank attitude at dinner, I removed his fingers from between my legs and placed them in my mouth to remove any juices from them. Then I tongue kissed him so that he could taste it because that is a major turn on for him. While doing so, I removed his erection from his pants and began to stroke him softly. I ended the kiss to wrap my lips around him, and his head met the wall as soon as my tongue met him.

I traced the head of his penis before taking him into my mouth completely. He touched the back of my throat with no effort, and I made sure to keep his testicles warm in my small hands. He held me by the back of my neck, pushing me down on him, and I silently thanked God for giving me skills, because an amateur baby-drinker would have choked.

I released his hold on my head and straddled him with my back facing him. I sat all the way down on his length, only lifting up a little before he was back in me. He held me by my waist as he met me stroke for stroke until he exploded inside me. It was the best five minutes I ever had. Afterward, he wiped me as best he could with the few napkins we had from the popcorn, and instead of letting the movie finish, we got into the car to go home. On the way home we stopped the car and parked behind a Dunkin Donuts where he bent me over the hood and handled his business. We continued our session in the shower and finished up in the bedroom where we got it on for like two hours. By morning I felt like I had ran a triathlon, but it was worth it.

I got up early and made breakfast while James was taking a shower. Me and the kids were at the table eating by the time he came downstairs. He looked tired, but thoroughly satisfied as he kissed me on the lips before taking the seat across form me.

"Oooooh, Mommy and Daddy kissin'," my four-year-old daughter Jaden said, covering her mouth in a cute giggle. Jalil, her fraternal twin brother, just giggled and continued to eat his French toast sticks.

"That's because Mommy and Daddy love each other, ain't that right, honey?" James asked after giving Jaden a kiss on the cheek and Jalil a pound. We were like the Cleavers in there that morning.

"Yep," I replied nonchalantly. I was itching to call Monica and was trying to hurry them out of the house.

"Daddy, can you take us to school?" our son asked as he crammed eggs into his mouth. I was just about to ask James that very question, but it sounded a lot better coming from Jalil.

"Sure, buddy. I'll drop you off," James said as he stood up to gather his belongings. "Last one to the car is a rotten egg."

Both of our kids jumped up, neglecting the rest of their breakfast, and ran to their rooms to get their jackets and back packs. While they were upstairs, James stooped down beside me. He just kind of looked into my eyes like he was trying to read my thoughts. I looked back, not wanting to seem like I was nervous about anything. He looked like he wanted to say something, but instead kissed me softly on my lips. I was just about to slip him some tongue when the kids came back into the kitchen.

"They kissin' again," Jaden tried to whisper to Jalil as they walked around the table to the door. James smiled at me and pecked me on my lips one final time before standing.

"Give Mommy a hug so we can go," James instructed our children as he took one last piece of bacon off the table. They both hugged me around the neck and kissed my cheeks. I kissed and hugged them back, and I could hear Jalil tell Jaden that you got cooties from kissing as they walked out of the door. James was going to have a time with them this morning.

Before leaving out for work, I decided to go ahead and call Monica up so she could say what she had to say and get it over with. I tried to prepare myself for the tears I knew would come, but her tears made me weak. I couldn't think straight and hold a level head when she was hurting. Although I came at her strong, it tore me up on the inside to see her like that. I was determined not to fall for her, and it took everything in me to hold it down. I had two kids to think about, and my career was not to be messed with. James was also the love of my life, and

I married him for better or worse. Something like that could snatch everything away from me, and that wasn't happening.

I had an hour and ten minutes before I had to be at work, so I decided to call Monica and get it over with. I knew I would need at least a half hour to deal with her. I got comfortable on the loveseat before I made my call, and decided that I would just get right to the point and let her know we couldn't see each other anymore. I reasoned that she had to be tired of me canceling on her all the time, and I was tired of the entire scenario anyway. I couldn't swing two lovers, and I knew my best bet was to stay with my husband.

When I called her, she picked up on the first ring. I didn't have time to practice what I was going to say, and she caught me off guard a little.

She didn't sound too upset, and that had me shook. If anything, she sounded too damn cheerful.

"Hey, Monica, it's me," I breathed into the phone. I was hoping to make a clean break, and didn't want her to start getting all hysterical on me.

"Hey, Jazz, what's good? What can I do for you?" I had to look at the phone for a minute to make sure I was talking to the right person. This didn't sound like the Monica I knew.

"Well, about yesterday . . ."

"Don't sweat it; it's cool," she just cut me off on some real nonchalant shit. I didn't know whether to be happy she was chillin' or ask her what the hell was going on.

"Okay, well, if you want I can make it up to you tonight."

"It's cool, no worries," she just kind of mumbled into the phone. Something was definitely up. I figured I might as well break the news to her so that we could be done with it. She didn't seem interested anymore anyway.

"I get off work at five tonight. Can we talk then?

"Actually, I was just about to call you to give you your dismissal papers."

"Excuse me?" *I know this chick isn't dissin' me.* I was starting to get an attitude.

"I've decided I'm done with this situation. After yesterday I realized it just wasn't worth it. So, you're dismissed." And she was serious.

"Are you kidding me?" I asked in disbelief. I knew this is what I wanted, but I didn't think it would go down like that.

"No, and actually I have to tend to my company, so I'll see you around. Don't worry about calling me back. After today this number won't work." Then she just hung up.

I must have sat on the couch looking stupid for like ten minutes. I knew I wasn't just handed my walking papers by needy-ass Monica! Then she had the nerve to get ignorant with the shit. I called back to give her a few choice words, but when her phone rang the operator informed me she had blocked my number. I tried calling from my cell phone, and that was blocked too. I had a numb feeling all over my body that I couldn't quite shake as I readied myself to leave for work. In a sense I was glad it was all over, but I was a tad bit salty because I didn't think it would end like that.

Camera Shy

It's been one hell of a day. My morning started off all wrong, and it's been going downhill ever since. James woke up with a pissy attitude, and has been for the last four months. It's almost like him and Monica had the same shit for breakfast, because about three weeks after me and her parted, his attitude went from sugar to shit. Every time I asked him what was up, he gave me short, one-word answers and some bull about being stressed out at the news station. I tried to be peaceful, but I didn't feel like the aggravation, so I just stayed away from him.

What pissed me off the most was I would still try to be courteous and make him breakfast when I fixed the kids and me some, but he would walk in the kitchen, kiss the kids good bye, and leave like I didn't even exist. I asked him on a couple of occasions what the hell his problem was, and he would just act like he didn't hear me say a word to him. So I just said "fuck it," and let it be.

I started to sleep in the guest room, but since me sleeping next to him made him miserable, I made sure to lay my head there every night and stayed with my ass on his side of the bed for good measure. I would throw my legs over his and elbow him in his ribs just to be smart, knowing damn well I was nowhere near sleep and it just pissed him off. When he would finally get out of the bed to go to the bathroom or something, I would stretch out in the middle so he would only have the edge to sleep on when he got back.

Instead of his stubborn ass asking me to move over, he would ball up on the very edge so he wouldn't have to touch me, and I would move closer to him so he had no choice. After a while he would get so frustrated that he would either lay on the floor beside the bed or go into the den and rest because he claimed it was too cold in the guest room. Who cared? If I had it my way I would pack the hell up and be over there with Monica in a heartbeat, but this wasn't television, so it wouldn't go as smoothly as that. I didn't want to, but every so often I would find myself thinking about Monica.

One day I wasn't even paying attention and was just driving home. Well, I thought I was driving home, but when I looked up I was sitting in front of Monica's house. Since she played me, I decided I wasn't going to deal with her anymore, but deep down I really did care about her. I just couldn't leave my family out of nowhere, and I don't think she understood that.

I started to just pull off when I noticed her porch light come on. I didn't want her to think I was a Peeping Tom or anything like that, so I started to put my Blazer in drive. For some reason my foot wouldn't step on the gas. I tried to be out, but my body wouldn't let me go. Before I knew it, she was down her steps and looking through the passenger side window.

I rolled down the window and looked at her. *She's even prettier than I remember,* I thought, and all of the good times we had flooded my mind. We looked at each other for what felt like an eternity before I got out of the jeep and walked around to where she was. Without any hesitation we stepped into each other's arms, and my tears flowed instantly. I cried because things were a mess at home and I felt powerless in trying to fix it. My heart hurt because I hurt her, and to my surprise I wasn't ashamed to admit that I was in love with her. I had been for some time, but I still couldn't say it.

"Let's go in the house and talk for a while," she offered as we stepped back from each other.

"Sure, let's do that," I responded through watery eyes and a weak smile. I didn't even realize I cared this much about her until we came face to face, and I hoped we could come to some kind of understanding before the night was over.

Her home was still beautiful, and I felt at peace when I sat down in her living room. Just like old times, she sat at the other end and gave me a foot massage while we talked. I didn't want to end up with her head between my legs, so I kept my thighs tight so that she wouldn't get any ideas. I was trying to clear my heart of some pain, and I really needed her to listen.

"So, do you think he's cheating on you?" Monica inquired while she worked her magic on my calves. Who knew someone with such soft hands could get a firm grip the way she does? I felt like putty in her hands, literally.

"I never even thought about it. Out of nowhere he started acting all crazy like the mere sight of me was killing him. A few times he was back to his usual five minutes, but it was only in the morning. Then when it got to be every time we had sex I asked him what the deal was."

"And what did he say?" she asked, sounding concerned. Meanwhile, her massage had found its way halfway up my thighs, and her fingers were damn near dipping inside me.

"He didn't say anything. He just gave me a dirty look and walked out of the room."

"Hmm, I don't know what to say about that. You know I would never do you that way."

"Is that so?" I asked just to be smart. I was trying not to go there, but she pushed me into it.

"Basically . . . My love for you is unconditional. I just wish I could get the same in return."

"If it's like that, why did you brush me off the way you did?" That was the million-dollar question I'd wanted to know the answer to for months.

"At that point I was just tired," she responded with a sad look on her face. I waited for her to continue, but she just went on with her massage.

"Okay, do you care to elaborate?"

"Well, even though I knew you had a family already, I still hoped that it could just be you and me exclusively. I know James is wonderful in the bedroom, but I pay more attention to your needs than he does. You never have to worry when it comes to me and satisfaction." She had a point there.

"Monica, I know all that, and that's why I love you. I just need you to understand that. What's wrong?"

Tears were threatening to fall from Monica's pretty eyes, and I had no idea as to why.

"You said you love me. Do you know how long I've been waiting for you to say that? I didn't think it would ever happen."

"Monica, I love you. I just need you to understand that I have a husband and kids at home. I just can't up and roll out like that. It's not just my life at stake here."

"Jazz, I know that. All I'm asking is that we get to see each other more often. James wouldn't know. He would think we're just hanging out. I just need you to be around."

"Monica, I wish it was that easy."

I didn't want to love her, but I did. Now I was all confused and I didn't know what move to make next. Who thought that me, Jasmine Cinque, would ever love someone of the same sex?

"It can be if you would just try it. The least you can do is think about it. That's all I'm asking you to do."

"Look, I'll think about it, but you have to promise to give me time to do just that. Give me room to make decisions, and don't crowd me like you usually do. All that does is push me away."

"I can do that. Just keep loving me."

"I will."

She kissed me softly on the lips while her hands explored the rest of my body. I was dripping wet by the time her fingers made contact with my clit, and I wanted more. Usually she did me first, but tonight I felt like getting into trouble. I pulled her thong to the side, and motioned for her to lie back on the couch. She put one leg over the back of the couch, and the other on the floor as I made myself comfortable between her legs.

I inserted two fingers into her and sucked on her clit softly the way she liked it. She grinded her opening into my face, and her body shook as she released herself on my tongue. That was amazing because I hadn't been down there that long. She was moaning like crazy, and just to make it up to her for being nasty toward her, I pushed her legs up so that they were touching her chest and dipped my tongue into her asshole until she exploded again. She had to practically beg me to stop, and I did after she had her fifth orgasm.

Monica got up off the couch on wobbly legs and asked me to follow her upstairs. I thought we were going into the bedroom, but she walked passed that door and went into the one at the end of the hallway. When she opened the door and flicked the switch, the room seemed to glow from my viewpoint. Upon entrance I saw that she had several cameras set up ready to take pictures. The room was all white, with a few photos here and there.

"Take off your clothes, and lay right there," she said pointing to a large area rug in the center of the room.

"Monica, I am not in the mood for taking pictures," I said, a little irritated. Shit, I was ready for back-to-back orgasms. We could play "photographer" another day.

"Just a couple, I promise. These are for my private collection so I can look at you when you're not here."

"Let me end up on the Internet, and see what happens," I said to her as I disrobed and made myself comfortable on the floor.

"Panties too," she said, pointing at my thong.

"I thought I could get away with that," I smiled sheepishly as I took them off and tossed them where my clothes were laying.

"Now, I want you to relax. Look seductive, as if I'm tasting you right now. Play with yourself and cum for the camera. The flash is off so it won't distract you. Just act like I'm not even here."

I started out leaning up on my elbow and stroking my clit. I held my lips open with my thumb and middle finger while my forefinger dipped into my cave and teased my clit. My eyes were closed. My head rolled back. Thoughts of James kept trying to surface, but I blocked them out and pretended my finger was Monica's tongue.

In the background I could hear Monica make comments on how I was doing, and she got so close a few times I thought she took a picture of my uterus or something. I could feel the camera lens press against me. I spotted a bowl of wax fruit and vegetables on a table in the corner, and walked over to see what I could use. Selecting and oversized cucumber, I stretched back out and continued my journey. Using the cucumber made for some very interesting pictures.

"Let's take this to the shower."

I got up without saying a word and followed her to her bedroom. She was still snapping pictures as I bent over to turn the shower on and then fixed my hair in a bun so it wouldn't get wet. After adjusting the water temperature, I stepped under the steady stream and began to seductively lather my body with the loofah that was resting on the side. I sucked on my own nipples, moaning in the process. She was moaning too, but she never put the camera down.

After a few more shots she joined me and we devoured each other until the water got cold. Monica dried me off and laid me on the bed, and I fell asleep instantly when my head touched the pillow. I only planned to sleep for a little while, then I would go home. I knew taking the photos was a bad idea, but I wanted to make her happy. I didn't think she would use them against me, but that just goes to show how much you really don't know a person. I woke up to her kissing me on my stomach an hour later. Stretching to get the kinks out, I smiled down at her as she made her way down toward my feet.

"Sleep well?" she asked, helping me sit up on the side of her bed.

"Yes, I did. Thanks for asking."

I got up and noticed that my clothes were folded neatly in the lounge chair by the door. I walked over and started to get dressed. Once again I couldn't find my panties, and had to wonder what was up. *Was this an invasion of the panty snatchers or something?* It was like I was losing a sock in the dryer or something.

"Monica, have you seen my panties? They're not over here."

"Yes, I put them away for safe keeping."

"I need to put them on. I can't go home without panties on. James will know I was out doing something I had no business doing."

"I need them. That's all I have of you when you're away."

"That's fine, but every time I come here you keep them. You must have at least ten pairs of my underwear. How many memories do you need?" I was still getting dressed while we were talking, minus the undergarments. I just knew I needed to get home, and I didn't have time to argue.

"Are you mad at me?" she asked like she was about to cry.

"No, sweetie. I'm not mad, I just want you to keep what we talked about in mind."

"I am. I just wish you could stay."

I gathered my suit jacket and hair barrette and made my way downstairs. She followed behind me slowly and I waited impatiently by the door although my face didn't show it. I wanted to scream for her to move a little faster, but I didn't want to hurt her feelings. When she got to the door she had tears on her cheeks, and I wanted to drop my bag and never leave, but I had to go.

"Monica, don't do this to me. I need you to be understanding."

"I'm fine, I just miss you already."

"I'll be back, and I'll call you when I get home. Just don't cry, okay?"

"You do love me, right?"

"Yes, Monica, I love you."

"Okay, drive safely."

"I will, and I'll call you."

She watched me until I got to my car. I waved at her as I pulled off and jetted home to be with my family.

I said I didn't want this, but for some reason I couldn't walk away. She wouldn't let me. An old saying that my grandmother used to say to me came to mind as I went well past the speed limit on the expressway: *The first time you hurt me, it's shame on you. The second time, it's shame on me. All the times after that is plain foolishness.* I felt like a fool too. I knew that all this would blow up in my face sooner or later. What you do in the dark will come out in the light whether you want it to or not.

When I got home, James and the kids were in the den watching *Finding Nemo* on DVD. I kissed the kids on the cheek and said hello to James. He gave me a weak response, never taking his eyes off the television. I wasn't in the mood for his bullshit, so I went on upstairs and hopped in the shower. When I came out, he was already in the bed reading a magazine. I tried my best to ignore him as I moisturized my body so I could put some nightclothes on and chill. I saw him peeking at my naked body, and I also saw him rise to the occasion. *He better go to the bathroom and get to whacking, because ain't shit poppin'.*

I stepped into my knee-length chemise and climbed under the covers. Turning my back to him, I chilled on my side and closed my eyes, thinking about how I was going to deal with Monica. I almost didn't hear him talking to me until he repeated his question for the third time.

"What did you say?" I asked with my back still facing him. I wanted this to be quick and done with.

"I asked how was work?"

"Fine," and left it at that. He still wanted to talk, and I felt like we were playing *Jeopardy* with all the questions he was throwing at me.

"Is the case coming along okay?"

"Yeah."

"What's with the short answers?" he said, a tad agitated. I didn't even give a damn, and told him just that.

"I've been wondering that same thing for the past four months."

"I told you I was stressed at work."

"That's the same excuse I have then."

"You weren't at work. I called there six times."

"And, what? You're checking up on me now?"

"No, it's not like that."

"Then what is it like? You've been giving me your ass to kiss for months. Now all of a sudden you care about my well-being? James, please tell that shit to someone who gives a damn."

"I do care, I've just been going through stuff."

"I tried to help you."

"I know that, and I apologize. I just don't want to lose you to someone else."

"Like who, James?" I started to sweat a little because I thought maybe he found out about me and Monica, but I wasn't going to be the one to say it first.

"I don't know who, but I need to know that it's just me and you."

I turned to face him and asked with a straight face, "Have I ever cheated on you before?"

"No, but . . ."

"Then I have no reason to now."

"Are you sure?"

"Are you? Usually when you start pointing the finger it's you who's doing it."

"I would never do that."

"Neither would I."

"Then how come we haven't been having sex lately?"

"Because you've been acting shitty. That five minutes you dishing out I can do myself," I regretted it as soon as it left my lips.

"So, is that how it is? Is that what you think of me?"

"James, it's not like that."

"If it wasn't like that, you wouldn't have said it," he responded while he put on the sweat suit he had on earlier.

"James, why are you leaving?"

"I just need to clear my head. I'll be back. The kids are still watching the movie, check on them in another half hour."

I was left speechless with a dumb-ass look on my face as he walked out of the bedroom. I heard him get in the car and pull away, and I resisted the urge to jump in my Blazer and go after him. I wanted to, but I couldn't leave the kids by themselves, and by the time I would've gotten dressed and got them to the neighbor's, he would be long gone. Besides all that, I didn't want the neighbors in my business. I just sat on the bed and thought about the last couple of months and what our future held. At this rate it didn't look too bright, and I was hoping our vows, *for better or worse,* held up.

How It All Went Down . . .

Playing With Fire

James pulled up in front of Monica's house after riding around in circles for two hours. Just like Jasmine, he had no intentions of ever seeing Monica again. The creeping they had been doing for the past four months had started to wear him down and his relationship with Jasmine was suffering. Taking all of that into consideration, he walked slowly up the path to Monica's house. Standing outside the door hesitant to ring the bell, he finally leaned on it until she answered. He had no business being there, this he knew. He felt terrible, but the things his wife said made him feel even worse. He knew that if no one else in the world could make him feel wanted, Monica would.

When she opened the door, a pleasant smile spread across her face. She didn't expect to see James this evening, especially since she just had his wife earlier. Standing in front of him in crotchless, French cut boy-shorts and three-inch stiletto heels, she waited for him to stop staring at her exposed breasts and make contact with her eyes before she said anything.

"What do I owe the pleasure of seeing your handsome face this evening?" she purred in his ear as she ran her hands up under his shirt and across his nipples. James tried to act like he wasn't fazed by her actions, but his evident erection spoke volumes.

"I needed to get out of the house. Jazz is trippin' again," he said, remembering his reason for being out that time of night. His erection faded to nothing as he stood with his head bowed down, waiting for Monica to invite him in.

"Really?" she responded as if she hadn't seen Jasmine since the courthouse incident. "Want to come in and talk about it?"

"Yeah," he said stepping into her living room, brushing against her to get by.

Monica already had her mind set on getting some before he left and made sure that he knew it too. Before he knocked on the door, Monica was upstairs entertaining Sheila, Jasmine's secretary from the law firm. Neither Jasmine nor Sheila knew about each other, and that made for a perfect playing field for Monica. With Jasmine she got her cake, James gave her the ice cream, and Sheila was the cherry on top. It would make for the perfect sundae if she could get them all together at one time.

They sat down in the living room and she removed his sneakers before placing his feet in her lap and giving him a foot massage. He went into detail about what happened with Jasmine and how their sex life was next to nothing since he had been dealing with Monica. He went into how he didn't think he could continue the affair with Monica because he needed to make his home life work.

"Honestly, I don't know what to do," he said to Monica in a defeated voice.

"You know what your problem is?" she asked him softly. She didn't want to ruffle any feathers because she wanted to at least sex him one more time before he decided to stay away. She honestly didn't think they would hook up again after the threesome she talked him into having with Jasmine, but it kind of just worked out that way. He dropped three thousand on that night, and the money just kept coming. When he gave her the money for the threesome, that was supposed to be it, but months later he still found himself paying for her services.

"My problem?" he responded, sounding annoyed. "Why do I have to have a problem?"

"James, relax. I'm not saying a problem like that. I'm just going to point out what you're doing wrong. Shall I continue?"

"Please do!" he looked like he was ready to leave. After all, he hadn't come there to hear what he was doing wrong; he knew what he was doing was unacceptable.

"The issue is your sex life has changed at home, right?"

"Yeah, she doesn't do what you do. Not to say that she's not good, but with you it's always something new."

"Does she have sex with you every time you want it?"

"Yeah, even when she doesn't," James said, wondering where this conversation was going.

"Are you still doing the same things for her that you used to? And don't lie," Monica warned him. Her massage was now up to his calves, and James was having a hard time concentrating.

"I like to think so."

"The thing is, James, when a man cheats on wifey, he tends to neglect her because he's concentrating on his new toy. What you don't realize is your wife can do the same things I do, probably better if you took your time with her. Don't change up your sexual habits with her because all you can think about is how good I'll fuck you. That's exactly how wives always find out that men are cheating. You change, and that's not good."

"So what am I supposed to do?" he asked, wanting desperately to make things right.

Monica was good to him. James couldn't deny that, but Jasmine was his wife, the mother of his kids, his soul mate. He couldn't see messing up everything they'd built together over a booty call.

"After you're done here, go home and make up with your wife. Don't rush it, but let her see that you're changing. You can have your cake and eat it too. You just have to know when to do it."

"I understand that, but are you going to be okay with us not seeing each other for a while? I don't want to hurt you."

"I'm cool with it. I have someone else occupying my time right now. Want to go upstairs and unwind before you go home?"

"Do you think I should?"

"I don't see why not. You won't be here for a while, so you might as well get one for the road."

Monica stood up and walked toward the stairs. James followed like a little puppy dog, feeling kind of guilty on the inside. He started seeing Monica months before he brought Jasmine in on the threesome. He told himself that after they got together in the hotel that night he would be leaving Monica alone, and he did try. Monica just had a way of making you feel like you were missing out on something when she wasn't around.

He looked at the drawings on the wall as they walked by, and stopped when he noticed one of the men in the drawings looked like him. In the drawing he was laying on his back on pink roses, and Monica was riding him with her back facing him. Her head was thrown back and her arm rested on his chest for support. Monica's hair was long in the drawing and a rose rested at her temple. James didn't know what to say; he just kind of stood there gazing at it.

Monica made her way to the top of the steps and yelled for James to hurry up. He tore his gaze from the drawing and made his way up the stairs, a little puzzled at how he became a part of her collection. He knew Monica was an artist and that she drew black art and sold it for high dollars. He also knew she was a professional photographer and took pictures for a number of agencies. He never thought he would be in one of them, and was going to question her once they got in the bedroom.

When he walked into the bedroom, all thoughts of him questioning Monica left his mind as he laid eyes on Sheila. He remembered her face, but couldn't think of where he'd seen it. He was also stunned because he didn't know Monica had company. He wished he would come home one day and find Jasmine in his bedroom with a beautiful woman. He also knew Jasmine didn't get down like that, and that she only dealt with Monica that night to make him happy. James didn't have the nerve to ask her to do it again.

"Hello, so glad you could join us," Sheila said before she kneeled down on the side of the bed between Monica's legs. Monica closed her eyes and leaned her head back, enjoying the tongue-lashing Sheila was giving her. James undressed immediately then walked over and joined them on the bed.

He kissed Monica's lips briefly before finding his way to her chocolate nipples. Sheila's mouth had already wrapped around his erection, and he almost exploded instantly when her tongue ring made contact with the head of his dick. He remembered thinking she was better than Monica before he laid back on the bed, allowing Monica to sit on his face.

Monica held her lips apart as James flicked and sucked her clit until she came in his mouth. Standing up on the bed she motioned for him to move back so that his entire body was on the bed comfortably. Switching places, Monica straddled his length and Sheila sat on his face. The two women kissed and fondled each other until they all exploded together. James's seed dripped out of Monica when she stood up off him.

In the shower he was beating himself up on the inside because he never ever had sex with her without protection. He never bothered to ask Monica if she was on any type of birth control and feared it was too late to inquire now because he knew she would be offended. Sheila and Monica scrubbed him clean and helped him dress so he could get home.

"Where are my boxers?" he asked Monica while Sheila was putting his socks on his feet.

"I put them away for safe keeping," she responded nonchalantly as she pulled his undershirt over his head. Sheila already had his pants halfway up and was waiting for him to stand so that she could finish the job.

"Every time I come here you keep my boxers. What do you have now? About ten or twelve pairs?" he asked, a little annoyed. He could not go home without any underclothes on, and hoped his credit card was in the car so he could stop and get some on the way back.

"That's all I have to keep you close to me," Monica responded as she pushed him toward the front door.

When they got downstairs, he turned to get one last look at her. He gazed into her eyes and then down at the rest of her body, stopping at the red lace boy-shorts she had on. Kissing her one last time, he looked down at her underwear again, trying to remember if he'd seen them before.

"You know, my wife has a pair of panties just like these," he said while pulling lightly at the band around her waist.

"She has good taste," Monica said, smiling up at him.

"Yeah." James looked at the door and then turned to face Monica again. "About that drawing on the wall . . . I don't remember posing for it."

"You didn't. I remembered one of the nights you were here, and decided to put it on canvas. Is that okay?" she asked, daring him to say otherwise. If he had said it wasn't cool, she would have sent it to Jasmine in the mail to let her know he had been there. Lucky for him, he didn't have a problem with it.

"No, it's cool. Just don't let it get out, okay? You know, with my career and all," he said, his voice slightly quivering.

"It won't, now go home," Monica said while opening the door. She wanted James out, and he was starting to get on her nerves. James had already served his purpose. She didn't need him anymore, so there was no use in wasting her time talking to him about shit she didn't care about.

"One more question then I'm gone."

"What, James?" Monica spat at him, her annoyance showing.

"Is that woman Jasmine's secretary?"

"Yes, why do you ask?" she replied with a slight smile on her face.

"She won't tell will she? I don't want any trouble with them on the job."

"No, your secret is safe. Now go home!"

"Okay, okay. I'm going. I miss you already."

"Yeah, yeah. I miss you too, now go."

James slowly made his way to the car, trying to make sense of what had just happened. With him exploding inside of Monica and orally pleasing his wife's secretary, he was sure this wasn't the end of it. He just prayed he could fix things at home before shit got out of hand.

Sheila listened to everything from the top of the stairs and crept back to the room when she heard Monica closing the front door. She liked Jasmine as a person and didn't want anything to do with this bullshit Monica had cooking up. This was only her second time at Monica's house, and she was still surprised at how she ended up there the first time. She was sitting on the edge of the bed contemplating all of this when Monica walked in the room.

"So, Sheila, did you enjoy yourself tonight, sweetie?" Monica asked before she reached behind the mirror and pulled out the camcorder. Sheila didn't know they were being taped and didn't know what to do. She'd just gotten herself into some serious shit and was clueless as how to get out of it.

"Yes, it was nice, but I need to be heading out. I need to pick up my son from my mom's house before she starts calling around looking for me." Her son was at home with her sister, but she was trying to find any reason to leave. She knew she would never step foot into Monica's house again, but she had to get out first.

"No problem, sweetie. Call a cab and get yourself dressed. I want to download some of these pictures onto my laptop before I forget. Let me know when you're leaving," Monica replied before leaving the room. She never even made eye contact with Sheila as she talked.

Sheila got dressed as quickly as possible after calling a cab from Monica's phone. She sat in the living room as she was instructed, and didn't budge until the cab driver honked his horn out front. Monica came into the living room and gave her money to get home in one envelope and money for the evening in another. Sheila was confused as to why she was getting paid for being there, and it showed all over her face.

"Now, this night is our little secret, right?" Monica warned more than asked Sheila as she waited for her to reply.

"Yes, I won't say anything."

"Okay, I'll call you later. Be sure to answer the phone."

Sheila walked out of the house and Monica watched her from the doorway, not seeming to care that she was still topless. Just as Sheila was opening the cab door, Monica called out to her. Sheila looked at Monica puzzled at what she was calling her for.

"Just a heads up," Monica began with an evil look on her face. "Don't fuck with me!"

Sheila got into the cab quickly and instructed the driver to take her home. Her heart didn't slow down for a couple of blocks, and for once in her life someone other than her mother put fear in her. She never suspected Monica was crazy, just a little obsessive with all the pink and white going on. Now that she knew Monica was crazy, she had to find a way to tell Jasmine without her finding out she'd slept with her husband too. Sheila didn't know what to do and was in tears by the time she got home.

***

James had left his credit card in another pants pocket and didn't have any cash on him to replace the underclothes Monica took from him. He decided once he got in the house that he would hop in the shower and sleep in the guest room. He wanted to make up with Jasmine for the way he had been acting, but tonight wouldn't work. He smelled like he just came from Monica's house, and he didn't want Jasmine to even think he was stepping out on her.

When he walked in Jasmine was lying on the couch asleep. She must have been waiting for him to get back and dozed off. Looking at his watch, he saw that he'd been gone for at least three hours and knew that Jasmine was going to have a fit when she woke up. He also knew that if he tried to sneak past her and hop in the shower she would definitely know what he had done.

Stuck between a rock and a hard place, he decided to wake Jasmine up and try to apologize to her. He stood over her watching her sleep and silently wondered what he had gotten himself into dealing with Monica. He knew he had to stay away or Jasmine would find out he was creeping. He honestly couldn't think of a reason to cheat on his wife, and he did feel bad. He decided at that moment that he wouldn't contact Monica anymore.

From what he could see she was nothing but trouble—trouble that was easy to get into.

"Jasmine, wake up," he whispered in her ear, shaking her a little to get her attention. When she opened her eyes, she looked at him like she wanted to punch him out.

"What time is it?" she asked while she sat up on the couch and got herself together.

"It's one thirty in the morning," James responded while bracing himself to be cursed out. Jasmine had a sharp tongue, and she could slice you up with just words.

"So you've been gone for at least three hours. Why did you leave like that without letting me explain myself?"

"Jazz, I really don't know. You hurt me."

"I hurt you? You've been acting like you hate me for the last few months. How did I hurt you?"

"I know I've been treating you wrong. I've been stressed at work and tired when I get home."

"I'm tired when I get home too, but I make sure you and the kids eat, and if you want to have sex you get it no matter how late I'm at the office. I bend over backward to keep this house running smoothly no matter how stressed I am."

"Baby, I know, and I'm sorry about the way I've been treating you. I'm sorry I stormed out of here the way I did; I just needed to breathe for a second."

"James, I need to breathe, too. You say shit to me that I don't like, but I stay here and deal with it! I just can't up and leave because I have kids to think about. Mommy can't afford to have a breakdown when things don't go right," Jasmine said between her tears, partly because she couldn't get Monica out of her system and partly because she didn't want James to go.

"I know that, Jazz. I know I need to change, but I need you to stick it out and help me. I need you to love me like you used to."

"James that will never change, but you need to get it together. I can't do this by myself."

"Baby, I know. I love you so much, and I need you. Whatever you do, just don't leave." James was begging her, nearly in tears. He had to leave Monica alone, and he vowed to himself right then that he would never be alone with her after that day.

Jasmine was a little shaken up because she had just told Monica they could chill again. She knew if she wanted to work things out with James, she had to let Monica go, but she wasn't sure she wanted to. Monica seemed to complete her, and it just sort of worked out. Jasmine knew if she called Monica and told her they couldn't get together anymore, Monica would spazz out. She was temperamental like that, and she could be dangerous if rubbed the wrong way. So Jasmine decided to just fall back instead of talking to Monica, and only see her when she could.

On the other side of town, Monica placed the photos she'd downloaded from her camcorder into a hidden safe behind the picture she drew of her and the governor of D.C. She had her hooks in his wife also, and she decided it was about time to call for her money. He paid Monica to keep quiet about him sleeping with her on occasions, and he didn't know Monica was having sex with his wife and his oldest daughter. She also knew she had to keep Sheila in check before her paranoid ass messed up everything. She had work to do, and she went to relax in the tub before putting her plan into action.

Marital Bliss?

For James, staying away from Monica was nothing. He knew she was trouble, and to avoid losing his wife he avoided her. She called his cell phone on occasion to hook up, but he always had a reason why it wasn't a good idea. This, of course, frustrated Monica, and she wasn't one to let things go easily. Deciding to pay James a little visit at home, she got into her hot pink convertible Benz dressed in a trench coat and stiletto heels. Freshly done hair, perfect make up, and nothing underneath the trench coat was sure to get James's attention. She almost burst with anticipation as she zigzagged in and out of traffic on her twenty-minute ride to the Cinque household.

Deciding to park a block down from the house so James wouldn't hear her pull up in the driveway, Monica made her way to the front door, her heels echoing loudly on the sidewalk. Glancing through the window, she spied James sitting on the couch in boxers and a T-shirt watching television. Monica knew Jasmine and the kids were away because Sheila had informed her that Jasmine went to visit her mother in Virginia on a three-day-weekend vacation. James couldn't go because it was sweeps week at the station, and he had to be there to make sure everything ran smoothly.

Ringing the doorbell, she loosened the belt on her coat so that when he opened the door she could surprise him. She felt in her pocket for the pair of panties she had in there then posed for him once the door opened.

"Monica, what are you doing here?" James asked as he leaned out the door and looked from side to side to make sure none of his neighbors were out. Things with he and Jasmine were starting to get better, and the last thing he needed was one of his nosey-ass neighbors seeing another woman entering his house. They would tell Jasmine no soon as she set foot on the block, and that would be something else he would have to explain. They were finally talking out their differences, and although it wasn't back to normal, it was damn close.

"I came to see you. I miss you," Monica responded, revealing herself to James. The look on his face said it all, yet he hadn't invited her in yet. Rubbing her hands down her body, she looked James in the eye, waiting for him to say something.

"I told you we had to chill for a while. I thought you understood that," James responded with his eyes still roaming all over Monica's naked body. Her trench coat was falling off her shoulders while she fingered herself. James knew if he didn't invite her in she would be standing in front of him naked for the entire neighborhood to see. And with his luck, all his neighbors would come out as soon as her coat hit the ground.

"Yeah, but Jazz and the kids are out of town, and you know what they say," she responded as she walked up to him in the doorway, and took hold of his erection. *"When the cat's away . . ."*

"Monica, we can't do this. Jasmine would have a fit!" James tried to keep his cool as she was backing him into the house, but it wasn't working. Before he knew it, Monica had the door closed and him sprawled out on the couch with his boxers down around his knees.

"What she doesn't know won't hurt you. You know you want this."

She kissed him behind his ear and stroked his length against her clit at the same time. Her wetness covered the head of his penis, and James struggled to gain control of the situation.

"Monica, you shouldn't be here," James responded weakly as he pushed her back off him. He stood up, pulling his boxers up with him, and tried to clear his head. Monica was set on getting it whether he wanted to give it or not, and instead of arguing with him, she turned and went upstairs.

James was left standing in his living room with a hard dick and no idea of what to do. He went over and locked the door, hoping to God no one saw Monica come in. He knew Monica wasn't leaving until she got what she came for. He had no choice but to knock her off real quick, and decided he would get it done quickly so that she could leave.

By the time James came up to the room, Monica was spread out on the lounge chair by the window with both sets of her lips spread open. Her eyes were closed, and she didn't open them until he was right up on her.

"Monica, we have to make this quick. I don't know what time Jazz will be back, and she can't see you here!" He got down on his knees on the side of the chair so that they could talk face to face.

Instead of responding, she took her finger out of her walls and placed it in his mouth. His eyes closed as he tasted her wetness with a hint of chocolate body butter mixed in. He stood at attention immediately, and Monica moved up so the head of his penis was just inside her cave.

James moaned as her muscles contracted around his head and she grinded him slowly, not letting any more than that go in. She wrapped her legs around his waist, still not letting him fully penetrate her as she tongue-kissed his nipples and rubbed his back.

Slowly at first, they pushed and pulled on each other. Monica fed James her nipples one at a time as his strokes quickened inside of her, making her lean against the window sill for support. They moaned like crazy, and James had just begun to explode when he looked out the window and saw Jasmine's Blazer pull into the driveway.

"Monica, you have to go! Jazz just pulled up . . ."

James grabbed the Glade air freshener and started spraying the room to get the smell of sex out after pulling on his boxers. Monica grabbed one of Jasmine's blouses out of the closet and wiped the semen off her stomach leaving what was on her pubic area there. She knew if she got pregnant Jasmine would leave him.

She made her way to the kitchen and could hear Jasmine getting the kids out of the car. James had hopped in the shower and planned to stay there until Jasmine came upstairs looking for him like he was in there the entire time. Monica slipped out the back door just as Jasmine was opening the front, and she crept around the side of the house and down the street into her car unnoticed.

Pulling up in front of the house, Monica parked her car, grabbed the binoculars that rested on the passenger seat, and stared up at the window that led into Jasmine and James's bedroom. She watched James walk into the bedroom with a towel wrapped around his waist. Monica felt sick as she watched him embrace Jasmine and kiss her slowly. She wanted Jasmine to come home to her and to kiss her that way. Briefly, she pictured herself in Jasmine's arms, and before a tear could drop, she peeled off down the street and onto the expressway thinking of how to put plan B into motion.

James held his wife like he hadn't seen her in ages. Jasmine thought it was because they were apart for the weekend, but James was just relieved that Monica had made it out in time. He sat down on the side of the bed after he was sure Monica was gone. He saw her sitting outside the house from the window and knew kissing Jasmine would piss her off, but he didn't care as long as she was gone.

"I missed you, too," Jasmine said once James pulled back from the kiss. She smiled; she wasn't expecting this, and she was pleasantly surprised.

"What are you doing back so soon? I thought you guys weren't coming back until the evening," James said as he sat down on the bed to lotion his body. He didn't want any traces of Monica on him or in the room, and he sprayed cologne on his body just to make sure.

"It started raining pretty heavy down there, so I wanted to make it back before it started to flood. You know how it is down my mom's way with the dirt roads and everything," Jasmine responded, taking a seat on the lounge chair and leaning back. Her arm fell over the side, lazily making contact with the blouse Monica used to wipe her stomach off. James spotted it, but Jasmine was already leaning over to pick it up.

Holding the shirt up and feeling the stickiness on her hand, she looked at James puzzled. James continued looking down at his legs and lotioning his body like he didn't see her pick the shirt up off the floor. He wasn't going to say anything until she asked, and he hoped he could come up with a good excuse as to why there was a sticky substance on her favorite Donna Karan blouse.

"James," she said with a little attitude in her voice, holding the shirt close to his bowed head, "can you explain this to me?"

Looking up guiltily, he examined the shirt she was holding with her fingertips up to his face. He didn't really know what to say, and he didn't want to lie. He also knew he couldn't tell her he'd just finished having sex with Monica on the lounge chair she was laying on and had exploded all over her stomach when she pulled up, and just to be a smart ass Monica used her shirt to wipe off. That would get him jacked up for sure.

"Before you came I was thinking about what you did to me before you left. You know your riding skills are the bomb, and I wanted something of yours near me. I was handling business, and let off on your blouse because I didn't want to get it on the bed. I was gonna have it cleaned before you noticed it."

"Then why was it under the lounge chair?" Jasmine asked suspiciously. She thought that maybe she saw Monica's car as she was riding up the street, but she wasn't sure. She didn't know too many people with a hot pink convertible, but opted to pay it no mind. She chalked it up to just missing Monica and let it be, but now she wasn't so sure.

"Because that's where I was. You know how I do, and I would have exploded all over the place if I didn't have something to cover up with. I didn't think much about it, and was going to put it in the bag for dry cleaning when I got out of the shower. You pulled up as I was getting out, and it totally slipped my mind. I can buy you another one though, two if it'll keep you from being upset with me . . . I just missed you, that's all."

With all that said, he bowed his head down like he was in some serious trouble and waited for Jasmine to snap. Instead, she just threw the shirt in the hamper by the door, and moved closer to her husband. Lifting his head up by the chin, she kissed him, softly straddling his lap in the process.

"Okay James, it's cool. The next time use something that didn't cost so much, please. Semen isn't all that easy to get out of silk," Jasmine replied with a smile before standing up. "I'm going to put the kids down for a nap. Be ready to make it up to me when I get back.

"I will," James responded as she left the room.

He didn't know how he made it out of that one, but he knew he would be staying as far away from Monica as possible. That girl was trouble with a capital T, and if he didn't play his hand right, Jasmine would leave him without thinking twice about it.

Jasmine came back in the room dressed in a pink thong and sandals that strapped to her knee of the same color. Hitting the power button on the stereo, the slow version of "Sumthin' Sumthin' " from the *Love Jones* soundtrack played right on cue. Jasmine danced her way over to the bed, sensuously keeping constant eye contact with her husband. Topless, she crawled up to him on her knees, kissing his body on the way up. James couldn't help but think that the show he was watching was something that Monica would do, but he was glad to see his wife broadening her views on creative lovemaking.

Squatting down onto his erection, Jasmine rode James slowly with her hands on the headboard for support. While they tossed and turned into different positions, James recalled thinking about Monica only once, and said to himself that it was going to be one hell of a night.

Monica ate ice cream and waited for the results of the pregnancy test she'd just taken. Who knew two minutes could be so long? She paced outside of the bathroom door trying patiently to wait for the timer to sound, indicating her time was up. When she got home, she did a headstand for about three minutes, hoping whatever semen was on her would find its way to her insides. Never mind most of it was rubbed off on the way home. Thinking rationally was not the issue here. Having James's baby would be a scandalous thing, but Monica could care less. She lived for drama, and scandal was her favorite pastime.

Finally the buzzer sounded, causing Monica to almost drop her dessert on the floor. Walking quickly into the bathroom, she sat her pint of Ben and Jerry's on the vanity and stared down at the test on the back of the toilet. Not sure what the line meant, she picked up the box to read the directions.

"One strip means not pregnant, two strips means baby on board," she said aloud. Looking down at the test, she only saw one line.

"This is bullshit! Is the nigga shootin' blanks or what?" Monica said to her frustrated reflection in the mirror. She knew James could make babies because he had twins now. She made sure he was inside of her the first time, and the second time he pulled out, but she still got some on her. She felt pregnant, or so went her imagination.

"Maybe the test is old," Monica said. "Who knows how long they sit in the back before they are put out for sale?"

Grabbing her jacket, she decided to go to the drugstore near her house. Pulling up with a screeching halt, Monica jumped out of the car before it stopped moving completely. Going directly to the feminine products aisle, she picked up four different brands of pregnancy tests just to make sure there wouldn't be any issues. The cashier looked at her kind of crazy as she rung the items up, and Monica gave her a "don't go there" look as she paid for her stuff and ran out of the store.

On the way home she hit ninety miles an hour, and as soon as she turned the corner to her block, a police car was right on her tail with flashing lights going off. She pulled over mad as hell and not wanting to stop, and at one point thought about jetting off. When the officer got to her car, she made sure to keep her hands on the steering wheel just in case this one was trigger-happy. She didn't want to become a statistic because of speeding and a few pregnancy tests.

"Can I help you, Officer?" Monica said to the cop standing outside her car door. She hoped he would make it quick; she had things to do.

"Ma'am, are you aware of how fast you were going?"

"No, sir I'm not. I have to pee and was in a rush to get home. I only live a few houses down on this side of the street." She gave him her most pitiful look, but he didn't seem to be buying it.

"License, insurance, and registration, please," the cop said, looking into the car window.

"Sir, please. You can't give me a ticket. I just got this car. Let me make it up to you."

"Ma'am, are you soliciting me? I'm an officer of the law, and I can lock you up for prostitution."

"I'm not a prostitute, sir! I'm just trying to get out of this ticket. I only live a few houses down. No one has to know but me and you."

The officer looked at her for a second to see if she was ser-ious. Monica started unbuttoning her shirt, exposing her chocolate breasts to the rookie cop. Monica had already slept with most of the guys on the force, and she didn't remember seeing this one before. He started thinking about how things were terrible at home, and his evident erection let Monica know she had him hooked. That was exactly how she got the mayor to sleep with her, and her little flash trick worked here too.

"Pull up to your door and go in," the officer said. "Leave the door unlocked; I'll be coming in right behind you."

Pulling off, Monica made her way down the block and parked her car in the driveway. Doing exactly as she was told, she went inside and stripped down to nothing as she waited for the cop to come in. Forgetting about the pregnancy and her earlier dilemma, she sat on the floor in front of the fireplace with her legs open, tugging on her clit. When the cop walked in, he spotted Monica and almost came on himself right then. Undressing quickly, he joined her on the rug, his head falling directly between her legs.

"Eat up, Officer," Monica spoke to him while holding on to the back of his head.

The cop kissed his way up her stomach, inserting himself unprotected as he kissed her breasts. Not even a minute later, he spit his seed inside of her, collapsing heavily on top of her. Monica held her breath and waited for him to move.

Rolling off her, he snatched her shirt from the floor beside them, and wiped himself off before stepping back into his uniform. Monica looked up at him from the floor with a smirk on her face.

"Now, be careful how you drive for now on. I wouldn't want you to tear that pretty car up," he said as he placed his state-issued hat on top of his bald head.

Monica just looked at him, wishing he would hurry up and close the door. After all, she was ass-naked, and there was a cool breeze outside, even for the middle of May. Officer Hill looked back at her once more before closing the door. Getting up to lock it, Monica almost laughed aloud at his silly ass.

"He had the nerve to look like he just did something," she said on the way upstairs. Totally forgetting about the pregnancy test, she filled the tub with hot water and soaked her tired body. Jasmine and how she was going to steal her from James was still on her mind as she rinsed off and went to lie across her bed. Before she knew it, she was drifting off to sleep, already making up her mind to visit Jasmine in the morning.

The next morning Monica was parked down the street from Jasmine's house waiting patiently for James and the kids to leave. She knew they rotated mornings on who took the kids out, and she hoped it would play in her favor today. Dozing off for a minute, she woke up in time to see James and his twins get in the car and pull off. Ducking down some in her seat so he wouldn't see her when they passed by, she waited about five minutes before she got out of the car and went up to the door.

Monica was dressed similarly to what she had on for James, but this time she had on the red French-cut boy shorts that Jasmine liked to see her in. Tying the belt tighter around her waist, she rung the bell and waited patiently for Jasmine to answer. When Jasmine came to the door, all she had on was a bathrobe, and half her hair was pinned up because she was curling it. Half dressed, she still looked like a goddess to Monica, and she wanted so badly to just have her to herself.

"What are you doing here?" Jasmine asked, looking both ways to see if anyone was outside. She didn't want to have to explain to James later why Monica was there.

"I came to see you, silly," Monica replied playfully. "It's been a while since we—you know, and I decided to catch you before you left. Maybe give you something to smile about while you're at work."

"Okay, Monica, that's cool and all, but what if James were here? How would I explain that?" Jasmine said, a little frustrated although she was getting wet just thinking about what Monica would do to her.

"I figured he would be gone around this time; that's why I waited. I'm sorry if I caused a problem," Monica began looking like she was about to cry. "I just miss you, and I needed to see you, so I came over."

"Look, don't cry," Jasmine said after the first tear fell. "Come on in, but we have to be quick because I have to get to work soon."

"No problem, just lay back and let me make you feel good."

Jasmine, still a little irritated, went upstairs to the bathroom with Monica following close behind.

While Jasmine was in the bathroom, Monica checked behind the bed to make sure the panties were still there. She also felt in her jacket pocket for the clay she brought with her. She knew a guy that made keys, and he told her all she needed was a good print of the key she wanted duplicated and he could make her one. She hoped Jasmine's house keys would be lying around somewhere so she could get a print, and was looking around from her spot on the bed.

Jasmine entered the room naked and took a spot on the bed next to Monica. Scooting over in the middle of the bed and spreading her legs, she waited for Monica to do whatever she was going to do. She hoped James wouldn't turn around and come back to the house for anything as Monica began at her toes and worked her way up.

Monica had already taken off her panties and had them on the side of the bed. Pleasing herself in the process, she spread open Jasmine's lips with her free hand and immediately took hold of her clit, making Jasmine explode instantly. Holding her legs up, Jasmine held on to the back of Monica's head while she devoured her. Moaning like crazy and exploding all over the place, Jasmine took her nipples into her mouth one at a time, adding to the excitement that was already playing all over her body.

Monica made sure to put her tongue inside of Jasmine, lapping up all of her honey until there was nothing left. Jasmine started squirming under her, indicating that another orgasm was fast-approaching. Taking her hand from her own clit,

Monica licked off her juices before inserting her fingers inside of Jasmine's tightness. Jasmine's body was barely on the bed as she rained all over Monica's hand and tongue.

Reaching over into her coat pocket, Monica pulled out the strap-on she'd brought with her and stepped into it. Getting as close to Jasmine as possible on her knees, she threw Jasmine's legs over her shoulders, plunging into her deeply and hoping that she was doing a better job than James. Jasmine held her lips open, begging Monica not to stop. Monica threw her legs over to the side, taking her that way, with Jasmine holding on to the headboard.

"Whose pussy is this?" Monica asked in a low tone, but loud enough for Jasmine to hear her.

"It's yours," Jasmine replied between breaths. Monica was doing the damn thing to her, and she was shocked because it was almost better than what James did the night before—almost.

"Tell me it's my pussy! Say it!" Monica came back, enjoying the control she had over Jasmine at this point. If Jasmine had any doubts that a woman could please her the same or better as a man, Monica wanted to make sure that she knew she could have the best of both worlds.

"Monica, it's your pussy. It's yours, baby," Jasmine responded as Monica turned her body so that she was on her knees in the doggie style position.

"It better be."

Monica started kissing Jasmine down her back, and running her tongue up and down her spine, making Jasmine go crazy. Using some of the KY-Jelly from off the nightstand, she applied some on Jasmine's asshole, never losing her rhythm with Jasmine throwing her ass back like crazy. She slowly pushed her finger into Jasmine's ass and slowed down her stroke; Jasmine's back stiffened.

"Jasmine, just relax. I won't hurt you, just enjoy it."

Every time Monica pushed in she pulled her finger out, and vice versa building up an orgasm so big Jasmine just about passed put from the explosion. Feeling satisfied that she'd handled her business, Monica pulled out of Jasmine and stepped out of her strap-on. Jasmine was lying face down on the bed trying to catch her breath as Monica dressed. Smiling to herself, she walked around the side of the bed and kissed Jasmine on the forehead.

"I'll call you later," Monica said before leaving the room, "and I'll lock the door behind me. Don't oversleep; it's nine o'clock."

Jasmine just kind of grunted her good bye and remained sprawled out on the bed, trying to get herself together.

When Monica got downstairs, she spotted the peg block hanging by the door. Coming closer to it, she saw several keys hanging from it. There were numerous tags listing what the keys were over each peg, and the last one that read "Spare House Keys" had two of the same keys hanging from it. She started to just take a key, but that would be too easy. Testing the key in the door to make sure it was the right one, she did as she was told and pressed the key firmly into the clay; the shape and name on the key came out perfectly. Smiling to herself, she slid the clay into one of the sandwich bags on the table and left the house whistling.

On her way back home, she went by the locksmith's office and dropped the imprint off. After knocking him off quickly, he told her she could come back and get the key that afternoon. She went home, and all of a sudden felt very sleepy and decided to take her shower after a nap.

Jasmine finally got out of the bed a half hour after Monica left. Pulling the sheets with her, the pair of underwear that Monica planted there popped out as planned. Jasmine, not wanting James to know that Monica was there and thinking that those were the panties Monica came there in, put them in the bottom of the hamper, mentally writing herself a note to get them out later before James saw them. Already late for work, she quickly dressed and headed for the office, smiling all the way there, just as Monica said she would.

Dancing With The Devil

An hour later, Jasmine walked into the office with a smile so bright she could be the star of a Colgate commercial. Unusually friendly to everyone, she practically skipped into her office, flopping down in her chair when she got there. Not that she was a mean person, but Jasmine was very professional all the time, and it was rare that she was giddy and carefree like she was now. She didn't know Monica had it in her to turn her out like that, but she was hooked. Never in her wildest imagination did she think a girl could leave her feeling sore and completely drained at the same time, but then again Monica wasn't just "any woman," and you could never be too sure of her capabilities.

"Sheila, can I see you in my office please?" Jasmine called from the intercom. She had several meetings she needed to attend, and if Sheila could download a couple of subpoenas for her by the time she got back, it would take a few hours off her day.

When Sheila walked in, her face was red and her eyes were puffy like she had been crying all morning. Trying to hide behind her hair, she sat down with her pen and notepad ready, looking into her lap and not at Jasmine like she normally did. Monica had been harassing her all week because she was avoiding her calls, and even went as far as sending her photos of her and Jasmine's husband when they were at her house. Somehow she took her face out of the pictures and put Sheila's there as if she was the one having sex with him. All she and James did was exchange oral pleasantries; there was never any penetration between the two.

She didn't know what Monica would do, but she did know she couldn't afford to lose her job. She already felt bad about what she did with her boss's husband, and Monica was only making it worse.

"Sheila, are you okay?" Jasmine asked, concern etching her face and stealing her once-jolly mood away completely.

"I'm fine." Sheila started to cry again. "Let's just get on with the meeting."

"If you were fine, you wouldn't be sitting here in tears." Jasmine decided to ignore her attitude and go around to sit in the chair opposite of Sheila with her tissue box in hand. "I'm a lawyer, I can help you."

"It's nothing, really; just some issues I have to work through, that's all," Sheila said, trying to steer the conversation away from her.

"Sheila, whatever it is, you can tell me. I'll try my best to help you, and I know others who can also. Is it your son's father? Is he abusing you?" Jasmine went on, at the same time going through her mental Rolodex thinking of who could help Sheila out with the situation she thought Sheila might be in.

Sheila just wanted to go home. As much as she wanted to tell, Jasmine could not help her out of this one. She had to do what was necessary to get Monica off her back, and although she didn't know what her solution was just yet, she knew she had to think fast before things got out of hand.

"No, I'm fine, really. I think I may end up taking a half-day if you don't really have anything for me to do. Honestly, my head is pounding and I probably won't be any good around here anyway."

"That's not a problem. All I need you to do is pull up and send out a few subpoenas for the files in the corner over there, then you can head out. Leave me a note on top of them when you're done, and your number so I can check on you later."

"Are you sure? I can stay if you need me."

"No, Sheila, go on. Every so often a woman needs to just lie down and rest for a second. You have my cell number; call if you need me."

"I will. Are we done now?" Sheila asked, wanting to get out of Jasmine's face. She felt like shit because the one person who was showing her the most concern should be whipping her ass for sucking her husband's dick. She got up to leave before any more tears fell.

"Yeah, we're done. I'll give you a call tonight, okay?"

"Cool."

Jasmine gathered a couple of folders for some cases she had to view and put the one she was about to start with on top. On her way out the door, she walked slowly by Sheila, looking to see if she was okay. Sheila was having a heated debate over the phone, and it was getting loud. Knowing how the senior partners were and not wanting Sheila to lose her job because of her personal problems, she waited by Sheila's desk for her to end the call.

"I told you to stop calling here!" Sheila said sharply through the phone. Monica was getting on her last nerve, and she had already hung the phone up twice on her. Something Monica said made Sheila freeze up. She was holding the phone tightly to her ear, tears streaming down her face.

Jasmine touched her shoulder to let her know she was standing there, and that she was starting to get weird looks from the other workers in the office. Sheila held up one finger to indicate she was almost done with her conversation, and she wanted to talk to her.

"I'll meet you there, but this is the last time," she said to Monica on the phone.

"Be there or else," Monica said then hung up.

Sheila placed the phone back on the hook slowly and followed Jasmine back into her office. After twenty minutes of convincing Jasmine that she would be okay, Jasmine recommended that she take some time off to get herself together. She informed Sheila of the procedures for a sick and a personal leave, and told her to let her know what she would do by the next day.

"I'm just looking out for you," Jasmine said while offering Sheila more tissue for her never-ending tears.

"I know, and I really appreciate it. If you could get the paper work for me, I'll come in tomorrow and fill it out so you can put it through." Not that Sheila wanted to leave work, but Monica was too much to handle emotionally and physically, and if any shit went down between Monica and Jasmine's husband, she didn't want to be there for it.

"No problem, just go on home. I'll get one of the temps to do the subpoenas for me and we'll talk tonight, okay?"

"Okay," Sheila responded after giving Jasmine a hug.

Sheila gathered her stuff and followed Jasmine out to the elevator. On the way down to the street level, Jasmine offered her a ride to wherever she needed to go.

"That's okay," Sheila said. "You've already been a big help."

"Just let me know if you need anything."

"I will."

As the elevator doors opened, Sheila tried to quickly step through them and managed to bump her right arm against the door. She winced and dropped the folder she was carrying. The photos Monica sent her scattered across the floor.

Both women bent down at the same time to pick them up, but before Jasmine had a chance to put her hand on one Sheila scooped them all up in a big pile. Jasmine peeped a few, but not close enough to notice her husband in any of them. Jasmine handed Sheila the hat she dropped.

"You sure you don't need a ride?" Jasmine asked one last time.

Sheila pulled the folder close to her chest. "Yeah," she muttered. "I'll just take the bus." She waved, turned, and walked off.

By the time Sheila got to Monica's house, she was a nervous wreck. She opted to take the bus over there for two reasons. One because she needed time to clear her head; she had to put Monica in her place, or at least try to. She was determined to make Monica understand that she wanted no parts of the bullshit she was brewing up and that she wanted to be left out of the entire situation. The second reason she caught the bus was because she knew Jasmine and Monica were cool—not exactly how cool they were—but she knew they were friends and she didn't want Jasmine to know she was chillin' with Monica like that.

Walking up the block slowly, Sheila made her way to the only pink house on the block. Monica's house stood out, seeming to make the neighborhood look a little brighter. Approaching the door, she raised her hand to knock. Monica swung the door open before Sheila's fist could make contact with the wood, and she accidentally punched Monica in the mouth. Monica immediately covered her mouth with both hands, caught off guard by the blow. She knew it was an accident by the look on Sheila's face, but she snapped anyway.

"Monica, I'm so sorry." Sheila reached out to hold Monica's face, but Monica stepped back. The hit wasn't as hard as Monica was making it out to be, but being the drama queen that she was, she milked it for all it was worth.

Instead of answering, she just turned around and went toward the kitchen to get some ice for the non-existent swelling she thought would take place. Sheila was so close on her heels that when Monica stopped suddenly Sheila bumped into her, causing the back of Monica's house shoe to flop off. Trying to keep her cool, Monica kicked the shoe off and continued to the freezer to get the ice. Sheila waited silently at the kitchen table for Monica to wrap her ice in a towel, put on the house shoes that were by the back door, and examine the back of her foot.

"Monica, I'm so sor—"

"Bitch, just be quiet! You done just about worked my last nerve, and you ain't been here that long. Fall back!"

That shut Sheila's ass right up. Monica was a tad on the demanding side, but she'd never talked to her in that tone before. Sheila wanted to say something, but for reasons even she didn't understand, Monica scared the hell out of her. Even if she wasn't scared, she couldn't think of a snappy comeback in time anyway, so she did as she was told and fell back. After about five minutes of silence and Monica giving her dirty looks, she finally joined Sheila at the table and got down to why Sheila was there in the first place.

"I need you to help me out with something," Monica began in a matter-of-fact tone like she dared Sheila to say she wouldn't do it.

"What is it?" Sheila did not feel like the Monica drama, but she figured if she just agreed to do whatever she wanted, she could leave and not hear from her again.

"James keeps asking about you, and he wants to know if you're down with a threesome. I told him you would do it," Monica closely watched Sheila's reaction.

Monica had spoken to James about a threesome when she was at his house the night before, but he said he didn't want anything to do with it. Since she stopped by his house that day, she had to find some way to have sex with him again if this pregnancy thing was going to work. She had taken two pregnancy tests so far and both came up positive, but she wanted to be one hundred percent sure before she visited her gynecologist.

"I'm not getting into that with you. Find someone else; you know his wife is my boss," Sheila said with her arms folded across her chest. For the first time, Sheila was seeing just how crazy and deranged Monica really was.

Monica came around the table and stood close to Sheila. She bent down so that the two were face to face.

"You'll do it," she whispered, "because if you don't, every step you take I'll be right in your ass. Trust and believe that life for you will be nothing wonderful when I'm done with you."

"Monica, what are you going to do? So what you sent pictures to the job? Your bedroom is in the background, and they weren't even clear shots," Sheila responded, feeling confident all of a sudden. She tried to play the same role Monica was playing and hoped that Monica would be somewhat intimidated.

"Dear Sheila, a lot of shit has changed," Monica said while walking circles around the table. Her facial expression seemed to turn sinister.

"The photos I sent you were that way because I knew you would underestimate me. I have photos of you giving him head and everything. I can take your picture and put it anywhere I choose—even e-mail them to Jazz if I wanted to take it to that level. How much of a job will you have then?"

Trying to hold her ground, but close to breaking down, Sheila was determined not to be a part of the nonsense. Jasmine was looking out for her in a major way even though she already violated her by sleeping with her husband. She couldn't bring herself to cross Jasmine again, and was damn near about to cry. She couldn't understand how Monica could act the way she did and not care about the lives of the people she was hurting.

Monica took her seat across from Sheila and waited for her to reply. In Monica's mind she couldn't take it far enough to get Jasmine. She wanted her as much as she wanted her next breath, and she was determined to have her by any means necessary. Sheila would be the perfect source to get Jasmine to leave James, and she figured she would have James's child so they could both have him in common. Sick and twisted? Yes, but she didn't care and was getting fed up because it was taking too long to get what she wanted.

"How do you plan to get James to come by? He's obviously happy at home. Jasmine came in the office today looking like he put some serious work in this morning," Sheila said hoping to throw Monica off.

Monica almost laughed. "You let me worry about that," she said, smirking. "Just be ready when I set up the meeting. I'll call you the day before. Now leave, your presence is making me feel sick."

Sheila wanted to grip Monica's ass up, but she decided it wasn't worth it. Monica could call until the cows came home. Sheila would be changing her phone number the very next day, and would be staying at her mom's house during her leave of absence from work. Monica was crazy, and Sheila decided to let her be crazy all by herself. Not wanting to reveal how she would pull off her disappearing act, Sheila readied herself to leave.

"I need a ride home," Sheila said to Monica on her way to the door.

"There's money on the table in the living room. Call a cab, and wait outside for it. I want you gone before I start getting pissed."

Sheila just gave Monica a look like she couldn't believe how she was acting and walked away. In the living room Sheila found about two hundred dollars sitting on the table next to receipts from Neiman Marcus and Strawbridge's. It only cost about seven dollars for her to get home, but Sheila opted to take the whole two hundred. Instead of calling a cab, she walked until she found one. Calling her sister over to help her with her son once she got home, she gave her sister half the money to tell Monica she wasn't there no matter how many times she called. Sheila knew getting away from Monica wouldn't be easy, and she needed her sister there just in case she needed backup.

Before morning, Monica was ringing Sheila's phone off the hook. Sheila didn't think she would be calling that soon, but she did take her money and instantly regretted it. Between Monica's calls she called the phone company, but it was after hours, and she would have to wait until nine the next day to do anything.

Sheila told her sister as much as she could without incriminating herself, and her sister decided that she didn't care how many times Monica called, she would have to get over it and move on.

"Hello, can I speak with Sheila?" Monica asked in her sweetest voice. She was calling to set up some time with Sheila for the next night, hoping she could get her to help persuade James into having the threesome.

"She's not available, can I take a message?" Sheila's sister replied just as nicely. She knew it was Monica from her calling the house before, and whatever reason her sister had for not wanting to talk to her was a good enough reason for her not to like her. There was something about Monica that she couldn't place her finger on, but she knew it wasn't good.

"What do you mean she's not there? I suggest you find out where she is and have her call me back!" Monica screamed into the phone, frustration wrinkling her brow already.

"Excuse me?" Sheila's sister had to look at the phone to make sure she heard right.

"I said Sheila needs to be contacted ASAP," Monica came back with even more attitude. She didn't know who the girl was on the other end, but she did know she didn't want to talk to her.

"You need to get a better attitude before calling someone's house!" she said and hung up.

Monica was pissed. She almost dropped her phone in the tub she was so mad, and she slipped while she was getting out, damn near breaking her ankle. She didn't know who answered the phone at Sheila's house, but she didn't play those games and would be over there in a flash if Sheila didn't answer the phone.

Sitting on the edge of the bed, she dialed Sheila's number again, and this time she was ready. Sheila didn't know who she was dealing with, and Monica would make her life a living hell if she didn't act right. The phone rang ten times before Sheila's sister answered again.

"Put Sheila on the phone!" Monica demanded from the other end.

"Bitch, please! When you learn some manners, call back," and she hung up again.

This was just pissing Monica off more, and it took a lot for her not to go over to the house and snatch this woman up. Dialing the number one more time, she decided that if Sheila didn't get the phone, her life would be hell from there on out.

From Crazy To Insane

Three weeks had gone by, and Monica still hadn't heard a word from Sheila. When she called the office, a temporary assistant answered the phone, informing her that Sheila was on an indefinite leave of absence. Monica had been trying to keep her cool, but this was the last straw. Getting dressed in a sweat suit and sneakers and pulling her hair back into a ponytail just in case she had to whip someone's ass, she got in her car and raced over to Sheila's apartment to see what the problem was.

Double-parking her car in front of the building and not giving a damn that she was holding up traffic on a busy intersection early on a Saturday afternoon, she took the stairs two at a time all the way up to Sheila's third floor apartment. Knocking turned to practically trying to break the door down as Monica screamed and hollered for Sheila to show her face. She figured Sheila was inside hiding from her.

Monica was making so much noise in the hallway that Sheila's neighbors started to come out in the hall to see what all the ruckus was about. After all, Sheila didn't exactly live in the ghetto, and it was normally quiet in the overpriced, working class renters' apartment building. Monica kicked and banged on the door for a half hour, thinking Sheila would come out eventually. She was so into it that she didn't see one of Sheila's neighbors walking toward her.

"Ma'am . . . Ma'am, are you looking for someone?"

Monica turned around to stare at the elderly Caucasian guy standing a few feet from her. Almost doubling over in laughter, she tried to control her smile as she stared at him. He reminded her of the cartoon character named Mr. Burns off *The Simpson's* television show, teeth and all.

"Would I be banging on this door like a madwoman if I weren't looking for someone?" Monica asked, her smile disappearing. After thirty minutes of kicking and banging, she decided if Sheila hadn't come to the door by now, she wouldn't be.

"Well, Ma'am," the senior citizen responded like he was getting an attitude, "it's just that you're making a lot of noise, and some of us are trying to sleep."

"Does this look like the face of someone who gives a fuck?" she asked him, looking him dead in his eyes. "I'm not here for you, so take your old wrinkled ass back to your apartment before you write a check your half rich ass can't cash."

"Your attitude is not necessary, young lady. I was just simply stating . . ."

"Simply stating what?" Monica replied, approaching the elderly man like she was going to strike him.

"That you need to take that hood shit back to the hood; this is a peaceful building and . . ."

"Old man, save it! I do what I want when I'm ready. What are you going to do to stop me?"

"I . . . I'm going to call the police," Sheila's neighbor responded, taken aback by what Monica said.

"Yeah, you do that. I'll be waiting right here for them," Monica shouted at his turned back as he shuffled down the hallway and into his apartment.

She could hear him making the call to the police department and perched her tired body into one of the chairs to wait for the cops to get there.

Not even ten minutes later, who but Officer Hill and Monica's other favorite officer of the law, Officer Collins, came strolling up the hallway to investigate the situation. Looking at Monica like he wasn't sure if he knew her, Officer Hill proceeded to knock on the neighbor's door to see what happened.

"Someone report a disturbance?" he asked the frail old man. He looked visibly shaken, and was afraid to step foot into the hall.

"Yes, that woman right there," he said pointing at Monica, "was making all kinds of noise and threatened me when I asked her to stop." Monica just sat there with a smirk on her face.

"Ma'am, is this true?" Officer Hill responded, taking a closer look at Monica. As he got closer to her, he recognized her and smiled in spite of the situation.

"No, Officer, it isn't. I'm just waiting for my sister to get home. This guy seems to get nervous around black people or something," she replied, smiling seductively at the cop. He remembered the night they spent together and started blushing.

"That's a lie!" the elderly man spat out between his dentures. "She was kicking the door and everything. Look at it, you can still see her footprints on it." Everyone looked at the door at the same time, and there were scuff marks on the bottom half of it. Monica just laughed softly to herself.

"Officer, those marks were on that door when I got here. My sister was supposed to meet me here, and I've been waiting for her for about ten minutes. That's my car double-parked out front. I haven't been here for that long." Staring at Monica's breasts and not really paying attention, Officer Hill didn't hear much of what she said.

"Sir, do you have any witnesses?" Officer Collins asked the man, reluctantly turning his gaze away from Monica.

"This is ridiculous," the neighbor said. "What do you have to do to get a good cop nowadays?" Without looking back, he walked into his apartment and slammed the door. Monica and Officer Hill stood in the hallway looking at each other and smiling. Monica was hoping they would just leave, but she was sure it wouldn't go down that way.

"And for the record," the Mr. Burns look-a-like said inching his door back open, "this is a quiet building. Take all of that ruckus back to your hood," he hollered before giving the door one final slam, clicking the locks loudly.

Both law enforcers turned to face Monica. Officer Collins couldn't even look at Monica for fear that he might snatch her up. He had dealt with her for only a short time, and she had managed to almost destroy his marriage. He too fell for the Jedi Pussy Trick, falling head over heels for the sexy vixen with amazing control of her vaginal walls.

"Hill, wrap this up; I'll meet you downstairs," Officer Collins said as he walked quickly down the hall opting to take the stairs before his good intentions escaped him. Monica hid her smirk as she turned her attention to the obviously horny Officer Hill.

"So, Ms. Anderson, how have you been?" Officer Hill said to Monica while backing her into Sheila's door. His erection, as small as it was, was pressing against her abdomen, clearly showing his intentions.

"I've been good, Officer Hill. How have you been?" Monica replied seductively, hoping he would get a call on his radio or something. She was not in the mood for him tonight, and knew it wouldn't be easy to just dis him.

"Better, now that I see you."

"How's the wife and kids?" Monica shot at him as he leaned down to kiss her neck. That caught him off guard, causing him to stand straight up.

"My wife an . . . and kids?" he stuttered, trying to remember if he ever told her about his family.

"Yes. You know, your wife Cynthia, and your kids Thomas and Jessica. How are they doing?" Monica smirked and waited for his reply as his erection faded to nothing. She got information on his background from the captain in his district. He owed her a favor, and wanted her to keep his secret from his wife, also.

"They're doing great. Thanks for asking," he replied, backing away from her and adjusting his pants. "So, are you about to leave?" he asked, already walking down the hallway toward the exit.

"Yeah, my sister doesn't seem to be home."

Looking back at the door one more time, she followed Officer Hill out the building. He waited for her to get into her car and pulled up beside her in his squad car. Lust was jumping off him like fleas on a dog as he stared at Monica, trying to think of a way to get over to her house.

"You go on ahead. I'll follow you to make sure you get home safely," he said, staring at Monica's painted lips. Monica almost laughed at his attempt to get a booty call.

"No, it's cool," she replied through the window, "I'm not going straight home, but I'll call you when it's okay to stop by."

"Don't wait too long," Officer Hill practically begged. "I don't think they have a twelve step program for getting over beautiful women."

Instead of responding to his lame advances, Monica pulled off as quickly as possible, jumping on the first exit she saw, not knowing exactly where she was heading. She wanted to get away from Officer Hill as quickly as possible. It was a nice Saturday afternoon, and she did not feel like his bullshit or his thirty seconds of so-called *lovemaking*.

Skipping her exit, she decided to go shake things up at the Cinque household. She was interested in seeing how the two would act knowing they were both separately sleeping with her, but neither knowing about the other. She thought maybe she could talk to James about that threesome on the sly if Jasmine left them in the room by themselves. Smiling wickedly, she jumped off I-76 at the Lincoln Drive exit and made her way to the Mount Airy section of the city to stir up some shit.

Parking in the driveway, Monica got out of her car and peeped in the window on the way past. Seeing Jasmine and James cuddled on the couch gave her an instant attitude, and she almost snapped. James was stretched out on the couch and Jasmine was lying on top of him with her head on his chest, both watching television. They didn't see Monica in the window, and when Jasmine leaned up to give James a kiss, Monica's temper went from zero to sixty in three seconds.

"I know he's not hugged up on my girl," Monica said to herself while she looked in the window. "Doesn't he know she belongs to me?"

Knocking on the door like she was the police, she waited for someone to open it, hoping it would be James. Putting on her game face, she waited patiently for the lovebirds to separate and finally answer the door. She wanted to scream through the window that the same lips that were kissing James were all in her treasure chest not too long ago. She hated the fact that no matter how hard she tried to separate them, they always found a way to be together anyway. "Who is it?" Jasmine's voice sounded from the other side of the door. She sounded frustrated, but Monica didn't care. She hoped she messed up their little make-out session because she didn't want James sleeping with Jasmine anyway.

"It's Monica," she said into the door. She didn't know how Jasmine would act to her popping up again, but she didn't exactly care either. She banged Jasmine's back out rather nicely a few weeks ago, so she figured Jasmine was aware of her capabilities by now.

"Who?" Jasmine asked not sure if she heard correctly. She swung the door open with tons of attitude.

"Hey Jazz," Monica said, acting like she didn't notice Jasmine's mood.

"What did I tell you?" Jasmine said getting right to the point. "Didn't I tell you not to be just popping up whenever you felt like it?"

"Yeah, but . . ."

"But what?" Jasmine said getting heated. She liked Monica a lot, but if she kept doing the stuff she was doing, she was going to mess up everything.

"I just wanted to take you shopping. I was on my way to the mall and I didn't want to go by myself," Monica replied, coming up with the lie quickly. She hoped she had at least one credit card on her, because if she didn't Jasmine would know that wasn't her reason for being there.

"Honey, who's at the door?" James hollered in the background. He was lying on the couch with a granite pipe waiting to serve Jasmine properly. Pissed because he told Jazz not to answer the door in the first place, he was wondering what was taking her so long to get back.

"Look, you have to go," she said to Monica, ignoring James. She wanted Monica to leave before James got up to see who knocked.

"We won't even be gone that long, just a quick trip to the mall," Monica replied, stalling for time. She wanted James to see her and wished he would hurry up.

Like he heard her thoughts, James finally got up to see what was going on. He wanted Jasmine wrapped around him in more ways than one, and he was ready to go now. When he got to the door his facial expressions went from shocked to scared as hell when he saw Monica standing there. He was just with Monica two days ago, and he still hadn't put the money he paid to her for the sex they had that night back into the account.

Monica was good, but she damn sure wasn't cheap. That night cost him seven hundred dollars, and it was getting harder to replace it. Yeah, she gave him a couple of free shots here and there, but most of the time she wanted her money up front if he wanted her to stay quiet. She was already pissed because he insisted on using a condom, and with that, up went the prices. Monica got even more pissed when he insisted on bringing his own condoms because he thought she was putting holes in the ones she had.

"Monica, long time no see," James said, feeling the heat between the two ladies.

"Hey, James. I was just asking Jasmine if she wanted to go to the mall with me. You know, sort of a ladies' day out. You don't mind, do you?" she asked James with a smirk. Blowing him up would be blowing herself up, but Monica didn't care about consequences.

"Well, we were about to . . ." James said looking down at Jasmine for support. He didn't want to be the one to say no and hoped Jasmine would say just that.

"Before you came we were . . . um . . . enjoying each other's company," Jasmine began, not caring if she hurt Monica's feelings, "so maybe next time you can call first and we can set up something, okay?"

"Are you telling me no?" Monica asked with a surprised look on her face before quickly checking her attitude. She didn't want to put herself out there just yet.

"I'm telling you maybe next time," Jasmine said, backing up so she could close the door. Monica looked like she was going to cry, but it wasn't working this time.

"Okay then, you lovebirds get back to each other. Jazz, I'll see you around."

Instead of responding, Jasmine closed the door in Monica's face with a hard thud and a loud click of the lock. Stunned, Monica stood looking at the door for about five minutes before she turned around and numbly walked to her car. She thought for sure she had Jasmine in check, especially after that last session, but now she wasn't too sure. James totally took her by surprise, and she knew she definitely would have to get him back for trying to play her.

"Hiding behind wifey," Monica said to herself angrily as she got into her car and peeled off from the curb. "She won't be yours for too much longer, James."

Not knowing what to do with herself because she was so mad, Monica rode around aimlessly trying to get her temper under control. For some reason things weren't working out the way she planned. At this phase, Jasmine should be ready to leave James, but they seemed more in love now than they did before.

Monica felt sick, and not sick like the morning illness she had been experiencing lately, either. She wanted to get pregnant, she wanted James's ass gone, and she wanted Jasmine now. Slamming on the breaks at a red light, she was fixing her mouth to curse the guy in front of her when she looked to the side just in time to see Sheila, accompanied by her mom and her son, come out of the Pizza Palace.

"This must be my lucky day," Monica said as she maneuvered her car into the right turning lane so she could pull into the lot before they drove off.

Running the red light, she pulled around the entrance and stopped next to Sheila on the passenger side of the car just as the door closed. Catching Sheila off guard, Monica had to control herself to keep from snatching Sheila through the car window.

"Hey, Sheila, it's been awhile," Monica began with a false smile. The only thing that kept her from snapping was the fact Sheila's son was in the car.

Sex, Lies, and Videotape

"Hey, Monica, how have you been?" Sheila sat in the car feeling caged in because Monica was the last person she was expecting to see. She figured since three weeks had gone by, Monica would have found someone else to bully by now.

"Sheila," Monica responded mocking Sheila's high-pitched voice. She wasn't in the mood for pleasantries, and her face showed just that. "I've been trying to catch you for a while. Where are you on your way to?"

"Home. My son is tired after all that playing," Sheila responded, gesturing to her sleeping son in the car seat. She knew what Monica wanted, but she wasn't in the mood to give in.

"Why don't you let your son go ahead with . . ." Monica said looking passed Sheila to her mother. "Is it good to assume that's your mom?"

"Yes it is," Sheila's mom replied in the background, "and you are?"

"Please excuse me for being rude. I'm Monica. Me and Sheila are good friends from the office," Monica replied, planting a fake smile on her face. She made eye contact with Sheila, daring her to say otherwise. Sheila's mom wasn't aware of what went down with Monica, and once Monica figured that out, she used it to her advantage.

"Yeah, we worked at the firm together before I went on leave," Sheila responded unconvincingly.

"I was about to go into the mall. Want to hang out for a while?"

"I really shouldn't," Sheila began. "I need to put Devon down for a nap, and I'm a little tired myself."

"Girl, that's nonsense," Sheila's mom said. "I can put Devon in bed. You've done nothing but cater to him since you been on leave. Go ahead with your friend. You need some adult time for a while. I have your cell number. I'll call you if I need you."

Sheila was determined not to be alone with Monica ever again in life, and now her mom had made that virtually impossible.

"But, Mom, I need to . . ."

"Nonsense, now go and have a good time. Your son will be here when you get back."

Trying to cover her attitude in front of her mom, Sheila gathered her belongings and got out of the car. Before closing the door, she leaned in and kissed her son on the forehead, looking at him like that may be her last time seeing him. She didn't want to be with Monica, but knew if she didn't go, Monica's persistent ass would just keep following her until she gave in. The way Sheila saw it, if she just got it done and over with maybe Monica would leave her alone, but deep down she knew it wouldn't be that simple. She had to find a way to turn the tables on Monica, and she vowed to find a way to do just that and still have her job intact.

After Sheila got into Monica's car, her mom wasn't even out of the parking lot good before Monica was back out on the street. Sheila didn't have to ask because she knew they were on their way to Monica's house, and her thoughts were confirmed when she saw the only pink house on the block standing out from their spot on the corner. Neither said a word on the drive over, and Sheila decided she would let Monica do all the talking while she tried to figure out how to get out of the mess she just happened to become a part of.

Walking into the house a short while later, Sheila excused herself and went upstairs to use the restroom. Noticing the open door at the end of the hall, curiosity took over as she crept to the door to get a peek inside. That door was normally shut tight and locked down. Taking notice of her surroundings, she began looking at the canvas placed in the corners around the room. She knew Monica was a photographer, but she didn't know Monica painted as well.

Sifting through the stacks of paintings, she noticed that the woman on the paintings looked just like Jasmine. She knew Jasmine and Monica were cool, but not to that extent. She figured Monica was probably just lusting after Jasmine too, and painted what she thought Jazz would look like nude because there was no way her boss was bisexual. Leaving it to an assumption, she turned around to leave the room only to find Monica in the doorway watching her.

"Monica, I was just . . ." Sheila began, holding her chest from the shock of seeing Monica standing there. She hadn't even heard her come up the steps.

"Being nosey as hell!" Monica began taking a step into the room. "Find what you were looking for? From what I recall the bathroom is nowhere near this room."

"I . . . I saw the door cracked, and . . ."

"You want to know why you see Jasmine on those paintings?"

Shocked by Monica's ability to read her thoughts, she stood in silence just looking at her. Sheila knew she was in some shit before, but it was just sinking in as to how deep the shit really was. Monica was one powerful chick, and Sheila was feeling the seriousness of what was going on around her.

"Follow me," Monica said, turning from the room and going into the master bedroom. Sheila's legs felt like lead as she walked behind her, stealing glimpses at paintings of James and what looked like the guy from the hardware store in her neighborhood.

Walking down the hallway seemed to take forever as Sheila continued to take notice of the people in the paintings hanging on the walls. All of them featured Monica, but each man was different, making Sheila wonder how many men and women Monica had actually been with. Furthermore, she wondered if she bothered to use protection with any of them, because she and Monica never had.

Upon entering the room, she took a seat on the edge of the bed as Monica hooked up the camcorder that she hid behind the mirror to the television. Sheila didn't want to know what was on the tape for fear of who she might see. It was obvious that Monica got around, and Sheila was sure that she might know some of the people.

Monica took a seat beside Sheila and turned her face so they were eye to eye. Sheila thought she saw flames shooting up behind Monica's hazel eyes like she was the devil reincarnated. Too scared to move, but curious at the same time, Sheila waited to see what would happen next.

"Sheila, I'm going to show you this tape because I trust you. This recording is one of many, and what you see here can never leave this bedroom. Do you understand me?" Monica asked with a straight face. There were no traces of vengeance in her voice, but Sheila did detect a hint of sadness—maybe even weakness—that Monica wouldn't normally show. Sheila's mouth wouldn't move, so she just nodded her head in agreement.

At this point Monica was tired of the runaround. Going to Sheila was pretty much her only option, because she had Sheila tucked safely in her back pocket. If Sheila told, she would be putting herself out there, and Monica doubted that she would do that. Besides, it was becoming too overwhelming trying to hold everything in.

"I also want you to understand that if this does get out, it won't be wonderful for you. Get my drift?"

Without waiting for a response, Monica pushed the play button and stood by the window to wait until the tape finished playing. Monica couldn't watch the tape again because, in spite of what everyone thought of her, it was painful for her. She wanted Jasmine more than she wanted life, and she just couldn't seem to grab hold of her no matter how close she got. It was like someone was dangling a carrot in front of her and she just couldn't reach it.

Monica spotted Jasmine long before she slept with James. Jasmine had represented Monica's former lover, Tanya, in the murder case for her husband. Tanya and Monica, much like her and Jasmine, were seeing each other. Monica fell in love with Tanya, and her husband had to go—by any means necessary. Tanya didn't want to break it off because of the children they shared, even though Monica had more money than either of them could count.

Monica was getting restless and fed up, because just as James was doing now, Tanya's husband Marcus was sleeping with her also. Although Marcus treated Monica like a queen, he was very abusive toward Tanya, often leaving her with black eyes and broken bones. Deciding enough was enough, Monica went to Tanya's house one night to see if she could lure Marcus away. When she arrived, she found Marcus going through one of his many drunken fits, and he was beating Tanya unmercifully.

Monica used her spare key to get in, and she tried to help Tanya out. In a raging fit, Marcus then began swinging on her, leaving her no choice but to take the small revolver out of the pocket of her trench coat and *off* him right there. The one shot to the head would have done it, but Monica unloaded the gun into his face, reloaded, and finished him off until there was nothing left but a shell of what used to be his head.

Tanya broke down and Monica fled the scene, promising Tanya that she would get her the best lawyer money could buy. Before Monica could act, Tanya was appointed to the extremely sexy Jasmine Cinque. When Monica saw her it was love at first sight. She went through the motions of finding out who Jasmine was and if she was married. Getting info from her favorite judge down at the courthouse, she found out about James, later seducing him and talking him into the threesome with Jasmine. Now it was only a matter of time before she got Jazz, and hopefully without having to get rid of James permanently. Tanya quickly became a distant memory as Monica left her rotting in jail for a crime she didn't commit and made Jasmine her replacement.

Monica snapped out of her memories when she heard Sheila gasp. Sheila stared at the television with her mouth wide open in shock at the things the tape revealed. First, she saw James, Jasmine, and Monica at the hotel. Then there was Monica and James, including the two exchanging money. Then, there was Monica and Jasmine with the ice sculptures.

Sheila almost fell off the bed when she saw Officer Hill on the tape in front of the fireplace. Monica didn't know Officer Hill was married to Sheila's oldest sister because their last names didn't match.

Sheila was feeling sick to her stomach as she watched Monica have her way with the obese mayor of Philadelphia. She almost lost her lunch when shortly thereafter a threesome, including the mayor's wife, Monica, and the mayor's daughter flashed across the screen.

Just as the tears began to form in her eyes, Monica came over and clicked the stop button on the DVD player. Sheila didn't know what to do as a steady stream of salty tears stained her cheeks and the front of her blouse. Monica seemed to be oblivious to Shelia, as she was dealing with her own pain and memories of Tanya. Breaking the monotony, she turned Sheila's face around so she could look into her eyes as she talked. She wanted Sheila to understand the significance of the situation before they moved any farther.

"Now, Sheila, I know that may have been a bit much to view at one time, but I need you to understand the caliber of what's happening here. I'm in love with Jasmine and I need your help. I don't want to blackmail James, but that may be the only way to get him out. Either that or kill him, and who wants to deal with that again?"

"What do you want me to do?" Sheila said through her tears. Monica had her on tape, and she was sure she had more than one copy.

"Not right now, but I'll need your help down the line. I just need to know that you got me on this."

"I can't do that to Jasmine. She helped me out in more ways than you can imagine. She's been good to me."

"I can get you a job better than that. I know people in high places. You can start tomorrow," Monica stated like that issue had no importance. She could just call one of the many judges she was sleeping with around Philly and have Sheila in a higher paying position the very next day.

"Monica, please, just give me some time."

"I don't have time!" Monica snapped, losing her cool for a second. She was not in the mood to negotiate with Sheila; she wasn't asking her for help, she was telling her what she was going to do. "You will do it or else."

"Or else what?" Sheila asked, not really wanting to know the answer. Monica calmed down a little before answering because now was not the time to lose control of the situation.

"Fuck with me and find out," and with that said, she put the DVD back in its case and put it in the safe that she had built into the wall behind a painting of herself in a two-piece sheer thong set.

Sheila didn't know what to do about Monica or her pounding headache, so instead of arguing, she moved farther up on the bed so that she could rest her head on the pillow. She didn't know what to do with the information she had just received, but she knew she had to do something. Before drifting off to sleep, she took one last look at Monica standing by the window. Monica seemed to be struggling with her own thoughts, and for the first time she looked vulnerable. Sheila could understand her pain, although she couldn't understand why she had to drag so many lives into it.

For a second she saw Monica as a child, which she thought was comical because she didn't know her then. She saw Monica looking out the window dressed in a pink and white baby doll dress with her long, thick hair pulled up into two pigtails held together with pink and white flower-shaped barrettes. Holding a bunny rabbit tightly in her little arms, she seemed to be at a happier time in her life then. Sheila wondered if that was when her obsession with the color pink began.

As she stared at her, Sheila saw the teenaged Monica, braces and all. Acne covered her face and this Monica looked sad like she had no friends to speak of and was teased because of her absence of curves like the rest of the girls her age had. This Monica looked like the last thing she wanted to be was alive, and her face was etched with pain and worry for reasons unknown to anyone but her.

Then she turned into the evil, conniving adult Monica, and Sheila could have sworn she saw devil horns sticking up through Monica's wrap hairstyle. Chalking it up as fatigue setting in, she closed her eyes in an effort to stop the little man from dancing on her temple. She hoped by morning she would figure out some way to stop this madness for good.

"When did you and Monica start hanging out?" James asked curiously, trying to get the heat off him. He didn't want Jasmine to even begin to think he was involved with Monica in any way, shape, or form. He was still scraping up the money from the last James and Monica private party to put back into their joint savings account they had for their twins. Keeping her quiet was expensive, and he often wondered why he kept going back.

"We hang every once in a while," Jasmine responded, choosing her words carefully.

"Since when? You acted like you didn't know who she was when we saw her at the courthouse that day." James tried to turn his guilt into anger, not realizing that he was making a done situation worse for himself.

"I didn't recognize her then," Jasmine replied with the beginnings of an attitude. "I ran into her again after that and we exchanged numbers. We only had lunch a couple of times and she picked me up from here twice. Is that a problem?"

"Are you sure all you had was *lunch?*" James asked Jasmine with a straight face. If he could get Jasmine to say she slept with Monica again, it would lift some of the guilt off his shoulders.

"What the fuck is that supposed to mean? Are you implying that there should be something else?" Jasmine came back almost at the boiling point. She wanted to continue what they started before Monica came, but James was messing it up with his accusations.

"No, I'm just saying that Monica can be very persuasive. You act like you don't know she has the hots for you."

"How would you know, James? We only shared one night. How many times were you with her since then?" Jasmine shouted, cleverly tossing the ball back into his court.

James automatically saw that he put his foot in his mouth. His reverse psychology didn't work, and he should have just let it go. He had been trying to stay away from Monica, but since day one he was drawn to her like a magnet. Deciding to bow out of the situation, he tried to come up with a lie to cover his ass before his cover was completely blown.

"I only see Monica in passing. A young lady that she's dealing with works near the station, and I see her sometimes when I'm on lunch break. She asks about you all the time, and once asked if you were interested in getting together for another threesome."

"And what did you tell her?" Jasmine asked with her arms folded tightly across her chest. James's story didn't add up only because she had been with Monica on more than one occasion, and the possibility of a threesome was never brought up.

"I told her that I didn't think you would do it because that's not your style. You only did it that one time because I asked you to."

"And she was okay with that?" Jasmine didn't sound convinced. If she knew anything about Monica, she knew that she didn't bend easily, and once she set her mind on something, that was it. She also wondered if James ever went back for more, because that story he told her about how they met just didn't add up.

"She didn't say anything otherwise, and it's been a while since I've seen her."

"How long has it been exactly?" Jasmine asked to see if he would lie about it. The night they got into the argument he came home without his boxers, and the only person she knows that keeps your underclothes after you've slept with them is Monica.

"A couple of weeks . . . She hasn't been coming that way for lunch lately, I guess."

"She told me you went there the night we got into the argument," Jasmine said, testing his credibility. She and Monica never discussed that night to that extent, but James didn't know they even talked like that.

"That's bullshit. I don't even know where she lives exactly besides the information she gave me to put the packet together for our threesome. I haven't looked at that since then, and that was so long ago."

"James, this conversation is over for now," Jasmine said while retreating up the stairs.

"But what happened with us making love on the couch?" James asked as his erection began to appear through his boxer shorts.

"You fucked that up when you decided to play detective."

"But . . ."

James couldn't get another word in as Jasmine disappeared up the steps and into the bathroom. He heard the shower running and thought about joining her. Deciding against it, he knew he had to figure out a way to leave the house so that he could go talk to Monica. He didn't know if Monica really told

Jasmine he was over there or if Jazz was just calling his bluff, but he was getting to the bottom of this once and for all.

Racing up the stairs to grab his keys off the dresser, he walked in on Jasmine applying lotion to her skin. Trying not to stare at the beads of water still on her freshly showered skin, he slipped into his boots and searched his jacket pocket for his cell phone. Jasmine took note of all of this as she continued with her task. She was not in the mood to argue with James, but she did want to get some before she went to sleep. It wasn't often that the house was child-free.

"I'll be right back," James said without even a glance in Jasmine's direction. He was going to confront Monica before his marriage was destroyed.

"Where are you going and why are you leaving now?" Jasmine was a little disappointed. She was going to make it up to James by *putting it on him,* but he was leaving the house.

"I have some business to take care of."

"On a Saturday afternoon? What kind of business?"

"Business . . . I'll be back."

"Sure you will. Tell Monica I said hello."

Without bothering to respond, he walked out of the house and jumped in Jasmine's Blazer, hoping to throw Monica off a little because she wouldn't be expecting him in his wife's car. He had to set things straight if things were going to work out between the three of them, and he had to do it today.

Jasmine watched from the window as James pulled off in her Blazer, wondering why he didn't take his car. She didn't really think James was fooling around with Monica, but felt guilty as hell because she was. Changing the sheets and taking clothes out of the hamper, Jasmine found the pair of panties that she threw in there a few weeks ago. She took them out holding them to her nose, still smelling the faint scent of Monica's chocolate body butter.

Deciding to toss them in the trash so James wouldn't suspect her of foul play, she cut them up into little pieces and made sure they were at the bottom of the trashcan. Taking the rest of the stuff to the laundry room, she busied herself with washing clothes as she tried to think of a way to let Monica go without ruffling her feathers.

Trouble With a Capital 'T'

When James first met Monica, he was in complete awe of how sexy she was. Standing outside of The Grill, a fast food restaurant that serves 90 percent of the businessmen and women in Central Philadelphia, he spotted Monica at one of the tables outside eating alone. After placing his order, he contemplated going outside to talk to the pretty-in-pink vixen dining alone. He and Jasmine were going through *it* at home, and even though he never really entertained the idea of stepping out of his marriage, if he did, Monica would be perfect.

Hesitant at first, he stood to the side while his food was being prepared, just watching her eat. She took petite bites of her grilled chicken salad as she simultaneously sipped home-made lemonade and flipped through her copy of *Complex* magazine. She had the cutest heart-shaped lips, the bottom slightly fuller than the top.

Watching her movements, James thought she made eating almost look sensual even when she looked up a couple of times, catching him glancing her way. Her facial expression didn't change as she looked back down at her magazine and continued to enjoy her meal. James noticed that her salad was almost gone, and he wished the cooks would hurry up so he would have a reason to go over to her. As if reading his thoughts, his number was called and he made his way through the crowded restaurant and outside just as Monica was preparing herself to leave.

"Is this seat taken?" James asked, flashing his most charming smile. His smile was what attracted Jasmine to him.

"No, and actually I was just leaving," Monica said as she pushed the remainder of her salad to the side and searched her pocketbook for her car keys.

"You can't leave . . . I mean, please stay. Your company is appreciated."

Monica looked at James—his physique, his jet-black wavy hair and goatee connected perfectly on his smooth face, his eyes that looked like pools of warm caramel that made you just want to strip down to nothing and dive into them. The handsome man intrigued Monica.

"No thank you, maybe next time," Monica replied as she dropped a twenty on the table and walked away.

James was speechless as he watched her in silence, her sway hypnotic. James almost ran after her, but knew if he did it would just scare her off.

The following day Monica was seated in the same spot. This time James had already ordered, and instead of asking her permission, once his food was done he went and sat down at the table with her. Monica looked up from her magazine, no indication of a smile present. James began cutting his grilled chicken into bite-sized pieces, totally ignoring the look of disdain on her face.

"I don't remember offering you a seat," Monica began, clearly annoyed. Although the man in front of her intrigued her, she didn't like the fact that he took the initiative. To her that showed signs of being pushy and inconsiderate, and she didn't tolerate that.

"Oh, I do apologize. It's just that all of the other tables are taken, and I figured sitting next to someone as beautiful as you would make all of the other men here jealous," James responded with a lazy smile. He could have easily occupied one of the tables where other men were having lunch alone, but he wasn't trying to get with them.

Monica already knew who James was from her little investigation the day before. After taking the liberty of doing a background check on Tanya's sexy lawyer, she was surprised to find out the handsome man at lunch yesterday belonged to her, and devised a plan to get next to her through him. She had to make him think she wanted him badly if she had any chance of meeting Jasmine outside of the courtroom. James was sexy, but Jasmine was a dime. Monica knew if she got the chance she would turn Jasmine out in more ways than she could handle.

"Flattery will get you everywhere," Monica flirted back openly. "What's your name?"

"James . . . James Cinque, and you are?"

"Monica."

"Monica what? I gave you both names, so now it's your turn."

"Monica will do for now," she replied with a slight smirk, satisfied that this was the correct James Cinque from T.U.N.N. The last name was not common, so she knew it had to be him.

"Okay Miss 'Monica will do for now'," James joked, "What inspires you? What do you do for entertainment?"

"A little of this, a little of that," Monica responded flirtatiously. She thought James's gullible ass was going to be easy as she picked at her salad.

"Cute . . . real cute. Well, what do you do for a living? Or does the answer remain the same?" Instead of responding, Monica placed a business card on the table. James picked it up, taking in the fancy script and pleasant smell like the cards were sprayed lightly with Breathless by Victoria.

"*Specializing in You*. Are you independently contracted or what? What exactly do you do?" James asked as he stared at the black card complete with a long stem pink rose and lettering of the same color. The card looked very chic but classy, just like Monica and completely unlike his wife's boring business cards that the firm supplied her with.

"I'm a photographer," Monica offered without further explanation.

"Family portraits, children, pets," James inquired getting a sexy laugh from Monica. "Please, elaborate for me."

"I photograph stars for several different magazines. *Essence, Complex, Sister 2 Sister, Ebony, Vibe,* things like that. I also paint and sell my work for high dollars."

"Wow," James said taken aback by Monica's forwardness. "So how do I go about getting a private session?"

"A private session, huh? Is that a wedding band I see on your finger?" Monica asked, already knowing it was.

"One has nothing to do with the other," James replied, trying to avoid the question. "How can a nice brother like myself take a sexy woman like you out to dinner?"

"Sorry," Monica replied. "I don't frolic with the talent. Have a good day, Mr. Cinque."

Without waiting for a response, Monica dropped another twenty on the table and left as quickly as she came. Looking down at the business card, James saw that she wrote her home number on the back of it. Tucking the card inside of his wallet, James wrapped his lunch to go and made his way back to the office.

Slamming on the breaks, James almost ran a red light as thoughts of Monica clouded his memory. He was clearly intrigued by Monica's beauty, but now he couldn't help but think that bringing her into his marriage was a huge mistake. He thought back on the threesome with his wife and wondered if she and Monica ever got together after that. He also thought about all the times he and Monica had unprotected sex and wondered what exactly he would do if she did get pregnant. How would he explain it to Jasmine? That threesome happened well over six months ago. The amount of money he spent on her was already an issue Jasmine could not find out about, and he was set on ending what they had today.

Pulling up to Monica's door, he parked behind her convertible and walked quickly through the closed door. Monica was elated that Jasmine came to see her until she saw James exiting the vehicle. Wondering what the purpose of his visit was, she took the steps two at a time, hurrying to answer his persistent banging on her cherry wood door.

"Why are you banging on my door like you're the police?" Monica said as she swung the door open.

"We need to talk," James replied coldly as he brushed past her, not waiting to be asked inside.

James missed the dirty look Monica gave him as she slowly closed the door and made her way to the sofa. She had just taken a pregnancy test, her third in three weeks, to confirm that she was still pregnant and the test worked. She had a gynecologist appointment in the morning that she was dying to get to. She was planning to share her good news with Sheila once she woke up, but James's unexpected visit deterred her for a second.

"What do we need to talk about, James?" Monica inquired, already bored with his presence. She thought briefly about waking Sheila up and having that threesome just to make sure she was really pregnant, but she decided to wait. Just in case she wasn't pregnant she would need him to come by again.

"Monica, I can't do this anymore," James began while pacing back and forth in front of the couch. He knew if he sat down he wouldn't get anything said. Sitting too close to Monica was dangerous at a time like this. He needed to keep a level head to get this done.

"You can't do what, James? How many times are we going to go through this?" Monica asked as she stood up and pressed her body against his. "Are you starting to feel guilty again?"

"Did you tell Jasmine I came over here to talk about her when she made me mad that night?"

"I haven't seen Jasmine in a long time," Monica began, trying to see where he was taking this. "Why? What did she tell you?" Monica asked, taking her seat again because she was starting to feel sharp pains in her side that took her breath away.

James didn't want to put it out there if it wasn't said, and chalked it up as Jasmine trying to call his bluff. He would deal with that once he got home, but for now he had to break things off with Monica.

"She didn't tell me anything. I wanted to know if you opened your mouth to her."

"Well, I didn't." Monica said between breaths. The pains in her abdomen were getting sharper, causing her breath to come in spurts.

"Good, keep it that way. I just came here to tell you that we have to chill. I can't see you anymore. Things at home aren't right, and being here is not going to . . . Monica are you okay?"

James was so into his story he didn't see Monica doubled over in pain on the couch until he turned to look at her. His back was to her, and he was mainly focused on how to get things with Jasmine back on track. She was clutching her stomach with tears streaming down her face, a pool of crimson blood forming around her on the beige sofa. James ran over to her not knowing what to do.

"Monica, it's okay, baby, I'm calling for an ambulance now," James replied while trying to hold her up and dial 911 at the same time.

"James, tell them to hurry. I don't want to lose my baby," Monica said between her tears.

"Baby? What baby?" James said as he waited for his phone to connect to the police station.

"Your baby, now hurry up," Monica replied, as the circle of blood grew larger beneath her.

James explained the situation to the cops, and he talked to Monica once they were on their way. As cruel as it may sound, he hoped deep down that the baby didn't make it. That way he wouldn't have to explain his adulterous ways to his wife.

By the time the ambulance showed up, Monica was laid back on the couch barely able to move. James did what he could to keep her comfortable, but he was getting more nervous by the second because of the amount of blood on the couch and on the floor in front of it. The ambulance walked in and checked Monica's vitals as they questioned James on what happened.

James tried as best he could to explain what went down as they wheeled Monica out to the truck. He heard Monica, as low as her voice was, telling the EMT to hurry because she didn't want to lose her baby. Monica had lost a lot of blood and was miscarrying as they spoke.

Not knowing what to do as the ambulance pulled away, James turned back to the house so that he could clean the mess up. When he walked in, he saw Sheila standing up the top of the steps with tears in her eyes.

"I didn't know you were here," James said, surprised to see Sheila. The last time they got together they were in a very compromising position, and it made him feel a little uncomfortable with her in the room.

"We were just talking and I dozed off," Sheila replied, not wanting James to know that she heard bits and pieces of what they were talking about. She thought she heard Monica tell James she was pregnant, but by the looks of things she might not be for long.

They stared at each other for a while, James taking a seat on the arm of the chair to collect his thoughts.

"Look, about the last time I was here," Sheila began suddenly feeling like she had to cover herself. She didn't know what James thought of her, and she wanted to tell someone what she knew before it killed her.

"Don't worry about it. Let's just clean this up. I don't want her to come home to this mess."

Without words they both grabbed towels and cleaners and got the mess up as best they could. They couldn't do anything about the blood on the couch, but they made sure the floor was spotless, and threw the soaked pillow away so that Monica wouldn't have to deal with it when she got home.

Sheila went back and forth in her mind about whether she should tell James about the videotape as he drove her home. She had taken one from the wall safe that Monica had left unlocked, and it was now burning a hole in her pocket. He didn't look her way once, his eyes appearing glazed over as the tragedy played repeatedly in his head. James was going through his own shit, and was praying hard that the baby didn't make it. After dropping Sheila off, he went home to talk to his wife, deciding that would be the last time Monica saw him.

By the time Monica arrived at the hospital, they had to take the three-month-old fetus from her and give her a blood transfusion to help her survive. She was carrying in her tubes, and they caught it just in time. If she had waited any longer, her tubes would have burst, killing her in the process.

Pulling into his driveway a half hour later, James walked slowly up to his front door after noticing his bedroom light was still on. Debating whether he would share what just happened with his wife, he put his key in the door, not really knowing how to handle the situation. Figuring it would probably be best if he just came clean, he took the long trek to his bedroom to clear the air between him and his wife once and for all.

When he walked in, Jasmine was sleeping quietly under the covers. James saw that she had fallen asleep with the television on because the house had to be pitch black and quiet for Jazz to get any kind of rest. She said it was so she could hear the kids, but James knew better. Smiling for a second at how beautiful his wife was, he had to wonder again how everything went wrong. They had been soul mates since day one. She gave him what he asked for without any questions, and never really gave him a reason to step out. The issues they had were minimal and could have been worked out had he been a little more patient with her.

Turning off the television and light and turning on the radio, James got into the bed and wrapped himself around his wife as sounds of Luther's "So Amazing" started to play from the radio. Jasmine snuggled up closer to him.

"Jazz, I'm so sorry I hurt you baby. I never meant to." James was trying to control his tears as he talked to his wife. He knew she was no longer asleep because she was crying as well. He felt her tears splash against his arm. Baby, I know I messed up. I just need to you help me. I need you to be here for me. I can't do this by myself. You and the kids complete me."

"James, it's okay. I'll never leave you, baby. I want this to work just as much as you do, but I need the truth. I need to know what happened when you left here. I need to know everything from day one."

As the quiet storm played on the radio, James told Jasmine everything about Monica from day one, leaving out the money, the baby, and a few other details that he didn't think Jasmine could handle. He knew he was still telling lies, but it felt good to get some of the stuff off his chest. He was determined to be done with Monica and get his family back on track. Afterward they held each other until they both fell asleep, making promises to each other to work it out the best they could.

Finders Keepers, Losers Cry

Monica had been in the hospital for three weeks trying to recover from the loss of her child and her near-death experience. James and Sheila didn't show their faces, and it was taking a toll on her mentally and emotionally. For the first time since Monica was a teenager, she truly felt alone in the world. In fact, ever since her mom had passed away—rather, since her mom's life was taken—it seemed as if no one in the universe cared about her.

Her depression only made her condition worse, and the doctors didn't see any sign of life in her outside of the healing of her body. All Monica did was cry day in and day out, and she wouldn't eat, so the doctors had her tube-fed so her body could get some type of nourishment. Her weight was at an unsightly low, almost making her look skeletal as she pitied herself for not taking the time to make things right in her life.

She slept most of the day, fighting off nightmares of her uncle and her sister's father molesting her as a teenager and the unforgettable incident from the tenth grade with Keith and his friends. Every man she cared even remotely about always ended up hurting her, breaking her heart.

Monica wallowed in self-pity day after day to the point where the doctor suggested she seek counseling so she could better deal with her anxiety and bouts of depression. Monica was falling apart at the seams, unlike the Monica that everyone knew.

On her last day at the hospital, after she signed up for therapy sessions and the doctor saw that she was eating and actually keeping her food down, Monica sat in her room thinking of ways to get her life back. She knew she had to get James and Sheila back because she felt like they abandoned her, and she also had to get Jasmine before it was too late. Monica was tired of sleeping alone, and she had to move fast if things were going to work.

While waiting for her discharge papers, Monica took her time putting on the new sweat suit and sneakers one of the guards purchased for her to go home in because the clothes she came in with were soiled. All he wanted was her number and dinner, and she obliged. Anything to get the overbearing, underpaid security guard out of her face.

Watching *Jenny Jones* on television while waiting for the nurse to come back, she almost fell off the bed when she saw Sheila walk through the door. Fixing her face to say something smart, Monica thought better of it, thinking she may need Sheila to help her later on down the line. Sheila came in with a small teddy bear and flowers, her facial expression showing how nervous she was in spite of her smile.

"Monica, I'm sorry I haven't been to see you. I've been so busy with . . ."

"Sheila, it's fine, no explanation is needed. I'm just waiting for my discharge papers so I can blow this joint," Monica said as she turned her attention back to the television.

Sheila took note of how frail Monica looked. Placing the teddy bear and Monica's house keys on the bed beside her, Sheila took one last look at her before she turned to leave. Nearing the door, she turned the knob, not knowing what to do and kicking herself for coming up there in the first place.

Just as she was closing the door, she heard Monica call her name. When she looked back into the room, Monica was holding the teddy bear in her hands with tears in her eyes. Sheila waited at the door for her to speak.

"Thanks for coming up here. I really appreciate it."

"It was no trouble. Just get better soon," Sheila replied and turned away quickly so Monica wouldn't see her tears.

Once Monica was sure Sheila was gone, she held up the teddy bear and took a long look at it. Ripping the head from its shoulders, she dropped both pieces in the can next to her bed. She continued watching her show as if nothing happened. She didn't need stuffed animals; she needed Jasmine, and that's all she was concerned about.

After signing her discharge papers, she walked out of the hospital and got into the waiting cab that was to take her home. The driver tried to make small talk, but Monica just stared out the window taking in the city, everything looking new to her. To her it felt like she was in the hospital for three years instead of three weeks. She couldn't wait to get home so she could lay down in her own bed and not the hard hospital one that she had been in.

Once the driver pulled up to her house, she paid him and exited the vehicle quickly so she could hurry up to her room. Upon entrance, she could smell the stale blood in the air from her recent loss. Avoiding the stained sofa, Monica all but ran up to her room, throwing herself on the bed in a fit of tears once she got there. She couldn't understand why things weren't going her way. She briefly thought about praying, but cast the thought aside after determining God wouldn't hear her for all of the dirt she'd done.

Drifting off to sleep once her tears subsided, she thought about ways of knocking James off quickly so she could finally have Jasmine to herself. The baby wasn't all that important to her, but if all else failed, Monica decided she would try getting pregnant again as a last resort. As bad as things were going, something had to give, and she hoped it would give soon.

Monica slept well until the next afternoon, the ringing phone waking her from her slumber. Upset about the interference of her much-needed sleep but glad to be awakened from the nightmare she was having, Monica answered the phone with a groggy voice lacking any type of enthusiasm. She thought it was still morning and wondered who would be calling so early.

"This better be good," Monica barked into the phone as she struggled to sit up in her bed. She was still having slight pains in her abdomen, and it wasn't easy for her to maneuver around.

"You have a paid call from an inmate held in Muncy Correctional Facility. If you attempt to use three-way calling or any other features, this call will be disconnected. To accept this call, press three now," the computer voice spoke into the receiver.

Monica glanced at the clock, realizing it was the afternoon, and wondered who got locked up and was calling for her assistance. She had just bailed her sister out only two months ago and hoped she wasn't sent up again. Her sister was a petty thief, and Monica was starting to think she preferred jail to having freedom. Pressing three, she spoke into the receiver ready to hear some member of her dysfunctional family beg for help.

"Who needs my help now?" Monica spoke into the phone once the call was connected. She didn't plan on helping whoever was calling, and was going to make this short and sweet.

"You seem to have forgotten about me," the voice came through on the other end, sounding angry and ready to explode.

"I forgot about who?" Monica replied, thinking her mind was playing tricks on her. She hadn't spoken to Tanya since the day she was sent up for her husband's murder almost two and a half years ago. Wondering why she decided to call now, Monica didn't hide her disbelief as they continued their conversation.

"After all we've been through you don't know who this is?" Tanya came through on the other end like she wanted to snatch Monica by her neck.

"I know who it is," Monica came back with an attitude. She was over Tanya and didn't feel like the bullshit. What was Tanya going to do for her from prison? Besides, she had her eyes on a bigger prize and didn't plan on being distracted by anyone.

"Why am I still in here? You told me a couple of weeks, and that's it," Tanya said, sounding like she was starting to cry. "I been in here for damn near three years waiting for you to get me out of this hellhole. What the fuck is the problem?"

"What do you mean what's the problem? I told you there would be some time served," Monica came back with just as much attitude.

As far as she was concerned, she didn't owe Tanya shit. If anything, she did her a favor by killing her abusive husband. Who wants to live in fear every day for the rest of their life not knowing how their man was going to act when he got home? You can't be cute with a black eye and broken ribs. Ain't nothing sexy about it. Monica came to the conclusion that if she didn't kill him he would have killed her, and it's as simple as that. No, she didn't think about the situation she put Tanya's son in, but Monica was never good at looking at the big picture.

"So what am I supposed to do? I didn't tell on you because I thought you had my back. I thought you loved me," Tanya screamed into the phone, her emotions getting the best of her, causing the other inmates to look in her direction. Even though she told herself she wasn't going to cry, she couldn't help it. She wanted out of the stone cage she was forced to be in, and she was ready to do whatever necessary to make it happen.

"What did I tell you about trusting people? Didn't I tell you no human was trustworthy? Didn't I tell you that *you* were the only one who had your back?" Monica shot the questions at her back to back, not giving her enough time to answer in between. "You come into this world alone and you leave alone. How many times have we had this conversation?" Monica was getting frustrated with the entire scenario and was about to hang up. Her main focus was Jasmine now, and she didn't want to hear shit Tanya had to say. When was the world going to understand that it was all about Monica and what made her happy? No one else mattered.

"So you just gonna leave me here?" Tanya said in a quiet voice, not believing the turn of events. She thought Monica was her soul mate, and thought about all the nights they were wrapped around each other, professing their never-ending love. The Monica she was talking to now was a complete stranger.

"Tanya," Monica began, feeling kind of bad because she was the reason Tanya was in jail in the first place, "I'll make some calls in the morning and see what I can do for you, okay?"

"Monica, listen. I need to get out of here. I can't watch my son leave another visit. It's driving me crazy knowing that he's too young to understand. All he knows is he wants his mom. He cries every time he has to leave. Can't you understand the pain I'm going through?"

Monica began thinking about her own loss and the loss of her mother years ago. There were so many times when she needed to talk to her mom, but couldn't. So many times she wished she had a gun so she could stop her stepfather from beating her mom in his drunken state. So many times she begged her mom to leave, only for her mom to tell her it was okay as she limped to her room after being beaten nearly unconscious for reasons she didn't even know. So many times she wished she had the courage to stop him that one last time as she watched her mother's spirit leave her body, her attacker still kicking and punching her until she stopped moving.

Brushing back tears, she got herself together as she listened to Tanya's soft cries and her pleas to get her home to her son. All Tanya wanted was a second chance, and she needed Monica to help her get it.

"Tanya, please stop crying. I'll be there soon, and I'll make some calls for you today. I'll get you home, okay?"

Before Tanya could respond, her time had expired on the call and they were disconnected. Monica held onto the phone long after the dial tone had stopped, and the operator was instructing her to either hang up or make a call as tears stung her eyes. She didn't want Jasmine's situation to turn out the same as Tanya's, or worse. Calling up Judge Stenton, the same judge who presided over Tanya's case, she set up an appointment to meet with him in private so they could discuss a few things. He owed her a favor, and there was no time like the present to cash in on it.

What I Wouldn't Do For You

James had been standing outside Monica's house for at least twenty minutes, several times resisting the urge to hop in his car and stay away forever. Hating to admit that he may be slipping again, he had called the hospital earlier just as he had for the past three weeks to check with the nurses to see if Monica was okay, not wanting to talk to her directly. He kept tabs on her progression the entire time, telling the nurses he was her brother from out of town.

Upon finding out that she was discharged, he took off from work early to check in on her and find out if she was still carrying the baby because he didn't have the heart to ask the nurse about it. Stopping to get soup and juice for Monica, he stood outside peering up at her windows, the sun relentless on his already chocolate skin. Finally taking a deep breath to boost his courage, he went up and knocked on the door, announcing his arrival to her home.

On the other side of the door, he could hear Monica racing down the steps. His heart beat just as quickly as her footsteps on the hardwood floor. Waiting in anticipation for her to open the door felt like an eternity; his voice came out weak and soft when she asked who was on the other side.

Monica took a step back, pausing before opening the door. James was just the person she was looking for, and she was prepared to read him the riot act for abandoning her the way he did. When she pulled the door open, James all but jumped back, gasping out loud at the woman standing before him.

Her cheeks and eyes were sunken in and her bones showed under the once tight shirt she was wearing, Monica looked like she had been binging on coke for the past couple of days. Gone was the sexy smile and mischievous eyes. Standing before him was a Monica he didn't recognize as a million questions flooded his head at once.

"Are you going to stand there and stare at me, or are you coming in?" Monica quizzed, frustrated that he caught her looking her worst.

Following Monica into the kitchen, he sat the contents in his hand down, taking a seat before his face became acquainted with the floor. James breathed heavily, trying to control the lightheaded feeling he was having. Monica leaned against the sink taking it all in, contemplating offering him a glass of water to ease his anxiety.

"So, James," Monica said while examining her nails, "what brought you to this side of town? I thought maybe your fingers had been broken or you had amnesia."

"It wasn't like that," James began, deciding against telling her that he had checked on her every day while she was in the hospital. "I had to keep things tight at home. Maintain balance with my own family. You know how it is."

"No, I don't know how it is! As you can plainly see, I am the only occupant under this roof. Or have we forgotten already?" Monica stated sarcastically, causing James to get on the defensive.

"Look, I didn't come here for all that . . ."

"Then what are you here for? To see if I'm still pregnant with your child?"

James didn't want to just bust out and ask her the obvious even though she had hit the nail right on the head.

"Monica, you need to slow the fuck down," James said, all of a sudden feeling strong and taking Monica by surprise. "I heard you were out of the hospital, and I came to see if you were okay. I bought you some stuff so you wouldn't have to leave the house because I was concerned. I know you're not used to people caring about your well-being, but I can do without the sarcastic bullshit."

"I just know you done lost your mind!" Monica stepped away from the kitchen sink and toward James like she was two seconds from pouncing on him and ripping his heart out his chest with her bare hands.

"You know what, Monica?" James said, backing away from the table and making his way to the front door. "This shit is for the birds. I don't want or need the drama!"

As he walked to the door, his one step equaling about four of Monica's, he could hear her playing catch-up behind him. Regretting turning his back to her, he hoped she wasn't running up on him with a knife or something. Monica had major screws loose, and he didn't feel like having to explain it to Jazz later. He was supposed to be at work anyway.

"James, wait," Monica said as she came up behind him.

"What?" James said, still facing the door with his hand on the knob. He just wanted to know if he was going to be a father again or not. Anything else was irrelevant.

"I lost the baby. I don't know how happy that makes you, but it damn near killed me. That's all I had to keep you near my heart, the only thing I could call mine. Someone to finally love me," Monica said through her tears. She didn't want James exactly, but knew that a child would give her unconditional love regardless if he was around or not. It would make her and Jasmine's family complete.

"All you would have done was caused problems. I don't need another kid right now, and even if you had kept it we still wouldn't have been together."

"Who said it's you I want, James?" Monica said before catching herself. If James knew she was after his wife, he would never come back over.

"Then who do you want, Monica? I don't think you even know."

Without continuing the conversation, he opened the door. The brightness of the sun blurred his vision for a few seconds as his eyes adjusted to the light. Monica stood in the doorway watching him walk away, not really feeling any remorse. She knew she looked a horrible mess, and that was the only reason James resisted her, but that wouldn't be for long. Closing the door and heading to the kitchen, Monica began making a feast as she calculated how she could get pregnant by James again.

Five Months Later . . .

Pulling up to the news station, Monica let the pimple-faced adolescent park her convertible after retrieving the picnic basket from the back seat. It was a nice fall day in The City of Brotherly Love. A slight October chill could be felt on her bare skin under the trench coat she wore, making her wish for a second that she had worn more than a thong and a garter belt. Placing her free arm across her chest, she pressed down against her erect nipples as she made her way into the building from the parking garage.

It had been a while since she'd seen James. The little scene at her house during his last visit played repeatedly in her mind as she worked at getting her appearance back to what it used to be. Her once sagging breasts were back to their perky selves, sitting at attention as they brushed against the underside of her soft pink trench coat.

Her hair was braided up in micros, set on straws with a flower on the side, giving her a carefree summer look even at this time of year. Monica's thigh-high boots peeked out of her trench coat every time she took a step across the marble lobby of The Urban News Network. Every eye was on her as she walked like a high fashion model, confidence dripping off her with lots left to spare.

When she reached the desk, the security guard was speechless as he sat looking in awe at the beauty in front of him. His erection was about to break his zipper.

"I need you to do me a favor," Monica said to the flashlight cop in a tone only he could hear. "I'm visiting my husband in the engineering department and I don't want him to know I'm here. Is it possible for me to get a key to his office so I can surprise him when he walks in? His name is James Cinque."

The guard couldn't answer; his tongue caught in his throat when Monica touched the side of his face, the front of his pants sporting a wide circle from his ejaculation. Passing her the keys, he couldn't take his eyes off her as she kissed him on the cheek, leaving her Revlon Passion Fruit mouth print on the side of his face. She walked slowly away from him, letting him take in all of her in as she boarded the elevator, opening her coat for him as the door was closing, giving him a frontal view of what he would never have.

The elevator took her to the eighteenth floor quickly; she stepped off the elevator thankful that no one got on as she came up. Finding James's office without a problem, she drew the blinds shut tightly so no one could look in. After she set up her candles and picnic lunch, she stretched out on the leather sofa in her outfit awaiting his arrival.

James, not paying attention to the sudden darkness in his locked office, opened the door, finally looking up at the scene. Noticing Monica mostly naked on his sofa, he closed the door abruptly, being sure to put both locks on.

"What are you doing here?" James asked, taking in Monica's smooth body stretched out before him. Gone was the skeletal Monica who was nothing more than a bag of bones the last time he saw her. What lay before him was a curvaceous ebony sister, thick in all the right places. This Monica was ten times better than the Monica before her skeletal state, her body radiating heat that he could feel from his spot at the door.

"Well," Monica said as she opened her legs for him to see the crotchless thong she was sporting, the candlelight bouncing off her pierced clit. "It's been a while since the last time I saw you and I wanted to remind you of what you were missing."

Getting up off the couch, Monica looked to make sure the mini-camera was on that she placed beside the picture of him and Jasmine he had hanging from the wall. Walking up to James, she began unbuttoning his shirt, kissing him on the neck in the process.

"Monica, what are you doing?" James came back trying to get some control over the situation, his manhood standing at attention and giving away his real thoughts.

"I'm letting you know what you've been missing."

Sliding down to waist level, Monica unzipped his pants and pulled out his thickness, marveling at the evenness of his skin tone. Circling the head with the tip of her tongue first, Monica took just the head in. James leaned against the door for support.

"Monica, we can't do this," James said weakly as the effects of the brain job he was receiving took effect. "I'm at work."

"Then that means you'll have to be quiet then, huh?" Monica replied between kisses as she swallowed James up, his seed dripping from the sides of her mouth showing his excitement.

Pushing James over to the couch, he sat down with a thud, as Monica stood over top of him, holding him by his tie.

Squatting down on his length, she moved slow and then fast, contracting her vaginal muscles around his shaft, causing him to explode inside of her almost immediately.

Monica being a pro, she kept him inside of her, working her muscles until he was stiff again, bouncing up and down on him like she was auditioning for a rap video. James held on to Monica's waist as he sucked hard on her nipples, adding to her pleasure. He reached between her legs and softly tugged on her clit ring until she threw her head back in pleasure. They climaxed together, evidence of their session all over his stomach and pubic area.

Monica got up and stepped away from him, bending over to remove all of their juices from his penis with her mouth, causing him to explode in the back of her throat one final time.

Allowing James to catch his breath, she stepped over to his desk and retrieved the chilled bottle of Moet she brought for their meal. Pouring the clear liquid into two flutes, Monica offered one to James, opting to remain standing in front of him. He didn't even bother to adjust his clothes, downing the champagne like it was spring water.

Finally daring a look at Monica, his length rose to the occasion again at the sight of her. He knew he was dead wrong, especially since he and Jazz had just made love that morning. Once again he didn't use protection, and that alone had him knocking himself in the head. Turning her back to him, Monica straddled James again. With his head leaned back against the sofa, he just enjoyed the ride, deciding to worry about the consequences later.

"James . . ." Monica moaned softly. Her body movement slowing down as her orgasm approached. "Can I cum, papi?"

Instead of responding, James pumped back harder, causing Monica to almost fall off him. Motioning for her to stand up, he stayed inside of her as he bent her over his desk, recklessly driving into her, trying to hurt her purposefully. Monica was staring at the photo of him and his family the entire time, in her mind replacing James's image with her own.

"Monica," James said as he banged her back out like a madman, "make this your last time coming to my office. It's over, you hear me?" Monica took too long answering, so James drove into her harder, her breasts bouncing against the side of the desk.

"I said do you hear me?"

"Yes, I hear you. Please . . . you're hurting me," Monica came back, still surprised at James. He had never sexed her with so much intensity, and for once, she couldn't handle it.

Instead of stopping, James continued his barrage against her swollen cave, holding her up as her knees tried to buckle under her. Hitting it hard, he didn't pull out until he was about to explode, doing so all over her braids and back. Stepping away from Monica's crumpled form on the floor he stepped back into his clothes, afterward taking a sandwich from the basket.

"Have my office back to normal by the time I get back," James threw over his shoulder as he gathered his keys and made his way to the employee shower room at the end of the hall.

Monica sat for a moment longer, gathering the feeling back into her legs. First disconnecting the camera and checking to make sure she had clear footage of what took place, she put what little clothes she had back on and straightened the office back up, leaving a sandwich and soft drink on his desk before exiting.

On her way out the door, she noticed Jasmine at the front desk talking to the old white lady that should have been there when she came in. Not wanting to be noticed, she walked quickly toward the side exit, tipping the still smiling guard on the way out, and then the valet as he pulled up in her convertible.

Screeching out of the parking garage, she sped all the way home, leaving the basket in the car as she raced to her room so she could do a headstand before any of James's semen seeped out of her. It could be her last chance at getting pregnant, and she didn't want any problems making it happen.

Reality Check

The short walk from the car to the menacing gates of the correctional facility seemed to take an eternity as the sun beat down on Monica's head. On the inside she felt like she deserved the torture because she knew she easily could have been the one behind those four stone walls, calling this place home for many years. She tried to harden her heart as she approached the desk, but her soul wouldn't allow it.

This visit wasn't like the many times she'd visited her baby sister because she had committed some petty crime. This was a matter of life, death, and the well-being of a three-year-old who didn't understand his mother's predicament. This was reality, coming face-to-face with the real. Her legs told her to leave, but her soul made her stay.

Approaching the desk slowly, she took in the rough faces of the security guards—both male and female, but some hard to tell the difference.

"Who you here for?" the slightly overweight guard barked from behind the podium. Monica looked into her bulldog-like face and almost vomited on the paperwork that sat in front of her from the stench of the guard's breath. The only way she knew it was a woman was from the tone of her voice and the fact that she had breasts.

"I'm here to see Tanya Walker," Monica responded as another whiff of the guard's foul breath made her take a step back.

The guard didn't seem to notice as she searched the books to make sure Monica was on the visiting list for Tanya. Searching her purse for the identification Tanya said she would need to get in, Monica placed it on the desk while the guard called over to the holding block to have Tanya come down. Monica checked her attitude as the guard looked over her ID and then set it on the desk as if it wasn't handed to her.

Taking her seat after she put her belongings in a locker and turned her twenty-dollar bill into coins so that she and Tanya could have something to eat from the snack machines, Monica sat patiently waiting to be called to the back. Monica was lost in her own thoughts for a second, trying to steady her nerves. It had been over three years since she'd laid eyes on Tanya, and she hoped she could handle being that close to her again.

The commotion broke into her thoughts as she witnessed two women up front having a shouting match and the guards doing nothing to stop it. Being nosey, Monica eased a little closer so that she could hear what the drama was about.

"Family for Ms. Tanya Walker!" the manly female guard called out, getting everyone's attention. Holding her change purse tightly in her hand, Monica walked up to the front, following the guard who was escorting her to the back.

Halfway down the hall, the two came to another waiting area where Monica was fingerprinted and checked for contraband. The bulldog-looking guard came back and told Monica to step out of her shoes and clothes so she could be searched for anything illegal that the detectors didn't pick up.

"You want me to take my clothes off?" Monica asked the guard, surprised at her request. Had she known she would be going through all this, she wouldn't have made the trip.

"All of them so I can see those pretty titties," she came back with a dirty look on her face like she wanted to eat Monica alive right there.

"Where is that in the rule book? I was never told about a strip search," Monica came back, angrily refusing to take any article of clothing off. She didn't know the law like that, but she knew she had some rights.

"Leave the girl alone, Tommy," a guard said from behind her. "Miss, put your purse in the tray and walk through the detector, please."

Thankful for the interruption, Monica was more determined to deal with the guard when she came out as she took one last look at her. Somehow she would get the info needed from one of the visitors or guards before she left. She would have a nice little surprise waiting for her once she left work.

Entering the room, Monica spotted Tanya immediately. From across the room she could see Tanya's sad expression as she sat at the table with her arms folded in front of her waiting for Monica to come over. She didn't stand when Monica approached the table, and Monica had a little salt on her shoulders because she was waiting to give Tanya a hug. Taking the seat across from her, they said nothing as they studied each other.

Prison was not going well for Tanya. Her once long, jet black hair that flowed past her shoulders in a stylish wrap was now braided into cornrows straight back off her face. Although her skin was still clear, she now sported a small, jagged scar above her right eyebrow, no doubt from a fistfight behind these walls. Her acrylic nails that always had a fresh French manicure were now bitten down way past the cuticle, and her pretty, pedicured feet were sporting Tims.

Monica resisted the urge to cry as she sat looking at her former lover. She instantly regretted having Tanya in this horrible place, but not the circumstances she was there for. Had she not murdered Marcus he would have surely murdered Tanya, putting her six feet under instead of in these human cages.

"When am I getting out of here?" Tanya spoke, skipping the pleasantries and getting right to the point, catching Monica off guard. Monica leaned back in her seat to get a good look at Tanya, not expecting their visit to go like this. Tanya was usually soft-spoken, unlike the angry woman sitting in front of her now.

"Well, I talked to the judge yesterday, and he's working on your paperwork now," Monica said in a calm voice, still not liking the direction their conversation was taking.

"Do what you do best, I just need to get out of here."

"What the hell is that supposed to mean?" Monica said, her temper rising quickly.

"It means," Tanya began in a slow deliberate voice, "that I don't care if you have to fuck him, suck his dick, and take back shots from all of his judge friends in the same night. I want out of this hellhole. I want to be with my son," Tanya responded, trying to control her tears. She said she wasn't going to cry, and she was determined to hold it down.

"Well, Tanya, I'm doing the best that I can, and . . ."

"Fuck the best, Monica!" Tanya came back almost knocking the chair back. "Do you know what it's like to be in here?"

Tanya began telling Monica how it was to have someone tell you when and how to make every move. How privacy was nonexistent as you showered, went to the bathroom, and lived your life in front of five thousand other inmates. How she had to fight the women off in the beginning because she was what they considered "fresh meat."

She drilled into Monica's head about all the nights that she laid in her cell and cried because she could no longer come and go as she pleased. How she would never see her son's smiling face. She told Monica about her fear of her son forgetting who she was because he was only a couple of months old when she was put away. She reminded Monica about all the birthdays she missed, and her child's first steps.

She told her of the pain she was in when she miscarried her second week in jail because she had gotten into a fight with one of the other inmates, and she didn't know she was pregnant. It tore her up carrying around a secret inside of her because she thought Monica would come back for her, and she had left her hanging in there to rot, not giving a damn what happened to her next.

Monica shed tears as she listened to Tanya's story, thanking God on the inside that she didn't have to go through such torture. Monica was a crazy bitch, but not half as crazy as she thought. They would have eaten her ass up on the inside, and she knew it. If she didn't know before, she definitely knew now that being behind bars and being taken away from your family was some serious shit, and she had to do what she could to get Tanya out.

"Tanya, I know sorry isn't enough, and I will see the judge again in the morning so we can speed up the process. I'll do what I can to get you out of here."

"Monica, I loved you, and you don't know how it hurt for you to do what you did to me. I'm willing to let bygones be bygones, just get me out of here."

"Tanya, I will . . . I will."

The two women embraced for what felt like an eternity as they calmed their wildly beating hearts. The two spent the rest of the visit catching up and making amends as they ate snacks from the vending machines.

Before Monica left, one of the visitors from the waiting room approached her. She had peeped the altercation between Monica and the female guard, and shared her disdain for her. On the way out she showed Monica where the guard's car was parked, and both the women slashed all four tires, getting into their respective vehicles only after the woman poured a bag of sugar into the tank of the beat-down Honda. She had already planned on messing the car up anyway because the guard had given her a hard time on her last visit, and after seeing what she did to Monica, she thought Monica would want her revenge too.

The two women exchanged numbers, both seeing that they had a lot in common from the way they dressed to the vehicles they drove, hers canary yellow and Monica's hot pink. As if the world needed two women like Monica. The women exchanged brief hugs before getting into their respective vehicles and driving away. When Monica got to the stoplight, she took one last look at the card before putting it into her glove department.

"Shaneka Montgomery, World Class Photographer. Who would have thought?" Monica responded as she sped off before the light could turn yellow, glancing at her cell phone and ignoring the thirty-seven calls she'd received from Sheila since that morning. She had to go talk to the judge, and tomorrow would be too late.

Payback's A Bitch

Breaking record speed, Monica pulled up to the judge's hideaway, searching for her key in the glove compartment before she exited her vehicle. Calling the judge before she got there to make sure he would show his face, she popped her trunk and grabbed her duffel bag with tapes of him with several women just in case she needed some extra reinforcements.

Upon entry into the judge's small house his wife knew nothing about, Monica frowned at the dusty room, she could tell no one had been there in months.

Removing the dust covers so it could look more like home, Monica placed them in the washing machine located in the shed kitchen so they could be ready to be put back once they left. Stomach growling a little, she instantly regretted not stopping for groceries; she grabbed one of the menus off the counter to order something to eat.

Monica turned the television on to occupy herself. She flipped through channels as she waited for her food to arrive. A few minutes later she heard a key being inserted into the door, and the judge's face appearing soon after. Not bothering to greet him, she turned back to her task of turning the channels, deciding on *Wheel of Fortune* and checking her watch to see how much longer she had to wait to eat.

Judge Stenton was a handsome man, not looking anywhere near his fifty-something years. The little patches of gray at his temples showed signs of age, but the judge in full form looked good enough to eat. Judge Stenton was well put together, and many women were killing themselves for the chance to have one night with him. How he and Monica hooked up was not that much of a mystery, but what kept them together was a sin.

Ignoring Monica completely, the judge walked past her and up the stairs to put away his clothing in the master bedroom.

Placing condoms in the drawer next to the night stand on his side of the bed, he disrobed in front of the mirror so he could check out his body in the process. Satisfied with his appearance, he jumped into the shower in no rush to find out why he was summoned by Monica. He figured she wanted a favor as usual, and he wanted to be right when it came time for her to serve him for it. He knew all too well what Monica was capable of, and his length grew just thinking about it.

Resisting the urge to satisfy himself in the shower and deciding Monica would surely do a better job, he washed quickly and wrapped a towel around his waist before going downstairs to see what Monica was doing. From the stairs he could see Monica engrossed in *Jeopardy* and snacking on vegetarian shish-kebobs. Walking up to her, he placed his lips on the butterfly tattoo on her neck and surprisingly got no reaction. Continuing his journey, he reached around to caress her breasts. Monica stood up as if he wasn't even touching her and took her plate into the kitchen.

Confused at first, he stood there looking at her as she walked away. Walking behind her, he caught up to her bending over in front of the refrigerator as she retrieved ice cubes from the bottom of the freezer. When she stood up his erec-tion was pressed against her back, his full length very impressive. When she turned around, he tried to kiss her lips, but she turned her head, his mouth landing on her cheek.

"What's up with you? Why the cold shoulder?" Judge Stenton asked as she squeezed from between him and the icebox, making her way back into the living room.

"I'm not here for that. We need to talk," Monica said from her spot on the couch, turning the television off and waiting for the judge to join her.

All hopes dashed of getting at least some head before they got into anything serious, the judge dragged his body over to the couch, plopping down on the cushion across from Monica, his once very full erection down to nothing. Taking a good look at Monica for the first time since he came in, he saw the sadness in her eyes.

"What's on your mind?" The judge straightened the towel around his mid section, suddenly conscious of the way he was dressed.

"I need you to work a miracle," Monica began without hesitation. She didn't have time to be bullshittin' with him; she needed him to be on the same page.

"A miracle like what? You already know what it's hittin' for," the judge came back, letting her know what she needed to do without actually saying it.

"It's for a friend," Monica began, choosing to ignore his underlying message. "I need you to get her out of jail."

"What she in for? Murder?" the judge asked jokingly, not realizing how close to the truth he was.

"Yeah. She's in for the murder of her husband. It's been about three years now."

Not knowing what to say and shocked that his joke was actually a serious matter, the judge sat with a numb look on his face, not knowing how to react. After all, he was only joking, and on the inside hoped she was too.

"Well, what . . . what happened?" He wasn't sure he really wanted to know.

"Her husband was abusive."

"And that's a reason to kill him? Why didn't she just leave?" he asked. He had a wife at home, and every so often he had to knock her in the head to get her to understand, but that was to be expected. He didn't see the harm in running a firm household.

"He was abusive to the point where he left bruises that took weeks to heal. Broken bones and shit like that."

"Then why didn't she leave?"

"Because I promised to save her."

"And how, pray tell, did you 'save her'?" the judge asked, trying to get to the bottom of the story.

"I killed him."

The room got silent. You could almost hear a pin drop on carpet as the two dared to take the first breath, one shocked at what was said and the other shocked having said it.

"And who is your friend?" the judge asked, not really wanting to know.

"You should know, you sentenced her," Monica stated sadly as she waited for him to search his memory for recognition.

"The Walker case?"

"Exactly."

The judge looked at Monica for a long time, not knowing what to make of her. He knew she was a freak and pleased him in every form imaginable, but he had no idea he was dealing with a possible murderess. Sweat began to form on his creased forehead; he tried to rationalize as a million questions swam through his head.

"So, you were the one that emptied the clip into her husband's face? Why did you do it? How do you know Mrs. Walker?"

"We were lovers," Monica began. "She was supposed to be leaving him to be with me. I met him first through a colleague at the art gallery, and I liked him. We fucked often, and he treated me like a queen until I met his wife Tanya. It was like love at first sight. She was a little quiet and a lot timid when we first saw each other. They had just had their first child, and she was glowing from motherhood.

"It wasn't hard to talk him into getting her to have a three-some, and after that first night she was hooked. It surprised me when she approached me the morning we were leaving the hotel asking if we could possibly get together for a private session. I agreed, not thinking much of it, but wondering how far she would go because my girl was a tigress in the bedroom. Anyway, we started hooking up, and she began telling me how she wasn't satisfied at home and how she wanted out. We would hang out all the time and Marcus didn't know because we would just tell him we were out shopping when on the real we were at my house eating each other up. Excuse my French."

She went on to tell the judge how they ended up falling in love and how Marcus became jealous of their "friendship," not wanting to share his wife with the woman he was still sleeping with. Marcus always had a problem with alcohol, and when he got drunk he would beat Tanya for things she hadn't done, or he thought she was doing, often leaving bruises for Monica to clean up. Tired of the whole situation, Monica went over to the house to lure Marcus away so Tanya could leave, and she walked up on him beating the life from her.

Monica told the judge how in that instant she went back to the day her stepfather was beating her mother in his drunken state and killed her right in front of her. Not able to distinguish the present from her past, she ran in to help Tanya before it was too late, doing to him what she wished she'd had the nerve to do to her stepfather all those years ago. Before the cops got there, Monica left the house and left Tanya there. She took the gun with her, and after cleaning her fingerprints off it, she sold it to a drug dealer just to get it off her hands.

She and Tanya had an understanding that when it came time for her to go down for the murder she wouldn't tell the investigators where the murder weapon was, so they placed her before the Honorable Judge Stenton to receive sentencing. Monica left out the part about her falling for Jasmine and abandoning Tanya for the last three years, figuring that was info he didn't need to help her out.

"So what exactly do you want me to do?" the judge asked, not really knowing what to make of the situation. After all, he had been having sex with a murderess, and now she wanted his help to get her naïve friend out of prison. He was also hoping she wouldn't turn on him if he declined.

"I need you to get her out. That gun has a lot of bodies on it by now, I'm sure. Just arrest the guy I sold it to, pin the gun to that murder, and set her free. It's simple."

"It's not that easy. We have to catch him in the act of a sale with a large amount of product on him, and . . ."

"I can set that up for you. To make it sweet I can get him busted right at his house where he keeps everything. You ain't said nothing but a word."

"Who is the guy?"

"Rico. I know you've been trying to get him for years. I can help you."

"How soon can you do it?" the judge said, becoming excited about catching a known felon he wouldn't otherwise be able to touch. The police department had been trying to get him for years, and putting him away would surely get him a seat on a higher court. His eyes looked like dollar signs when he turned back to Monica.

"Set it up for this weekend," he said. "I need to make a few calls."

"That can happen, but I need to know that I have your word on this. She's in jail for a crime she didn't commit, and her son needs her."

"You take care of me like you been doin', and I'll take care of you. I need to make a few calls. Be naked and ready by the time I get upstairs."

Monica went upstairs to prepare for the judge, hoping she was doing the right thing. While she bathed, she could hear the judge on the phone making connections to bring down Rico and get Tanya out of jail. Making sure her diaphragm was in properly, she laid back on the bed and waited for the judge to join her.

A half hour later he came into the room full of excitement. Monica didn't know if his energy came from the case or from her naked body as he pounded into her with an intensity she never felt before. She was thankful she didn't have to tell him to put a condom on as she watched him put on two for extra safety. Monica spent the sex session thinking of a way to hook up with Rico so they could set the plan in motion.

How To Catch A Convict

"Wassup, ma? Long time no see."

Rico had spotted Monica jogging through Fairmount Park about a week after her talk with the judge. Monica had put the word out that she was looking for him, and as sure as gossip spreads, he found her.

"Hey Rico, how you been?" Monica asked as she caught her breath from the mile-long sprint she was engaged in. If things were going to work, she had to be absolutely irresistible, and her body had to be tight.

"I been good, ma. I hear you been trying to find me. Are you finally giving in and becoming mine?" Rico joked as they took a seat on a nearby bench so that they could talk.

"Stop playin' with me. You know you don't want me like that," Monica responded, blushing. Her acting skills were in full gear.

"Ma, I been trying to get at you since I first laid eyes on you almost five years ago. You just never wanted to give me any play," Rico came back, getting comfortable on the bench, but at the same time watching his back just in case the cops chose that day to take him down.

The cops had wanted Enrique Casarez, or Rico to everyone that knew him, for years now. They could never catch him with anything major to hold him, and everything he owned was in his mother's name, so his papers were legit. Although he lived in the Mount Airy section of Philly, he stayed on the west side where he got his hustle on and made his name famous.

Rico had West Philly on lock. Just about every block was covered with workers making his money, and he knew if he were ever caught that would be one for the books. He stayed clean, never carrying too much money or product on him just in case he did get pulled over by some hatin'-ass cop. They hated how he was able to floss right in front of them and couldn't do anything because half the police force was on his payroll.

"So, word has it that you been tryin' to find me. What's that about?" Rico quizzed, looking Monica in the eyes. His mother taught him when he was young that when you want the truth, look into a person's eyes when you ask a question. The eyes tell you what you want to know, but Monica wasn't the average storyteller and his little trick wouldn't work here.

"Well, I needed your assistance in getting some protection. You know I stay by myself, and there has been someone lurking around the neighborhood, and I want to be prepared just in case he decides my house is his lucky pick one night," Monica said with a sincere look on her face like she might really be afraid.

"Why didn't you go to the guy you got your first burner from? The one you asked me to get rid of that night?" Rico asked, still trying to make sure Monica wasn't up to any bullshit. As pretty as she was, he knew she had to have some sneaky ways about her, and he didn't want to find out the wrong way.

"He's locked up."

"I see, and you don't know anyone else to get some heat from?"

"No one I can trust, and I knew you would take care of me," Monica replied, hoping her story worked.

"If you let me, I would treat you like the queen you are," Rico said, sizing Monica up. He had been trying to get her for a while, and he needed someone in his corner who he could trust with everything he owned. Monica was already established, so he knew she wouldn't be on no gold digging type of mission; she would be loyal to him.

"Rico, it's not that easy," Monica replied, happy he had played right into her trap. It was easier than she thought, and she was bursting at the seams with anticipation. All she had to do was find out how his operation worked and then she could end all this madness.

Keeping in mind the time frame the judge gave her to make this work and knowing they were on twenty-four-hour surveillance, she agreed to let him take her to dinner later that night so they could discuss the possibility of a future together.

Rico walked her to her car, and after making sure she was safely inside, made his way to his jeep, looking over his shoulder to make sure the feds weren't on his neck. Speeding off, he went to tie up some loose ends before going back home to get ready for his date with Monica. He knew he had to come correct when dealing with her, and he didn't want to give her any reason to think he couldn't step up to the plate. He was also feeling good because he had just broken up with his girl that morning, and snagging Monica was a major step up.

On the way back to her house, Monica called the judge to inform him that the plan was set in motion.

Over the next three weeks, Rico spoiled Monica, happy he'd finally found someone to hold him down. Trusting Monica with his very life, he put her on to how his operation was ran and told her enough to satisfy her curiosity so she wouldn't feel like she had to sneak behind his back. He couldn't honestly tell her everything—he wasn't a fool—but he wanted her to know that there was definitely a level of trust there on her behalf.

Good pussy will do that to you, and Rico found himself getting more relaxed around her and not worrying about the feds as much. He was slipping up in a major way—exactly how Monica had planned it.

"Rico, instead of having your money in your house, did you ever think about hiding it somewhere else? I mean, just in case the feds did come here. You could lose everything. Maybe you should put it in a Swiss bank account or somewhere untraceable."

Monica and Rico had just finished round two of their lovemaking, and she was wrapped in his arms like he would never let her go. For the first time in Rico's life he was at peace, and it felt good. He was able to be himself around Monica, not having to lock everything down before she got there. He left bags of money out, not concerned that any would be missing because in his mind his money wasn't any of Monica's concern.

"I ain't putting my money in no bank. You can't trust those cats," Rico replied, pulling Monica further into his embrace. His manhood was awakening slowly but surely, preparing for round three. At that moment he didn't want to talk about money, he wanted Monica bent over the side of the bed with her ass in the air.

"Okay, I understand your apprehension, but I'm just saying, baby, if you at least purchased a safe you could keep it in my house. Only you and me would know the combination, and if you were ever raided, I could pay your lawyer with no problem. At least do that for the time being until you figure something else out. It would be a much safer option for you."

Hitting on a nerve, Rico contemplated the scenario Monica laid before him, not sure what he should do.

"Let me sleep on it, ma, okay?"

"Okay, baby. I'm just looking out for you, you know."

"I know, boo. Now turn over so I can get in there," he replied, referring to her wetness. By the time Monica got done turning him out, they were dressed and at Home Depot that night purchasing a safe to take to her house. By morning the safe was stored in her living room closet, and Rico deposited a little over a million dollars in ten and twenty dollar increments into the safe. Monica made sure to keep the combination in a safe place, and after making love in front of her fireplace, they enjoyed breakfast and made a trip to the mall on him.

All this time, Rico was buying Monica little odds and ends, from clothes to jewelry. She would put it up in the hall closet for Tanya. She wanted her to be set when she got home, and not have to want for anything. Rico trusted Monica completely, and on the days he gave her his credit cards she purchased gift cards and clothes for Tanya's son, telling Rico they were for her baby sister. Not really knowing her family, he went along with it, not finding a reason not to trust his girl. After all, she would never lie to him.

Time was winding down, and Monica had just about everything set up for the bust. Rico gave her a key to his home in Mount Airy and a key to the apartment he rented in West Philly where he did business. Monica made sure he separated his money in amounts of ten thousand, giving him the excuse that it would be easier for him to keep track of. Rico didn't know that he was dividing the money up for the cops who were in on taking him down. Love will make you do crazy things, and his whole demeanor was in chill mode because he felt Monica had his back. With her by his side, nothing could go wrong.

When You Least Expect It

"Monica . . . girl, what chu tryin'a do to me?" Rico moaned as Monica rode on top of him. He still couldn't believe how he lucked up and got her. He had been trying to get with her for the longest, but nothing he said or did worked, and it had him wondering what he did differently now.

"Turning you out, boo, ain't that what you wanted?" Monica responded as she contracted her walls around his shaft, making it virtually impossible for him to speak. She didn't expect him to answer as she continued to work her magic on top of him. Monica made sure to double up on the protection with Rico because she didn't want any mistakes this time.

This might be the only chance she had left, and when the test came up positive, she knew she had to do whatever was necessary to hold on to it. She had to be only a few weeks since she was sure it happened at the news station, and she took the liberty of scheduling an appointment to her OB/ GYN so she wouldn't have a repeat of the last pregnancy.

Today would be the day. She had Rico spending mad cash on her, and she was doing what she could to get him to take her to his place. The feds had been watching their every move from day one. They were going to put them in separate cars when they raided the place, but once they drove off, Monica would be set free. The plan was to bust in on them having sex so he wouldn't have any guns on him.

Monica's body shook from anticipation. Tanya would be set free upon his capture, and Monica would be walking away with a little over a million dollars, enough to set up wonderful living arrangements for Tanya when she came home. Monica didn't want Tanya back, but figured the least she could do was provide her a lavish place to call home. The house she planned to purchase was from a guy she knew in real estate who owed her a favor, and he cut her a nice deal on a three-bedroom home in the Over-brook area of Philadelphia.

Looking at the clock across the room, Monica saw that she only had about ten minutes before they were busted, and she made sure he wasn't going to cum any until then. She had given the judge a key to Rico's place so they could get him without breaking the door down. The judge was concerned about her being nude at the time of arrest, but Monica assured him it was perfectly okay.

After all, half the police force had already seen her in the buff, so what difference did it make?

The feds had already set it up for him to be picked out of a lineup for the murder by some guy they had paid off. It didn't matter that the guy didn't even know Marcus, they just needed someone to say Rico killed him. They had a jury ready to go made up of officers on the squad and all, and even the lawyer he would be appointed was in on it because they were all walking away with a nice amount of cash in their pockets. Rico's money had money, so there wouldn't be any problems dishing out the dough. Judge Stenton would be presiding over the case, and Rico was getting the death penalty by lethal injection as soon as he came in. Everybody would be eating for years off this one, and they couldn't wait.

Monica maxed out all of his credit cards in the last couple of days by paying off her house and car note, and had him purchase a cotton candy pink Ford Explorer in her name for the winter months, paid in full at the dealership. Rico was blinded by all the attention Monica was showing him, and pretty much did what she said.

At exactly two o'clock in the morning the feds started entering the house while Monica and Rico were in the room getting it on. Monica had the radio on as planned so Rico couldn't hear the front door open. They turned the lights off in the hallway so when they opened the door it wouldn't shine into the apartment. After the building was properly surrounded and they were in the house, the plan went into action. Monica pulled him into her, making him explode just as the feds kicked open the door, catching him off guard. Literally snatching him out of the pussy, Monica played her part as she screamed and tried to cover up her body. Placing Rico in handcuffs, they let Monica put pants and shoes on him as she cried fake tears asking the feds what was going on.

They took Rico down the steps and put him in the car with Monica not too far behind with the handcuffs loosely placed around her wrists for appearances. Rico went off when he saw Monica being placed in the car next to his. He was trying to tell the cops she had nothing to do with it, but no one was listening to him. As they pulled off, he twisted into the seat screaming for Monica at the top off his lungs.

Rico wasn't allowed to make his first phone call for almost two weeks after he was put in placement. His thoughts stayed on Monica, constantly wondering if she was okay. He didn't know if she was brought in, but in the back of his mind something kept nagging at him. He didn't want to think it because he was truly in love with Monica, but something smelled like a setup. He just couldn't put his finger on it. The thought stayed on his mind well after he went to sleep, causing him to toss and turn at the thought of his love betraying him.

When he woke up the next morning, he went through the motions of washing and getting dressed, Monica still on his mind. The way things went down was just way too coincidental. He would have never gotten caught ass-naked like that.

The thoughts stayed on his mind, damn near driving him crazy by lunchtime. When the guards came by to check their cells after lunch for count, he noticed the female guard from the day before. She was always giving him flirtatious looks, and he wondered to himself if she could get him at least one call.

"Excuse me, miss lady," Rico called to the guard as she walked by. She was sexy as hell, but he couldn't see it as he tried to make sense of his situation. The guard smiled at him, relieved that he finally noticed her.

"You talking to me?" she asked as she flirted openly with the inmate. Rico saw this and immediately took advantage of it.

"Yeah, I had something to ask you," he flirted back as he got up from the hard mattress, flexing his muscles for her viewing pleasure. She leaned against the bars after she looked around to make sure none of her coworkers were around. One of her colleagues had just gotten fired for getting caught having sex with one of the prisoners, and she was not trying to go down like that.

"I was wondering if you could help me get a phone call," Rico said as he talked close to her ear so that no one around them could hear their conversation. He breathed softly down the side of her neck before catching her earlobe between his teeth, making the guard's panties wet instantly. He knew if he got caught he would be sent to the hole, but he was willing to chance it.

"What's in it for me?" the guard asked as she thought of ways to make it happen. She was sure she could get her cell phone or someone else's for that matter.

"What you want? It's only so much I can do in my situation, you know?" Rico said as he passed the back of his hand over her tight fitting uniform shirt, lingering around her nipples before making his way to her neck.

"Let me see what I can do, but you prepare for some me and you time once it's done," the guard said before walking away, neglecting to check the rest of the cells so she could put her plan in motion.

Almost two hours went by before the guard came back. She opened his cell door and handcuffed him before leading him to the back of the building, using the cuffs to keep up appearances. Her captain was on vacation, so while everyone was out in the yard and in the recreation room she made use of the office where no one would be able to see her.

"You can use the captain's phone, but make it quick," the guard said quietly as she locked the door behind her, keeping the lights off so no one would know they were in there. "You have to be as quiet as possible, though."

Rico was already dialing his right hand man, paying the silly-ass guard no attention. He knew he would have to twist her back out, but he had to get this phone call before she got scared on him. His partner's phone rang five times before he picked up, each ring sounding longer than the last. Rico was trying to make it quick, and so was the guard as she stepped between his legs to untie the strings on his pants.

"Yo, it's me man," Rico said into the phone, trying to control his breathing as the guard pulled his penis out of his pants and began to perform orally on him. He leaned back in the chair, making it easier for her as he continued his phone conversation.

"Rico, my nigga. Don't worry baby, I got your lawyer handling everything," Rico's man said into the phone, glad to hear from his friend. He didn't know what to do and didn't want to make any noise the night Rico got caught. He was just turning the corner to go to Rico's place when he saw the law parked outside. Watching everything from across the street, he didn't leave until he saw them put Rico into the squad car, not knowing if he had stayed a little longer he would have seen them let Monica go.

"Good looking, man. I really appreciate it. Now, this is what I need you to do . . ." Rico continued to tell his partner about the way things went down and his suspicions of Monica. His partner agreed that it sounded like a setup and told him he would keep his eyes open.

In the meantime, the guard went from giving Rico head to riding him with her back facing him. Ending the call, Rico held the guard by her hips and thrust back as hard as he could until he finally exploded. Knowing he just made a huge mistake, he pulled his pants back on, unable to look the guard in the face. He wiped his fingerprints off the phone and she straightened everything up. They made their way back to his cell quickly, Rico lying down on the cot so that he could gather his thoughts. Shit just got heated, and he was not in the mood.

Word traveled fast on the streets, and when Rico's partner went to his apartment and saw everything missing, he knew for sure his man was got. Moving fast, he got in contact with his cousin Philippe who was locked up in the same jail as Rico. He mailed Philippe a letter to give to Rico.

One night after a poker game, Philippe had one of the prison guards take a letter over to Rico explaining everything that he knew. The same guard who made it possible for Rico to make the phone call tucked the note into her back pocket, promising she would take it to him before she was off duty.

A couple of hours later while everyone was in the cafeteria she noticed that she didn't see Rico so decided to go up to his cell block to pass the letter on. When she reached his block, it just seemed a little to quiet for her. Something wasn't right and she couldn't quite put her finger on it as she made her way past the empty cells. Rounding the corner to Rico's cell, she almost fell out as the sight of his dead body hanging from the ceiling. Screaming uncontrollably over the radio, she called for backup as she struggled with the key, unsuccessful at getting the bars open.

Everyone was put on lockdown as guards swarmed Rico's cell, everyone crowding the bars of their own cells as Rico's dead body was wheeled through the corridor. The guard didn't know what to do, totally forgetting about the letter in her pocket. She was going to reveal to Rico that she was pregnant that very evening, but he had hung himself before she got the chance.

The night before Tanya's release, Monica had Rico's apartment cleaned out, giving all of the furniture and clothing to Goodwill. The money he kept in the three safes he had in his house went to the law, each taking their share of the pie. Monica pawned all of the jewels after taking the diamonds she wanted for herself, adding another five hundred thousand to the money she already had.

When morning came, Monica was up at the prison in the office where Tanya would be released. After about two hours' worth of paperwork and fingerprinting, they were ready to go.

When Monica saw Tanya approaching, she stood up, ready to receive a hug. Tanya acted like she didn't even see her as she walked past her and pushed the button to call the elevator. Monica, hurt and confused by Tanya's actions, walked with Tanya to the car quietly, not really knowing what to say. They drove for a couple of blocks before Monica could say anything to her, not knowing what to expect from Tanya.

"Do you want to stop for a bite to eat?" Monica asked, hoping Tanya would lighten up a little.

"I just want to see my son," Tanya replied, not taking her eyes off the road. She was glad to finally be out of that hellhole she called home for the past few years and just wanted to see her family. They didn't know she was getting out, and it would be a pleasant surprise.

Before taking Tanya to her son, Monica decided to show her the house and the car she purchased for her. Pulling up to the single-family home, she got out of the car and walked around to let Tanya out. Tanya just sat there looking at Monica and not budging.

"Monica, this doesn't look like my mother's house. I haven't been gone that long to not recognize it," Tanya said from the seat with a frown on her face.

"I know that, Tanya. This is your house, for you and your son."

Stepping out of the car, Tanya took a good look at the peach and white house with the black Acura sitting in the driveway. Walking slowly up to the house, she noticed a key taped to the mailbox of her new home. Looking back at Monica, she opened the door, not knowing what to expect. Upon entry Tanya saw that the house was fully furnished, and very tastefully. It looked nothing like her old home, and she was glad because she had no desire to go back there. Every room from top to bottom was decorated, and Monica turned the back bedroom into an office for Tanya, complete with a computer and printing system. She would show Tanya the restaurant she purchased for her the next week.

Getting back into the car, Tanya still had nothing to say, but at least she had a smile on her face. Dropping her off at her mom's, Monica decided not to stay for the reunion. Once she got home, she took a bag of money from the safe before she went upstairs, sitting it by her bed as she ran a bath. After cleansing her body, she laid down in the middle of the bed not knowing what to do with herself.

Tears came from nowhere as she reached for the bag of money. Taking a handful and throwing it up in the air the money slowly floated in the air landing on her wet skin and around her on the bed. She rolled around on the money until it stuck all over her body while she cried for reasons she didn't even know. Finally falling asleep, Monica felt a little peace for getting Tanya out, and wondered what she was going to do about her and Jasmine's situation.

The Setup

"James, you already wore that shirt this week. Why can't you just wear a different one? What's wrong with the one you got on?" Jasmine said to James, tired of the entire disagreement. They had been arguing about that damn shirt all morning and she didn't want to hear anymore about it.

"I don't want to wear another one, I want that one. I told you I had a meeting today, and that's my lucky shirt. Every account we've ever landed at T.U.N.N., I was wearing that shirt," James replied while adjusting his tie in the mirror.

James had since put on a different top, but his irritation at the situation hadn't lessened any. He didn't really care about the shirt, he was just picking a fight with Jazz so he would have a reason to not come straight home. He was meeting up with Monica to discuss "business," and didn't want Jazz to know his whereabouts.

"Well, I don't know what the hell you want me to do then, James. I apologized for not getting the shirt cleaned, what else do you want?"

"I want you out of my presence. The sight of you is sickening me," James replied, still looking in the mirror. He knew he had gone there, and was waiting for Jasmine's reaction.

Jasmine had to step back for a minute to register what she had just heard. James hadn't turned from the mirror, and that pissed her off even more. Before she knew what happened, she had taken her shoe off and aimed it toward James, the heel hitting the back of his head with a dull thud. Before he could grab the back of his head, she was already on the other side of the room.

"I know you done lost your damn mind!" Jasmine yelled into James's face as he caressed the knot on the back of his head. "I don't know who you thought I was, but if you ever mistake me for one of those flunky bitches at your job again, shit will get ugly real fast."

Walking away, she grabbed her blazer from the bed and put her shoe back on before grabbing her briefcase. James was still shocked by her reaction. He was expecting her to snap, but not like that, and he would never admit that it scared him a little bit.

"Oh, and by the way," Jasmine said before exiting the room, "the five minutes you gave me last night sickened me. Get it together because I'm tired of being a damn actress. I went to school to study law, not to fake orgasms with your trifling ass."

James didn't get a chance to respond as she exited the room. Watching her from the bedroom window, he saw her get into her Blazer and realized after she had pulled off that she didn't have the kids with her. Racing down the stairs, he stopped at the kitchen entrance, his angels sitting at the table eating breakfast while watching cartoons on the thirteen-inch color television.

"Now she know damn well I didn't have time to take these kids to school," James said as he raced upstairs to gather his stuff, hoping God would spare him a traffic jam so he wouldn't be late for his meeting.

Once he got the kids settled in the car, he searched for his cell phone and almost side-swiped a school bus as he zoomed through his neighborhood well past the speed limit. Dialing Jasmine's number, he waited until the answering machine picked up before hanging up and dialing again. It took three calls before she answered the line.

"What, James?" Jasmine said still obviously irritated.

"Why would you leave the kids with me knowing I was already running late?" James barked into the phone, getting even more frustrated at the snail's pace traffic movement.

"You should have thought about that before you changed your shirt four times," Jasmine responded nonchalantly, knowing it would get under his skin even more.

"How many times I changed my shirt is beside the point! You knew I had something to do this morning." James glanced at the clock on the dashboard and the sea of cars in front of him, the scene making him madder by the second.

"Nigga, I do that every morning, so deal with it!" Jasmine just hung up. James, hating not having the last word, dialed her number right back waiting for her to answer.

"Don't you hang up . . ." before James could finish the sentence Jasmine had already fed him the dial tone. Moving to call one more time, he looked up to see his children's school up the block and decided to call after he got them situated. He didn't like arguing in front of the kids, and was upset that they had seen him angry with their mother.

After walking the kids to their respective classrooms and giving each a hug and five dollars because he felt guilty about arguing in front of them, he jumped back in his car and raced toward the expressway. His eyes just happened to catch the reading on the gas gauge; the red arrow wasn't that far from the E. Not wanting to be any later than he already was but not sure if he would make it to the city on what little gas he had, James reluctantly pulled into the gas station, calling his boss before he got out of the car.

Fidgeting around for his wallet as he apologized repeatedly to his boss, James almost lost it as he remembered leaving his wallet on the kitchen table. Having given his last ten dollars to his kids, he thought he would go crazy as he searched frantically for a credit card, knowing he wouldn't find one in the car. Not knowing what to do, the first person he thought to call was Monica as he rested his head on the steering wheel in an attempt to calm down. Calling Jasmine instead, he waited for her to answer her phone as he rationalized what to do next.

"What, James?" Jasmine talked into the phone, sounding like she wasn't in the mood for his shit.

"I need you to come give me gas money. I left my wallet in the house, and gave the money I had to the kids."

"And I care because of what?" Jasmine came back as she entered the law firm and made her way to her office, surprised to see Sheila and not the temporary secretary who was occupying the space the week before. Jasmine had been in court all week, and didn't know Sheila was back in the office.

"Jazz, come on with the bullshit. I'm not working with a lot of gas here. What's in the tank won't get me to work," James said with desperation creeping into his voice.

"You better take a cab, my trial starts in a few minutes."

"I just said . . ." Jasmine hung up.

Not knowing what to do, James began dialing Monica's number. Before he could finish dialing, he looked up just in time to see Monica roll into the gas station at the pump next to his. Silently thanking God for looking out, he rushed over to Monica, explaining the situation he was in. She didn't hesitate to pass over her gas card as James promised to make it up to her later while he filled up his tank. Not having time to talk, he gave her a kiss on the cheek and hopped in his car, arriving at work just as the presentation for new business was beginning. He made it by the skin of his teeth, and knew he would hear it later, but by the time he sealed the deal and had their newest client sign on the dotted line, all of that would be forgotten.

Snapping her cell phone closed, Jasmine signaled Sheila to meet her in her office so they could talk. Sheila grabbed a pencil and paper after getting Jasmine a cup of coffee. Stepping into her office, Jasmine held up one finger indicating she would be with Sheila after she finished her call. While listening, she graciously took the cup of steaming liquid, silently thanking Sheila for the beverage. Sheila occupied herself by drawing little knife and bullet wounds on a sketch of Monica as she waited for Jasmine to end her call. Ten minutes later Jasmine hung up, finally able to talk to Sheila.

"So, Sheila, how have you been? I didn't know you were coming back into the office today," Jasmine said as she searched her briefcase for the files she had placed there this morning. She was glad to have Sheila back. Not that the secretary she had wasn't doing her job, but it's smoother when you have someone who already knows what to do.

It had been a while since Sheila had been to work, and her first week felt kind of awkward. Now that she knew everyone's secrets, it was harder to look at Jasmine in the face every day and not have the urge to tell her what was really going on. She wondered if she and Monica were still sleeping together, and what could she do to get her out of the picture.

Yeah, Monica treated her like shit, but Sheila figured that was the only way she knew how to show her true feelings toward her. Monica could be very aggressive when she wanted something, and Sheila chalked it up as her not knowing how to express herself.

Sitting in Jasmine's office waiting to take notation for a court-ordered child support document, Sheila kept her fake smile in place while Jasmine told her all about how things were going with her and James.

I wish this chick would come the fuck on, Sheila thought to herself. She was waiting to hear from Monica, and was already developing an attitude because she hadn't returned her call yet. It was already lunchtime, and she had called Monica's cell phone at least seven times since eight that morning.

"So, what do you think I should do?" Jasmine asked Sheila in the midst of correcting notes for the document Sheila would be typing up.

"I'm not sure," Sheila responded partly because she hadn't heard a word Jasmine had said.

"Well, do you think I should go with the sexy cream dress, or the magenta pant suit? I look good in either one, but . . ." Jasmine continued, unaware that Sheila was once again paying her no mind.

"I think you should go with the cream, but why all the trouble?" Sheila asked, trying to jump back into the conversation she had missed. She wanted everything cool so when she put her plan into action everything would work to her benefit.

"Because we said some hurtful things to each other this morning, and I really want our marriage to work. This on-again, off-again relationship is not working for me. I need something more solid." Jasmine thought about the latest events in her life. She wanted things to be how they were when she and James first got married, but she didn't have the slightest idea of how to get there again.

"Maybe do something that shows you're trying to work it out. An 'I'm sorry even though it's your fault' gift."

"Please explain." Jasmine laughed as she gathered her papers on her desk. This had to be good, and she wanted to give Sheila her undivided attention.

"Well, what was the argument about?" Sheila asked again because while Jasmine was talking to her she wasn't paying her any mind.

"I forgot to get his lucky shirt cleaned for his business meeting today. He wears it every time he signs a deal," Jasmine said recapping her morning.

"Okay, since he already decided to wear a different shirt, as a gesture of kindness add two more shirts to his wardrobe. Men in James's position can never have too many button-down shirts with him having to wear suits all the time. What's his favorite sport?"

"Basketball," Jasmine said, wondering what she was getting at.

"Buy him two tickets for tomorrow night's game and make reservations for dinner at his favorite restaurant. After all that, break him off real nice and put him to sleep. He'll be fine in the morning."

"That sounds good, but when will I find time to do all that? I have to be to the courthouse in twenty minutes and . . ."

"Look, I'll go get the shirts and tickets during my lunch time. Start tonight by making him dinner to see if it'll soften him up a little."

"That may just work. Will four hundred dollars do?" Jasmine said while searching her pocket book for a MAC card so she could use the machine in the lobby.

"Sure, I'll go over to Business Men, Inc. and see what they have on sale. Maybe I can find ties to match too, and I can order tickets over the phone for the game and pick them up before I come back. I have connections so I can probably get him courtside seats," Sheila said while gathering her paperwork from the desk. She planned to spend the afternoon shopping at Jasmine's expense, and would be walking out the door right next to her.

"That'll work. How fast can you have it done? I'll be back in the office by four."

"Are you extending my lunch break?" Sheila wanted to know so that she could cover her ass if something went down.

"Yeah, take as long as you need. Just have it by the time I get back."

"I will, don't worry. Now get going. I have some calls to make."

Taking her seat as Jasmine raced out of the office, Sheila sat down to call Monica one more time before leaving. This not answering the phone thing was making her mad, especially since she found out that Tanya was out of jail. Sheila was under the assumption that Monica and Tanya were together and that's why Monica wasn't answering her phone.

Nothing could be further from the truth. Monica hadn't heard from Tanya since the opening of the restaurant she had purchased for her. Monica was too busy trying to get pregnant again by James so she could put her plan into action, and Tanya was the furthest thing from her mind. The pregnancy test she took already confirmed the obvious, but Monica wanted to be extra sure this time. It just so happened that Monica was about to call Sheila when her phone began to ring.

"Just the person I wanted to hear from. What's good with you?" Monica said into the phone like everything was cool. She wanted Sheila to come over to her house when James got there so they could have the threesome. There was no way James could resist both of them at the same time.

"I've been calling you all week. Why haven't you returned my calls?" Sheila responded, heated because of Monica's nonchalant attitude. Sheila was tired of playing cat and mouse with Monica and Jasmine. She wanted to end this nonsense as soon as possible so she could move on with her life.

"I've been extra busy, sweetie. I'm sure you understand and I am so glad you called."

"Why are you glad, Monica?" Sheila wanted to know. She was so frustrated with Monica she didn't know what to do with herself.

"James is coming here later. We can do what we talked about."

"Well, I have a better idea," Sheila said, sure of her plan.

"What can be better than what I came up with? We both know who the mastermind is on this team, Sheila."

"If it were you, you would have Jazz by now, right?" Sheila stated boldly as she listened to the silence on the other end. "That's what I thought. Now this is what we're gonna do . . ."

Sheila told Monica about the incident this morning and how Jazz planned to make it up to him.

Monica shared what James told her at the gas station, and told Sheila how she got him to agree to come over there and about their episode at the news station. She didn't tell Sheila she was pregnant because she didn't want to jinx it this time, but she did want them to meet up later.

"It would be better if we did it at their house, Monica. What woman wouldn't freak over that?"

"Yeah, but what if she snapped on all of us? That would defeat the purpose," Monica said, unsure if Sheila's plan would work.

"Look, trust me. When she comes back to the office she'll do some paperwork for about an hour and it will take her an hour to get home from the city. We could already be there. Just have James take you to his house when he comes there, and let him know that you know for sure Jazz is working late."

"How will I get him to go there? He doesn't want his wife to know he's cheating, idiot."

"It's simple," Sheila said checking her attitude before she snapped on Monica. "Tell him you're fumigating your house or something. You know he has no money from this morning's incident so suggest that you go over there. Give him some head in the car or something, and he'll do it. Believe me, he'll do it."

"And what if he doesn't?" Monica said, for the first time doubting herself.

"It'll work, you know how to get shit done."

"What time should we be at the house?"

"We should be in the house getting it on by six. She'll be there no later than six thirty. I'll meet you there. After y'all go in I'll knock on the door like I'm looking for Jazz. If you can, try to keep the door unlocked so I can come in without him actually answering the door. Y'all should already be having sex, I'll just join in."

"Sounds flawless, talk to you later."

"Monica, one more thing. I need you to call your man at the ticket office. I need two courtside seats for the married couple for tomorrow night."

"Done, anything else?"

"What's James favorite food?"

"Caribbean. We always order from this place called a Taste of the Islands that's near their house."

"Okay, that sounds perfect," Sheila responded as her mind raced from one thought to the next as she put her plan in order.

"Anything else?" Monica asked, ready to get off the phone. For some reason she was a little nervous about how this evening's events would end up, and she wanted to get her head together so she would be ready for James when he arrived.

"Don't be late."

After the two hung up, Sheila went on her shopping spree, getting James's shirts and ordering dinner for Jasmine so all she had to do was pick it up later. After getting an outfit for herself, she made her way back to the office just in time to see Jasmine enter the building. Coming up behind her, they caught the elevator together as Sheila explained her plans to her.

"So, all you have to do is pick up the food from A Taste of the Islands on the way home. I put the order in and paid for it earlier. I told them you would be there by six to get it."

"A Taste of the Islands, but that's all the way on the other side of town," Jasmine complained as she inspected the shirts that Sheila picked out. Satisfied with the selection, she took a peek at the tickets for the game, impressed at the courtside seats. James would love it.

"Yeah, but it's closer to your house so the food won't get cold before you get home. You and I know there ain't no heating up Caribbean food once it's gotten cold."

"Yeah, you have a point there. What did you order?" Jazz replied while starting her paperwork. By the time she finished noting her files, she would go get the food and be home in time to put the kids to sleep and spend the night making up with her husband.

"All of James's favorites with beef patties and fruit punch on the side. I also got a bottle of mango rum just in case you decided to get creative with the fruit punch, if you know what I mean," Sheila responded like she put a lot of work into it.

"Thanks, Sheila. I really appreciate this. You're leaving right?"

"Yeah, I have to go pick up my boy. See you Monday?"

"See you Monday."

Sheila got her purse and stuck what few personal items she had inside it because she knew that would be her last day after what would be popping off that evening. She knew she would miss working for Jazz, but this was the only way she could see getting Monica off her back.

Calling Monica once she got into the car, Sheila let her know everything was a go as she dashed across town to get her son and take him to her mother's house so she could get to Jazz's house in time. Everything had to go as planned or shit could backfire in everyone's face.

Not wanting to take his children anywhere near Monica, James sighed as he came to a stop in front of her house. He'd made plans to be with Monica, forgetting that he had to pick his babies up from school. He knew Monica would have a fit, but he hoped she would stay cool in front of his children. They were sleeping in the backseat, and he hoped they would stay that way until he pulled away from Monica's door. He knew kids had a tendency to repeat what they saw and heard, and he didn't want Jazz to know he was anywhere near Monica. Ringing the bell, he stood outside the door with a sad look on his face, hoping Monica would understand his situation.

"Hey, sweetie. I missed you," Monica replied while trying to wrap her arms around his neck. He stopped her advances, and stepped back, taking a look into his car to see if Jalil and Jaden were still sleeping.

"I can't stay. I forgot I had to pick my kids up from school. Can I make it up to you tomorrow?"

"I'm leaving town tonight. Why can't we do it tonight?" Monica asked, crossing her arms over her chest and pouting.

"I just told you why. Why can't I see you when you get back?"

"Because, I want you now; I can follow you to the house, and come in after you put the kids to bed. Come on James, I need you today."

"What if Jazz comes home and catches us, then what?"

"Have we ever gotten caught before?" Monica asked, getting impatient with the situation.

"No, but now could be the time."

"James, come on with the bullshit. We doing this or what?"

"Look, just follow behind me and wait until I tell you to come in."

Monica said nothing, just reached behind the door for her keys and locked the door as James made his way to his car. Following him to his house, Monica found a parking space a few houses down while James pulled into the garage and got the kids into the house.

A half-hour later, James motioned from his bedroom window for Monica to come into the house. As she walked down the street, she noticed Sheila's car pulling up into James's neighbor's driveway. Not wanting to bring attention to Sheila, she walked past and went into the house, leaving the door unlocked so Sheila could come in.

Monica found James in the kitchen standing by the sink drinking a soda. She said nothing as she walked up to him, taking the bottle from his hand and sitting it on the counter. Walking James around to the other side of the table, Monica began to undress him as she sat him in the chair by the entrance with his back to the door so he wouldn't see Sheila come in.

James took it upon himself to strip so they could get it done and over with. The last thing he wanted was for Jazz to walk in and catch them in the kitchen having sex. She would go off for sure. He had left his condoms upstairs, but it didn't matter at this point because Monica was already undressed and riding him like the true rodeo queen she was.

James melted instantly as her walls contracted around his shaft, almost causing him to ejaculate prematurely. His kids being in the house only crossed his mind once before he stepped up to the plate. He didn't lock them in the room because if something happened he wanted them to be able to get out, and normally when they were asleep, it was for the entire night. He figured he would do Monica and get her out the house before anything serious jumped off.

Taking her nipples into his mouth, James closed his eyes and enjoyed the taste and feel of her wrapped around his body. He didn't hear the door open, but Monica saw Sheila walk into the house. She turned and started riding James with her back to him as Sheila neared the kitchen.

"What's going on in here?" Sheila asked as she made her way around the table. James didn't know what to do because even though they were caught, Monica never stopped riding.

"Sheila, you know what it is," Monica said as she leaned back into James so she could take him in deeper. "Care to join us?"

James was at a loss for words as Sheila stood there contemplating whether she was going to be a part of this threesome or not. Looking at her wristwatch, Sheila knew Jasmine would be pulling up in a matter of minutes, and she was deciding if she should duck out to keep her name clear or go with the plan.

The look Monica gave her helped make her decision as she undressed and climbed up on the table positioning herself so Monica could feast. All her nervousness subsided as Monica devoured her, her legs wrapped around her head and her hands gripping the table's edge. Sheila forgot about time as Monica brought her one orgasm after the next. The trio was so into it they didn't even hear the front door open.

Revelation . . .

What's Done In The Dark

No matter how much you think you are in control of a situation, you can never prepare yourself for the unimaginable. Even the most detailed person can be shocked into speechlessness. I don't even think a word exists to describe what I saw when I walked into my house earlier. So it was ten after six in the evening, and when I pulled up to the door I saw what looked to be Monica's car parked a couple of doors down from my house. I didn't think anything of it, thinking maybe she was visiting someone else on the block, taking into consideration that I told her of my plans before I left the office.

After parking my car and getting all my purchases out of the backseat, I saw Sheila's car parked in front of my neighbor's driveway. Now the hair was standing up on the back of my neck, and all of a sudden I felt like something wasn't right. I refrained from dropping the bags as I moved as quickly as possible to my front door. All of the lights downstairs were on, but the upstairs was dark as hell. There was no sign of the kids besides their backpacks sitting in the corner. I knew James was home because his car was in the driveway.

My stomach was knotting up even more as I sat the bags down on the loveseat. Walking toward the kitchen, it sounded like I heard voices, and not my husband's. Hesitant at first, because I was not in the mood for any more bullshit, I damn near fainted once I reached the doorway.

On my brand new oak wood kitchen table, the shit that cost me almost two thousand dollars because James said it had "chemistry," the place where my kids and I enjoy several meals a day, the spot where I haven't parked my ass yet because I'm trying to be a fuckin' lady was the murder scene . . .

James sat in the chair while Monica rode him with her back facing him. Sheila was sprawled out on my table like she was a dish at the Old Country Buffet, and Monica's face was so far up her ass it looked like she was touching her uterus with the tip of her tongue. James's eyes were closed, and all of them were moaning like they were at a hotel some damn where.

"What the fuck is going on here?" I said in an even tone that surprised even me. My face was as red as a Crayola crayon, and my fists were balled up so tight at my sides that my fingernails cut into my palms.

Scaring the shit out of all of them, James exploded inside of Monica from the shock, and when he pushed her up, I saw he didn't have on any protection. Sheila fell off the side of the table and crawled underneath to stay away from me when she saw the expression on my face. Monica stood looking at me with a smirk on her face that I was so damn close to knocking off.

"Jasmine, what are you doing home so early?" James said in a 'damn, I done messed up' voice as he tried to cover his stiff as granite member with a potholder. The fact that he was rock hard made the situation worse.

"What the fuck is going on here? Where are my kids?" I said as I tried to keep control of my breathing. I took a few more steps into the kitchen, causing everyone that was already there to step back.

"The kids are cool, just calm down. It's not how it looks," James began in a scared voice. He knew I was about to snap, and I wondered if anyone else could sense it.

"Where are my kids, James? This is my last time asking you," I said evenly as I made my way over to the drawer where I kept my butcher knives.

"They're upstairs. They should be sleeping," James said as he watched me pull out the two largest knives without turning my back to them. "Jasmine, just calm down and let me explain."

"You had a threesome in my kitchen with my secretary and my friend on my brand new table and you want me to stay calm? My fuckin' kids are in this house, and you want me to stay calm?"

Before he could respond, I threw one of the knives at him, grazing his thigh and sticking in the wall. Monica's smirk fell off her face like a tick off a dog as I reached into the drawer to replace the knife I just threw.

"Jasmine, fall back. Why you trippin'?" Monica managed.

Instead of answering, I turned and grabbed a handful of knives and began throwing them at the trio one at a time, barely missing them. I wasn't going to really stab any of them, but they would feel my wrath.

"Jasmine, please let me explain," Sheila said from her spot behind Monica under the table. Sheila was scared as shit and feared she would be cut next, especially since she was the one who went and got all the stuff for this so called 'perfect' night. James tried to get under there with them, but there wasn't any room. Blood was running down his leg and it formed a puddle that he slipped on as he tried to join the ladies and get out of my path.

I took a good look at them looking like they were all about to shit on themselves as they cowered under the table. I didn't even have the words to say anything, and I didn't want to hear any excuses. Taking a look at them, then around the kitchen, I suddenly felt dirty. Dropping the remainder of the knives on the floor, I turned and ran quickly up the steps, not stopping until I got into my children's room. Thankfully they were still sleeping when I got there because had they witnessed any of this evening's events I would have to definitely cut somebody up.

I didn't pack any clothes; I just scooped my babies up and headed downstairs. When I got down there, Monica, Sheila, and James were clothed and standing in the living room waiting for me. I said nothing as I struggled to keep my tears in, not believing these bitches would do me like this. I trusted both them hoes, and they cut me deeper than any knife ever could. Gathering my keys and my pocketbook, I juggled the twins in both arms as I finally got the door open, and prepared to walk down the driveway.

"Jasmine, you just can't leave like this. Can we talk?"

I turned to look at James, then the other two. Sheila looked like she was about to pass out, and Monica wouldn't make eye contact. James looked like he was trying to make himself cry, but at that moment any love I had left for him was nonexistent. I could feel the ice form around my heart as I turned away and made the long trek to my Blazer.

James knew he was wrong, and he just stood in the doorway watching me strap the kids in. Monica was in one window and Sheila was in the other. Proud of myself for not snapping, I got in my car and pulled off. I kept my tears in check all the way to my brother's house by blasting my Tupac CD because I didn't want to hear any slow jams. I didn't want anything replacing the hate I was building up in my heart for James. The scene in the kitchen replayed constantly in my head. It wasn't until I pulled up into my brother's driveway that I let my tears fall.

I was a complete mess as I told him what I had just witnessed and what I had done to them with the knives. He was ready to go over there with a 9mm and off all of them, but I talked him out of it. I put the kids in the guestroom, and then I stretched out on the couch, contemplating what went wrong in my life.

Back at the house, James and Monica argued as Sheila sat on the side taking it all in. She didn't know what she was going to do about money now that she had sealed her fate with Jasmine. At the same time she was glad that Jasmine found out so Monica wouldn't have any power over her anymore.

Slipping out the back door as the argument got heated, Sheila snuck by the window just in time to hear Monica tell James she was pregnant with his child. Her steps faltered a little as the revelation of what really happened popped in her head. Monica went about getting Jasmine the wrong way, and even if Jasmine were to take James back, Monica was carrying his seed.

Shaking her head in defeat, Sheila made her way to her car and pulled off, trying to come to grips with how she was going to survive from here on out. She wanted to talk to Jasmine, but knew it wasn't a good time to do so. Everything seemed like a dream as she drove on the quiet streets seemingly moving at a snail's pace. She hoped to never see Monica again, and even never would be too soon . . .

***

Through Monica's Eyes: Three Months Ago

"i knew you when i had a friend. very deeply love lived within, but somehow we got loose from what was oh, so tight. somewhere we went wrong when we were oh, so right . . ."

"What the fuck is going on here?"

I was so wrapped up in the moment that I forgot my own plans on having Jasmine catch us in the act.

James practically threw me off him, but I felt him cum before he had a chance to get me off him completely. Sheila fell off the side of the table and crawled underneath it. I smirked a little and said nothing as I let James explain for all of us.

"Jasmine, what are you doing home so early?" James asked her in a frightened tone. I was thinking she was right on time as I watched him try to cover up his erection with a damn potholder. I wanted to go over to Jasmine's side, but I was naked too.

"What the fuck is going on here? Where are my kids?"

"The kids are cool. Just calm down. It's not how it looks."

I looked at him like he was crazy. What did he mean it wasn't how it looked? We were fucking on her table! I wanted to smack him in the back of his head for saying that stupid shit, but I refrained for the time being.

"Where are my kids, James? This is my last time asking you!"

I could see that Jazz tried to stay as calm as possible in this situation, but her anger level was quickly rising on the charts. If she didn't get an answer soon, all hell would break loose. James was standing there looking like he was about to shit on himself, and I was starting to feel scared my damn self. Jazz was on the verge of snapping, and the look in her eyes told me she had checked out of reality a long time ago.

"They're upstairs. They should be sleeping. Please, just stay calm and—"

"You had a threesome in my kitchen with my secretary and my friend on my brand new table and you want me to stay calm? My fuckin' kids are in this house, and you want me to stay calm?"

I was enjoying the show. James kept digging a deeper hole for himself. Looking back at Jazz, I went from enjoying the scene to being scared as hell. This bitch spazzed the fuck out and started throwing knives and shit. I jumped behind the table after she threw the first knife so my ass wouldn't get cut. Jazz had the snaps, and for the first time I felt bad. I fucked up her happy home, but what could I do now?

"Jazz, fall back. Why you trippin'?" I managed. She didn't answer. She just kept throwing knives.

I mean, who actually had that many? She had to have thrown at least fifty of them, and they were still coming.

"Jasmine, please let me explain," Sheila spewed out of nowhere. I wanted to punch her in her throat for bringing Jazz's attention to us under the table. She was doing perfectly fine trying to chop James's ass into little pieces, and now this bitch got her focused on us. At that point I just wanted to get out alive.

Jazz stopped and looked at all of us for what felt like an eternity. I kept my damn mouth shut and looked at her, wondering how I would make this right. She took one last look around the kitchen before she dropped the knives she had in her hand and ran out of the kitchen, I'm sure to get her children.

I jumped up to put my clothes on, and James and Sheila followed suit. By the time we got dressed and moved to the living room, Jazz was down the steps and on her way out the door. I decided I would wait until she left to let James know my secret.

"Jasmine, you just can't leave like this. Can we talk?" he pleaded.

Jazz gave him the look of death. I had to turn my head because the pain in her eyes was unbearable. Sheila looked like she was going to piss on herself. I hated her right then. Listening to her dumb ass got us into this shit, and I would make her pay dearly. Jazz continued to secure her children in their car seats before jumping into the driver's seat and pulling off. James stood at the door and watched her until we could no longer see the taillights on her car.

James slammed the door and we started arguing about the situation. I saw Sheila slip out the back door. I would get her ass soon, but I just had to tell James what was going on.

"James, I'm pregnant."

"By who?"

"By who? I'm pregnant by you. It's your child!"

"Monica, you need to get the fuck out of my house. I don't need any more shit out of you, and if you *are* pregnant, then get rid of it."

"But, James, I thought you wanted me!"

"This is my last time asking you to leave. Next time I'll snatch you by your neck and throw you out. Now go!" he said angrily.

I decided not to argue. Quickly grabbing my shoes and keys, I left. I fell into a heap of tears when I got home. I would make this right. If I didn't do anything else, I would make this right.

We now return you to your regularly scheduled program, already in progress . . .

Jasmine D. Cinque

At one point in my life I thought I had everything under control. I ate my vegetables, pleased my husband, looked after my children, and went to work every day. No one told me that one day you could look up and your life would be a disaster. My momma never told me to beware of marital mishaps and conniving women. I thought if I did everything right the first time and kept everyone happy, I would be blessed with a marriage like the one my mother and father had.

Shit, they'd been married for thirty-six years and I couldn't ever remember the silent treatment being passed between them. Even when I look at them now, they appear to be in love as much as they were when they first laid eyes on each other, if not more. Why couldn't I have that?

I felt like someone had ripped my heart out with their bare hands. The only thing that gave me the will to live was my children. I gave that bastard everything, and this was how it turned out for me? Every time I looked at my son I saw James, and I couldn't help but cry. One day my son would be some woman's husband. Would he break her heart the way his father did mine? Or would my poor little girl reap the sins of her father?

Every time I looked in the mirror I wondered what had happened. Years ago, I saw a smart businesswoman with nothing to lose and everything to gain. At the age of thirty-seven I could still drop it like it was hot with the younger crowd and "Electric Slide" with people my own age. I was a tigress in the bedroom, living room, garage, and anywhere else my husband decided to be creative. But as I looked in the mirror, all I saw was a woman scorned, and I didn't know how to fix it.

Yes, I was partly to blame since I had agreed to let another woman enter the sex life of me and my husband. But so what? I mean, just because I agreed to it, does that mean I deserved to be totally disrespected and humiliated? I don't think so. Like I said, I didn't know how to fix my jumbled feelings, but one thing I did know was that I was fully capable of medicating my feelings of scorn and bitterness.

The way I saw things, I figured what better way to medicate my feelings than to flip the script by allowing myself to indulge in some freaky and disrespectful sexual behavior the same way my husband had done by violating our kitchen with those whores!

Ever since the day of that ugly and unfortunate episode that I had witnessed taking place in my kitchen, I had not been able to get the picture of my husband screwing two other chicks out my head. It was like I could see the whole incident replaying itself in slow motion. I can even remember the smell of sex that was in the air that day, and no matter what I do, I can't seem to shake that smell or dislodge that thought from my mind.

The only thing that seemed to work was when I found myself in Bally's working out, running on the treadmill or something. And since James and I had been apart, I found myself visiting the gym regularly, at least four times a week. I would go to the gym after work to get my mind off things.

In fact it was at Bally's where I decided to hatch my plan for vindication. Not total vindication, but vindication that would leave me feeling somewhat satisfied.

There were these male twins who I'd met at the gym. Things developed from an informal hello how-are-you-doing type of relationship to a more casual, us talking about our workdays type of relationship. In between there was always a bunch of flirting on their part, but I never paid it any mind.

That was then, but now that I had found myself not as happy in my marriage, I decided to indulge in their flirtatious ways.

I called over to one of the twins. "Hey Donnie, can you spot me?" I asked, while lying on my back getting ready to do incline bench presses.

"Jasmine?" Donnie asked with a question mark in his voice. "What you know about bench pressing? Incline at that?"

"Well, I know that it's the best thing to keep my tits from sagging," I said while totally catching Donnie off guard.

Donnie laughed.

"Come on, I gotchu," he stated as he lifted the forty-five pound bar off the rack and helped me get my workout on.

Before long Donnie's twin brother Rahmel walked over to where the two of us were and began talking. "So you only doing one set?" Donnie asked while also informing Rahmel that I was doing bench presses to keep my tits from sagging.

"Say word?" Rahmel stated as he began laughing.

I could have continued on with the conversation going in that direction, but to be honest, my plan was already hatched in my head and I was ready to set it in motion.

"You know what, I always see the two of you whenever I work out and I have been meaning to ask one of y'all for the longest time if you do personal training."

Donnie and his brother looked at each other and they smiled.

"Yeah, we do. Why?" Rahmel asked with a sinister smile on his face.

"Because I'm looking for someone to train me. I mean, the gym is good and all, but I have a gym and equipment in my house and I know I could get in better shape if I had someone to stay on top of me and keep me in line."

"So you're saying you want a personal trainer to come by your crib and train you?" Donnie asked.

"Yes, that's what I'm saying."

There was a brief awkward pause.

"Well, it's not that serious. I mean . . ."

Donnie cut me off by smiling and saying, "No, I gotta keep it real with you. We workout, but as far as personally training somebody, we ain't no personal trainers or nothing like that."

"Well, that's ok. Like I was getting ready to say, it's really not that serious, meaning I really just need somebody to come by the crib just to keep me motivated. I know y'all can help motivate a sister, right?" I said while adjusting the drawstring on my spandex workout pants.

Donnie and his brother agreed to both personally train me. We never spoke about price or anything like that, yet they agreed to come by my house on that upcoming Friday morning. They both would be free since they worked the graveyard shift, so they had no problem committing to the time.

I, on the other hand, knew that I had to finagle some things in order to free up my time, especially considering I was planning on having the twins show up at my house. See, I had walked out on James and was staying with my brother, so I didn't know what James's schedule would be like on Friday morning. I didn't know if he would be home or not, but since he worked 9 to 5, I figured he would be at work and that I would be ok.

Still, the thing was James and I didn't have a lick of workout equipment in our house and that was OK, because in spite of the wedding rings I noticed on Donnie and his brother's hands, I was determined to get it on with both of them. I don't know if Monica's ways had rubbed off on me or what, but in my desire to medicate my bitter feelings, I was willing to stoop to the level of getting it on in a threesome with two men, married men at that.

The way I looked at it was James had totally disrespected me by bringing two women into my kitchen and fucking them while my kids were in the house, so why couldn't I bring two men into my house and get it on with them at the same time in the same kitchen?

When Friday morning rolled around I had made it to my house and James wasn't home. I figured he had left for work. It felt eerie walking into my own house and as soon as I walked in, those scenes of Monica and Sheila sexing my husband instantly came back and gripped me. It was at that point that I decided not to even step foot into my kitchen because it would bring back too many memories.

I entered the living room and for a brief moment, I contemplated what I was planning on doing with the two unsuspecting twins when they arrived. And I figured I could get one up on James by bringing them right into the same bedroom that James and I once shared.

Before I could give it much more thought, my doorbell rang and it was the twins.

Taking one last look around the room, and solidifying my decision to use the bedroom, I put on a brave face and opened the door without asking who it was. I mean, who else could it be at that time of morning?

"Hello, fellas. Thanks for coming through." I smiled as I stood back to let them in, suddenly happy I opted to wear the shortest skirt I owned with no panties underneath. I wanted this to be as easy and quick as possible.

The twins looked puzzled at first, and I'm sure they were wondering why I didn't have any workout gear on. After locking the front door, I signaled them to follow me up the stairs.

"Follow me, fellas. The workout room is this way."

I took the liberty of walking ahead of them on the steps, making sure to give them a good view of my bare ass. I had gone to get a Brazilian wax the other day just to ensure that the entry would be smooth. I didn't look back to see if they followed, and used the sound of their boot clad feet hitting the steps as indication that they were close behind. Opening the door to the room James and I shared up until the recent events, I entered and stood in the middle of the floor, watching their faces to see what they were thinking. Just as I thought, Donnie was the first to speak.

"Jasmine, what's all this about? You said you wanted us to help you train. I don't see any exercise equipment in here." He nervously looked at his brother, then to the bed, and then back at me. A wicked smile spread across my face as the thought of getting back at James rang like sweet revenge in my ear. To ease Donnie's mind I walked closer to him and stood breast to chest, noticing his quickening breath as I ran my fingers down his arm.

"There's exercise equipment in here, sweetie. Big enough for all of us to work out at the same time."

Backing up slowly, I began to strip out of the skirt and shirt I had on and placed my naked body in the middle of the bed for display. Opening my legs wide, I spread my lower lips apart and inserted my middle finger into my wetness, working it in and out for a few seconds before taking that very same finger and putting it into my mouth and sucking it clean of my own juices.

Donnie and Rahmel were still standing in the same spot with looks of shock on their identical faces. Rahmel looked like he was ready to get it on, while Donnie, on the other hand, didn't look like he was too sure about going through with it.

I continued to please myself, allowing soft moans to escape my lips, hopefully enticing them to join me. Donnie was the first to take his wedding band off and undress, placing his face between my legs. Rahmel stood watching us for a while, not sure what he wanted to do.

Donnie flipped me over with ease, entering from the back and pounding me with long, hard strokes that made my breasts bounce against my stomach and caused my breath to escape from my lungs. Not long after, I saw Rahmel's naked form on the side of the bed, and I didn't hesitate to grab his dick and place it inside of my warm mouth. I had yet to see what Donnie was working with, but from the feel of it these guys were really identical from head to toe.

Rahmel was ready to join in the fun and signaled for his brother to let up so he could lie on the bed. After he got comfortable, I straddled his length and after a few strokes I paused for a quick second so Donnie could enter me through the back door. We moved like synchronized swimmers, our collective moans sounding like a swarm of honey bees. By the time I came down on my fifth stroke, Rahmel had come inside me, but my constant movement kept him from going down.

We switched from one position to the next, and at one point both men were standing in front of me while I gave one head and one a hand job until they both came all over my face and neck. I had to lay on the bed and get myself together after that workout, but the fellas quickly dressed and headed out, promising to meet me at the gym later that day.

I didn't even bother to change the bed linens, I just merely fixed it back to the way it was, threw the clothes I had on in the dirty laundry hamper, and proceeded to the shower. My nipples and clit were still warm and a little tender from the work Donnie and Rahmel put on me, and I smiled while I got dressed in an outfit from my closet and made my way out, happy to enjoy the rest of my day.

James D. Cinque

Where did I go wrong? The Creator gave me everything I had ever asked for. I was on top of my game. Most men envied me. I climbed the corporate ladder quickly and remained humble when I reached the top. I had it all. I was given a wonderful woman who loved me unconditionally, and the blessings kept coming when we found out Jazz would be having twins. But as I looked at my reflection in the mirror, I had to wonder what the hell went wrong.

Thinking with my "other" head was what went wrong, but could you blame me? Monica wasn't just any woman. The girl had to have put a root on me or something, because not in all the years I'd been married had I allowed anyone to interfere with my relationship with my wife. The little flings I had on the side were kept under control, and Jasmine never knew about them. Somehow Monica turned the tables and messed up everything. Not only did I not have my wife, but I'd gotten another woman—who I didn't even want anything to do with—pregnant.

I was surprised when Jasmine's brothers didn't come banging my door down waving guns. I wanted them to because there was no way I deserved to live after all that. Hell, I already felt dead inside, so they may as well have taken my body. Maybe I needed to suffer, because even though I was going through a horrible time, I could only imagine how my wife was feeling. And that damn Sheila . . . that one really surprised me. I guess Monica had us all under her spell.

All I knew was that I needed to get my home back in order, and I needed to do so as smoothly as possible. The transition wouldn't be pretty, but I was more than willing to take the risk. I couldn't breathe without my babies, and I needed to hold my wife in my arms. If I got another chance I swore I'd make it right, but for now I figured I'd start by purchasing a new kitchen table because that would be one less thing she had to deal with if she came back home. I didn't even feel right eating meals there myself, so how could I expect her and my kids to?

Yeah, I wanted to do right by my wife and the new kitchen table would be a small start. But I knew that if I really wanted to do right I would have to do a complete one-eighty when it came to the way I thought about sex. I mean, sex sort of dominated my mind and my life. To me it was like everything I saw in certain porno movies I felt like I had to live it out. But it was just something about the threesome thing that really just had a vice on me.

While Jasmine and the babies were at her brother's house, I knew that that was the time I had to use to just focus and get myself right, but at the same time I sort of felt the freedom of a bachelor. And that freedom was something I hadn't felt in a long, long, long, time.

I knew I had been wrong by letting myself get too wrapped up with Monica from an emotional standpoint and I would never make that mistake again.

With my newfound freedom I decided to take one more stab at the threesome thing just so I could finally get it out of my system.

There were two strippers from the Cat House stripclub who I'd arranged to meet at my house. One was a black chick named Desire and the other one was a Spanish chick named Ina. Both were into the girl on girl thing, which for me was a must.

Earlier in the week I already had it setup for Ina and Desire to meet me at the crib at eight o'clock. I was showered and smelling fresh in a silk robe with nothing under it. They arrived right on time, and we didn't waste any precious minutes making small talk. They were there to get paid and laid, and then they could move on.

Once we entered the bedroom, Desire removed my robe and instructed me to lie on the bed. I did as I was told, and tried to control the smile spreading across my face as the two women danced and grinded on each other in front of me.

Ina was the color of hot cocoa, and Desire was the color of cocoa when wet. They looked delicious together. Where Ina had a nice round ass that most women of Spanish descent were known for, Desire was blessed with the most beautiful set of breasts, with nipples that looked like they were dipped in dark chocolate. My man stood at attention just thinking about the possibilities.

As the music played the women kissed and touched each other, and I watched through eyes at half mast with my right hand working my strength. Ina came and laid down on her back between my legs with half her body hanging off the bed. Desire mounted her so her pussy sat right on Ina's mouth, and she rode her tongue while she swallowed me whole. The rhythmic motion of her head bobbing up and down, and the feel of her mouth as she blew down on my dick and clamped her jaws tight on the way up made me come all in her mouth, and she sucked me back into an erection in no time.

Desire's body shook with release shortly after mine, and Ina moved from under her to a position behind, spreading her ass cheeks and making her face disappear from my view as she tongue fucked Desire in the ass. I just sat back and let them work for their money.

Switching positions, Ina got up from behind Desire, and after sliding a mango colored condom on me, in an anal entry she began riding me while Desire got comfortable between her legs. She switched from eating Ina to juggling my balls in her mouth. The grip Ina's ass had on me was beyond words, and soon after, I busted my second nut of the night.

Ina removed the condom and tossed it in a small bag they placed on the dresser. The idea was for them to never leave any evidence behind, so they took everything with them when they left. Used condoms and all.

Desire put another condom on me after working me up into the ready position. She rode me and Ina sat on my face. The two women fed from each others' breasts until we all exploded in a simultaneous climax. That shit was off the damn chain.

I allowed the ladies to clean up and we had a little more fun in the shower before they had to go. As promised, I paid their fee for the night in cash, and saw them to the door. I waited until they were in their car before I locked up and turned in for the night. The last thing I heard before drifting off to sleep was the night time newscaster from T.U.N.N. telling viewers to get ready for the nine day forecast. If what just went down didn't get a threesome out of my system, I didn't know what would.

Monica L. Tyler

What had I become? I just knew I had everything on lock, but somehow I messed up along the way. I was supposed to be a part of a happy family. Jasmine, her children, and I were supposed to be filling the space under my roof. I had succeeded in getting pregnant, so James was no longer an issue. For the life of me I just couldn't put my finger on where I had messed up.

And that damn Sheila! Lord knew I didn't want to talk about her. She said her plan was foolproof. Why in the hell did I listen to her? I mean, what woman wouldn't be mad if she walked into a threesome on her kitchen table? I was surprised Jasmine didn't cut us all up into little pieces. I honestly think the only thing that saved us were the kids being in the house.

I wanted to call James to see if he had a number for Jasmine, but I knew he wouldn't cooperate. I had to find a way to get around things and get back into his good graces. Maybe now that Jasmine wasn't an issue, he and I could hook up. Shit, who was I kidding? That man wanted me dead and his unborn child with me. If only I could just get him to listen to reason . . .

I had a doctor's appointment the following Monday, and I was hoping she'd tell me something good. I've tried carrying before, and it didn't work out, so I was hoping this pregnancy would be followed all the way through and the baby would be born healthy. I was also wondering if she could tell me about the nightmares I'd been having. I thought all of that had stopped once I got out of my uncle's hellhole, which was cleverly disguised as a house. My head pounded just thinking about it, and I couldn't even take anything because I was knocked up.

Well, one thing I could say was that I'd never been a quitter. I hoped if I could just talk to Jasmine she'd see things my way.

As I looked at myself through my mirror, I hoped what I saw was still appealing to her.

I would wonder about Jasmine on a daily basis and although I wasn't physically with her, that didn't stop me from being connected to Jasmine and being *with* her in my mind. In fact, on almost a nightly basis I would masturbate while fantasizing about being with Jasmine.

My routine and my fantasy was pretty predictable. Each night I would begin by lighting my candle and placing my favorite song, "Reunion," on repeat before making myself comfortable in my bed. "Reunion" was the first song I heard as I watched Jasmine and James dance on the night we met. The very night I fell in love with her.

I started out with my little silver bullet like always. I lifted my legs up and back so that my knees touched my ears, and my pelvis pointed toward the ceiling. In a slow circle, I started with the vibrating tool on low and traced my erect clit in small circles. The closer I got to my orgasm the more I increased the speed of the bullet, every so often dipping it into the puddle of juice that was quickly collecting at my opening. By the time I reached my climax my body would be shaking from the currents of pleasure running through my body.

I would imagine my tongue was Jasmine's as I placed my nipples into my mouth and fingered my clit until the shaking subsided enough for me to grab Hector, my ten-inch, hot pink dildo from the table. I always started out with slow strokes so I could tighten my pussy muscles around the shaft, making it almost difficult to pull it out. I would close my eyes, picture Jasmine's naked body in my mind, and start fucking myself harder and faster pretending I was doing it to Jazz until I squirted my love juice all over my sheets.

To finish it off I grabbed the Jackrabbit, a beaded vibrator that had a rotating head and beads that jumped around on the inside, causing all kinds of havoc. On the outside the little bunny ears rested on your clit, and once turned on, they squeezed and vibrated on your clit in conjunction with the inside action, causing my damn head to spin.

By the end of the night I was thoroughly fucked, but missing Jazz even more. I knew I couldn't have her to myself, but if I could just get her one last time . . .

Jasmine

Taking Baby Steps

"Mommy! Mommy!" my four-year-old twins screamed at me in unison while shaking my sleeping body. It felt like I had just fallen asleep, my eyes dry as a bone from all the tears I'd shed. It'd been about three-and-a-half months since the catastrophe at my house, and I still couldn't seem to get it together.

"Don't y'all see Mommy is trying to sleep?" I asked as I reluctantly opened my eyes to acknowledge them. My daughter gave her brother an "I told you so" look as she brushed her long braids away from her face.

"Mommy, are we going to see Daddy today?" my son asked, oblivious to the stares both his sister and I were giving him. I felt so bad because they had been asking me that same question every day since we came to my brother Dave's house.

It was killing me on the inside because they were too young to understand. It wasn't that I was keeping them away from James, but if I saw him at that time I may have ended up behind bars. Although he could have called to check on them himself, he made no moves to see about their well-being, and that pissed me off. For the first three weeks he called every day, pleading with my brother to get me on the phone. My brother said he was going to stay out of it, but I knew he wanted to go hurt James for the pain he had caused his little sister.

"Let Mommy get herself together, and I'll let you know in a bit, okay?" I said to them as I swung my legs around to the side of the bed so I could get up. I'd been feeling nauseous all week and the light-headedness was a bit much. I didn't even want to entertain the thought of being pregnant again. Not then anyway.

"Okay, Mommy," my twins said in unison before kissing me on my cheeks and walking away.

I sat there on the side of the bed for a second trying to figure out my approach. I wasn't ready to see James yet, but our kids were having a hard time dealing with the separation. Well, Jalil was. Jaden just seemed to go with the flow. She was the stronger one. I contemplated what I would say as I reached over and picked up the receiver. Dialing the number was painful as I thought about what had happened under that roof, but I had to do it for my children. I slowed my breathing as my heart pumped at top speed in my chest. I maintained my cool when I heard his voice. James answered on the third ring.

"Hello?" James's voice sounded a millions miles away to my ears. The man I loved with all of my heart and soul, the man who had hurt me the most.

"Hey, James, it's me," I said into the receiver. I could hear his breathing quicken at the surprise of hearing me through the other line.

"Jasmine, baby, I'm so sorry," he began, his voice sounding like he was holding back tears. I was struggling with my own tears as I finished with the call, making it as quick as possible.

"I was calling to see what you were doing this afternoon. The kids have been asking for you a lot. Maybe we can stop by." I kept it cool although I wanted to curse his ass out for doing me the way he did.

"Sure, please do. I miss all of you so much. Can we talk when you get here, please?"

"Only if we're talking about the kids, James. I'm not ready to relive that horror right now."

"Jazz, please don't be like this. I made a mistake, baby. Just give me a chance to redeem myself, please," James begged from the other end of the phone connection. He started sounding hysterical and a part of me really didn't give a damn. I wanted him to suffer. We definitely needed to talk, but I was not in the mood.

"James, right now I just want to bring the kids by to see you. We can talk when they're not around. Now is not the time."

"Jazz, listen to me. I want you to bring the kids, but is it possible you can get your brother to watch them tonight? Jazz, please, I can't live like this anymore."

"You should have thought about that when . . ." I couldn't even finish the thought. Pointing the finger at him would be pointing three back at me. I had to admit that I fell for Monica's bullshit, but I wasn't ready to take the blame yet. We had both messed up, but he got caught.

"Jazz, please just think about it. You can bring the kids now if you want, but I need you to come back tonight. I'm begging you, please give us a chance at starting over. I can't breathe without you and my kids."

"James," I began, letting out a long sigh in an attempt to keep my tears in check. We did need to air out our dirty laundry, so why was I procrastinating? "I'll be there in about an hour. I have to get the kids washed and dressed, okay?"

"Can we talk tonight, Jazz? Please?"

"I'll be there in an hour, James." I hung up before he could say anything else.

This was going to kill me, but I had to face him. I missed him so much and I didn't want our kids to suffer because of our problems, but I couldn't seem to get up the nerve to make things right. He had hurt me terribly. As I pulled out clothes for us to wear, thoughts ran through my head a mile a minute. There was so much I wanted to discuss, and I contemplated leaving the kids so we could say what we had to say, but I knew they wouldn't let me leave the house without having a fit.

I washed myself, then them, and got all of us ready. We piled into the jeep, leaving a note for my brother on the fridge. Making the trek across town from Mount Airy to Wyncote felt a lot longer than the half hour it was. The block seemed a mile longer than it did when I was under that roof. I blasted my Tupac CD all the way to the front door, keeping my head up just as the rapper suggested.

Before I was even out the car, James was out the house and unbuckling Jaden from her car seat. I avoided eye contact as I unstrapped Jalil and placed him on the ground so he could give his Daddy a hug. James looked like he was close to tears as he hugged our kids close to him, their little arms barely fitting around his neck. I stood back, taking in the scene and wondered why our family couldn't always be as perfect as it seemed at that moment.

We finally made eye contact, but I looked away first, keeping my tears in check as I walked around him and went into the house. As soon as I stepped in, it felt like all the oxygen had left the room as flashes of that night raced through my mind. I could still smell the food I purchased that night. Shaking off the dreary feeling, I removed my jacket, then turned to remove Jaden's. Jalil was already out of his and back in James's arms.

I wanted to have a seat, but I felt restless. I wanted to jump on his damn neck and bash his head in for being stupid enough to get caught. I too was guilty of playing on Monica's field, but damn. Why did it have to end this way? I knew she wanted me for herself, and at one point in time I was considering it, but in reality there was no way possible I would have left James to be with her. I'd been loving him for too long.

Before I had a chance to sit, James pulled me into the kitchen. That was the last place I wanted to be. That bitch was parked on my kitchen table like she had a right to be there. This meeting was going way too fast, and I was ready to take my kids and make a hasty retreat. Entering the kitchen I was pleasantly surprised to see that the table had been replaced. Ten cool points for James for making this a little easier. This gesture didn't make me forget the events that happened here, but at least we didn't have to endure the pain of dining on the same set that they used to have their freak fest. But at the same time I knew that I was one to talk because I had fucked two guys right upstairs in our bedroom. But, hey, at least I was smart enough to not get caught!

There was a spread fit to feed ten people. Our feast was set up as if we were at a picnic. All of us took our normal seats while James served us before taking his food. I didn't want to look at him, but I did notice he was looking mighty tasty in his crisp, white wife-beater and button-down shirt. His body looked more buff in his jeans, making my panties wet just thinking about the power underneath. He sported a fresh cut, his goatee and side burns lined perfectly. The smell of his Cool Water cologne was driving me crazy, but I chilled. It wasn't that kind of party.

We ate in silence . . . well, I did. James kept up a lively conversation with the kids as they gave him blow by blow of the weeks spent at their uncle's house. I sat in silence and let him have his time with them. Every time I looked up I could feel his eyes on me, but I pretended it didn't bother me. He wanted to see his kids, and I had granted him his request. I didn't want it to be said that I was trying to keep them away from him.

Jalil chatted away; he was so happy to see his dad. Jaden looked occupied by her own thoughts, playing more with her food than actually eating it. I wondered if my baby girl felt what was going on between her parents. She was definitely a daddy's girl, but lately she'd been kind of withdrawn.

We finished up and went to sit on the back patio so the kids could play on the swings and seesaw we had built to match their clubhouse. The neighbor's children were outside, so they were too happy to see their friends. I sat on the lounge chair opposite James so I could have a good view of the kids. They looked so happy and carefree as they raced up and down the slide and around the yard. I remembered similar days and longed for life to be that simple again.

For a while James stayed in his seat across from me, staring directly at me. I knew he wanted to talk, but I wouldn't be the one to initiate the conversation. I honestly didn't want to talk about it with the kids there, just in case I wanted to use a few choice words to get my point across. At the same time I wanted nothing more than for him to hold me in his arms and make the pain go away. I wanted to be a family again.

James got up and sat next to me, draping his arm across my shoulder, my head finding a place to rest on his shoulder out of habit. Nothing made sense to me at that moment. I still wanted to be mad at him for what happened, but I loved him so much I honestly couldn't stay upset forever. It felt good being in his arms, his chin resting on top of my head, his breathing like a lullaby. I closed my eyes and breathed in the scent of my man, wrapping my arms around his waist in comfort.

"Jazz, I'm so sorry things ended up this way," James began as we cuddled on the patio. My eyes remained closed as I listened to his words. His voice sounded deeper with my head pressed against his chest.

"James, can we talk about this later?" I wanted to talk, but I knew right then wouldn't be a good time.

I wanted to enjoy the moment before it got tense again. He breathed a long sigh, and his grip tightened around me. I held on to him like my life depended on it as I watched the kids play, so innocent at that age. Jaden was the bossy one and Jalil was a natural born leader. I smiled on the inside at what I was able to bring into the world. As hectic as my life had been lately, when I looked at our children they reminded me that peace still existed on this twisted planet we call home.

James put his finger under my chin, lifting my face up to meet his. At first I thought he was going to kiss me, and I wouldn't have resisted. To my surprise he just stared at me, tears threatening to fall from his pretty brown eyes. I wanted to put his soul at ease and let him know everything was okay, but we both knew it wasn't.

"Jazz, I know I messed up, baby. Just know that I love you more than life itself and I'll do whatever I have to do to make this right. I know you don't want to talk right now and I respect that. I just want you to know that I need you in my life. I need my children, and I need us to be a family again. I love you, Jazz, I really do. Can we please just work this out? I feel like I'm suffocating."

Our tears dropped simultaneously when he leaned his head down to kiss my lips. I could feel the electricity pass through my body into his as our tongues explored familiar territory. For a second I forgot how crazy everything was as I kissed my husband, the man I swore to love through sickness and health until death parted us. The man I bore children for, the love of my life.

As our kiss ended I knew that it was almost time to come back home to our house and live as a family again, but we had so much to talk about first. The closet was now wide open and skeletons were practically sprinting out of it and dancing on Broad Street. It was time for us to do some soul searching and come clean. Myself included.

For the next couple of hours we just sat and held each other, engrossed in our own thoughts. It wasn't until the sky turned burnt orange, indicating the end of another day, that I gathered the kids up so we could leave. They had a fit as we put them into the jeep. They did not want to leave their father. There were too many things left unsaid, too much hurt. James kissed the kids good night, then walked around to the driver's side where I was standing.

We embraced for what felt like an eternity, neither of us wanting to let go. We kissed one last time before I got into my jeep to leave. He leaned into the window to kiss me again. I pulled away, my tears making me see double for a second.

"Mommy, I miss Daddy. Will we be going back home soon?" Jalil asked as he and his sister yawned, trying to fight sleep. Their time in the yard had exhausted their little bodies.

"I miss Daddy too, baby. But don't worry, we'll be home soon enough."

That answer must have been good enough for both of them as we continued our ride back to my brother's house, but as I listened to the Quiet Storm on the radio, my thoughts wandered to a happier time in my life when everything felt like it was perfect. I wanted to be there again, but things had to be smoothed out first. It was going to take some time for us to completely heal and bounce back. We had to learn how to trust again, and that might be our biggest hump to get over.

I let the melody from the radio take me back to a time when I had no doubts. Now doubt was all over me like a second skin. I wanted to know so much, but in a way I didn't. Crazy thoughts ran rampant through my head all the way back to my temporary home. I wanted my life back, and was determined to get it, no matter what.

When I pulled into the driveway I could see my brother and his wife in the kitchen. I hated disturbing their household, feeling more like an intruder than a guest. Although my brother said he didn't mind the company, I felt like I was an added burden to their peaceful lives. They weren't used to kids, toys, and crayons everywhere.

By the time I turned the ignition off, my brother was outside helping me remove my sleeping babies from the backseat. I could see the concern in his eyes, and was thankful that he waited until the kids were in bed before he questioned me.

"So," he began with a sad look on his face, "how'd it go?"

I broke down in tears as I told him and his wife about my afternoon. It was so painful not being with my husband, and seeing him made it worse. I told him about the offer James made for us to talk tonight, and surprisingly my brother agreed. He gave me his blessing, assuring me that watching the kids wouldn't be a problem while I handled my business at home. He also warned me to keep my legs closed, reminding me that now wasn't the time to give in to lust. I kept his words and his blessing in my heart as I drove back to the city, back toward my husband, hoping to accomplish something positive.

James

Confessions

Okay, having an affair was a selfish act. Bringing Jazz into it made it worse, but that didn't mean I didn't love my wife and kids. It showed how stupid I was, and I was paying for it every time I stepped into my empty house.

Pacing back and forth in front of the couch was surely wearing out the carpet, but I couldn't rest. I wanted to hop in my car and follow her over, but I knew she wouldn't have liked that. I was trying to give her space so she could come to me willingly, but how much longer would I have to wait? It'd been like an hour and a half since she had left and I knew it didn't take that long to get to the north side. I wanted to call her brother's house, but I didn't want to seem too pushy. I felt like the walls were caving in on me as I tried to make sense of it all.

I got excited as I heard the sound of the doorbell and I figured it was Jazz.

I didn't want it to look like I was going through an ordeal. I wanted to look like I was chillin'. Taking a quick look around the room, I made sure the lamps were down low enough to set the scene. I pulled out the photo albums from our wedding day, her pregnancy, and pictures of the kids as they grew up, hoping they would aid in getting Jasmine to change her mind and come back. I had a bottle of apple cider chilled in a bucket with two glasses, not wanting any alcohol to cloud our vision and have us do something we would regret later. When I opened my door it was my neighbor reminding me to roll up my car windows before I turned in for the night.

A half hour later I found myself dozing off in front of the television. I was mad as hell that Jazz didn't show, but at the same time I didn't have a right to be mad. I got caught with my pants down, literally, and I couldn't really be all that upset that she didn't want to talk. Deciding to call it a night, I clicked the television off.

The moment I turned off the television I heard the sound of a doorbell ringing, but I wasn't sure if that had been a sound that the televison made before I turned it off.

Hoping for the best, I quickly rushed to the door, but I paused before opening it because I didn't want to seem too anxious. Then the bell rang again, so I finally decided to open it up and let Jazz inside the house.

Unfortunately, when I opened the door I got the absolute shock of my life. It wasn't Jazz who was standing at the door, it was the two strippers from the Cat House, Desire and Ina! The two of them were standing at my front door looking as strippered out as they could look, with the stilettos and all. They instantly got me aroused even though my heart had dropped to my feet because I knew Jasmine could be pulling up to the house at any moment.

"Hey, Papi!" Ina said in her thick, Puerto Rican accent. "We decided to stop by on our way to the club and see if you wanted us to hit you off before the night started." Ina continued while letting herself into the foyer of my house while simultaneously caressing my dick.

"Oh, shit!" I said while I smirked a devilish laugh that was combined with a nervous smile.

Before I could say anything else, Desire had also entered into the foyer and proceeded to make her way into the living room. She looked as if she was preparing to take off her clothes so that we could do the damn thing. She made sure that she reminded me that it had been my idea to have her and Ina "surprise me" as she stated in a somewhat mocking tone.

"Yeah, yeah I know what I said. But listen for real for real both of y'all gots to go! Not now but right now! My wife is literally on her way here as we speak. I thought it was her at the door when the two of y'all rang the bell."

"See, Desire? I told you he was a frontin'-ass nigga! We see them all the time in the club fronting like they got dough and shit but when it comes time to make it do what it do then they start frontin' and bitchin' up!" Ina stated.

"Nah, wait a minute. Fuck that! Yo' ass told us we could stop by here any night we wanted to to hit you off and you would hit us off with two hundred dollars apiece! Fuck that, I want my money! *Unannounced! Just show up and I got y'all!*" Desire stated as she mocked me by imitating what I had said to them one night. It had to have been the Hennessey that was talking for me when I had said that, but hey, I was in a jam and I had to think and act quick because if Jazz were to walk in on this then I could forget about it!

"Okay, okay. Look, I got y'all." I said as I reached into my pocket and pulled out a wad of money.

And just as I took out the money, sure enough I saw headlights outside.

"Ahh, shit! Motherfucker!" I yelled as I had looked out the window and confirmed that the headlights were indeed Jasmine's.

"Listen! Just take this and split it. I'm sure it's more than enough and I don't have time to count it. That's my wife who just pulled up and if she finds the two of y'all in here she will kill all of us!"

"You know, I really don't need this bullshit!" Desire stated in her ghetto accent. "We got money to make. We don't have time to be playing around with you and your clown ass!"

"Desire, listen. Both of y'all please just do me this solid and hide in this closet right here next to the front door. I'll make sure I leave the front door open and when my wife comes in I'll walk to another room with her and when y'all don't hear us talking y'all can come out of the closet and walk out of the front door and bounce," I said in a rushed and panicked tone while pushing both Ina and Desire toward and into the foyer closet.

"I can't believe this nigga!" Desire stated as Ina sounded as if she were cursing me out in Spanish. No sooner were the two of them crammed into the closet, than Jasmine was walking through the front door.

"Hey, James," she said as my heart raced a thousand beats per second.

I hesitated at first, but then held my arms open for a hug. She stepped into my arms without a second thought, and I closed my arms around her, hoping she didn't feel my thumping heartbeat. Although I was nervous as hell, it felt so good to have her body pressed against mine, her strawberry shampoo a familiar scent to me. She stepped back long enough to close the door and lock it.

We then sat down at opposite ends of the couch, leaving the middle cushion empty. Jasmine's back was to the foyer area where the two strippers were hiding. Neither one of us wanted to be the first to speak, but we both knew we had a lot of things to talk about. At this point I was ready to do whatever I had to do to have my family back. But as I looked and saw Ina and Desire tiptoeing in stilettos, making their way out of the closet and to the front door, I knew that if Jazz just slightly turned around that I could forget it as far as ever getting my family back.

"Well," Jasmine said as she looked everywhere but at me. *Thank God she didn't turn her head.* "I guess I should start by apologizing."

"For what?" I was confused. I was the one caught ass out on the table with her secretary and a woman I wasn't supposed to have any ties to outside of the threesome we had planned. All she ever did was try to be the woman I wanted her to be.

"For everything. The fact that you thought you had to step outside of our marriage to find satisfaction. If I was on point you wouldn't have had a reason to look anywhere else." I could see the tears welling up in her eyes, but what could I do? I could also see Ina and Desire safely making it out the front door and, man, was I ever relieved. I knew I could then focus on what Jasmine was actually saying.

"Jazz, listen, had I not pressured you into having the threesome in the first place, none of this would've happened. You only did it to make me happy, and it got out of hand. Monica was conniving anyway, and she wanted us to be at each other's throats. It's not your fault, Jazz."

"As true as that may be, James, I feel like we would have been cool if we had just talked. Tonight I'm going to tell you some things that may hurt you—things that you may never forgive me for—but I need to tell you what happened if only to clear my own heart so I can sleep at night."

"Baby, we don't have to get into all that now. We can take it one day at a time. I just need you and the kids back here with me. I can't live without you, Jazz." I was hoping my tactic was working because Lord knew I didn't want to tell her what really went down. She would be out of there for sure if she knew I wasn't straight with her about Monica and me from the beginning. And she would have really been out had I dry snitched on myself and told her about how I was wilding out with the strippers from the Cat House. And if there was one thing I knew, it was that there was no way in hell I was going to tell her about that.

We got comfortable—or as comfortable as was possible considering the situation—on the couch so we could talk further. The first thing she did was pick up our wedding album. I sat back and kept my mouth shut as she quietly flipped through the pages, some of the photos producing a slight giggle at the memory. She stared at some pictures a little longer than others. I let her take her time because I wanted things to be like they were then.

"So," she began after putting the album down, "let's get this done. I'll tell you everything you should know about the past year, and I want to know everything on your part. Answer the questions honestly no matter how hurtful, okay?"

"Cool." I was sweating already. What I had to say would cut deep, and I wasn't sure I was ready to reveal it. "Where do you want me to start?"

"The beginning. How did you really meet Monica?"

"I met her at a Bistro in Center City. She would always be there on my lunch break."

"So, the story about her being your friend's sister or whatever was a lie?" she asked as she got up and poured herself a glass of apple cider. The room seemed to get twenty degrees hotter in a matter of seconds. I didn't want to be questioned first, but somehow it was flipped on me, and I was stuck.

"Yes, I didn't want you to think she was just any ol' body off the street."

"So when did you actually start sleeping with her?"

"Maybe two weeks before we had the threesome," I lied with a straight face. It was more like two months before then, but I didn't want her to think she wasn't satisfying me for that long.

Yeah, I knew it was the time to lay all of the cards on the table so we could move on, but I just couldn't do it. Too much was at stake, and in keeping it honest, I really didn't think it was a matter of her not pleasing me. Jazz was a beast in the bedroom. I truly believed it was just one of those opportunities that maybe I shouldn't have taken advantage of.

"So, how did the threesome come about?" Jazz quizzed as she sipped from her cup. She didn't seem fazed by what I was telling her, but then again, who was to say she wasn't ready to cut me right then?

"Well, I was up front with her from the very beginning about being married. I guess she just kind of wore me down, and after I slept with her she kept pressuring me about bringing you in once I showed her a picture of you."

"I see. How many times did you sleep with her before we all got together?" Jazz asked with a straight face. She was too calm, and I wanted her to do something besides just sit there. I needed her to show some kind of emotion.

"Twice," I responded as I reached for a glass so I could drink something. She had only asked me a few questions, but I was already falling apart at the seams.

"So, after sleeping with her only twice she was able to convince you into convincing me?"

"Well, not exactly. I had been trying to get you to do it way before I met her, don't you remember? But it wasn't until she came along that I brought it back up, and I decided that if I had to share you with someone, why not Monica? You both looked beautiful together."

I was thinking I may have said too much because Jazz was looking like she was ready to blow. She was keeping her composure, but I could tell she was getting upset.

"How did Sheila become a part of the equation?" Jazz asked in a somewhat calm tone, but the look on her face and her body language showed she was ready to hurt somebody. I knew she said she wanted the truth, but I didn't think she wanted it as raw as I was giving it to her.

"Well, to be perfectly honest, I really don't know. After the threesome I saw Monica a couple of times when we happened to run into each other. Well, you know how persuasive Monica can be."

"Yeah, how 'bout that," she said as she picked up the other photo album and started flipping through it.

I could tell the conversation was getting to be too much for her, but at that point I agreed we had to get it done so we could move forward. We hadn't even begun to scratch the surface, and there was still much more to work through.

"Well, is there anything you want to know about me?" Jazz asked.

"Just tell me what you think I should know."

As she flipped through the album she told me about the flowers Monica kept sending to her office, and how the woman Monica was talking about the day I saw her at the courthouse was her. She said she even contemplated leaving me to be with Monica on several occasions, but she didn't want to do that to the kids.

"James, you know I love you with all of my heart, and even though I thought about leaving, I knew it was pure lust that was pointing me in her direction, but you or our kids didn't deserve that."

She went into detail about how she went to Monica's house on nights when I thought she was working, and that Monica was determined to make her fall in love with her. She said she was hurt because even though we both were wrong, the position I got caught in was unforgettable, and she didn't really know what to do to get past it. I listened as my wife poured her heart out, and I felt like shit because I still wasn't keeping it totally real with her.

"So, is there anything else I should know, James? We need to get this out and over before it's too late," she said as she wiped tears from her cheeks. I wanted to hold her, but I knew there was no way to stop the hurt.

"Well, there is one thing," I said before clearing my throat. I was only telling her this because I didn't want her to find out from someone on the low. Yeah, I had left out a lot, but this would make or break our marriage, and I wasn't sure I could live with that. "Okay, what is it?" she asked as she moved to the end of the couch to stand up.

"Jazz," I began, placing my hand on her knee so she would remain seated, because if she stood up she would surely fall back down.

"James, just go ahead and say it, baby. Whatever it is, I can handle it."

"Well, baby . . . Monica's pregnant."

Monica

May, 1991

Monica,
I've been liking you for a long time. Meet me behind the
bleachers at three o'clock so we can make it happen . . . I
think I love you.
Kevin

I got the note at nine in the morning when I went to get my
algebra book out my locker for class. I must have read it at
least fifty times during the course of the day, not believing
what I read. Kevin was the captain of the school football team,
and was fine as hell. He'd led the team to victory three years
in a row, and all the college scouts were on him like crazy. I
had been eyeballing him since I transferred to the Parkway
Gamma High School, but who was I to approach anyone?
That was my second year there, and he never looked my way
or said anything to me until now. Yeah, he laughed at the
jokes that I always managed to be the butt of, but he never
said anything mean to me.

Transferring to a new school was killing me. Between try-
ing to make new friends, which didn't seem to be working out,
keeping up in class, and keeping Uncle Darryl off me, I didn't
think I was going to make it. I felt like the chick from The
Color Purple, *and Uncle Darryl was Mister. The only thing*
I was missing in this situation was the pretty sister to help
me deal with the mess. She lucked up and got to stay with her
people.

All I wanted to do was get my education so I could get the
hell out of there. The people at school were not the least bit
friendly, and I'd gotten into a fistfight or two because of it.

Since I was considered the ugly duckling of the class, I was nowhere near popular.

Well, it was 2:53 p.m. By the time I put my books in the locker and walked across the field, Kevin should be there. Checking the mirror in my locker, I made sure my hair was in order as I put lip gloss on my lips and slicked down my eyebrows. I took only the books I needed and stuffed the rest in my locker, rushing out the school so I could make it on time.

As I walked across the field, all kinds of thoughts rushed through my head. Maybe he was going to ask me to go with him to the junior prom. I had heard that he and Ashley broke up, so this would be right on time. Ashley was head cheerleader and a damn snob. She could jump the highest and had the longest pigtails. Every girl wanted to be her or be her friend. She treated me like shit, so I stayed far away from her and the members in her crew. I hadn't even discussed the prom with Uncle Darryl yet, but I would get around to it when he wasn't drunk. Whenever that was.

As I approached the bleachers I spotted Kevin sitting on his jacket smoking a joint. His eyelids were already at half-mast from the effects of the illegal drug he was puffing on. I took all of him in as I approached. His body was toned. His T-shirt stuck to his chest from the warmth of the afternoon, defining his muscles. By the time I sat next to him I was a wet mess and nervous as hell.

"You looking real cute in them jeans, girl." Kevin was rubbing his large hands up and down my legs, squeezing my thighs in the process. My nipples were hard on my flat, boy-like chest, making me sort of embarrassed that I was responding in that way.

"Thanks, Kevin. I'm glad you like them."

"I like you. I've been watching you for a while, waiting to kiss those pretty lips of yours. You have a sex appeal about you that I just can't explain, but I like it. I like it a lot," he said to me through kisses on my earlobe.

I was too naïve to recognize game. All I knew was this didn't feel like what Uncle Darryl did to me on a regular basis. This felt real, like how it should be. I felt myself falling fast for him, and by the time his lips touched mine, I was in love.

Kevin Hall was six feet even, caramel-skinned, and handsome as hell. His slanted, hazel eyes had all the ladies salivating over him in hopes of one day being the one to wear his team chain and football jacket. I felt like I had just hit the lottery. I couldn't wait to see the expression on every girl's face in the school when I walked in with his jacket on, especially that damn Ashley. I would make it my business to see her.

"Look, it's getting kind of chilly. You wanna come to my house for a while? My parents won't be in until later tonight, so it's cool," Kevin said as he took one last drag off his joint before grinding it in the dirt with the heel of his boot. It was actually hot as hell under those metal bleachers, but if that was his way of inviting me to the crib, I would play along.

"Sure, that's cool, but I have to be home by five thirty or my uncle will have a fit."

"Not a problem. We'll be done by then."

I acted like I didn't hear his last comment as he helped me from the ground after dusting off the back of his jeans. We took the short way to the parking lot and hopped in his car so we could go to his house. His car was better than I'd expected. The engine was quiet on his 1990 Ford Tempo as we made our way down the street.

I melted in the leather seats as we listened to the Force MD's sing about tears falling like rain. He had me from then on. To me it made him look so much more mature, and it brought back memories of my mother and WDAS on the radio on Sunday nights.

He kept his eyes on the road, neither of us bothering to make small talk. I already knew what was going to happen, and I was trying to calm my nerves before we got there. My Uncle Darryl would have a fit if he knew I was with a boy and not at the library like I told him, but that was a chance I was willing to take. Out of all the girls he had, he chose me, and I was ready.

We pulled up to an enormous house not too far from the school. It was a single home with a well groomed yard and a beautiful flowerbed. By the time I got my seatbelt off, he was already opening the door for me. I smiled as I exited the vehicle, grabbing my book bag.

The walk to his house felt like it was a mile long as we seem-ingly moved in slow motion all the way to his door. I heard nothing—no cars or anything else that I would normally hear on a busy afternoon. As I walked into his living room, I blocked out the outside world. It was like someone had hit the mute button, taking all of the sound from the planet. My heart was beating so fast I could have easily had a heart attack. Kevin appeared cool as he turned on the radio, and the song we were listening to in the car drifted from the speakers.

He took off his button-down shirt and sat down beside me. I damn near jumped out of my skin, because unlike outside, there was nowhere to run, no bleachers to hide behind, and no one to help me get out of the situation. It was just me, him, and my sweaty palms. I didn't want to seem immature in his eyes, so when he leaned over and began to unbutton my shirt, I held my breath until he was done.

He took my small breasts into his hands before releasing them from my bra. The entire time I was wondering why we didn't just go up to his room, but I was too shaken to speak. He pushed me back on his couch, and before I knew it my pants were undone and one leg was out. By then I was start-ing to panic, but I didn't want him to think I was scared.

I tried to steady my breathing as he pulled out his penis. He was almost as big as my uncle, and Lord knows it wouldn't fit inside me without ripping me in half. I moved to pull my pants back on and tell him I couldn't do it, but before I could sit up, four of his friends, guys I recognized from the football team, came out of his living room closet, each grabbing a hold of me and pinning me down to the couch. One held a pillow over my face so no one would hear me scream, causing me to turn my face to the side so that I could still breathe.

The more I struggled, the harder they gripped me. The room was dark and my face was behind the pillow, so I couldn't see who was doing what, and after a while I just gave up the struggle as they took turns having their way with me. Uncle Darryl had only gotten the head in, but these boys tore into me like a bullet, the burning sensation unbearable. I just closed my eyes and cried silently as I listened to the Force MD's sing on the radio. My tears fell like rain that day, and after they shoved me out the door once I put my clothes back on, I knew I would need a good, long cry as I made my way home.

Once I got home it went from bad to worse. Uncle Darryl was drunk as usual on the couch. One of his lady friends was over, but that really didn't matter. I'm sure if she didn't stay all night, he'd be in my room before the sun came up. Uncle Darryl wasn't a bad looking brother, considering the kind of man he was. Standing six feet three inches with a solid build, skin the color of vanilla wafers, and jade green eyes, women were practically throwing themselves at him. That's why I couldn't see what he wanted with little old me.

I spoke a weak hello as I made my way by them and went straight to the bathroom. Locking the door, I stood in the tub after a painful urination and washed between my legs, removing the blood and semen from my earlier ordeal. I was still bleeding, so I grabbed a clean pair of underwear and a maxi pad from the closet before changing into a pair of sweats and a T-shirt. I then went to clean the kitchen.

I was in a daze as I simultaneously washed dishes and started dinner. While everything was simmering on the stove, I swept and mopped the kitchen floor before starting my homework. It hurt like hell to sit down, so I folded one of my legs under me to ease the pressure of sitting flat on the chair.

My mind was still in a state of shock as I calculated math problems and held back my tears. I really thought Kevin liked me. Had I known it would come to this, I never would have gone to his house, but how could I know? How would I face him in school the next day? All of these thoughts raced through my head as I fed my uncle and his friend, and cleaned the kitchen for the night, unable to eat anything myself. Instead of turning on my little black and white television, I lay in the dark until I cried myself to sleep.

I finally fell into a comfortable sleep. Just as I was going to turn over, I felt my uncle slipping into the bed next to me. My body stiffened automatically, and I held my breath as he grabbed roughly at my breast, the smell of liquor evident on his breath.

"Uncle Darryl," I said through slightly parted lips as I held on to my pants. He was trying to pull them down and I was trying to keep them up. "Uncle Darryl, we can't do this. My period is on."

"Girl, since when did that matter? You know my motto, don't chu girl? Don't chu?" he asked as he continued to pull on my pants and tears ran down the sides of my face.

"Yes, Uncle Darryl," I said between sobs. "I know the motto."

"Then what is it?" he replied after he finally got my pants down and his Johnson out. "Say it, bitch! What is it?"

"Walk through mud . . . fuck through blood," I said as he ripped my pants the rest of the way off and entered me fully for the first of many times.

"And don't chu ever forget it!"

For the next hour he forced himself inside me, my stiffness not a concern of his in the least. For what seemed like the hundredth time that night, I cried silent tears as he took advantage of me over and over again. When he finally left, I didn't bother to move as I watched his silhouette through the light in the door. He rumbled through his pockets and threw something on the floor.

It wasn't until morning that I discovered the two crumpled twenty-dollar bills and a Trojan condom wrapper. I picked the money up before I went to take a shower, only doing so after I made sure the coast was clear and Uncle Darryl had left for work. When I came back into the room I put that money with the rest of the money I got from him every time he did what he did to me.

In the back of my closet I had an old mayonnaise jar that I used to hide the money. Tears streamed down my face as I unfolded the six hundred dollars I already had there, adding the forty dollars to the bounty. One day I would have enough to move out, and hopefully that day would come soon.

When I got to school the next day, it felt like all eyes were on me. As I walked through the hallways in a daze, it seemed like everyone stopped what they were doing to look at me. I was still numb from the events of the previous day, so by the time I got to my locker I was unaware of the small crowd forming behind me.

After three tries I finally got the combination to my locker to work. When I opened it up piles of condoms fell out and landed at my feet. All I could do was stare as the crowd behind me burst into laughter. I didn't even know how the condoms got in there, and I made no effort to pick them up as I took out the books I needed, causing more to fall from my locker and onto the floor. Closing the locker, I turned to squeeze through the crowd only to find myself face to face with Ashley.

"Figured you may need those since you like the group thing," Ashley said, getting another round of laughter from the crowd. She had on Kevin's jacket and chain. That was another slap in the face.

Embarrassed, I pushed through the crowd before they could see my tears drop. I walked as fast as I could down the hallway, stopping to pick up the books that kept falling from my arms along the way, the crowd taunting me in the background.

"There's some plastic wrap here, too. Just in case you decide you wanna be a blow fish again," Ashley called out behind me.

I kept up the pace as I made my way to the principal's office. Taking a seat on the bench, I put my head down so I could catch my breath. It was obvious that Kevin and his goons came back and told the entire school that I willingly had sex with them yesterday. By the time the office aide noticed me sitting there, I was a mess. She told the principal I was out there, and walked me into her office so we could talk. I could hear "Tears" playing from the small radio on the principal's desk as she got up to close the door behind the secretary. I put my head on the desk and cried, wondering to myself how my life had ended up this way.

As the sun sets and the night comes around I can feel my emotions coming down. But now I pull the covers off my bed saying to myself, "Tonight I'll forget . . ."

Jasmine

Full Of Surprises

"So, you're telling me that Monica is having your baby?" I said to James with so much venom dripping from my voice it could have burned a hole in the floor. I know he didn't just tell me some bullshit like that. Honestly, I wasn't even sure why I was so surprised, because when they were propped up on my damn table there surely wasn't any protection popping off. I damn sure don't remember seeing any condom wrappers on the floor that day, so why would they have used one any other time?

"I'm telling you that's what she told me, but I haven't spoken to her since then, so I'm not sure how true it is."

"And if she is, James, what are you going to do?" At that point I felt like my world was crumbling around me. I swear, every time I thought I could pick up the pieces and put everything back together, another issue came around, messing it all up again. It was like I had a black cloud hanging over my head. Haters were always trying to knock a bitch back.

The fact that James was so cool about the situation was pissing me the hell off. If—and I stress the word "if"—Monica was indeed pregnant, she was not giving that baby up. She'd keep it just to make me miserable, and I'd be damned if I wanted that constant reminder in my face every day. James and I had our owns kids to raise, and not that we were hurting for cash, but her having James's baby would be another mouth to feed, even if it was only part time. Call it cruel, but I didn't want that baby anywhere near me and my kids. It was as simple as that.

Looking over at James, I wanted to knock that stupid ass look off his face. I was trying so hard not to place all the blame on him, but if he hadn't pressured me into that threesome shit, none of this would be happening. I wanted to jump on his neck and choke the shit out of him, but on the flip side I was disappointed in myself for letting it go that far. I honestly was trying to please my husband in the beginning, but then it got way out of hand. I had no business being over at that woman's house either, and I knew it.

Starting to feel lightheaded and a tad on the nauseous side, I took a seat on the arm of the couch so I could gather my thoughts and get my head on straight before I went back to my brother's house. More than ever I was hoping my black clouds did have a silver lining. I had to put my life back together before it was too late.

"James, we'll talk about this some more, but not today. Right now I don't have the energy," I said to him as I moved to make my way toward the door. I felt like I was moving in slow motion as the room began to spin violently around me. I felt like I was watching myself from the sidelines. The last thing I remember before the room went black was reaching for my coat and trying to remember where I had placed my car keys.

When I came to, my head was pounding. I finally focused in on James after adjusting my eyes to the light. He was looking down at me with a worried expression on his face. He was sweating profusely, and he appeared to have the shakes. I wanted to lift my head from the pillow, but doing so made my head pound harder. I looked around the room and tried to figure out where I was. I didn't remember James telling me he had painted our guest room. Still feeling delirious, I was trying to think if the bed had railings on it before today.

"Jazz, how are you feeling, baby? Are you thirsty?"

"No, I'm fine. My head just hurts. Where's my coat?"

"Jazz, you can't leave until the doctor is finished evaluating you."

"What?" For the first time I realized that I was not in the comfort of my own home, but I was in a hospital room instead.

"Yeah, you passed out at the house and bumped your head on the edge of the end table. We've been here for a couple of hours. I was scared I lost you."

"James, I . . ."

"Baby, just rest. The doctor should be back any minute."

Taking the cup of ice from James, I sat back on the bed, trying to gather my thoughts. I must be really stressed out because I'd never passed out before. This shit with James was working my last nerve. My thoughts flip flopped from wanting things to work, to wanting it all to be over. Just as I was dozing off again, the doctor walked in.

"Mrs. Cinque, I'm glad to see you're awake. How's your head feeling?" The doctor quizzed as he touched the bottoms of my feet to see if I was responsive before moving up to listen to my heartbeat.

"My head is pounding something awful, but I'll survive."

"That's good to hear, although you do have a nasty bump on your head. Do you mind if I ask you a few personal questions?"

"No, not at all. What do you need to know?" I responded as my heart began to pound wildly in my chest. I hope he's not about to tell me I have a deadly disease. I have enough shit going on in my life.

"Have you been under a lot of stress lately? When you came in your blood pressure was abnormally high."

"Well, things have been a little hectic lately, but nothing outside of the norm," I lied after taking a quick peek at James. I wish I could have told the doctor what the real deal was, but that was a little too much information, and I didn't need him in my business.

"When was your last menstrual period? Has it been coming on a consistent basis?"

I couldn't answer right away because it'd been at least two months since I'd seen it. I didn't really pay it that much attention, contributing its absence to all of the stress I'd been under lately, but now I wasn't too sure.

"It was maybe two months ago. I didn't have one last month, and it's a little late this month, but it'll come. I've just been stressed."

"Well, Mrs. Cinque, we took some blood when you first arrived and the tests show that you're pregnant. We're going to do an ultrasound to find out how far along you are. I'll have the nurse . . ."

I didn't hear anything the doctor said after that. Did he just tell me I was pregnant? I was stuck on what I should do next. Now was not the time to be having another baby. James and I had too much to work out, and I still hadn't found out if Monica was having James's kid. My life was pretty much spiraling out of control, and I had no clue as to what I should do to fix it.

"So I'll send the nurse right in and we'll see what's what, okay?"

I nodded, still in shock at what the doctor told me. When he left the room, James came over, stood on the side of the bed, and took hold of my hand. I was starting to feel sick all over again just thinking about what we were facing.

"James, I can't have this baby," I stated matter-of-factly, not caring what he thought. I refused to bring another child into the drama that was going on, and it didn't look like things would be getting better any time soon.

"What do you mean, you can't have the baby? Why not? I hope this has nothing to do with Monica," James practically screamed, nearing hysteria. For a few quick seconds I thought he was going to snatch me up.

"We already have issues we need to work through, and a baby would just complicate things."

"Things aren't that complicated, Jazz. How can you make that kind of decision for both of us?"

"Both of us? Did you think about both of us when . . ." before I could finish, the nurse walked in. James and I were steaming, but we managed to hold our tongues.

I was almost in tears as the nurse smeared a cool gel over my belly so she could perform the ultrasound. Flashbacks of when I was carrying my twins caused tears to spill over my eyelashes and run down the sides of my face. I wasn't ready for this. Not under these circumstances.

When I heard the baby's heart beat my tears flowed even more. As the nurse moved the monitor around on my belly I could see a figure the size of a tennis ball on the screen. I thought to myself about the possibility of having this baby, and how it would affect our lives. Was having this baby a good idea?

As I lay on the bed with my eyes closed, I could hear two heartbeats getting louder. Instantly I took it as my own and the baby's, but how could that be? When I opened my eyes to look at the monitor there were now two figures on the screen. I didn't want to believe my eyes. Could I be having . . .

"Well, Mrs. Cinque, it looks as if you're carrying twins," the nurse said happily. All I could do was stare at the screen and hope I was seeing double. As if one baby wasn't stressful enough, the size of my family had just doubled in a matter of minutes. "Did you say twins?" James asked with a cheerful voice. He knew I would have a hard time getting rid of one, so two was definitely out of the question. I'd never be able to do it.

"Yes, you guys are having twins. We'll be keeping you overnight for observation, Mrs. Cinque, just to make sure you're okay and no harm was done to the fetuses from your fall. The wait shouldn't be that long. I'm going to check for room availability now. The doctor will be in to talk to you shortly."

I was quiet as the nurse removed the gel from my stomach before readjusting my bed. On the way out she congratulated me and James on our new additions before closing the door to give us some privacy.

A million thoughts raced through my head as I turned to think of a way out of this. In my heart I knew there was only one, but I'd never do it. How could I? My babies deserved a chance at life . . . no matter how fucked up it may be.

James came and stood quietly by my side, and I continued to stare at the wall. What if Monica was carrying twins, too? That would be six mouths to feed! We had money, but damn. That would put a hurting on anyone's pocket. The thing was, Monica probably didn't even want the baby.

I lay there not really focusing on anything, but thinking many things at once. James laid his head on my stomach. I refrained from touching him because I wasn't ready to forgive him. I still wanted to be mad at him. Hell, I needed to be mad because otherwise I'd give in too easily.

"Jasmine, I can't apologize enough for everything I put you through. I was wrong, and I admit it, but please don't take my babies away from me. We can make it work. I'm sure we can make it work," James said as tears ran from his eyes and onto my belly. I could feel my heart tug on my emotions, but I couldn't give in just yet.

"James, we'll talk about it later."

He didn't respond. He just pulled his chair up next to the bed and kept his head on my stomach until the doctor told us the room was ready. When we got upstairs and were settled, the doctor gave me a prescription for pre-natal vitamins and iron pills. He gave me instructions to make an appointment with my gynecologist within the next couple of days just to make sure everything was going well. After wishing us a successful pregnancy, he went on to treat the many patients in the emergency room.

James put his head back on my stomach, and this time I rubbed the back of his head, thinking of my next move. They had yet to tell me how far along I was.

Reaching over, I decided to call my brother before he started worrying. I should have been home hours ago. After dialing the number, the phone rang three times before he answered it.

"Hello, Robinson residence," my brother Dave sang into the phone, sounding like he was in a really good mood. His wife, Sarayah, must have broken him off a little something. Despite the obvious turmoil my heart was in, I still giggled a little in response to my big brother's happiness.

"Hey, it's me," I spoke into the receiver, trying to hide my sadness. I didn't want to alarm him.

"Hey, Sugar Pop. How'd everything go?" he asked, calling me by my childhood nickname.

"Not as good as expected, but I'll live."

"Well, when it comes to matters of the heart, you have to take it one day at a time."

"I know," I replied, hesitant to begin my next sentence. "I called to let you know I'm in the hospital, and they're keeping me overnight."

"You're where? In the hospital? For what? Did that nigga put his hands on you?" he shot off.

"No, he didn't put his hands on me, silly. You know he wouldn't do that."

"So, how did you end up in the hospital, Jazz?"

"I passed out at the house and woke up in the emergency room. James said I accidentally hit my head on the side of the table."

"Damn, girl, you all right? Want me to come get you?"

"No, I'm okay. James is still here."

"Good. That's good to hear. So what did they say? Stress?"

"I'm pregnant," I blurted out before I lost the nerve. I felt funny saying the words out loud, and my body cringed at the thought.

"Say word. Are you serious?" he asked, full of excitement. I wish I could've mustered up half his enthusiasm.

"With twins."

"With . . ." the phone got silent for about ten seconds and I wasn't sure if he hung up or passed out.

"You there?" I heard rustling in the background and before I knew it, Sarayah was talking into the phone.

"Jazz, congrats! Now I know why you were sleeping all the time. Girl, you were getting a little thick," she yelled into the phone, just as excited as my brother. "Honey, I can't wait until we have ours."

"So, I take it the twins didn't drive you crazy?"

"Oh, no. We had a ball when they woke up. Those little angels are back to sleep now."

"Angels? My kids?" I said as we shared a laugh over the phone. It felt good to be happy about something finally, even if only for a moment.

"Well, Jazz, I do hope you feel better, and I'll see you when you get home, okay?"

"Okay, and tell your crazy husband I'll talk to him later."

After hanging up the phone, I lay back and stared at the ceiling. Telling my brother I was pregnant was my way of not doing anything stupid, like going through with the abortion. I cracked myself up talking like I would really do it, but right then I was stressed the hell out.

"Jasmine, I'm sorry I hurt you," James said, turning his head around so he could have his head on my stomach and look at me.

"James, we'll talk about this later."

"But baby, I just wanted to . . ."

"James, we'll talk later."

"Okay, later is fine."

"Okay."

I finally turned the television on, not really paying attention to the program that was playing. I had to get in contact with Monica sooner rather than later. We had a lot of things that needed to be discussed.

As I lay there I remember just wanting to scream to no end because life wasn't supposed to be like this. I lay there in a daze staring at the television, thinking to myself how I had a lot to discuss with Monica, but in reality who was I fooling? See, Monica was a major part of my problems, but I also knew that the twins from the gym, Donnie and Rahmel had ran all up in me and nutted up in me not too long ago and I didn't want to think it, but in my heart of hearts I knew that the twins that I had just found out that I was carrying weren't James's babies. Those babies inside of me had to be fathered by the twins from the gym! A woman knows who the father of her kids are; it's sort of like a spiritual, instinctual thing. I couldn't deny what I was feeling, and inside I knew that those kids couldn't be James's.

Lord, I can't take this drama! I remember thinking to myself. But no matter what, I knew that I could never let James onto the little secret I had which now had blossomed into a major secret being held inside my womb.

Carlos

It's A Small World: Today's News

News about Rico's suicide had been in the paper every day for the last three months. I was already stressing over the case I had. Yeah, they was trying to get me, but I kept my business as clean as possible so they'd need to try a little harder. Hell, Rico didn't even get props like that when he was walking the streets. Every time I turned on the television or picked up the *Daily News,* I saw his face plastered all over it, like his spirit wouldn't let me have any peace.

Shit, he had it coming! Every hustler in this game knew you couldn't get out. You either disappeared or died trying. Rico knew it was just a matter of time before he was slayed. He had enemies from here to the end of the earth, so his days had been numbered for years. Rico was a lot of things, but suicidal? Naw . . . he would never die a sucker's death. That dude was a soldier. He expired before my connect had a chance to get at him. I knew his supplier, but damn if I knew if he was willing to do business.

Bitches were practically throwing their panties in his casket at the funeral, and that Monica bitch didn't even have the decency to show up. She could have at least faked it 'til the very end. Damn! That bitch had no class, and it made her look suspect.

I just felt bad for Shaneka . . . sort of. She was ride or die for Rico, and he just tossed her to the birds like she never meant shit to him. That woman was a ticking time bomb, and I was just laying low, waiting for her to explode. They had broken up and got back together plenty of times, but that last time was murder. He scooped Monica's ass up quick as shit, and it was like a slap in the face to Shaneka. All I could say was when

Monica got dealt with, it wasn't gonna be nothing pretty about it. Monica played that "Oh, I'm crazy" shit, but Shaneka was certified. That girl got papers and was not to be fucked with.

I wasn't banking on Monica getting off as easy as she did. It seemed like she woulda taken the fall with Rico, but it didn't turn out like that. It was almost like she was fucking the judge or something. I'd be seeing Monica about some shit real soon.

Rico had gravy beyond your wildest imagination, and I knew she walked away laced. When his peeps came to clean out his apartment that thing was practically empty. I knew my man was living lavish, but you could never tell by how his place looked when his peeps rolled through. It was like he never even lived there. Clothes, shoes, jewels . . . everything was gone, like my man never existed. Like maybe he was a figment of your imagination. He never introduced Monica to his family, so no one knew who to look for, but I had my eye on her ass from the gate. Snakes recognize other snakes, and I knew her ass was kin. I was just mad she got to him before I could.

One day right after Rico had died I was on the block, trying to push this powder while I still could. The feds were trying to sweep the whole neighborhood on some bullshit, and I had things to do. I couldn't be sitting up in nobody's penitentiary doing time. Yeah, I was a hustler but, I wasn't made for that shit. Give that to the real gangsters. Yeah, I be out here bustin' them guns when necessary, but when it came to doing time, I was a wankster all damn day. You wouldn't have my ass scared to pick up the soap.

I was about to head back because the same cop car done circled the block three times. I didn't know who they were looking for, but if it was me, that day wouldn't be the day. On the way back to the crib I decided to stop and get me a sandwich and a Pepsi when my cell phone rang. Looking down at the caller ID, I decided to ignore the call. Blocked numbers didn't get answered, and whoever was blowing my hip up should've known that. My phone rang four more times before I got to the crib, and whoever it was never left a message. Oh, well.

I was sitting around trying to put a plan together. I'd been with Rico to visit his supplier plenty of times, but you just couldn't be approaching people like that, unless, of course, you had a death wish or something. I knew someone knew who did Rico, because personally I wasn't convinced he did it himself. Gangsters worldwide had been trying to get at him for the longest, and I just needed to find out what crew got him done so I could make my next move.

Taking a peek at my phone, I had twenty-seven missed calls from an anonymous caller, and it was working my nerves. Hell, it could be some chick I met recently or my worst nightmare on the other end. Either way, I wasn't interested. I was curious though, so I decided if the phone rang again, I might answer it.

Around seven thirty my anonymous caller buzzed my phone again I picked up the phone, my agitation clearly evident in the tone of my voice.

"State ya purpose, quick!" I growled into the phone. I didn't make it a habit of answering calls when I didn't know who was on the other end. I was knee deep in illegal shit, and the last thing I needed was the jakes on my ass. Only a handful of niggas knew the math, so for someone to call me with a blocked number spelled trouble.

"Carlos, it's me, Shaneka," the soft, feminine voice responded from the other end of the phone line. She sounded like she was crying, but that was none of my concern. The only nigga that gave a damn was dead now, so what did she want me to do? Instead of responding to her obvious cry for attention, I straight blacked on her like she was one of my many enemies.

"What I tell you about calling out my government, and why in hell are you calling me from a blocked number? You know I don't play those games."

"Well, C-Dogg, I had some valuable information for you, but since you want to act like a damn nut—" she spoke into the phone sarcastically. I could almost see the look on her face, probably a smirk with her eyebrows raised.

"Listen, speak ya piece, okay? If you got info, spill it. If not, get off my dime," I barked into the phone, cutting her off.

The part that killed me the most was that she acted like she was all bent out of shape over Rico's passing, but the entire time they were together I was tapping her ass to no end. Hell, the day he got busted I had just finished tearing her guts up before I went over there. She would come and blow me early in the morning, then later that day I'd see her tongue kissing Rico like my soldiers weren't just tickling her tonsils a few hours before. Snakes! Kin always recognized kin.

"Damn, since when has it been like that between us? You act like I never done you right."

"Shaneka, please tell me what I need to know, ma." I counted to ten to bring my blood pressure down. I had to refrain from banging on her ass because I swear we'd be arguing like we were a fuckin' couple. This girl was trying my last nerve early in the game.

"If you insist," she responded, sounding like she had shit in check. I decided to let her have that small victory for now. "Well, remember when I told you I thought I saw Monica before?" she asked, knowing damn well we'd already had that conversation.

"Yeah, I remember, why?"

"Well, peep this shit . . ."

Shaneka broke everything down from when she met Monica a while back up at the prison. The same guard Shaneka told me she was having problems with was giving Monica heat. As payback they did a number on the guard's car by slashing all four tires and putting a mixture of sugar, popcorn kernels, and Snickers candy bars in her gas tank. So even if the guard got new tires, by the time she started the engine, and that mixture started circulating, the car would be no good.

Come to find out Shaneka and Monica were visiting the same person. The men are housed about a mile down the road, but the visiting room is shared by both sexes to make it easier to keep track of the prisoners during visiting hours since none of the guards wanted to do any real work anyway.

Shaneka had been seeing a woman named Tanya for over a year and a half before Monica started to visit Tanya. Shaneka was rotating between seeing her brother one week and Tanya the next. Monica always visited Tanya on the week Shaneka wasn't seeing her, but Shaneka remembered what Tanya said about Monica's involvement with Tanya ending up on lockdown. It just didn't click in Shaneka's mind who Monica was until after Monica gave her a business card.

Shaneka met Tanya on a day she and her mom were visiting with her brother, and they had been cool ever since. She told Tanya that she would help her when she got out, and they became fast friends, and later on lovers. Rico never knew what was going on. Shaneka was practically running circles around him.

Her hate came about for Monica when they broke up and she found out Rico saw Monica that same day. Never mind that Monica knew nothing about Rico and Shaneka. Her vendetta was definitely personal on getting Monica back.

"So, what does all of this have to do with me?" I asked.

"I'm getting to that now," she sighed, getting a little attitude because I had cut her off again.

She went on to talk about all the similarities between them, and how they knew a lot of the same people with both of them being photographers and artists. I think I heard her say something about a pink bitch, but I wasn't sure. She rambled on for about another ten minutes before I had to cut her off again. The information she was giving me I already knew, or didn't give a damn about, so what was the purpose of the call?

"Shaneka, please get to the point, damn!"

"Okay, okay. Damn . . . so angry," she replied, afterward sucking her teeth. I didn't give a damn.

"Well, how about I saw her at the doctor's office this morning and you are not going to believe me when I tell you this!"

"Tell me what, Shaneka?"

"How 'bout that bitch is pregnant."

"And?" I said more than asked, confused as to why I should give a damn. Hell, it wasn't my seed.

"And? Nigga, I think it may be Rico's," she said, bursting into tears again. Now I knew why she was so upset.

"And you care because?"

"I care because that bitch stole my man, had him killed, and now she's having his baby."

"How you know she had Rico killed?" I asked, curious as to where she got her information. I thought maybe she knew something I didn't.

"I don't, but I think she did. Anyway, she's pregnant by my man. That's what's important."

"So what you gonna do?"

"Get her ass back! What the hell you mean what I'm gonna do?"

"I meant how, Shaneka, damn!"

"I'll get back to you on that by the end of the day, but I do have a tad bit of info that may work to your advantage."

"Word? What's that?" I asked, now bored with the conversation. I had my own neck to protect. Her shit was on solo this time.

"You know that cute little young girl that you be fuckin' all crazy over in Tasker projects? The one you got twisted on that coke?"

"Yeah," I said, now listening more to what she had to say.

"Well, if you're looking for a way to get at Monica, that's it. That pretty little young thing you got turned out is Monica's little sister."

Before I could say anything else, she hung up the phone, and I had a million questions I wanted to ask her. One thing I could honestly say about Shaneka was this: she may have been a little on the annoying side, but when she had some info she was usually on point—99.9 percent like a paternity test. I must say that shit she had just dropped on me was heavy, and I had to take a step back before I made my next move.

It's funny how small the world is, because I would have never in a million years connected Yoyo with Monica. Yolanda was a cutie for sure. Small waist, bubble butt, perfect breasts with kissable nipples, and the same heart-shaped mouth like her older sister. They were both dimes, the only difference being their last names. Maybe that's why I hadn't put two and two together.

As fly as Yoyo was, and as good as that pussy felt while she was riding me, she had one hell of a damn habit. My girl got her snort on, and was serious with it. Now, don't get me wrong, she didn't look like your average Joe Crackhead, but that girl would snort all day if the blow was available. And talk about wild sex! Man, that shit must run in the family because this chick was a beast.

One night I slid through for my waxing and she answered the door ass naked holding a silk scarf in one hand, and two pair of handcuffs in the other. My man came to life instantly, causing my pants to tent majorly in the front. She didn't say anything to me. She just dropped the handcuffs and scarf on the floor, and walked toward her bedroom in the back of the apartment.

Now, I ain't gonna lie, I was stuck on dysfunctional for a hot second. I knew she liked being creative, but sometimes she didn't give me a clue. I just had to walk in there and do my own thing. So now my mind was racing a mile a minute as I bent over to pick up the items from the floor before locking the door. She had a fly little apartment and she kept it neat, so I made sure to hang my coat up before going into the bedroom.

When I walked in, Yoyo was on the bed lying on her side with one leg up to her chest working a dildo from the back. Her other hand helped keep her nipples in her mouth as soft moans escaped her lips. I damn near exploded watching her in that somewhat compromising position. Shedding my clothes quickly, I joined her on the bed.

First turning her on her back, I tied the scarf she gave me around her eyes so she couldn't see what I was doing to her. Grabbing another scarf from the nightstand, I tied her hands tightly to the headboard so she couldn't move. I had to take a second and slow down before it was over, and it hadn't even started yet. Looking at her body stretched out on the bed, and my name tattooed across her pelvis where hair should be, almost had me wanting to wife her . . . almost.

Taking both pairs of handcuffs, after placing the keys in her hand, I first attached them to my wrist then to her ankles so she couldn't move. Yolanda was practically double jointed so I knew if I stretched her any which way she'd be able to conform. Normally, head was out of the question and never part of the equation, but that night I decided to show her what it was really hittin' for.

Since my hands were connected to her ankles I pushed her legs up and out as far as they could go comfortably. I would suck on her clit softly, making it real wet, then I'd blow on it until it got cold, warming it with my mouth and cooling it off repeatedly. It was interesting to sit back and watch as her cream began to rise to the top and gather at her opening.

I took the tip of my tongue and traced the edge of her tunnel in a complete circle before I stuck my tongue inside her, tasting her sweet, yet tangy nectar. I tugged on her clit softly with my teeth, leaning back so I could watch her juice spill over the sides and run down, my tongue catching it at her asshole.

Yolanda was practically begging me to slide up in her, but I wasn't ready yet. Pushing myself up on my knees I held on to her feet while I used my hips to rub the head of my man back and forth across her already sensitive clit. I would push just the head in, then pull it out and rub it across her clit again. Each time I went in, I pushed a little deeper until I was all the way inside her. I was killing the pussy with long, slow strokes, sometimes pulling out until just the tip of my dick was pressed against her, her walls gripping me like a Hoover trying to suck me back in.

Leaning in, I took her nipples into my mouth one at a time, since I couldn't push them both together with my hands. I grinded my hips into hers, causing another series of explosions.

"Now, I'm gonna untie you, but I'm not taking the handcuffs off. You ready to ride?"

Instead of answering, she threw her legs back farther so I could untie the scarves from her eyes and wrist. Once she was untied, I grabbed her by her ankles and she held onto my neck as I maneuvered our bodies so she could be on top. My girl did the damn thing to me, uncuffing me so I could hold on to her waist. Yolanda rode me until I was bone dry. Afterward she retrieved the eight ball from my coat pocket. She worked for that nose candy, so I just sat back and gathered my thoughts while she did her thing.

Thinking back, that was the last time I was over there, and from the imprint in my sweat pants, it was time to pay her ass another visit. While she worked me over I could see what info she would give me about her sister. They didn't appear to be close, and Yolanda was always out for self, so I was sure she could tell me something good. Making the call, she was all too happy to hear from me. We made plans to meet up before the week was out, and she made sure I knew what to bring with me.

Shortly after, just as I was reaching into my pants for a quick release, my cell phone buzzed indicating an incoming call. This time, Shaneka's number flashed across the screen. Peeping the time, I saw that it was ten o'clock at night. Damn, where did the time go?

"Yeah," I answered, feigning sleep. Unless she had more info, I wasn't in the mood to talk.

"Carlos . . . I mean C-Dogg, I need you to drop a package off at FedEx for me in the morning."

"On the real, Shaneka, I really don't want no part of whatever you tryin'a pull off. I got my own shit to deal with."

"Come on, C. You know I can't go into FedEx since I got into that fight with the manager."

"That's not my problem. Ain't nobody tell you to be in there on that hood shit. Go to another one."

"Come on! It ain't like you delivering a damn bomb. It's a gift for Monica."

"Oh, word? What is it?" I asked, curious as to how she was planning to get Monica back.

"It's nothing really. Just a little something to let her know I got my eye on her. Can you please drop it off for me, please?"

"All right, already. Bring the shit by tonight, and I'll drop it off in the morning."

"I'm on my way."

After hanging up the phone, I hopped in the shower. Since she was coming over, I thought I might as well get fucked nice. That should hold me until Saturday.

Monica

One Down, More to Go—1991

I ended up telling the principal only half the story because I didn't want to have to explain the previous day's events to my uncle. I used the excuse that I wasn't feeling well so I could leave early. I walked home so I could take time to think, and I became a new person with each step. I was tired of Uncle Darryl having his way, and having to deal with the ridicule from the students in school. I was determined it all would end that day. In my mind I hatched a plan that would get my revenge on every person who ever did me wrong—especially those snotty-ass cheerleaders and that damn Ashley.

When I got home I ran up to my room and dropped my book bag in the corner. Standing in the mirror I took a look at my hair, deciding to loosen the ponytails. I went to my stash, took out three hundred dollars, and left the house, moving quickly toward the strip so I could get everything I needed and be home before my uncle got in.

Stopping at the hair store first, I picked up a mild relaxer, a can of Isoplus oil sheen, electric flatirons, and a satin cap to sleep in. Once I paid for my items I walked three doors down to The Style Shop, a clothing store that sold fashionable items at cheap prices. I tried on outfit after outfit and finally settled on five pairs of jeans with matching shirts, shoes, and purses.

Clasping the bags tightly to my chest, I raced back home with three hours to spare. Hiding my new clothes in the back of the closet behind the boring clothes Uncle Darryl bought for me, I sat down to read the directions on the Dark & Lovely relaxer kit. I didn't want to risk my hair falling out from the procedure. Things were hard enough to deal with already without adding fuel to the fire. Following the directions, I worked the chemical into my hair until it was straight, and shampooed my hair three times to ensure all of the cream was removed.

After rinsing the conditioner and blowing my hair dry, I plugged in my brand new flatirons so they would be nice and hot when I was done cleaning up the mess I made in the bathroom. Taking a pair of scissors from the kitchen drawer, I trimmed my ends, afterward taking small sections of my hair and binding them into a soft, bouncy wrap.

Satisfied with my look, I then wrapped my hair into a bee-hive like I had seen my mother do to her hair many times, and tied a bandana tightly around it so it would be perfect in the morning. Getting rid of the evidence, I proceeded to clean the house and prepare dinner before my uncle arrived home. As I cleaned, I decided I would use a little more of the money I'd stashed to buy more clothes so I could keep up appearances.

I took the sharpest knife from the kitchen drawer, ran upstairs, and placed it under my pillow after I had made my bed. I didn't think I could kill my uncle, but if he came in my room again, he would get it. I would be buying a lock for my door tomorrow, whether he liked it or not. After finishing my homework, I ate dinner, cleaned up my mess, and took a bath. I put lotion on my skin so it wouldn't be dry, then got into bed to get some sleep.

My uncle came into the house around eight that night with one of his many girl toys. I woke up when I heard him come in, and I fed him and his company dinner, then cleaned the kitchen for the night. As I was walking by, he reached out and smacked me on my ass. I turned to say something, but before I got a word in, his lady friend was cursing him out.

"Darryl, you ain't got no business touching that girl like that. Keep ya hands to ya self!"

"Bitch, mind ya business! This here is family business."

"Oh, I know you ain't just call me a bitch? Nigga, I'll . . ."

While they argued back and forth I made my way upstairs. I felt relief for a second because I never had anyone take up for me. Everybody always acted like they didn't know what was going on. At the same time, I wished she would've kept her mouth shut because I'd have to pay for it later. Once I was upstairs, I checked the position of the knife, closed my eyes, and anticipated my return to school. I contemplated how I would get Ashley back. I felt like the Grinch from *How the Grinch Stole Christmas*, hatching his plan to steal everything from the residents of Whoville.

I was abruptly awakened from my peaceful sleep by my uncle standing over my bed with his pants unfastened. I tried to act like I was sleeping, but my heart was beating a mile a minute in my chest as I gripped the knife under my pillow.

"Little bitch, I know you not sleep. Open up for Uncle Darryl," he said as he dropped his pants to his ankles and stepped out of one pants leg before moving to climb on top of me.

Just as he settled on the side of the bed, I jumped up and put him in a headlock, pressing the knife blade to his throat.

"We're not doing this anymore, you hear me? We're family, and this shit just ain't right," I said to him as the knife began to dig into his flesh on the side of his neck. He was sweating bullets as he tried to breathe with me pressing on his esophagus.

"Baby girl, I just came to give you your allowance and thank you for dinner," he said as he tried to catch his breath. I'm sure he didn't expect me to snap the way I did. He was really trying to hit it before he went to sleep.

"Look, I'm tired of sleeping with one eye open. Why bring these women here and not sleep with them?"

"Baby girl, let me . . ."

"Don't 'baby girl' me. This shit is coming to an end tonight. Make this your last trip to my room." I held the knife to his back as he eased off the bed. When he got to the door he took a few bills out of his wallet and placed them on my dresser before closing the bedroom door behind him. I breathed a sigh of relief as I lay back in my bed and put my knife back under my pillow. When I woke up in the morning, Uncle Darryl was gone, but the money he left was still on the dresser. I counted two hundred dollars total.

Taking my time in the shower, I put on one of the new outfits I bought the day before and combed my hair down as I had seen my mother do. Adding the money my uncle gave me to the change I had from the day before, I stopped at the

*corner store to buy a lock for my door and purchased a bottle
of Nair hair removal lotion.*

*By the time I got to school my confidence level was through
the roof as I strutted through the halls like I owned them.
Removing the remaining condoms from my locker and gathering the books I needed for second period, I made my way to
the girls' locker room so I could get ready for first period gym.*

*Ashley and her crew looked at me oddly and laughed at
their own jokes, hoping to make me feel self-conscious. I paid
them no attention as I took off my new jeans and shirt, folded
them neatly so they wouldn't wrinkle, and then changed into
my blue gym suit. I applied a small amount of lip gloss to my
already shiny lips. Brushing my soft hair into a ponytail so I
wouldn't sweat out my wrap, I looked in the mirror one last
time before sitting on the bench to change my shoes. I waited
until I was the last one in the locker room before putting my
plan into action.*

*Every Tuesday like clockwork, Ashley washed her hair,
leaving it curly for the rest of the day. I laughed to myself as
I poured half the contents of her shampoo bottle down the
drain before replacing it with the Nair. After shaking it up
vigorously, I placed it back into Ashley's locker and put the
bottle of Nair in the bottom of my book bag. Tossing everything back into my locker, I made sure to put the combination
lock on before heading to join the class with a bright smile on
my face,*

*During gym, I heard all of the little giggles and sly remarks
from Ashley and the gang, but I just chilled and smiled,
knowing I would have the last laugh. I breezed through the
exercises and was the only girl able to climb all the way up
the rope and ring the bell. I noticed the stares I got from the
boys in my class as they watched my ass bounce in my gym
suit, but I paid them no mind. I had a mission to accomplish.
Before long, gym was over and it was time to hit the showers.*

*Casting my shyness to the side and removing all my clothes,
I put the plastic cap on my head the way the girl at the store
showed me so my hair wouldn't get wet. Moving toward the
showers, I made sure to get one near Ashley so I could watch
everything take place.*

I hung my towel on the hook under the showerhead so it wouldn't get wet and began to soap my body as I discreetly watched Ashley get into the shower. Getting a quick peek at her body before she closed the shower stall door that came up to just above her breasts, I saw that she had a nice pair of breasts—at least a 36C. I looked down at my A cups, then briefly glanced back at her.

I watched as she closed her eyes and put her head under the showerhead, soaking her hair so she could apply what she thought was shampoo. Before I could turn my head she caught me looking at her. My heart was beating fast as hell as she poured a huge amount of the concoction I made into her hair.

"Damn, what the fuck, are you lesbian now? First you fuck my man, now you wanna fuck me?"

Instead of responding, I rinsed my body under the water and lathered up again as she worked her hands through her hair with her eyes closed. When she stepped back under the water big sections of her hair slid off her scalp and ran down her body. She was oblivious because her eyes were closed. I turned my back to her, not quite believing that my plan had actually worked. She applied more of my concoction to her hair with her eyes still closed, and began to lather her hair again.

I was cracking up on the inside as clumps of her hair slid down her body. When she opened her eyes, clumps of hair were in her hands, and even more was at her feet. Ashley began screaming at the top of her lungs, causing a crowd of naked teenage girls to gather around her. The more she rinsed, the more her hair came out, causing Ashley to collapse in a crying heap on the floor.

Ms. Rhodes, our gym teacher, came to see what all the commotion was about. When she walked in she began screaming, asking us what happened and wrapping a towel around Ashley's head and body, calling the principal on her walkie-talkie for help. We were instructed to get dressed and immediately report to second period class. I kept my mouth shut, although I wanted to jump for joy at my silent victory. One down, many more to go, I thought.

Before the school day was over we received letters to take home to our parents explaining what had happened to Ashley, and to inform them that we would be taking gym last period because they were banning shower use at the school. I practically skipped out the school and all the way up the strip to get some more outfits and accessories for school.

When I walked into the house, Uncle Darryl wasn't home yet, giving me time to stash my newest purchases in the closet and put the new lock on my door. When I walked into the room, I was shocked to discover that Uncle Darryl had purchased me a new and bigger bed to sleep in. The comforter and sheets on the bed matched the curtains.

My little black-and-white television was replaced with a nineteen-inch color television with a remote. When I opened my closet a few of my old clothes were thrown out and my new clothes were hanging in their place, and my new shoes were lined up on the top of the closet. When I reached in the back my jar was still there, but when I counted my stash I had seven hundred dollars in it and I had taken three hundred out just the day before.

When I sat down on my bed I was surprised to find the knife still there. Under the other pillow was a note from someone named Stephanie telling me to find another hiding place for my jar, and to keep the knife in my room just in case. My uncle told her what I did to him and she helped him redecorate my room as a means of apology. I felt tears well up in my eyes at the gesture, and I did what she said.

Looking around my room, I noticed tons of new things, like the vanity that sat by my closet full of perfumes and feminine products, and an electric crimping iron accompanied by my new flat iron. I even had new clothes baskets, one for coloreds and one for whites. For the first time in my life I felt like a teenager should.

I raced downstairs and began to cook dinner so I could be done in time to watch a little television before I went to bed. I placed the bottle of Nair on my vanity and tossed the note from school in the trash. When I heard my uncle come in, I noticed he was with the lady from the other night. After fixing their plates, she winked at me before I went to clean the kitchen, letting me know she had my back. On my way upstairs my uncle stopped me before I reached the steps.

"Baby girl, I hope you liked your—"

"Darryl, leave the girl alone. She's cool. Right, Monica?"

"Uhhh . . . right. Thanks," I replied, shocked that she knew my name. She winked at me again before I went upstairs, and for the first night in a long time I felt at peace, even though I was almost certain it would be short lived.

That night I lay in my bed thinking of how I could get Kevin back. My plan was almost perfect. It would take me the rest of the week, but he had it coming. When I finally went to sleep I had a dream that I was in the shower at school, only my head was attached to Ashley's body. I was leaned up against the stall wall as she knelt down under the shower with her face between my legs. She was orally pleasing me beyond my wildest dreams, but as the water ran over her head, her hair was sliding off. I wanted to stop her, but she had my clit in her mouth and her fingers in my pussy, causing me to explode in one orgasm after another. I didn't know what the dream meant, but I smiled despite the situation.

On Friday I was ready to set my plan with Kevin into action. After this he would surely think twice before violating another woman again. I left a note for him to meet me at the same spot behind the bleachers on Sunday evening. I had to play my part, so I wore one of the new miniskirts I'd purchased, and a fitted shirt that showed my belly button. I made sure my hair was freshly flat ironed, and my lips were shining.

I was a little nervous about him not being there, but smiled instantly when I saw his car parked on the side of the gate by the field. I kept my bag close to me because I needed the contents if this plan was going to work. His face held a bright smile as I walked closer to him.

"Follow me. I got something to show you." I didn't bother to wait for him. I started walking toward the school as he scrambled to catch up with me.

On Sunday afternoons the side door was always open because they had adult GED training for a couple of hours. I led him into the building quietly and upstairs to our homeroom class. *Giving him full view of my bare bottom with my ass perched on the teacher's desk, I could see his arousal from the chair he sat in. Walking seductively toward him, I straddled his lap and gyrated my hips on his stiffness, the warmth from my opening heating his length.*

I kissed his lips, slipping the two GHB pills I paid a smoker to get from the drug house around the corner from my house from under my tongue and into his mouth. He swallowed them without a second thought. Continuing to move my hips, I eased his manhood out of his pants, rubbing it against my clit, but not allowing him to penetrate me.

Pretty soon the effects of the pills caused his eyelids to get heavy and his body to slump in the chair. Once he was completely out I went to work, stripping him naked and chaining his hands and feet to the teacher's chair. Class would start at 7:15 a.m., just in time for the pill to stop working and Prince Charming to wake up. I nailed the wooden legs of the chair to the old hardwood floor so it wouldn't topple over. Once Kevin's limp body was secure in the seat, I took a permanent black magic marker and wrote, "I AM A RAPIST" in big, bold letters all over his body, starting at his forehead and working my way down until his entire body was covered. I then Krazy-glued the outline of his feet to the floor. Once outside, I drove his car to the middle of the football field and spray painted the word RAPIST all over the inside and outside of his car, and left it running.

When I got to class in the morning a huge crowd was standing outside the door as the school principal, the school nurse, and the security guard worked to get Kevin unstuck and unlocked. They kept asking him who did this to him, but he kept his mouth shut as we made eye contact from my position in the hallway.

This fiasco made the local papers that evening with photos of his car and of him being led out of the school in a bathrobe on the first page. One more student out of school for the week. I was almost satisfied, but I had one more to go.

Carlos

Family Ties: Present Day

I had it all figured out by the time Thursday rolled around. I would spend the weekend with Yoyo and force her to tell me everything I needed to know about Monica. Besides, Yoyo was the type who would sell out God himself if Satan offered her enough dope to snort. She didn't give a damn about her family, and she made it known. She once told me that the only thing family was good for was giving her money and getting her out of jams.

So, late Friday afternoon, after I made sure my right hand man knew how to get at me if need be, I was off the scene and smiling up in Yolanda's face. She opened the door, and to my surprise, she was fully dressed. When I stepped into her place, she gave me a hug, then went back to watching television without saying a word.

Not knowing what to think, I hung my coat up in the closet and took a seat next to her on her sofa. My instincts told me to just get my shit and bounce, but I needed some info from her. We sat in silence for about ten minutes before I spoke.

"Yolanda, are you . . ."

"Hush nigga, damn. I'm trying to figure out the puzzle," she replied, sounding irritated and never taking her attention away from the screen. I wanted to jump in her ass for screaming at me, but I had to be nice to her if I wanted her to tell me what I needed to know.

When the show was over, she finally gave me her attention. I didn't know if she was getting high before I got there, but I was not in the mood for her bullshit. Yoyo could be a bitch sometimes, and I was hoping that day wasn't one of those days.

"So wassup, Carlos? What brings you to my neck of the woods?" she asked as if she didn't just snap on me a moment ago.

"Damn, ma, can I miss you? It's been a while since I've been through this way. How you been?"

"I'm good. You know how I do."

She stood up to stretch, my eyes catching every curve. Her ass bounced in her jeans as she pranced around the living room. She could have easily been an Apple Bottoms model. Yoyo was a damn dime from head to toe. She had the same smooth chocolate skin like her sister, but she had a little more thickness to her which filled out her jeans perfectly. Just the thought of her ass bouncing on my dick had me ready to bend her over the back of the couch, but I held it down. We'd get to that later.

"How's ya family?"

"My family?" she turned around stunned, like I had just asked her to kill for me.

I knew asking her that would stop her dead in her tracks. Everyone knew she didn't get down with her peoples like that. It was almost a sin to even bring it up in a conversation, but I knew she at least kept in touch with Monica. She was in and out of the pen too much not to have a source of help.

"Yes, your family. You know . . . your brother, Brian, and your sister, Monica. When was the last time you talked to her, by the way?" I was hoping it was recently.

"You know Brian don't fuck with us. And Monica be on some ol' other shit. I only call that bitch when I need to get out of a jam. Why, you tryin'a fuck her too?"

"Did I say all that?"

"You didn't have to. Now that your boy is out of the picture you can slide on in. She likes 'get money' niggas like you."

"Oh, so you brushin' me off? Ya family can get at me like that? I thought me and you were tight?" I asked, feigning like I was hurt. Yolanda obviously knew something I didn't, but I knew she would never just come out and say it.

"Yeah, we thick as thieves," she replied sarcastically with a smirk on her face. I knew what it was hittin' for, and her facial expression let me know she wasn't falling for the okey-doke.

"So what do you need me to do, or do you need me to find out some shit?"

"Damn, ma, you killin' me."

"I ain't killing you, I'm keeping it real. The only time you blow through here is when you want something, be it ass or info."

"Yoyo, you know it's not even like that." I got up and went over to where she was standing so I could look her in the eyes. Even though we both knew it was bullshit, I wanted to at least sound sincere. "You just always seem to have some info I can use, and you ride out for me. I know I always got you in my corner, ma."

"Is that so? So why are you here today?"

"Because I missed you . . ."

"And?"

"I need some info on ya sister."

"See, I knew it was some bullshit!" Yolanda said, breaking from my embrace. I tried to pull her back, but she was already turned around and facing me.

"What bullshit, Yoyo?"

"You only here to get the scoop on my people. You only using me!"

"And you're not using me? Did you forget so soon the price I have to pay to get what I want? Eight balls ain't cheap, or are you getting ya nose candy from someone else nowadays?"

That hushed her ass right on up. She stood there looking at me for a minute like she was contemplating a way to kill me, but then she plastered a fake-ass smile on her face like everything was cool. I watched as she went around the room turning out the lights and the television before I followed her back to her room.

She immediately began to undress when we reached her bedroom, her back facing me the entire time. I stretched out across her bed and watched, wondering when she had become so shy. Shit, this was the same chick who answered the door asshole naked on any given occasion, so why the sudden case of shyness now? I didn't even bother to ask as I watched her do her thing while I chilled fully clothed in her bed. She'd be working for the dick that night, for sure.

Yoyo wrapped a towel around her body before she went into the bathroom to turn the shower on. Normally, I would be naked and in there with her, but I just fell back and clicked on the television. She was stubborn, and I damn sure wasn't going to make it easy.

Forty-five minutes went by before she came back into the bedroom, and by then I was already sleepy. I watched her dry off through half-closed eyelids, feigning sleep while she started undressing me. I cooperated as she removed every stitch of clothing from my body with lightning speed.

Yoyo wasted no time getting into position and squatting down on the head of my dick. She was killing the game as she rotated between riding just the head and taking all ten inches. I swear this girl needed to bottle some of that shit because the pussy was tight.

"So, why are you here, Carlos? What do you want from me, huh?" Yolanda asked as she grinded her pelvis into mine, causing my toes to curl up from the grip her walls had on me.

"I . . . I need some . . . damn, girl," I could hardly get it out. She was doing the damn thing to me with her legs wrapped around my back pulling me closer to her with each stroke.

"What you need, boo? Talk to me."

"I need . . . I need some info on Monica."

"What kind of info?" she asked as she rotated her body so her back was facing me. I loved the view of my dick going in and out of her. I had to look away before I messed around and ended it all.

"What happened with Rico, and what really went down with the police. He was untouchable until she came along."

"I see, so what you gonna do for me?"

Instead of responding, I met her stroke with a hard thrust, causing her to moan louder. Quickly gaining control of the situation, I picked her up off me so she could lie back on the bed and I tore the pussy up. We pushed and pulled on each other until it was over for both of us.

When we were done, Yolanda retrieved the eight ball from my pants pocket, tucking it in her nightstand. I made myself comfy on the bed as Yolanda got a warm rag from the bathroom. I was excited but I kept my cool because I didn't want to let on how important this info was to me.

"Well, since you've been so nice to me I'll see what I can come up with. Just give me a couple days, but for now let me see what my loving sister is up to."

Monica

Pandora's Box

"Okay, Ms. Tyler, you are about twenty-three weeks pregnant and everything is looking good so far. Because of your past medical history, I'll be placing you as a high risk pregnancy until further notice, just to make sure everything is running smoothly. I need you to fill out these forms, and . . ."

The nurse must have gone on forever until I tuned her out. Honestly, I couldn't really focus on anything else after she told me how far along I was. Twenty-three weeks . . . that was almost six months pregnant. The crazy thing was I really had to put my plan into action before I started showing. Right then I had a little pooch, but you know how that could go. One day I'd be fitting my clothes, and the next I'd be big as hell.

I shook my head and gave her one word answers as I signed my life away on the papers she placed in front of me. I knew for sure that once this baby dropped, my ass would be right back in the gym, and I hoped to God I didn't get stretch marks. If only I could let this baby grow in a jar or something, I'd promise I'd come back to get it when it was ready. Hell, who was I kidding? This wouldn't be easy, but the sooner it was over, the better. And I couldn't wait to get back to the gym to confirm if the rumor that I had been hearing was true or not. Rumor had it that the twins from the gym had ran up in Jasmine at her crib while James wasn't home. I couldn't wait to drop this baby just to get the scoop straight from the horses' mouths about this one. It sounded like it might be just the thing I could use to finally tear Jazz and James apart. If my pregnancy alone wouldn't do it, I knew that there isn't a married man alive who would stay with his wife after two guys ran a train on her ass!

"Ms. Tyler, I asked you a question," the nurse snapped, annoyed that I was ignoring her.

"Oh, I'm sorry. I just have a lot on my mind. Can you ask your question again?"

"Will the child's father be joining you in Lamaze class, or will you be partnering with someone else?" she asked as she glanced at me over the top of her glasses, noting my chart at the same time.

"Ummm . . . no, I'll be attending by myself. My fiancé is extremely busy."

"Do you have a girlfriend or a family member who can come with you? You need to be partnered up."

"I said no," I responded, getting frustrated that she felt the need to constantly remind me of my predicament.

"Well, I'll see if we can partner you with one of the assistants at the facility," she replied hurriedly as she gathered the papers in a sloppy pile. She had just a little too much attitude for me, and I really wasn't in the mood for being pleasant.

"You can get dressed now. Make an appointment for four weeks from now at the front desk. Do you have any questions?"

"No, not right now."

"Okay, Ms. Tyler. I'll see you in a few weeks."

After she closed the door, I stepped down off the exam table to take a look in the mirror before I put my clothes back on. The skin on my belly was still smooth, but I was developing a little pooch from the baby growing inside me. As I turned for a side view I began to feel overwhelmed because my mom wasn't there to share the moment.

I wanted to hate my mom for not being strong enough to stand up for herself. I wanted to hate my mother for not protecting me from the hands of my brother and stepfather. Although neither of them ever penetrated me, what they made me do was unspeakable. I knew she heard my cries for help, but she never came.

I wanted to hate her for leaving me and not teaching me what I needed to know to survive, but how could she if she didn't know how to survive herself? I wiped my tears and put my clothes back on. Now wasn't the time for tears. I had things to do, and I couldn't be getting all soft all of a sudden.

After standing in line for all of fifteen minutes to pay my copayment and schedule my next appointment, I was finally on my way out the door. I bumped into some chick on the way out, but I honestly didn't care enough to look back. If I had, maybe I'd have caught the dirty look I'm sure she threw my way.

Getting home in record time I pulled up just in time to see the FedEx delivery guy pull away from my house. I didn't remember ordering anything. I sat the box on the table and took careful measures not to shake it up or cut the packing too deep since I didn't know what was inside.

Inside the FedEx box was a beautifully beaded pink box. It had jewels on it, and pink was my favorite color. I was puzzled and excited because I knew I hadn't ordered anything. I briefly wondered who sent it before taking the lid off.

The box smelled sweet as I pulled out the tissue paper that covered whatever was inside. My face went from a look of wonderment to shock as I viewed the contents of the box. Inside I found a little doll dressed in what appeared to be a black dress as if she were mourning. A knife was sticking out of what seemed to be her pregnant stomach. Further inspection produced a headless baby and a little car that looked like a hearse. Black rose petals filled the bottom of the box, and a card sat in the corner.

I was scared to open the card at first, but curiosity was killing me. Inside I found a card that had black roses on the front with a picture of an eye in the middle. The words "I'VE GOT MY EYE ON YOU" were typed right across the middle. I put the card down with shaking hands and leaned back on the couch to gather my thoughts. Who would be watching me? Why? I'd done so much dirt in my life that it was hard to tell who'd want to get back at me.

I sat on the couch stunned for what felt like hours. With the exception of Jazz and James, everyone else I did anything to got what they deserved. I didn't force myself on anyone. They came to me willingly. I don't know how long I sat there until the ringing phone startled me out of my thoughts. I hesitated to answer, not sure if I really wanted to talk. The person who sent the package obviously knew where I lived, so who was to say that he or she didn't have my phone number? I crept to the phone, not realizing how crazy I must have looked. I stood near the phone and allowed it to ring again before I answered.

"Hello?" I answered the phone, my voice barely audible. I don't know what the hell I was so scared of. Killers don't normally call first.

"Hey, big sis! How's it going?"

"Yolanda?"

"Please, call me Yoyo. Besides, how many little sisters do you have?"

"No, it's just that I wasn't expecting your call. Are you locked up again?" Not for nothing, I didn't mind hearing from my sister. I mean, we were family and all, but the only time she called was if she was in a jam or short on cash like I was a damn ATM.

I can't even begin to count the number of times I had to help her out.

"Damn, is that the only reason I can have to call you? Hell, I thought we were family."

"And when did family mean anything to you?"

"Look, Moni, I ain't call to argue with you."

"Okay, so you're not in jail. What do you need? Money?"

"Damn, Monica, can a bitch call and see how you doing without wanting something? Rico is gone, and you're there by yourself. I'm just calling to check up on you."

"Well, a bitch can surely call to check me out, but I have yet to see a female dog dial a telephone. And since when did you care about anyone's well-being but your own?"

"You know what, Monica, I tried to be civil with your evil ass. You're going to die a lonely, old, bitter bitch. That's why I don't fuck with you now. You've always been a—"

"Yoyo, I'm pregnant." I had to blurt it out before I lost the nerve. For the first time I was actually scared of what was coming. I knew I wasn't anywhere near being the motherly type. What was I going to do?

"What? By who?"

"You don't know him," I said as I walked back to the couch and flopped down. What the hell have I gotten myself into? James didn't want this baby, and since I was keeping it real, neither did I. My dumb ass done got caught up on Jazz's table so I knew that was a done deal, unless . . .

"Do I need to call Maury? He'll test you and all of your baby father possibilities."

"Yolanda, I didn't say I didn't know the father of my child. I said you don't."

"So, what's the problem?"

"I'm not sure if I want to keep it."

"Girl, you better hold it down. Your ass ain't getting any younger, and the least you could do is keep Rico's baby since he ain't here no more."

"Rico? I am not pregnant by Rico. Where you hear that?"

"I just assumed it was his since y'all were kicking it like that. Didn't you feel bad for getting him locked up?"

"First off, I was pregnant before that shit went down with Rico, and what I had with him was strictly business. I didn't know he was going to kill himself."

"So, if it ain't Rico's kid, whose is it?"

"You don't know him."

"Well is he at least claiming the bastard?"

"Yolanda, what did you call here for?"

"Just to see what's up."

"Well, if you're done with your twenty questions, I have some phone calls to make."

"One more before you go."

"What?"

"Can we go shopping or something? I need like three hundred dollars, and a new outfit to wear to Fat Daddy's party on next Saturday night. I saw these Jimmy Choo boots that I just have to have."

"You said that like you've ever done something for me. How much is your tab now?"

"Girl, as long as I owe you . . ."

"I won't be broke regardless. Call me next week. I'll meet you downtown."

"Thanks, Moni. You know I love you, right?"

"Yeah, right. You love me like I love a pair of Payless shoes. Good-bye."

I didn't wait for a response. I hung up. I had to start setting my plan into action, and I needed the help of a few old friends. I called Sheila and smiled to myself despite the situation. It'd been a while, and I hadn't heard from her since I got her that job as the judge's secretary. She owed me a favor or two.

Sheila S. Stone

I swear, life was such a bitch sometimes! One day you'd be sitting on top of the world, and the next day your ass would be getting crushed by it. My past had been haunting me like crazy, making it hard for me to move on. I was so mad at myself I didn't know what to do, but at the same time I was stuck between a rock and a hard place. That's why when Monica set me up to work with the judge I hopped right on it. I knew my job with Jazz was over. I wished I could call Jazz and apologize, but what was I supposed to say? I'm sorry for setting you up and getting caught fucking your husband on your kitchen table? I really did want to talk to her, but I wasn't ready yet.

My phone had been ringing nonstop all morning, and it was working my nerves. The judge was sleeping with half the women in Philly, but I just stayed my ass out of it, took messages, and smiled brightly when I saw his wife. The last time I tried to help someone my ass got caught up. I knew whoever this was calling now was persistent. The damn phone had rung ten times. I had to find a way to change the ring count so the answering service would pick up after three rings.

"Good afternoon and thank you for calling District Council Three. Sheila speaking. How may I help you?"

"Sheila, it's me, Monica. I need to talk to you about something."

Speak of the damn devil . . .

Carlos

The Scoop

"Damn, Carlos. For all that you should have called her yourself. You was all up on the phone like you dialed the number."

As soon as Yoyo hung up the phone I was in her ear about Monica. Hopefully, she got some info I could use, and they weren't just talking about some girlie bullshit. I tried to go pick up the other line in the kitchen so I could listen, but she wouldn't let me get out of the bed. I even tried to put my face next to hers on the receiver, but she kept pushing me away. As soon as she hung up, I was all in the business asking a million questions.

"So, what she say?"

"Nothing really. She's pregnant, and it's not Rico's."

"Oh, word?" Now, I already knew she was pregnant because Shaneka was crying about it earlier this week, but I didn't know it wasn't Rico's baby, which meant Shaneka was spazzing for nothing. She did feel like Rico betrayed her, though, so I'd just keep that bit of info to myself and let her get her shit off.

"So what happened with all that money Rico had?"

"Did it sound like we were able to discuss all that? Hell, you were practically on the phone with her your damn self."

"Well, it's shit like that that I need to know. That man had major chips, and I know she walked away with a nice piece of it."

"Maybe you should write a list of questions so I know what to ask her specifically. That eight you gave me ain't covering any detective work."

"Well, what it cover?"

"Good pussy, nigga. Who fucking you like I do? The information you want I can definitely get, but what do I get out of it?"

"What you talking? Chips?" I was trying to decide if it was worth the money and aggravation. It only took me three seconds to decide it was.

"Major chips, but for right now we have some unfinished business."

I knocked Yoyo off real quick and left. She was upset because we were supposed to be spending the weekend together, but she cheered her ass right up after I promised her a shopping spree. On the real, I had to get back on the block. I totally trusted my right hand man, but just like with me and Rico, a dude got to watch his back because your main man will be the first to do you in. Now that I knew what's good with this Monica chick, I needed something to get Judge Stenton off my damn back.

I also had to find men I could trust to watch Monica and not try to snake me for their own come up.

Monica

Speak of the Devil

"Sheila, I need a favor."

I knew I was definitely the last person Sheila wanted to hear from, especially since I'd been the sole reason for her demise, but she owed me. If it weren't for me, she wouldn't be in the position she was in. There was no way she would've been able to continue to work with Jazz, so what was she going to do for income? Like I said, she owed me—her life.

"Monica, I was wondering when you were going to call. It's been, what, four months now?"

"Just about, but enough of that. I need a favor."

"I'm done with favors, Monica. That's the reason I'm where I am now."

"You are in a way better position now. Did you really think you were going to advance at that law firm?" Now I was starting to get heated. I had saved her from an awkward situation, and she was making way more money now. Didn't she know who I was?

"It's not about me advancing, it's the principle. Besides, I'm sure you didn't call me to discuss my financial status, so what is it that I need to do now to pay my lifelong debt to you?"

"Oh, so we have a backbone this year. Cool, I'm just calling to see if you could be my partner in Lamaze class. I start next week."

"Lamaze class? You're pregnant?"

"What other reason would I have to go to Lamaze classes?"

"I'm just shocked. I had no idea that you actually got pregnant. Is it James's?"

"Who else's would it be? You know the history." I was getting sick of this conversation with Sheila. We were all on that kitchen table that night, and even before that when we had the first threesome she knew how we got down. So why was she acting all clueless all of a sudden?

"Why would you keep it? You know James is not going to want that baby, and Jazz is going to have a fit."

"Since when did you become president of the Jazz and James fan club? They don't give a damn about you, so why do you care?"

"That's not what I'm saying, Monica. All I'm saying is why bring a child in this world you know you don't want? That child didn't ask to be here."

"So what do you suppose I should do, since you like playing Dr. Fucking Phil? Tell me what I need to be doing." By now I was *extra* pissed. Like I needed her throwing in my face what I was doing. In the back of my mind I knew it wasn't right, but my heart still belonged to Jazz. I just needed to get her to see things my way, that was all.

"All I'm saying is it's cheaper to spend three hundred dollars now, than three million during a lifetime."

"What?"

"Get an abortion, Monica. It's better that way."

"Abortion? Are you serious? Look, I need you to help me at the Lamaze class, and it starts Monday. Will you do it?"

"I'll be there Monday. Where am I meeting you?" She sounded defeated, but ask me if I gave a damn.

"Meet me at the University of Pennsylvania Hospital on the fifth floor. It starts at four o'clock."

"I'll be there."

"Of course you will. See you then."

After hanging up I made my way to my room. I was always able to think better in there, and now would be the perfect opportunity to have some alone time. Rico had been on my mind lately, and I needed to find out what went down with him. From what I understood, he hung himself in prison, but my gut was telling me otherwise. Maybe I needed to take a trip up to the prison to see what exactly went down. I didn't want to call the judge again, but who else could get me up there without a problem?

I went past his house, and when I didn't see his wife's car outside I went to ring the bell. His car wasn't there either, but I was hoping maybe his son had it and he was really home. Pulling my cell phone out of my pocketbook, I dialed the judge's number, hoping his wife wouldn't answer. The phone rang five times before the answering machine came on. I didn't bother to leave a message; I just simply called the courthouse. I didn't want Sheila in my business, but she just may prove to be useful later on.

"District Council—"

"Sheila, put Stenton on the phone." I cut her off dead in the middle of her sentence.

"Who may I tell him is calling?"

"Who's calling? Girl, put the judge on the phone. You don't recognize my voice by now?" Sheila didn't answer; she just clicked over immediately. A minute later the judge's deep baritone voice came through the other end of the receiver.

"Monica, long time, no hear. To what do I owe the pleasure of this call today? Do you have the lead on any more drug dealing boyfriends I should know about?" the judge said with a hint of hope under his laughter. Busting Rico put him on the map, and he was rewarded handsomely, despite the money he took up front during the bust.

"Not today, Judge, I just need some info on Rico's stay in prison. I just need to know how he came to hang himself."

"Well, sweetie, I wasn't exactly there to witness it, but the guard on duty at the time said she found him hanging there when she was doing her rounds. He was in the cell by himself, so it was just assumed that he did it himself. Why? Do you think there was someone in there who wanted him gone?"

"He was a damn drug dealer—kingpin to the fullest. Of course there was someone who wanted him dead. Shit, plenty of people were waiting for that. I just need to know who got to him. You and I both know that Rico would never hang himself. Let's be real."

"Okay, so what do you want me to do? Have every man in the entire prison put on a lie detector? Monica, you need to explain yourself better than this."

"No, I'll just talk to a few people if you let me, but first I want to talk to the guard. She was the one on duty, so I'm sure they exchanged some kind of conversation."

"Listen, give me a couple of days to set it up for you. I have to clear it with the warden first. I just can't allow you to waltz up in prison and start questioning people. You act like you work for the D.A. or something."

"Do what you have to do, but get back to me by the end of the work day. And don't let the guard know I'm coming. I don't want to give her time to get her story together."

"As you wish, master," the Judge responded in a mock genie voice that almost made me laugh. Almost. "I'll give you a call by six."

"Looking forward to hearing from you."

"Yeah, I'm looking forward to sleeping with you, too." He hung up before I had a chance to respond.

I thought of what I could ask the guard, and not sound like I didn't know what I was talking about. The information she would be giving me could get a ton of people swept off the streets, and I needed to go about getting it the right way so I could make my next move. I raced home to wait for the package from Stenton. I knew this was my only shot at finding out what really happened with Rico, and I had to do it right.

The ringing phone woke me up from my sleep. When I looked at the clock it was six on the dot.

When did I fall asleep? I hurriedly reached for the phone, hoping it was the judge calling.

"Hello?" I answered, trying to sound alert.

"Monica, it's me, Stenton. I set the meeting up for tomorrow at ten thirty in the morning. The warden okay'd it, and the guard will just be starting her shift. She will be told to report to . . ."

The judge broke everything down for me on where we would meet and how much time I had to question her. He also told me what I should wear, like he really had to. He sent me a badge from the D.A.'s office via FedEx, and it arrived around seven that evening. He tried to get me to commit to seeing him over the weekend, but I rushed his ass off the phone, telling him I would get back to him soon.

The next morning I was up bright and early and on my way to the prison, stopping like a hundred times to go to the restroom. If being pregnant was like this I swore I would never do it again. I arrived at ten after ten, leaving enough time to go to the restroom once more and be seated in the office before the guard got there. I had a list of questions I would ask her and a small tape recorder.

At ten thirty the guard walked in looking like a deer caught in headlights. I had to give it to Rico, she was a pretty woman. A little on the shy side, but she was pretty.

The second thing I noticed when she walked in was her protruding belly. I didn't know if it was a beer gut or if she was pregnant, but I would find out in time. She said nothing, just sat down in front of me with a scared-ass look on her face and her hands folded across her stomach. She wouldn't look me in the eye, though. Her eyes shot around the room like she couldn't focus—nervous energy. The eyes told everything.

"My name is Samantha, and I just have a few questions for you. I will be recording our conversation, and if necessary this tape will be used in a court of law. Any answers you give need to be accurate to the best of your knowledge. Do you have any questions?" I spoke to her clearly and precisely, opting to use an alias just in case she had heard something about me.

"No . . . no I don't." Her voice was shaky.

"Okay, there's no need to be nervous. Just answer the questions to the best of your ability. I will be starting the recording now."

She looked like her heart would burst out of her chest and sprint halfway across town. I kept a straight face and questioned her like I was a damn detective.

"State your name for the record."

"Alexis Cook."

"How long have you been working in this facility?"

"Four years."

"What did you know about Enrique Casarez?"

She didn't answer right away. She sighed and held her breath like she was trying to hold back tears. I didn't know what all that emotion was about. Rico was only in jail for two months before he was found dead, so what kind of relationship could they have had?

"We only spoke a couple of times when he needed to use the phone. I would let him use the one in the supervisor's office. I knew about Rico way before he got here from what people said on the street and from what I saw the few times I saw him on the block. He seemed like a cool guy, so I didn't see the harm in letting him make a call."

"Who did he call? What was he talking about?"

"Well, it sounded like he was calling friends of his. He said something about being setup, but I really wasn't paying attention. While Rico would talk on the phone I would ride him backward until I came. That was my payment for me letting him use the phone."

"What about the setup? Do you know who was setting him up?"

"I'm not really sure. He mentioned some woman's name, and was telling a friend that he thought she was the reason why he got locked up."

"When did y'all last talk? Share what you feel comfortable in telling me, I just need to know the circumstances surrounding his death, and anything too personal will stay between me and you. I just need you to be as honest as possible."

"The last time we talked was right before Juan, or the Cage as we call him, gave me a letter to give to Rico. He found out some information and wanted me to pass the letter to Rico. I was going to see Rico anyway because I found out I was pregnant, and I wanted him to know he would be a daddy. When I got there he was hanging from the ceiling."

"Do you still have the letter?"

"Yeah, it's in my purse in my locker. If you'd like I can go get it for you."

"Sure, you can get it after the interview. How many months are you?"

"I'm sixteen weeks pregnant. I just found out I'm having a boy yesterday."

"Okay, thanks for your time, Alexis. You can go get the letter now."

I watched her walk out of the room. I was taking notes as we talked, but I would definitely be listening to the tape when I got home. By the time she came back I had already put everything in my bag, and was standing. She gave me the note and her phone number. She said if I needed to know anything else to give her a call.

When I got out to the car I unfolded the letter and began reading. Apparently, Rico felt I had something to do with his setup and got in contact with Carlos to investigate. I drove home in silence trying to decide what angle I would use to get at Carlos. I would definitely go see the judge to give him the info I had because my ass might need some witness protection after this. For now I was on my way to the Cinque household. If I waited on them they would never talk to me.

Jasmine

Truth Be Told

I was released from the hospital three days later with well wishes from the staff, tons of literature to look at for my pregnancy, and a whole lot of stress and anxiety thinking about what I was gonna do since I was carrying twins from what was literally a late morning quickie with two guys I hardly even knew.

At three months, I had a ways to go before I would begin buying anything, and I hoped that the time would go by as quickly as possible. I still couldn't believe I was pregnant with another set of twins, and I couldn't help but wonder how Jalil and Jaden would feel. But for obvious reasons, that was the least of my worries. Yes, it had just been them for the last four years. They were not accustomed to competing with other kids for our attention, but I was sure that wasn't the only problems I was facing. My mind was all over the place. I had to plan their birthday party in another two months, and Lord knew I didn't feel like being around a bunch of kids with a huge belly.

James had been extra attentive, but I was still not open to him. Yeah, I had now probably fucked up a whole lot worse than he had, but I was still bitter about everything that had went down between Sheila, James, and Monica.

Truth be told, I was ready to go home, but not to the home I already had. I was ready to start our life in a new place, but we had just bought our house five years ago. Although the events of late were overwhelming, we had so many memories in that house. I didn't know when, if ever, I'd get past it.

I still saw the image of Monica, Sheila, and James on my table when I walked in the door, but it was becoming a mere shadow, not as vibrant as my first time back home. The voices were getting quieter, and I truly did think we'd get through this. We had to. We had children to consider. But what was weird is that I had begun to replay the sexual payback stunt that I had pulled with Donnie and Rahmel. Damn! It had felt good getting fucked by two men at the same time, but I knew in many ways I would forever be cursed by that act of revenge.

James and I weren't in the house for two minutes before someone was ringing the doorbell. James made sure I was comfortable on the couch before he went to answer the door. I propped my feet up on a few pillows and leaned my head back on the arm rest so I could rest my eyes for a few seconds.

For a second it sounded like James was arguing with someone at the door, but I wasn't really sure. I got up off the couch and made my way to the door only to receive the shock of my life.

"Monica, what are you doing here?" I had to force myself to keep my mouth from hanging wide open. I wanted to see her, but not now. The pain was still too new.

"Jazz, I came to apologize to both of you, and to talk to you personally. I just figured the longer we waited, the harder it would become to get past this problem. I wanted you to hear my side of the story."

Before I could say anything James was pushing me back into the house and closing the door. Monica just stood there like she was about to cry, but I held the door just before it closed shut. I had to hear what she had to say.

"James, we should at least hear her out."

"Baby, I don't want that woman in my house. She's the reason why we're in the shit we're in."

"No, you wanting to be greedy is the reason why we're in this shit. Open the damn door. We need closure."

I knew this could be the biggest mistake I ever made in my life, but I needed to hear what she had to say. Maybe if I looked her in the eye, I could understand how she had so much power over people to make them do things they really didn't want to do. There was no denying her skills in the bedroom. On that note she was a phenomenal woman. When she was around you couldn't think rationally. For my own curiosity, I just needed to know.

"You better make this quick, and make this your last damn visit. You're not welcome here," James said to her as I walked away from the door and resumed my position on the sofa. I didn't offer her a drink or anything because I didn't want her to get comfortable. She needed to state her purpose and keep it moving.

"Monica, what brings you here today?" As she made herself comfortable on the loveseat, I noticed the bulge in her shirt. It could easily be overlooked if you weren't looking for it, but I was dead on it. This bitch was pregnant by my husband, or so we assumed.

"Jazz, first I want to apologize for all the problems I've caused your family. I should have gone about trying to get you in a better manner."

James and I looked at each other and back at her. I didn't think she would come right out and say that she wanted me. I thought for sure she would deny it and take it to her grave, but then again, Monica never failed to amaze me.

"So, you're saying what exactly?"

"I'm saying that I fell in love with you the very first time I saw you, and I thought if I could get close to you maybe I would have a chance. Sheila put it in my head that I could get you if I tried hard enough. She set everything up from the beginning. It was her idea to come here. I would have never thought of it. I could have easily had either of you over at my house."

Still speechless, James and I sat wide-eyed and stared at her like she was a television set. I couldn't believe what she was saying, and if I wasn't there to hear it, no one could have ever convinced me.

"So Sheila put it in your head that it was cool to climb your ass up on my table? Better yet, tell me, Monica, how many times did you and James see each other before I became involved?" I had agreed to move past that, but something was telling me that James wasn't being straight with me. That was our biggest problem, the fact that we were never straight up with each other. But oh well, I still needed to hear it from the horse's mouth.

"We started seeing each other maybe six weeks before he finally decided he would ask you, but we slept together at least thirty times before that night. James couldn't get enough of me."

"And since that night?" I don't think I really wanted to know the answer, but my mouth said it anyway. A part of me did want to know, but another part would rather do without the details.

"We got together at least twice a week. Sheila had him too."

James just put his head down in his hands and shook it from side to side. My breathing felt labored, but I needed to know one more thing.

"Monica, how many months are you?"

"About five-and-a-half."

Before I had a chance to react, James jumped up off the couch beside me and knocked Monica backward out of the chair. By the time I got up he had already punched her in her face once, and I had to practically jump on his back to keep him from swinging again. I don't know where the strength came from, but I was able to pull him up and stand between them so Monica could get up off the floor. She looked stunned, and even though I hated her, I hoped nothing happened to her or her baby. It wasn't the child's fault.

"Get the fuck out of my house! Get the fuck out!" James kept yelling it at the top of his lungs as Monica made her way to the door slowly.

"Jazz, don't be mad at James. He was at my house as much as you were."

Now it was James's turn to hold me as I charged at her like a bull. She was able to open and shut the door before I could get to her, and by the time I got the door open I could see her making her way to her car. She turned and looked at me and stopped me dead in my tracks with her words.

"Oh, Jasmine, I forgot to mention that you really look good since I last saw you. I don't know what it is, but maybe it's those *private personal training sessions* that you've been having at your house with the twins Donnie and Rahmel from Bally's. Girl, whatever you do, keep those personal one-on-one sessions going because they really got your body looking tight!"

After she said that there was dead silence as I could not believe that those bitch ass twins from the gym had opened up their mouths and gossiped like straight-up bitches!

I wanted to literally kill Monica for having pulled my card like that. But I had to give it up to her, the bitch was vindictive as hell and she was good at it.

James looked at me with a confused look on his face.

I shook my head and asked, "What the hell is she talking about?"

Then all I could hear was her car screeching down the street. I just fell to my knees in the doorway and cried, not knowing what to do next. I would be paying her ass a visit. That was for sure. I just hoped I could be civil when I saw her again. Yeah, we were all at fault, but this entire situation just pissed me off. I was hoping that James didn't question me about what Monica had said about the twins training me.

Thankfully, somehow we made our way up to the bedroom where we lay in silence for what felt like hours. I don't know if either of us were ready for what was said, especially me. I was upset that she put James out there, but I was even more upset that she told him my business. And I was even more livid with the twins from Bally's.

Yeah, I had already told James what I wanted him to know, and I'm sure he did the same, but I guess now he knew where all of my panties had been disappearing to.

As I lay next to my husband, I tried to think of what my parents would do in a situation like this. My heart was telling me they would stay together. I needed to move back home. This incident would stay between us, and it was as simple as that. And I would keep my sins a secret for as long as I could.

I rolled over to face James, and he looked just as lost as I did. The only way to get our marriage back on track was for me to move back home and deal with our problems together.

Monica

Revenge Is Best Served Cold, August 1991

When I woke up, the pain in my stomach was unbearable. It definitely didn't feel like the usual menstrual cramps, but what else could it be? I could barely lift my head off the pillow, and when I was able to, and I saw the amount of blood on the bed, it scared me even more. Something wasn't right, and I needed to get help as soon as possible. I tried to stand up, but my legs felt like wet noodles under me. The pain was getting worse by the second, and all I remember was making it halfway down the hall on my hands and knees before I passed out. Waking up in the emergency room, I was scared for real. I wanted to ask what had happened, but the pain in my stomach and the tubes down my throat prevented me from speaking.

I kept my eyes closed as I listened to my uncle and Stephanie argue about who was going to clean the blood up in the hallway. He wanted me to do it, but she said I wasn't feeling well enough. I hated him, and I couldn't wait to get out of his house. Instead of dwelling on their nonsense, I closed my eyes and sifted through my own issues.

By the end of the school year I had successfully gotten even with two other girls from Ashley's crew: Jessica and Samantha. How I caught Jessica was priceless. Since Ashley and Kevin hadn't returned back to school, the school staff took it upon themselves to plan our junior prom. I was cool with that and happy because I was finally able to talk my uncle into letting me go.

Although I had about twelve hundred dollars stashed in my closet, I still took on a few afterschool babysitting jobs to get some extra loot so I wouldn't spend all my money getting what I needed. I decided I would go to the prom by myself. After all my efforts to raise cash, Stephanie offered to take me to New York to get my gown so no one would have one like mine. My gown fell right above my knees and went up around my neck like a halter top. I had a detachable train that fell to the floor and doubled as a shawl just in case I got cold during the night. We bought my shoes and handbag from the same boutique, and I decided on a single pink rose to match my dress for my corsage.

She took me to the guy who did her hair, and taught me how to apply my makeup properly so it would have a natural look. My uncle rented a Benz for the evening, after arguing with Stephanie about it for three days straight, and he decided that since she wanted to be so helpful, Stephanie could take me to the prom and pick me up when it was all over.

To lower the ticket cost, the prom was held in the school gymnasium, which made it convenient for everyone. I had butterflies in my stomach something serious because this was my opportunity to get Jessica's ass. I knew she would come to the prom like she was the shit, and I'd make it my business to show her she was, literally.

I was dropped off at the prom about an hour after it started. I got there just in time to get my picture taken before the camera crew packed up for the evening. Once the prom got popping I went to the ladies' room to make sure the coast was clear. The day before I'd stashed a bag of items in the bathroom vent.

I put "out of order" signs on the stall doors on the ends so that the only restroom available was the middle stall. After hiding my bag in the first stall, I left the bathroom and waited for Jessica to come in. When I saw her go to the bathroom, I waited for a minute before I went in and locked the door behind us.

She was standing at the mirror on the other side when I walked in, so I snuck into the stall and circled the toilet seat with clear super glue. I went into the first stall after using a towel to crawl under the door. Just as I hoped, she walked in and plopped her nasty ass right down on the toilet seat. I took the cup I had in my bag and filled it with water from the toilet. After taking a peek over the top to see what she was doing, I tossed the cup of water over the top.

She screamed as I threw three more cups of water on her. When she realized she couldn't get off the toilet I took the opportunity to crawl back under the door, depositing my bag back in the vent and exiting the bathroom unnoticed.

While I was getting some punch I saw a crowd of students running toward the bathroom. I made my way over, almost the last one there. From my viewpoint I could see Jessica still trying to get off the toilet with her dress and hair drenched, and her panties around her ankles. I should have pissed in the cup.

When we got back to school the following Monday, the school paper was passed out during lunch. On the cover, much to everyone's surprise, was a picture of Jessica stuck on the toilet looking a hot mess. I just laughed to myself as I finished eating my lunch in silence. For the first time in all of my sixteen years I could honestly say life was good.

Opening my eyes for a brief second I saw the doctor who was working on me. He was telling my uncle that I was pregnant in my tubes and the tube burst, which was the reason for all the pain and blood. I was grateful, but not really. I was upset about the tube part, but if I had the baby who was to say it didn't belong to my uncle? And that shit that Kevin and his boys did still gave me bad dreams, so I was glad it was gone.

I heard the doctor whisper that although the tube was repaired, I wouldn't be able to pass eggs on that side, so it would be a little difficult for me to conceive again. My dumbass uncle asked the doctor if they could give me a hysterectomy, but of course they wouldn't do it. The effects of the morphine were making me sleepy again, so I let it do its magic as I thought about my revenge on Samantha.

***

We were having a festival at our school for our last day. I volunteered to help set the yard up for the fair. In the back of our school there were woods that some of us usually cut through to get to the strip quicker. Jessica wasn't in school to walk home with Samantha, and the rest of her girls went the other way, so I knew if I was going to get her I had to act quickly.

I snuck off while the other volunteers weren't looking and hid my book bag in the woods. Inside my bag I had stuffed my uncle's overall jumpsuit so I wouldn't mess up my clothes, a bandana to cover my face, and a pair of Tims. I had some rope, duct tape, a pack of cigarettes, a jar of honey, and a rechargeable pair of clippers so I didn't need a plug. Her ass was going to catch it, and I couldn't wait.

The day of the festival was hot, but not the type that carried high humidity. I had on my booty-hugging shorts, and a matching red and yellow tank top that looked nice on my tanned skin. My body had filled out a lot in the past couple of months. I had Stephanie take me back to her stylist to get my hair done for the day. I wanted to be cute from head to toe. I finished my outfit off with a pair of red, low top, classic Reeboks and yellow socks with red balls on the back. I must say I was looking rather tasty.

I noticed how the boys in my class had been watching me lately, but wasn't shit poppin'. After that mess with Kevin, I decided that not another soul in this school would get within sniffing distance of this stuff. I took the compliments they dished out and kept it moving. There was no need for small talk.

I chilled the entire day playing the games and getting my fill of hot dogs, cotton candy, and soda. I flirted with some of the guys, and kept my lips glossy just to make the girls mad. I made sure to keep close tabs on Samantha, and when she left I was right behind her.

I kept ten paces behind her, ducking behind trees to make sure she didn't see me. I had a padlock and four heavy rocks in a sock that I had gathered together before I left the fair. I knew I would have to knock her ass out to tie her to the tree, and I was sure that would do the job. Just as she was about to step over the old tree that lay on the ground, I ran up on her and knocked her in the back of her head. Her body folded like a paper bag.

I left her there while I fished my bag out the hollow part of the tree, shaking the bugs off before I put my overalls on over the outfit I had on and stuck the honey and clippers in my pocket, putting my sneakers inside the bag and placing the bag back in the log. Taking Samantha by her ankles, I dragged her body over to the tree.

Propping her body up as much as possible, I tied a rope to her wrists, and then connected the ropes in the back of the tree in a tight knot. While she was still out I took the clippers and shaved off sections of her hair, letting them fall in clumps on her lap. Satisfied with my hair cutting skills, I then lit a cigarette and began burning circles on her skin until she woke up.

When she came to, all she could see was a person in a jumpsuit with their face covered. I Krazy glued her lips together. She struggled in terror as I took cigarette after cigarette out the pack, and burned her with them. After about eight cigarettes, I opened the jar of honey and stood over her, pouring it on top of her head and watching as it ran down the sides of her face and the rest of her body. Once the entire jar was poured out, I began digging holes around her so that any bugs that were in the dirt would come out and feast.

Stepping back to admire my handiwork, I made sure to clear all evidence that would trace this back to me, and I left her there. I changed my clothes back near the fallen tree and stuffed all the evidence in my book bag, then continued my walk through the woods, stopping back at the festival to get a snow cone and cheese pretzel before heading home.

On the news the following morning I could hear Samantha's mom talking to the reporter in a tearful voice because she hadn't come home the night before. They began searching in the woods behind our school where they found her tied to the tree. She had huge black lumps on her skin where the bugs *had bitten her, and her wrists were almost cut to the bone from her struggling to get loose.*

I laughed to myself as the reporter flashed Ashley, Jessica, and Kevin's case on the news, trying to figure out who was the cause of all the terror that had struck Parkway High School that year. I snickered as I turned over and went back to sleep, enjoying the first day of my summer vacation.

I woke up later in a hospital room with the tube removed from my throat. Although the pain was still there, it wasn't as bad as the effects of the drugs they kept pumping in my system. My uncle was no longer there, but his girlfriend was asleep in the chair next to my bed. I have to honestly say that I didn't like her very much in the beginning, but she had definitely looked out for me since she'd been in the picture. I closed my eyes and rested. When I got out I would take advantage of the rest of my summer because school would be starting in just another month, and I still had some planning to do.

Tanya C. Walker

I must say that I was pleasantly surprised at how Monica had hooked me up when I got home. I was thankful, but she owed it to me. I spent years in the joint fighting bitches off me while she lived the good life, and after one visit I was free to go? It was like I got a get-out-of-jail-free card or something. That just made me wonder if she was really trying to leave me for dead all that time.

Now, I know I was stupid for taking the rap, but at the moment I couldn't think straight. She killed my husband right in front of me, and had no remorse as she popped cap after cap into his face. Marcus was abusive, but damn. I didn't think it would go down like that, so I took the rap, not knowing I would do that much time.

I spent almost four years locked up, but I must say she laced me pretty lovely when I was released. A brand new house, car, and my own restaurant were just a few of the trinkets I received. We had yet to talk, but I couldn't help but hate her. Yeah, she had hooked me up, but she was fucking up too many lives, and when Shaneka told me about the whole Rico thing I almost lost it.

Monica just didn't get it. My new love, Shaneka, had it in for her ass, too. She promised me she would get Monica back, and when she did, I couldn't wait to see the look on her face. When bricks started falling, the building would eventually fall down, and I couldn't wait to see it tumble on her ass. She'd be just like the wicked witch from the *Wizard of Oz* with her damn feet sticking out from under the building, and I'd be right there to take those ruby slippers the hell off.

Jasmine

Curiosity Killed the Cat

I waited until about two weeks after Monica came to my house to go visit her. Even though she had caused all kinds of problems in my life, I needed to know if I still had feelings for her. Call me crazy, but my heart still kind of went out for her.

Things at home were still on shaky ground, but the babies and I were finally settled, and they were happy. James and I had had sex numerous times, but I couldn't get Monica off my mind. Pretending it was her on top of me instead of James was the only way I could cum. Sad, but true.

Being back at work from my three month leave of absence gave me plenty of work to do, but I couldn't concentrate on any of it. My life had changed so much in the last couple of months. For a while I didn't know whether I was coming or going.

All morning I had been trying to get my files in order. I stayed locked in my office because every time I walked past Sheila's old desk I wanted to scream. Why would she do that to me? I mean, no, we weren't the best of friends, but I thought we at least had mutual respect for each other. It was crazy how it all went down, but something was telling me that Sheila really didn't have a choice in the matter. I heard she was working for Judge Stenton now. Maybe I'd pay her a visit, too.

After looking at the clock for the thousandth time I decided it was time I took a lunch break. The senior partners had been absolutely wonderful to me by making sure I had fresh fruit and plenty to drink for the babies, but I needed to get out and get some fresh air. I stopped to let Trish, my new assistant, know I would be taking an extended lunch. I put on my jacket and left with all intentions of getting something to eat and checking on the kids.

On my car ride over to the school I found myself going in the direction of Monica's house. I had planned to just stop and say what was on my mind because I was still pissed about the entire episode that happened at the house. I also wanted to know just what she knew about me fucking the twins, but when she opened the door all of that went out the window.

Monica answered the door in a white wifebeater and pink cotton shorts that barely covered her ass. She had specks of paint on her clothes and skin, and her hair was pulled back into a sloppy ponytail. Her skin glowed and my clit jumped when my eyes made contact with her hard nipples. My mouth watered a little as I remembered how she tasted. Her belly appeared bigger than it was the last time I saw her, and it made her look even more radiant. Guys always said that pregnant pussy was the best pussy, and I was hoping that I would find out if that was true.

We stared at each other without saying any words. I had to keep repeating in my head that she was pregnant by my husband, but it damn sure wasn't working. Maybe if I just tasted her one more time . . . "Hello, Jasmine. To what do I owe the pleasure of this visit?"

Monica flirted openly from the doorway, and for the first time I noticed her holding a paintbrush as I averted my eyes away from her face. I had to keep a cool head about this.

"I just stopped by to talk to you and see how you were holding up. Do you mind if I come in?"

"No, not at all. I was just about to make something to eat. Would you care for some?"

"Sure."

I followed Monica into the house and into the kitchen after she hung up my jacket. Whatever she was in the midst of making smelled delicious, and as I made myself comfortable, she placed a bowl of beef stew and a tuna sandwich in front of me. I wasted no time digging in.

We ate in silence, looking at each other periodically. I guess neither one of us could believe we were here like this.

"Listen, I was upstairs painting. Care to join me?"

"Sure."

I followed her up the steps, glancing at the photos on the wall on the way up. I thought I recognized James in one of them, but I wasn't sure. I made a mental note to look again on my way down. I stood at the door as she took her seat, the memories flooding my mind at a rapid pace as if they had happened yesterday. Not too long ago I posed for pictures in this very room. Now it looked totally different.

Where there were stacks of paintings, easels, and camera's, now only housed drop cloths, cans of paint, and brushes. The once white walls were now mint green with yellow borders, and Monica was in the middle of creating a mural.

"Do you want a change of clothes so you can come in?"

"Huh?" I was so lost in the mural I didn't hear her say anything at first.

"I said, do you want to change your clothes so you won't get paint on your suit?"

"Sure, that sounds perfect."

When she opened her bedroom door I moved straight toward the bed. It was almost like there was a magnetic force pulling me over to it. The pleasure I had received on top of these sheets was unbelievable. I wanted to lay on them one more time, and . . .

"Monica, can I use your phone?"

"It's by the bed."

I called Trish at the job and told her something I ate upset my stomach so I'd be in the next day. She wished me well, and that was that. I set Monica's alarm clock for four thirty so I'd be up to get the kids from daycare. While Monica was in the closet I took my clothes off and stretched out on the soft comforter. It was now one o'clock, so I had some time.

I kept telling myself that I just needed to know if I felt anything for her, but I already knew I did. When she came out of her walk-in closet, she dropped the clothes on the floor, surprised at what she saw.

"Jasmine, I was just . . ."

"Come here. Let me show you how much I missed you."

She was hesitant at first, but I gave her a reassuring look as she began to undress and make her way to the bed. I allowed her to lie on her back and spread her legs.

Taking one of the chocolate pieces from the table next to her bed, I had a brief flashback of the ice sculptures that sat there on my first encounter with Monica. Looking back at Monica, I got into a comfortable position between her legs. Opening her lips with my thumb and index finger, I rubbed the chocolate against her clit, the candy melting on her hot skin, making her clit look like a chocolate-covered cherry.

Taking my journey a little farther, I took the candy and circled the outside of her opening, licking it all off and starting over again until all the chocolate was gone. Monica moaned and gyrated her hips against my tongue until she came, depositing her honey on my face. I didn't care. I kept her clit trapped between my lips until her shaking subsided.

Kissing a trail up her body, I made sure to pay special attention to her protruding belly, no longer mad that it may have been my husband's child. I decided we would cross that bridge later as I moved to her side and pushed her nipples together, blessing them with my mouth. As soon as I touched her with my tongue, rain began to hit the window panes.

I let Monica touch my clit and finger my pussy with the same rhythm my fingers pleasured her with until we both erupted at the same time. Damn, it'd been a long time since I felt like this, and I wanted it more often.

We fell asleep in each other's arms after I licked her tears away, accepting her apologies and apologizing for the bruise James had left on her beautiful face. We woke up at four, giving us time to have fun in the shower, and giving me time to get dressed.

Before we went downstairs, Monica showed me the middle room, which she'd made into her studio, and a few pictures of the baby furniture she would be ordering. We sat at the table for a second just staring at each other as I waited for the rain to subside.

"Before you go, I have something for you." Monica got up and gave me a box that she had stored in her kitchen. It was light in weight. I was skeptical.

"It's not a bomb, is it?" I said while shaking the box playfully, but serious at the same time.

"No, but you can't open it until you get home." She giggled.

"Okay, I can live with that. Now let me go get the kids and get home before James gets there."

"Okay."

When we got to the door, I put my jacket on and grabbed the box from her. She looked like she was about to cry. After giving her a hug and promising to call her, I ran to my car, trying to dodge as many raindrops as possible.

When I pulled up to the school I opened the box out of curiosity, and was shocked by what I saw. Pulling them out one at a time, I counted thirteen pairs of underwear, belonging to both me and James. Damn, I guess we were both over there an equal amount of times after all. I decided I wouldn't say anything to James. I'd just put them in the dirty clothes before I started dinner. It didn't make sense to cause any more problems.

When I walked in the house James was already there, and he had started dinner. The kids ran upstairs to wash their hands and change their clothes so I could help them with their homework before dinner. Jalil ran right to James for a hug, but Jaden made a beeline for the steps. I pretended I didn't notice. I left the box in the car when I saw James's car in the driveway. I didn't want to answer any questions, and he'd surely have some once he saw the contents.

I sat down at the table, kicked off my shoes, and waited for the kids to come back down. James walked over to me and tried to kiss me, but I faked a cough before he got too close. I had since washed my face and brushed my teeth at Monica's house, but I didn't want him to get too close and possibly smell her on my skin.

"How was your day, sweetie?" James asked as he stirred the contents of the numerous pots and pans he had on the stove. He looked good in his dress slacks and button-down shirt, but I barely noticed because I had Monica and our afternoon together on my mind.

"It was okay. I just tried to catch up on some work."

"Are you sure? I called your office to check on you and the babies, and your secretary said you left early with an upset stomach."

I was stunned to silence for a split second because I wasn't expecting him to come at me with that. I didn't factor that into the decision to leave early. I shook it off and came back with a lame excuse.

"Yeah, I went to Grandma's Kitchen for lunch, and I think the greens were a bit much. I went to my brother's house to lie down for a while because it was closer from there to get the kids than coming all the way home."

Okay, so I told a boldfaced lie, but so what? He'd been lying to me for months. Plus, I knew he'd never call my brother to confirm my stay, but I'd be sure to call and give them a heads up just in case.

"How are you feeling now?"

Before I had a chance to answer, the kids came running into the room, saving me from having to lie again. I immediately began helping them with their homework, thoughts of my afternoon with Monica heavy on my mind. I decided I would continue to see her, but James could never know. I wouldn't see her as much as I used to, but I would still see her.

James set the table after the kids were done with their homework. He served all of us before he sat down. We all lowered our heads to say grace, looking like a fake-ass happy family. I didn't know how all of this was going to end, but I was sure the outcome wouldn't be good.

I listened as my husband and kids conversed. After our meal was done and we had dessert, I bathed the kids and put them to bed. I took a shower and put on a pair of comfy pajamas before getting into bed. Normally, I would have put on something sexy, but I didn't feel like pretending tonight. I wanted to go to sleep with the feel of Monica's touch on my skin.

Not long after I got in bed, James joined me after taking his shower. I lay in his arms and he rubbed my belly until I went to sleep. My last thought before I submitted to slumber was to remember to get that box out of the trunk of my car. It was his turn to take the kids to school, so I'd have time to go out there and get it after he left in the morning.

James

The Saga Continues

Since all of this craziness had been going on, I'd been trying my damnedest to keep Jazz happy. Lately, Monica had been on my mind a lot, and I badly wanted to grip her by her damn neck. We had an understanding from the beginning. I would let her have sex with my wife once, and that would cover any charges for three sessions. That was the entire reason for setting up the damn threesome, but come to find out they were getting it on like crazy. Jazz had already told me they were, but it didn't hit home until I heard it from Monica's mouth. I'd been looking at Jasmine sideways ever since.

I don't know what came over me when I hit Monica. I guess I was just so mad I couldn't help myself. Jazz pissed me off too, asking Monica questions when I had already told her what I wanted her to know. That conversation was supposed to be over, and there she went bringing up old shit. If we were ever going to move past all of this, then we needed to let it the fuck go. Why keep talking about shit we couldn't change?

Then Jazz jumped on me like I did something wrong—like she was taking Monica's side. Now, don't get me wrong, I ain't no woman-beater or no shit like that. My father brought me up to have the utmost respect for women, but that bitch was running her mouth and saying shit she had no business speaking out loud. Okay, she was pregnant, but I didn't hit her in her stomach, did I? Hell, her face wasn't pregnant.

After that Jazz started acting all funny and shit, and when I called her at work to check on her, Trish said she had already left for the day because she wasn't feeling well. I called her brother's house and her cell phone, but no Jazz. She said she went to her brother's before she got the kids. I guess she got there after I called. I didn't bother to call and confirm because they were family, and I knew he'd just go with the flow. But something wasn't right. I could sense it. I had been trying my hardest to remember what that comment was that Monica had mentioned about some personal trainers for Jazz. I didn't know what that was about because Jazz didn't have any personal trainers that I knew about, but Monica was trying to hint at something. I don't know, maybe Jazz is going to the gym and she doesn't want to tell me. I don't know.

After I called Jazz at the office that day I drove past Monica's house. I thought I saw her car parked on Monica's block, but I knew that it couldn't have been and I made up my mind to ignore it. And if she was indeed there I'm sure it was for a good reason. She seemed a little uneasy when she came in, but I just let it go. If I was going to forgive her, there was no need to keep reliving the past. The trust had to start somewhere.

My morning had been a hectic mess.

After barely getting through my morning, I called my wife to see if she wanted to hook up for lunch. It'd been a little tense at home for the last two weeks, so I figured this would be a good icebreaker. A man could only go for so long without getting his dick wet, and I was lying next to some ass every night, yet lately I couldn't seem to get none. Something had to give, and soon. I wouldn't step out on her again, though. I'd learned my lesson from the shit I was going through with Monica, and how I almost got busted with those strippers, so I was cool on that note, but what was I supposed to do?

When I called her office the first time, her secretary said she was in a meeting, so I opted to call back as opposed to leaving her a message. I wanted to talk to her personally. A half hour later I was connected to her, but she sounded like she had an attitude. I had my own shit going on, and I didn't feel like all that, but I guess she was having a bad day too.

"Hey, sweetheart, how's your day going?" I asked extra cheerfully, trying to change her mood. Both of us didn't need to be angry at the world.

"I've had better mornings. What's up with you?"

"Nothing. I had a little time to spare so I was hoping we could meet up for a quick lunch. Maybe check out that new soul food spot that just opened up in University City."

"Which one? Tondalayah's?"

"Yeah, that's the spot. I heard the food is banging, and the iced tea is off the chain."

"Your treat?"

"Of course."

"I'm game."

"Cool. I'll meet you outside your job at one thirty. Tell Trish you're taking an extended lunch. I just landed the account with Nabisco, so we have a reason to celebrate."

After hanging up with her, I went to talk to my boss for a few, and he gave me the rest of the day off for pulling off getting the account in spite of the disasters from this morning.

I straightened up my desk, took one last look at the photo of me, Jazz, and the kids, left the office, and made my way across town to meet my wife for lunch. Hopefully, the rest of my day would go smoother.

Sheila

Old Flames

Early Monday morning, I was waiting outside the hospital for Monica. Initially, she told me the class started at four, but she called me back yesterday to let me know she would be taking the ten a.m. class instead. She pulled up ten minutes late in a cute, hot pink jumpsuit, her belly a bulge at the bottom. I said nothing to her as she took her time getting out the car and passing the valet her keys as if she wasn't already late.

All of the memories from the previous year flooded my mind as we took a quiet elevator ride up to the tenth floor of the building. Monica still looked the same, yet different. I could still see her devil's horns, but her eyes looked like those of a scared child. I was sympathetic, but determined not to get caught up in her shit this time. Hell, she was carrying a married man's child, and I wanted no part of the fiasco. If I was going to hell I'd like it to be for some shit I did, not because of someone else's.

I was almost positive it was James's baby, but with Monica, you just never knew. I still needed to talk to my sister about the shit that went down with her husband, Hill, and Monica, but I hadn't found the time or the nerve. Hill was a cool dude and all, but there was always something sneaky about him that I didn't particularly care for. Now I knew why. During the class, I helped Monica learn her breathing exercises, but I wasn't committing anything to memory because I would not be there to help her deliver. Lamaze class was one thing, but childbirth was another. We went through the motions of counting breathing repetitions, but on the real, all of that shit went out the window when it came time to push. That was the number one reason why I only had one child. The shit hurt like hell. I guarantee if men had to carry children and give birth, we'd be an endangered species.

After class, Monica invited me to brunch at Tondalayah's, a new soul food restaurant that opened up a while back in University City. I kept planning in my mind to get down there, but I never got around to it. I was really ready to go home and chill since Monica fixed it so I had a paid day off.

"Sure, I'll go, but you're driving."

During the ride over my heart was beating a mile a minute. It'd been a long time since I'd been this close to Monica, and I wasn't sure if I liked the feelings I was having. She turned my life completely upside down in less than a year, but my pussy was throbbing like everything was cool between us. I kept telling myself not to fall for her, but my body was betraying me. Just thinking about the things her mouth could do had me spent.

We chatted about various things on the way over, avoiding the obvious. I damn sure wasn't going to be the one to bring it up. My sister warned me this morning about helping her, but I was just trying to pay my debt so I could move on. She cursed me something horrible when I told her where I was going.

"It is that serious, Sheila. Ain't this bitch killin' people and shit? You go right on ahead, but don't dial my number when the block is hot. If anything happens to my nephew, that's your ass. Don't take it as a threat, because that ass whipping is promised. Put ya check on it."

My sister's words echoed in my head non stop, but I figured Monica had to have calmed down at least a little bit now that she was pregnant. Her stomach was definitely showing her pregnancy, so I didn't think she'd be making too much noise, but then again, with Monica you never knew.

We pulled up to the restaurant twenty minutes later, and the smells from the kitchen had my mouth watering. I had neglected breakfast because I was in a rush to meet Monica and get it over with, but the growling noise in my stomach gave away my hunger to everyone in the place.

Tondalayah's was a nice spot. The whole place looked inviting, even from the outside. I just loved the ambiance in the place. After seating us and filling our glasses with mixed fruit iced tea, the waitress took our order and we were served hot, buttered biscuits.

At first we looked around the restaurant, avoiding eye contact. I glanced her way a few times when she wasn't looking, and I had to say that pregnancy brought out the best in her. She appeared to be glowing from the inside out, and it looked like her hair had grown a lot in the last couple of months. My coochie was talking to me again, but I wasn't having it. After the James and Jasmine drama, I knew I could never get that deep in someone else's issues again.

Before the moment could get any more awkward, our food was served and we began eating. She talked a little about a mural she was painting in what would be the baby's room, and invited me to come see it. I just looked at her like she was crazy. I didn't give a damn if Noah was building a new ark on top of her house and we had to go there to avoid the flood. I'd be a drowned bitch before I stepped into that house again. Ain't no way I was going over there, come hell or high water.

Our conversation was improving, and we were really enjoying ourselves until Monica practically jumped out of her seat, sprinted across the restaurant, and ended up in another woman's arms. Was I jealous? Not really, but when I saw her reaction I felt something. They exchanged words, and a few minutes later they started walking toward the table. The woman looked familiar, but I couldn't remember where I had seen her face. Monica was all smiles like she had just hit the damn Powerball. I mustered up a weak smile as they got closer to the table, but I was feeling sick to my stomach at the sight before me.

"Sheila, this is Tanya Walker, a good friend of mine. Tanya, this is Sheila, one of my many associates."

My face almost cracked and fell on the floor at Monica's introduction, but I got my shit together real quick and reached out to shake Tanya's hand. Her face frowned up a little when Monica said they were friends, but I let it pass, not really knowing the meaning behind it.

"Nice to meet you, Tanya."

"Thank you so much. I hope you're enjoying your meal."

"Oh, I am. It's delicious."

Monica rudely pulled Tanya to the side and they continued to converse while I attempted to finish my meal. Not sure what made me glance out the window, I nearly spit my food across the table when I saw James helping Jasmine out the car. I crossed my fingers and tried to cross my toes, hoping to every god on the planet that they were not coming here. All hope went out the door when James opened it and the couple walked inside.

I watched Monica's face for a reaction. At that same moment Tanya walked away. It then hit me where I knew Tanya from. I remembered seeing her face on the front of the newspaper when all that shit went down with her husband being killed. I couldn't really remember the story at that second, but I made a mental note to research it when I got home.

In the meantime, Monica, Jazz, and James were stuck on stupid, standing there staring at each other. I got up to go to the bathroom in an effort to avoid any unnecessary chaos. On my way to the back of the restaurant I was stopped by Tanya in the walkway by the kitchen.

"Let me talk to you for a second."

I said nothing. I just followed her into the storage room so we could talk. I was nervous because I didn't know what she was going to do. I didn't remember seeing Monica's name in the article, but I was assuming they were once lovers.

"How long have you known Monica?" she asked as if she had a big secret.

"About a year or so. Why?"

"Honey, you are walking around with trouble, you hear me? Run while you can."

For some reason I trusted Tanya at the moment, and figured if we both put our heads together maybe we could get Monica's ass back. I wasn't sure what role Monica played in Tanya having to serve time, but I was sure it was all her fault. I'd also been sitting on the tape I'd taken from Monica's for a couple of months, and I needed to share what I knew with someone. Maybe she could help me out.

"Listen, is there a way we could meet up after business hours? I have a feeling we need to talk," I said.

"Here's my home, cell, and restaurant number. Contact me as soon as you can. This is serious." Tanya scribbled her info on the top page of her receipt book. I folded the paper and stuck it in my back pocket, careful to stick it all the way down so I wouldn't lose the number. Some serious shit was about to pop off. I could feel it.

I pretended I was drying my hands on my jeans when I walked out to the front. Jazz and James were seated at a table, and Monica was standing by the door waiting for me. Our food had been put into carryout containers, and our tea in sports bottles. I was hesitant to walk past Jazz and James, but I had no choice. It was the only way out the restaurant.

As I walked, I kept my eyes on Monica, avoiding eye contact with Jazz and James. I was going to walk by without a word, but I couldn't. In my mind I felt I owed Jasmine an apology, and now would be the perfect time, just in case the opportunity never presented itself again.

"Jasmine, I don't want to interrupt your meal, but I just have one thing to say." I was an emotional mess at this point. I literally had to blink back tears as I stared into Jasmine's angry face. I knew I had to make amends somehow.

Jasmine's entire face scrunched up like she had smelled something foul. Monica, I'm sure, was boring a damn hole in the side of my head, but I had to get it out. James just sat there and looked straight ahead, his hands tensing up into tight fists on the tabletop.

"Sheila, what can you say? The damage is done."

"I know, and I just wanted you to know that I never meant to hurt you. I'm sorry for all the confusion I caused."

"Listen," James said abruptly. His eyes appeared to be shooting red flames, and it was clear he was trying to keep his composure. "My wife is pregnant and doesn't need any extra stress. What's done is done. Let's not keep reliving the past."

My mouth dropped. I was at a complete loss for words. Jasmine was pregnant? Who would've guessed that? I turned to see the look on Monica's face, but all I heard was the chime on the door as I saw her wobble quickly across the street. I apologized once more and rushed out the door, barely making it to Monica's car.

Monica said nothing the entire ride, and I offered her no condolences. All I could do was hope that Jazz would hear me out one day. I knew I should let it go, but I just couldn't. I was indecisive about what I would do to get back at Monica, but I knew once I got a chance to talk to Tanya everything would be cool.

Monica dropped me off at my car in a huff, barely letting me get out of the car and close the door before she pulled off. I had a plan forming in my head, and I couldn't wait to get back to the restaurant. I had to beg my sister to watch my son a little while longer. Finally, she agreed to an extra hundred dollars and a platter from Tondalayah's as payment for watching my son.

Before I left the house I grabbed the tape I took from Monica's, stuffed it in my bag, and made a beeline to the other side of town. I had some business to take care of that couldn't wait until the end of the day.

Sheila

Stolen Secrets

I pulled up to the restaurant about an hour later, my heart beating wildly. I had to count to ten and get my head together before I could get out of my car. Some serious shit was about to go down, and I had to be on point if it was going to go down right. When I walked into the restaurant James and Jazz were gone. That alleviated some of the stress. Tanya saw me when I walked in. I took a seat at the closest table before I ended up stretched out on the floor from an anxiety attack.

"Tanya," I said to her between breaths. I was really trying to keep my composure but it was killing me. "I know you said to come after closing hours, but I couldn't wait that long. Is there a way we can go somewhere now to talk? I don't think I can make it until the end of the day."

"Sure. I was just saying to my mate that I couldn't wait that long either. Let me just get my stuff from the back and we can roll out. Smitty can handle everything here for the rest of the day."

I sat there attempting to get my head straight. I noticed that Tanya said her 'mate,' and I was curious to see if it would be another woman. A few minutes later she walked out with a beautiful woman next to her.

This woman resembled Monica in so many ways it was scary. They had similar looks, and although their faces weren't exactly the same, they could have easily been cousins. Her style of dress and the way she wore her hair was nearly identical to Monica's. If I hadn't just left Monica not too long ago, you couldn't have told me she wasn't standing before me. The only thing missing was the pregnant belly.

"Sheila, this is my soul mate, Shaneka. Baby, this is Sheila, the woman I told you about earlier."

"Nice to meet you," we said in unison, causing a slight smile to spread across our faces. That definitely relieved some of the tension between us. I was grateful. For the first time I felt like I was doing the right thing, and I couldn't wait to get started.

"Tanya, I'll follow you guys. I hope you have a VCR at your house. We'll need it."

The three of us left the restaurant and hastily went to my car. I couldn't wait to get this shit out in the open . . . finally. A half hour later we pulled up to a beautiful house in Wyncote, a suburb of Philly. The neighborhood was so quiet I felt that if I breathed too loudly everyone would hear me. We got out of the car and headed toward a stunning peach and cream house that sat so far back off the street you had to drive up to get to the door.

"Tanya, your house is beautiful," I exclaimed. I had never in my life seen a community so tranquil. This could definitely be a place to raise my son.

"Thanks to Monica. It was her hard-earned money that paid for it."

Something told me there was more behind that statement, but I didn't question it. I knew we were about to get into some heavy shit and all would be discussed in a matter of time.

The inside of her home was just as impeccable as the outside.

We went straight to the back of the house and down a few steps to an entertainment room. I dug through my bag and nervously gave the tape to Shaneka. She and Tanya sat on the couch. I sat in the chair.

You could cut the tension in the room with a knife as we patiently waited for the tape to rewind and start. I took one last deep breath as I watched the tape begin to play.

I had never watched the tape, besides the parts that Monica had shown me, and I had no idea what I had missed. The tape opened with James and Monica in what appeared to be a hotel room.

She had him blindfolded and tied to the bed, his dick standing straight up in the air like a thick, black pole. She rode him in positions I didn't even know were possible. I found myself getting a little turned on by their actions, but I quickly checked myself. That wasn't what I was there for.

The first segment of the tape ended with Monica balancing her hands on his stomach, and stretching her legs out like a gymnast would on a balance beam. She then proceeded to push her body up and down with her arms, riding his dick until his ejaculation slid down the sides of his dick. The camera was zoomed in so close you could see his dick pulsate as his seed spilled from the head and into Monica's eagerly awaiting womanhood. I was amazed at her skill.

A scene with her, Jazz, and James followed. James was leaning against a dresser in a different hotel room stroking his dick while Monica and Jazz performed on the bed. Jazz looked a little hesitant at first, but after some coaching, she got into it. As the tape played I went from being amazed, to being upset, to not believing what the hell I was watching.

She had the mayor of Washington, D.C. in all kinds of compromising positions. Tanya and Shaneka just sat there with their mouths wide open, not knowing what to say.

A couple of scenes went by with people I didn't recognize, and a few more of Jazz and James. My sister's husband, Hill, popped up with a quick episode by the fireplace and a few other guys from the police force who I recognized from last year's Christmas party were acting a fool on camera too. Monica must have a camera setup in every room of her house. I just sat there in awe, not believing what I saw.

I almost lost my lunch when I saw Monica and Stenton on the tape. She had him handcuffed to the bed in the doggie style position, blind folded, and dressed in a maid's outfit giving it to him from the back.

After the tape was done, Shaneka got up and started pushing buttons on one of the many remotes that lay on the front case of the entertainment center. After about five minutes, two tapes popped out. She gave me one, and labeled the other before putting it away in a drawer by the bookcase. I knew at that moment that she had made a copy for herself, and I briefly wondered if I had done the right thing.

I waited for them to get situated, because that was truly a lot to take in at one time. We sat in silence for what felt like an eternity. I briefly flashed through my life over the past five years wondering why I always ended up in situations like this. The sound of Tanya's voice interrupted my trip down memory lane as I came back to deal with the situation at hand.

"Sheila, I just want to thank you for stepping forward with this matter. Knowing how Monica is, that took a lot of courage on your part, and I want you to know that as of this moment you have no need to fear her again. Trust me on that."

"I want to get my life back. I can't live like this, constantly looking over my shoulders, wondering if she's going to jump out of the damn bushes on me."

"Listen, when I first met Monica I fell for the bullshit, too. She was sexing me crazy and had me thinking that we could truly be together. Even after she killed my husband I knew she would be there for me, but she never came."

Tanya went on to tell me how Monica killed her husband and then convinced her to take the blame for it.

"She looked possessed when she was pulling the trigger. Like she went back in time to another point in her life or something," Tanya said with a spaced-out look on her face.

We all talked for a little while, and then Shaneka brought it all together so it made sense. We had to get Monica back, but we would wait for the baby to be born. That way, we wouldn't be imprisoned for harming a fetus and we could just handle our shit and not have to worry about an unborn child.

"That sounds like a good plan, Shaneka, but what do we do right now?"

"Now we go to see James and Jasmine. They need to know what kind of shit they were pulled into. Revenge should be sweet, and I'm sure they'd want a piece of it too."

"Are you sure that's a good idea? I honestly think all they want is to move on and put their lives back together. I don't think they would want in on it." I tried to persuade them to think otherwise, simply because I wasn't ready to face Jazz and James again, but it was apparent they weren't trying to hear that.

"Let's at least show them the tape," Shaneka argued back. It wasn't until she told me about her beef with Monica and Rico that I understood what she was trying to do.

"Okay, you guys can follow behind me. We might as well go and get it over with."

During the drive over I tried to envision how it would all go down. I mean, I was a lover, not a fighter, and I didn't know if Jasmine could take seeing me twice in one day. I was on that tape giving her husband head. I didn't exactly sleep with him, but that was damn close. I knew if it was me, I'd be ready to go on a head-smashing spree. On the flip side, I think she needed to know. James was wrong, there was no doubt about that, but even Jazz knew how persuasive Monica could be.

When we got there I let Tanya ring the bell. If Jazz was going to swing, I didn't want it to be on me. I knew she was going through a tough time, especially being pregnant. What were they going to do with another kid, and with Monica possibly carrying James's child? I didn't want to be there when that shit went down. When Jazz opened the door her face let us know she didn't feel like the nonsense. I stayed in the back behind Shaneka while Tanya explained our reason for being there.

"What tape are you talking about? Where did you get it from?" Jasmine had yet to open the door fully. I didn't see James's car, so I figured she would be apprehensive about letting us inside because she was home alone, but the last thing I would allow was for her to come to any harm.

"I took it from Monica's house the night she was taken to the hospital for a miscarriage," I explained to Jazz. "I just wanted to have some proof of what she was doing."

Jazz looked at us like we were crazy, but she eventually let us in. The place looked different. I didn't know how I would react to seeing her again, but I was glad she gave us this time to talk. Once we were all seated, I mustered up enough courage to finally say something to her.

"Jazz, I know you don't necessarily want to hear anything I have to tell you, but after you watch this tape, maybe we can discuss some things."

"Sheila, you know you hurt me the most. I understand that we weren't close, but damn, you set me up in the worst way, and in my eyes that's unforgivable."

"It wasn't even my idea. I was trying to talk Monica out of it. She wouldn't hear anything I had to say."

"That's funny, because she blamed it all on you when she came here."

"Did she? Well, since when could her word be taken as the truth? She's a manipulator. She'll say whatever she needs to say to get you off her back."

"As true as that may be, it doesn't excuse you.

You knew what was going down, that's why none of your shit was on your desk when you left for the day. I knew something was up, but I didn't expect to come home to your raggedy ass on my kitchen table."

"Look, we're not here for all that. Y'all can rehash the past once we're gone. I just need you to look at this tape," Tanya explained.

Both of us looked at Tanya like she was crazy. I said nothing after that. Jazz got up, snatched the tape out of my hands, and popped it in the VCR. I just sat back and watched her face as she watched Monica in action. There was going to be some shit when it was over. I could feel it. All hell was about to break loose, and for the first time in my life, I couldn't wait.

Tanya

Playing Catch Up: Through Tanya's Eyes

Seeing Monica on that tape brought back so many memories. At the time we were together I was in love with her, and I couldn't see how mentally sick she was. I, too, was caught up in her web of lies and deceit, and for a brief time in my life I wanted to believe I was in love with her. She presented a stability that I couldn't get at home, and I craved to live life on the other side of the fence. I soon found out that the grass wasn't as green as I thought it was.

I met her at an art demonstration down at CCP (the Community College of Philadelphia) during fashion week. She had a few pieces on display, and I was in awe of the detail displayed in her work. Before I knew the woman in the picture, I was intrigued. Her eyes drew you into the painting, having you believe that she could see into your soul, taking the breath out of your lungs.

I was standing there in a trance staring at a painting of her lying on a chaise lounge the color of fall leaves. The fireplace strategically placed off in the corner of the painting looked lifelike. Her use of colors was impeccable. I must have zoned out because I didn't realize she was standing next to me until she spoke. Her voice sounded like a rushing waterfall. I was hooked from day one.

"My living room used to look like that just last year, but I went with a new color scheme for the New Year."

I turned toward the direction of the voice, surprised to see her face to face. She looked almost angelic . . . almost. There was a hint of mystery behind her eyes I couldn't figure out at the time, but now I know it was nothing but the damn devil. If I knew then what I know now.

"So, you're the artist? It is truly a pleasure meeting you. I must tell you that your work is absolutely wonderful. I'll be purchasing this one for my living room," I said to her while shaking her hand. The skin of her palm felt like silk, and I could only imagine how her hands would feel on the rest of me.

"Thank you so much. I appreciate the patronage." She blushed, looking away for a brief moment before resuming eye contact. I smiled to myself and turned my attention back to the painting on the wall.

"Listen, what are you doing after the demonstration? There's a café down the street, a few doors away. Maybe we can chat over an espresso," Monica invited.

"That would be nice. I'll meet you at the entrance when it's all done."

"That's fine, and don't worry about paying for this painting. I'll be sure that you get it before you go."

"You don't have to do that. This painting costs five thousand dollars. I can't let you pay for that."

"Did you forget I painted it? It wouldn't cost me anything," she replied with a cute laugh that made me follow suit. I burned her smile into my memory at that moment.

"Okay, I'll meet you at the door."

She said nothing. She walked away and began mingling with the other guests. I made my way to the door to avoid the crowd that was sure to come. There had to be nothing but ballers in here, because these painting were a grip, but all of the money made went to The Sanctuary, an organization that extended their hand to teenage girls who had been molested. It was a good cause that brought out plenty of supporters with big bucks. I saw the mayor of D.C. and his family there, as well as a few other bigwigs in political positions, and many members of the police force.

I wasn't waiting long before I saw her making her way through the crowd. We had yet to exchange names, so I couldn't call out to her. I waved my hands in the air until she saw me. Her smile blessed my eyes once again.

"You ready?" she asked as she pushed her way through the door.

"Yep, let's get out of here."

We made light conversation on our way down to the café, and once we got inside we grabbed a table by the door. After our orders were placed, we were finally able to converse, exchanging names before we moved along in line.

She told me all about her life as an artist/photographer, and I actually remembered seeing some of the covers she did for *Essence, Sister2Sister,* and *Vibe* magazines. I wanted to ask her why she started The Sanctuary, but it was obvious she had been hurt coming up so there wasn't any need to go there.

I told her about my job as head chef at The French Quarters, and my dream of one day owning my own restaurant. My husband wouldn't allow me to work after our son was born, and I became a stay-at-home mom, but I didn't think she needed to know all of that. I let her know I was married, choosing to be up front about my status. It was obvious she was trying to get to know me on a personal level. I was open to all the possibilities.

"This is my son, Tyler, and my husband, Marcus." I showed her a picture in my wallet from the days when we were a happy family.

When Marcus and I first got together he knew I was into women, and he was all for it as long as I brought them home so we could share. I figured we could do the same with Monica, but I didn't find out until much later from a friend of mine that Marcus already knew Monica before I did. That was the reason he purchased the ticket to the art demonstration. It was all a setup to get us together on his terms. I was the only one who didn't know about it.

Giving it to her straight, no chaser, I told her what my husband and I were into and that I thought she would be perfect for an evening of adult pleasure. She agreed, but only after I agreed to meet with her one-on-one beforehand. She said she didn't mind sharing me with my husband, but she wanted to see what I was about first. We set a date to meet the next night.

I knew Marcus wouldn't go for that, so I told him I would be out with a few girlfriends and I needed him to watch the baby. Of course he objected, stating that if I got to go out why couldn't he? It wasn't until I told him I'd see about bringing a woman home that he agreed.

I called the number Monica gave me and we set a time. I was to be at her house by eight that night and I was pulling up at seven fifty, eagerly knocking on her door.

We walked straight upstairs to her bedroom. We didn't waste time on formalities or anything like that. I knew why I was there, so we needed to make it happen. This girl could do things with her tongue that you would never believe unless you had a Monica experience yourself. I thought I was Spider-Woman, and it was obvious that Monica thought she was Spider-Woman, too, because every wall I climbed, she climbed up right behind me, never taking her tongue from my clit. I thought about my husband for all of four seconds before the next wave of orgasms came crashing down and wiped him from my memory. We tossed and turned and climbed all over each other for hours, causing me to miss my curfew.

When I returned home it was obvious that Marcus had been drinking. He staggered into the living room when I opened the front door. An empty Hennessy bottle was on the table. I moved to check on the baby, but he grabbed me by my neck and pinned me against the wall. The smell of his breath made me want to vomit, but I forced it down while trying to catch my breath at the same time.

"You were supposed to be in this house. Where were you, and why did you walk through my door by yourself?"

"I . . . I can't," I attempted to answer him, but the tightening of his fist around my throat made it difficult to breathe and talk at the same time. At the very moment I thought I would black out, he let me go. I fell to the floor on my knees, gasping for air. The room spun around in circles for a while. I barely had time to recover when I saw stars from the impact of his fist connecting fiercely with the side of my face.

"Get on your knees," he demanded, pulling me up by my hair. I obliged, if only to stop the stabbing pain shooting into my head from the grip he had on my roots. I didn't know how much longer I could take this abuse. Something had to give, and soon.

"Marcus, can you please let go of my head? I can't see."

"You don't need to see to suck a dick. Just open your mouth." I had no other choice but to do what he said. He forced his dick into my mouth repeatedly, causing me to gag on several occasions.

I did the best I could for the three minutes it took him to explode. He came so much a good amount of it shot out of my nose, and the rest I either swallowed or spit out. I spent the next minute or so sputtering on the floor trying to catch my breath. He left me there for dead, warning me not to come in late next time, and especially by myself. That was just one of the scenarios that pushed me closer to Monica, and ultimately led to his demise. I saw Monica a few times after that, and once we had the threesome we started hooking up even more. Of course, Marcus didn't like it, not believing the story I gave him about us just being shopping buddies. He would whip my ass, and she would heal my wounds. This went on for a few months until finally she got tired.

We had decided that my son and I would move in with her and be a family. By this time Marcus had already cracked one of my ribs, tried to slit my wrist, and had pulled a patch of hair out from the side of my head that I now covered with a weave track. They were threatening to fire me from The French Quarters. Between Marcus calling there a million times a day for absolutely nothing, and me missing days from work because I was hiding injuries, it just wasn't working out, and my life was spiraling downhill quickly.

Three more weeks went by and he punched me in my face for not having dinner done, breaking my nose in the process. That night Monica decided I would leave him. I went home to pack my stuff while he was at work, but he came home in the middle of me packing my son's stuff.

We were in the living room arguing back and forth because I was trying to leave. I had more than enough money in my checking account to start over, and decided I would just leave whatever belongings I had there. He wouldn't let me leave, and even after I grabbed my son to keep him from hitting me, he still continued to batter my body with wild blows from his heavy hands. I balled up in the corner to cover my face and the baby, and just when I moved to punch him in his private area, Monica burst in through the front door.

I can't remember what she said to him, all I knew was he moved in her direction to swing at her and she unloaded her gun into his face, afterward reloading and finishing him off. When she was done there was nothing left of his head.

I was devastated. Yes, I wanted him gone, but damn. I was stuck, literally. I couldn't move at first. The cries from my son brought me back to reality. I held his small body close to mine in an effort to quiet him as I stepped closer to my husband's dead body. The tears were uncontrollable as the reality of what happened set in.

"What did you do? Monica, what did you do?" I screamed after I sat the baby down in the crib. I couldn't believe he was gone. Now what would my son do for a father?

"What did I do? Bitch, I took you out of your misery."

"Monica, you just killed a person. Do you know how much time you get for murder?"

"Tanya, you won't be in there long. I have connections who will have you out in no time. Just tell the police it was a break-in that went bad."

"What do you mean *I* won't be in there long? I am not taking the rap for this. Fuck what you heard!" I was back on my feet and ready to beat Monica's ass. I wasn't doing time for anyone, damn the jokes. Who I look like, Boo Boo the Fool?

"Tanya, listen to what I'm saying to you. If I do the time, how can I take care of you? The most you'll spend is a few hours at the precinct for questioning. Call me when you get down there and I'll come get you. Okay?"

For some strange reason I believed her, and followed her instructions. I should have known she wasn't shit. When I got down to the precinct and tried to call, she didn't answer her phone. Yeah, she got me a bomb-ass lawyer, but I spent damn near four years in the bricks before she came for me. I was in there fighting bitches off, ending up with a damn scar on my face from some of them creeping up on me late at night trying to rape me. When I got out she laced me, but by then Shaneka told me she had a lot to do with Rico getting axed.

As Shaneka drove us home from Jazz's house that night I let my head rest on the seat while I tried to get my thoughts together. We'd lay low for a while until Monica had her baby. It was only right.

I looked over at Shaneka and watched her as she concentrated on the road. She had held me down from the first day we met, and I wasn't sure I would have made it without her. I owed my very sanity to her, and her patience. She made me complete, and her love was unconditional. She gave me exactly what I thought I got from Monica—love and attention. Monica's day was coming, and soon.

When we pulled up to the house I waited until she opened the door. We held hands as we walked up to the house, and once inside we connected as one in front of the fireplace. She scratched my itch and I scratched hers until the sun rose. Love definitely made things happen.

Carlos

Flash Forward

"Bring that nigga in here. It's time to end all of this right now."

Jesus, Hector, and I had set up the block about three months ago to see what Arturo was up to. And now we finally had him where we wanted him. When we met back up that night, I have to say my feelings were hurt to find out that Rico trusted Arturo more than me, even though I was supposed to be his right hand man. I had asked Rico on many occasions to introduce me to his connect, just in case some shit went down, but he never did. Then I found out that this nigga, Arturo, done been to see him at least five times since Rico was done in.

Jesus and Hector had spent the last hour beating Arturo nearly to death. Killing him wouldn't get me the information I needed, so I had to keep him alive for at least a little while. They brought his bloodied body into the living room, sitting him in one of the kitchen chairs and securing his hands and feet to the arms and legs. Honestly, I don't think Arturo would've taken such a harsh beating had he gone one-on-one with them. Hector would have been an easy win for him, but Jesus would have definitely taken his life.

"So, Arturo, what do you have to say for yourself?"

It took him a minute to focus on me. I'm sure the room was spinning, no doubt from the multiple blows to his head. I'd decide later if I wanted him around. Dishonor meant death—no more, no less.

"Listen, Carlos, all I did was what Rico told me to do."

"What did he tell you?"

"He told me to make sure that chick he was fucking with took care of his shit. I think her name was Monique or Monica or some shit like that. We went ring shopping and everything for her, man. He was really in love with her, and he was leaving Shaneka to the birds."

"What did that have to do with his connect? How did you get to meet him?"

I was trying to put two and two together, but it wasn't making sense. I knew Rico had it bad for Monica from back in the day, and Shaneka was supposed to take her place, but I didn't think it was that serious. Yeah, he started to slip a little with the spending, but I knew Monica kept the jakes off him for a little while because she had connections. This nigga was riding around town like he was the fucking President of the United States or something, like his ass was untouchable. But I knew something had to be going down, so that's why I started to investigate as soon as shit started looking suspicious.

"Well, one time we went out shopping for a house for Monica and he told me how it was better to put a safe in her house and keep the money there, so if the cops ever searched the apartment they wouldn't find anything. That's how she got the cash, and all his shit. The day after he got locked up, she told me to help her move all of the stuff out before the cops came back, and as payback for helping her she'd take me to the connect to re-up on the supply."

"So, she knows who the connect is?"

"Yeah, she directed me to the house and waited in the car while I handled business in his mansion. Rico said he couldn't trust you, that's why he never took you over there. He felt you were always trying to stick him."

That hurt like hell to hear those words spoken out loud. Rico and I have been to hell and back. I shot dudes dead for him on more than one occasion. Before all of that we came from grade school together, sharing clothes and barely eating. I loved him like a brother, even though I felt like I needed to take charge, but I would've never brought harm to his doorstep.

"What happened when Rico got to jail?"

Arturo broke it down how once word was out that Rico got knocked, Juan had his boy who was on the same block as Rico set shit up while everyone was at dinner. Rico was sleeping with one of the guards for phone privileges, and he called me to find out what the word was on the street. He had suspicions that Monica had set him up, and I remember vividly the day he called me with his concerns.

I believed every word Arturo said because that was exactly how it went down. Now all I had to do was get him to take me to the connect and he could be done with. I was considering sparing his life, but I wasn't sure yet. After all, he just did what the boss told him to do, but now he needed to understand that there was a new sheriff in town, and things were about to change.

"So, where is the connect?"

"In D.C., right outside the White House. He works for the President. His coke is flown directly to him without any interruptions. The staff says nothing. It's like everyone is in on it."

"Arturo, this is what I'm going to do for you. If you are willing to work with me I'll spare your life. Understood?"

All he could do was nod. He was badly beaten, and I knew a good sleep would do him justice. I walked over and stood directly in front of him so he could see that I meant business. Hector and Jesus completed the circle around him. We all looked at each other before I spoke again.

"Okay, Hector and Jesus will take you to the hospital. I will give you a few days to get yourself together. Come see me Friday morning. We'll go see the connect and get down to business. Understood?"

"Understood."

"Oh, and Arturo, I have the world watching you right now. Don't try to skip town or you really will end up missing."

I drove around the block, then I made my way over to Yolanda's house. She was supposed to get information for me from Monica, and since I hadn't heard a peep from her, I took it as she wasn't moving until I came up off that shopping spree.

Turning my car toward South Philadelphia, I got to Yoyo's house a half hour later.

Checking my hip to make sure my heat was secure, I parked my car in front of Yoyo's apartment and moved to her door swiftly, looking over my shoulder on the way up the path. No telling who was watching. Even your own will do you in. I knocked on her door like I was the police, and turned my back to it just in case someone tried to walk up on me. Since Rico's demise, fools had been testing me.

"Who is it knocking on my door like the damn police?" Yolanda yelled from the other side of the door, obviously upset. I didn't give a fuck.

"It's C-Dogg, mami. Open the door."

I heard some movement on the other side, and a few minutes later she came to the door dressed in a cut off tank top and boy shorts. My mouth dropped open at the sight of her ass bouncing as she made her way back to the couch. Yoyo had a lot of legs, and I wanted to dive between them.

"Carlos, when did you start popping up unexpected? Did you lose your phone or break your finger?" Yolanda knew she looked good, and I could tell from the look on her face that she was really feeling herself. Her hair was laid, so she must have just gotten it done. And the polish on her fingers and toes looked fresh. I acted like I didn't notice either as I took a seat on the couch across from her and turned up the television.

"It's nothing like that, ma. I was just wondering what was up with you since I haven't heard anything from you in a while. Did you get that information I asked for?"

"That would be no."

"Why not? Yoyo, you know how important this is to me."

"Did you come up off that shopping spree? I think not, because I don't see any new boots in my closet."

"Come on now, mami. You know it's never that serious with me coming up off a few thousand dollars. I just need to know that you're going to ride for me, that's all."

"You know I'll ride for you, C. I just don't think I feel the same love coming from your end."

"Yolanda, you're killing me. Tell me, what I need to do to make this happen. Tell papi what to do."

"Take me to get those Manolo boots I saw, and maybe we can talk."

"Damn, Yoyo, is it like that?"

"Oh, it's like that."

"Okay, listen to me. We can go out right now if you'd like. I just need you to call your sister."

"You know damn well by the time I get dressed and make a call the malls will be closed, and you ain't taking me all the way to New York on a Tuesday night, and you ain't fuckin', so no."

I got up off the couch and walked over to her, dropping to my knees in front of her. She kept eye contact, refusing to be the first to turn away. She was looking good. Her lips were all shined up the way I liked them, and her nipples stood at attention through her cutoff tank top, the skin on her belly was smooth like a baby's ass. Forcing myself to stay focused, I made my eyes connect with her eyes and tried to talk to her sensibly. I could definitely see myself making Yoyo a steady, but she had to clean herself up. I couldn't have her around me, knowing she was liable to sniff up half a brick at any given moment.

"Yolanda, listen to what I'm saying. If you call your sister right now and see what's up, I'll take you anywhere you want to go this week. We can leave in the morning, but we have to be back by Friday. I have some things I need to take care of."

"So, what will you do for me right now?"

I said nothing. I just simply moved the crotch of her panties to the side and began making my acquaintance with her clit. I had to hold her down by her legs to keep her still after she eventually took one of her legs out of her panties. I had Yolanda's legs trapped under me so she couldn't move, and she was trying hard to get away. Switching between sucking on her clit and pushing my tongue in and out of her she was losing her damn mind. She begged for the dick, but I refused to give it to her. I needed her to handle business for me, and she could get broke off after that. A half hour later she was on the phone with Monica getting the scoop.

"Listen, before I dial her number I need you to promise me one thing."

"What now, Yoyo?" I asked her while I washed her essence off my face. She was a wet one.

"I know Monica has probably gotten into some shit she had no business being in, but you have to promise me one thing."

"What is it already, damn!"

"You have to promise me you won't hurt her. She's pregnant with my niece or nephew, and she needs to be here for her child. I don't want him or her to go through what Monica and I went through as kids."

"You have my word. I just need her to give me some info on Rico; then I'll call all the dogs off, even Shaneka."

"What beef Shaneka got with my sister? Yo, I know she don't want none. That bitch ain't as crazy as she thinks she is."

"Calm down. She thinks Monica is carrying Rico's baby, that's all."

"Okay, but I already told you she's not, so make her aware of the situation before I have to."

"Yoyo, you have my word. Shaneka will not be a problem. Just call your sister, please."

She looked at me like she was leery, but after I started counting out hundred-dollar bills on the countertop, she slowly began dialing the numbers to her sister's residence. Yoyo was really taking me through it this time, but I had to do what I had to do.

"Hey, Monica, how's my little niece or nephew doing?"

I couldn't hear what Monica was saying to her on the other end of the phone, so I just sat back and tried to read Yoyo's facial expressions. I listened as they chatted about baby shit and some kind of mural that Monica had completed for the baby's room. They talked about baby furniture and all that jazz. Monica must have promised her something because she started smiling. I started taking back hundreds, making her face frown up. She gestured for me to hold up.

"So, did you hear more about Rico?"

I wasn't sure what Monica said, but I knew it wasn't good when Yolanda's face frowned up. I wasn't in the mood for no bullshit until I heard Yolanda tell Monica to grab her cell phone and call the ambulance.

"Don't worry, sweetie. Your water just broke. I'll hold on. Just call nine-one-one so someone can come get you. I promise I won't hang up."

For the next twenty minutes I listened to Yolanda as she coached Monica. This bitch was about to have a baby, and I needed some information from her. I'd be calling Tony the locksmith sooner than expected. I wouldn't ransack her house, but I would be paying it a visit very soon.

Monica

Nobody Has to Know

As I felt the pain of the contractions I wondered if the pain I was enduring was worth it. I had been in labor for ten hours now. Yep, I was getting ready to deliver the baby James and I had conceived, and the physical pain from the contractions was almost so unbearable that I began to wonder whether or not getting pregnant by James in the first place had been worth it. While I contemplated my present plight, my mind began to drift back to the emotional pain I had endured during my childhood and adolescent years. I didn't know which pain had been worse, but while the physical pain would eventually end, it seemed I would forever be plagued by emotional pain. Of all times, why during labor was I thinking about my dirty-old-no-good uncle? I could still hear his voice.

"Monica, open this damn door! What I tell you about locking my damn doors around here?"

I was on the other side, fearing for my life as I hurriedly dressed before my drunk uncle broke down the door. I didn't want him to see me undressed, especially knowing what would happen if he did. I zipped up my pants and tucked my shirt in tightly. I unlocked the door and opened it just before he was about to kick it down.

"Who you got in this room, girl? Who you tryin'a hide?" Uncle Darryl said, barging into the room and almost knocking me into the wall.

I stood as far away from the bed as possible, not wanting to give him any ideas. I didn't know how I ended up in this never-ending nightmare, but I knew that when I got old enough I would leave. In my heart I vowed that no man would ever touch me once I escaped. Not like this.

"I was 'sleep and didn't hear the door," I replied in a barely audible voice. I didn't want to upset my uncle anymore than he already was.

"Let me find out you lying," he responded with a snarl, "Ain't nobody hittin' that but me, and as ugly as you is won't nobody want cha anyways. Get cha ass downstairs and clean that kitchen. I told you I wanted that done before I came home from work."

"Okay, Uncle Darryl, I'm right behind you," I stated, looking around the room for something to do so I wouldn't have to walk past him.

"I said I want it done now. Move ya ass!" Hesitantly, I moved by him as quickly as I could, almost running. I wasn't fast enough because he reached out, grabbed my pants pocket, and pulled me back by my shirt collar. He reached into my shirt and fondled my young breasts. I grimaced as he rubbed himself against me and kissed behind my ear. I did everything I could to hold back the tears, hoping he wouldn't make me go back into the room.

"Nobody betta not be hittin' this but me. Ya hear?" he whispered into my ear as he continued to explore my underdeveloped body.

"Yes, sir," was my only reply as I made my way downstairs after he released me.

For the life of me, I couldn't figure out what a grown man could see in me. Boys my age thought I was hideous, so I couldn't understand why I had to practically beat my uncle off me at least five nights a week. He seemed to get off on just rubbing the head against me. I gagged every time. I knew the slimy stuff he left behind was not supposed to be there, and I honestly thought the only reason he didn't actually do it to me was because it wouldn't fit.

I found myself on a few nights holding a mirror between my legs so I could look at myself to see if something was different. There was barely any hair there, and it didn't look appealing. But that didn't seem to keep his mouth off it. Uncle

Darryl had threatened to kill me if anyone found out, and my fourteen-year-old mind believed it, so I took the abuse, hoping he would die or leave me alone. Who could I tell anyway?

I didn't know what to do about the red bumps that hurt like hell when I went to pee, but I knew I had to do something soon because I couldn't take the itching and burning anymore.

I cried. I wished my mom were still alive. My mother was killed by her lover and I was powerless to help her. My feet felt like lead, like they were glued to the floor. I watched my stepfather beat my mother to death.

When the cops came that day, my sister, the baby of the family, was taken to go live with her Aunt Joyce over in West Philly. My brother, the middle child, was taken to his grandparent's house, and I was stuck with drunk ass Uncle Darryl. I didn't know if I was going to make it out alive, but I knew if I did, every man would pay dearly for what I went through. I thought the abuse would be over when my mom passed away. At least then I wouldn't have to worry about my stepfather trying to sneak into the room late at night, and my mom acting like she didn't know. But I jumped out of the frying pan and into a big ass fire. Uncle Darryl was bold, and the fight was no longer easy. He would pay when the time was right. He and every man after him would get what they deserved.

A sharp pain in my side quickly brought me back to reality, and soon after my son was born. The doctor said it was too late to give me an epidural, so I had to bear the pain of childbirth. When he came out I didn't want to hold him. The nurse cleaned him up and put him in a crib next to my bed. I was upset that I couldn't take a shower right away. My legs felt like wet spaghetti, so even if I wanted to get out of the bed, I couldn't.

My first instinct was to leave my son in the hospital and let them deal with it. But my heart wouldn't let me. For two days straight I stared at him, letting the nurses feed and change him. I refused to hold him, but I had the nerve to get an attitude because the doctor made him cry during his circumcision.

He looked so much like James and Jazz's son Jalil that it wasn't funny. I knew James didn't care, but I decided to call him anyway to let him know his child was born.

It was nearly three in the afternoon, so I called James's job. I was going to take the sucker way out and leave a message on the stations answering machine, but at this point I just felt betrayed. It wasn't really about me anymore. It was about his child. I felt that I needed to talk to James for my son's sake. I dialed the station. The phone rang twice before the nosey old lady who sits at the front desk answered.

"Good afternoon, and thank you for calling The Urban News Network. How may I direct your call?"

"Can you connect me to James Cinque, please?"

"Who may I tell him is calling?"

"His new baby's mother, bitch! Just connect us. Damn all the questions."

The line got quiet for a second, and I thought she hung up on me. Just as I was about to snap the fuck out I heard James's voice come from the other line."

"Thanks for calling T.U.N.N. This is James speaking. How can I help you?"

"I had a boy."

"Excuse me? Who is this?"

"James, don't play stupid. It's Monica. I had your son two days ago."

It got quiet on the other line, and if it weren't for his breathing I would've thought he had hung up the phone. A part of me felt bad for James. I knew this baby was the last thing he wanted, but this was the consequence of having sex without protection. In the beginning he came to me willingly. It wasn't until later on that he decided to fall back, and that wasn't working too well with me.

"Hello? James, are you still there?" I had a slight smile on my face from his discomfort, but it really wasn't a funny situation. James could shell out all the money in the world. At the end of the day I was the one stuck with a crying baby. I would definitely be getting a live-in nanny. I didn't do diapers.

"Monica, what hospital are you in?"

"The University of Penn. Why, are you coming to see your newborn son?"

"No, I'm coming to get a blood test. This ain't no *Jerry Springer* shit, Okay? I'll be there within the hour."

He didn't give me a chance to say anything else. He just hung up the phone. I placed the receiver back on the base and sat up on the side of the bed to look at the baby up close. They had finally let me shower, so I was able to move around a bit.

I carefully took him out the crib and cradled him to my chest so I wouldn't drop him. There was no doubt in my mind that this was James's son. He had his eyes and everything. Tears gathered at the corners of my eyes, but I refused to let them drop. If I was going to move on to a normal life I had to stay strong.

I laid the baby on my chest and rubbed his back. I giggled as I watched him suck his thumb. It then hit me that there was no turning back. I was a mother. I stared at him for what felt like an eternity. I had no idea how much time had elapsed, but when I looked up and saw James standing in the doorway I knew it was time to face reality, and there was no turning back. It was time to take care of business.

James

Here and Now

I look in your eyes, and there I see what happiness really means. The love that we share makes life so sweet. Together we'll always be . . .

I stood outside the door and watched Monica and our son for a few minutes before I walked in. I say "our" son, because deep down inside I knew he was mine. Yeah, I truly believed that Monica was a slut, but why lie about something like this?

When I walked into the room she looked at me like she was shocked I had shown up. I stopped at the gift shop before I came up to the room and got her a few "It's A Boy" balloons, and flowers for the side table. I wasn't sure why I made the effort, but she looked appreciative.

I stood at the door for a few minutes, capturing the moment in my mind. Inching closer I slowly made my way to the side of the bed, looking at my son for the first time. Damn, there was no denying him. We had the same face. He looked just like Jalil when he was first born. I blinked back tears, keeping the reason why I was there at the forefront of my mind.

"So, do you believe me now?"

"Monica, I never said I didn't believe you. Any man would have doubts in this situation. Look at the circumstances."

"Fuck circumstances, James. Look at him! This is your child."

Monica began to cry and it was breaking me down. I almost gave in, but I thought about how I got here in the first place. Plus, I needed to come correct with Jazz. Her stomach was growing more every day with our children, and it was only fair to her that we knew how to proceed from here on out. I was a lot of things, but a deadbeat dad wasn't one of them. No, I didn't want Monica in my life, but we had a child together, so I had to do what was needed to make things right.

"Monica, can you buzz the nurse in for the blood test? We need to get this done."

"Blood test? Are you telling me that you are still going to go through with it even though it is clear that James, Jr. is yours?"

"James, Jr.?"

"Yes, James will be a junior. He might as well carry on the family name."

"Monica, Jazz is going to make our son a junior if she has one. You have to change his name."

"It's first come first served in this game. She's just going to have to think of something else."

"Look, Monica . . ."

Monica cut me off as she stated, "You come up in here talking about a blood test and all this other bullshit but what you need to do is bring that blood test shit to your wife because she's probably not even pregnant with your fucking baby!"

Monica was a sick, twisted, manipulative bitch and this was a perfect example of her bipolar ways. But I wasn't trying to fall for her tricks. I knew that those babies Jazz was carrying were my kids. There was no way in hell Jazz would have stepped out on me and gotten pregnant! So I quickly dismissed what Monica had said.

"Look! Call the damn nurse in so we can get this over with. I have to get home to my wife and kids."

Monica paused and looked at me and shook her head.

"So, you're going to go through with this?"

"Either you push the damn button, or I go get her. It's your choice."

As Monica went to her bed to push the button, I walked across the room and leaned my head against the window, trying to think of a way to propel myself into the rush hour traffic that crowded the street fourteen stories down. For a brief second I wondered if my dad was like this and my mom never said anything. Did I have brothers and sisters out there who I didn't know about? How was I going to explain this to Jaden and Jalil? How do I tell them that they have a brother and it's not from their mom?

I took a seat until the nurse came, making myself as comfortable as possible given the situation. Periodically, I would look over at Monica. She put Junior back in the crib and was looking at television. The curiosity was killing me. I had to hold him.

I tiptoed over to him and leaned over to get a good look at his face. Gently picking him up and holding him close to my chest, my heart soared when he reached up and wrapped his hand around my pinky finger. The last time I felt like this was when the twins were born, and I almost forgot how it felt to be surrounded by innocence.

Taking my seat again, I studied his face for signs of another man, but it was like I was looking into the fountain of youth. The nurse came in to let us know that she would be ready for us in a few minutes. As she was walking out the room a very stunning woman walked in. She was gorgeous, and my man began to rise to the occasion.

"Girl, you look good considering you just pushed out a baby! Where is my darling nephew?" Still in shock, I stared at the woman who was obviously Monica's sister. She was the bomb, and I had to remind myself that I had a wife at home.

"His father is holding him, but he'll be leaving soon so you can hold him then. We're waiting on the nurse to come back so she can do the blood test."

"Blood test? For what? Didn't you just say he was claiming him?"

"Yeah, but he has to explain it to his wife, I guess."

"His wife! Monica, are you serious?"

"First of all, you two aren't going to talk about me like I'm not here. If you have any questions about me, or my family, ask me. I have nothing to hide. Monica was a terrible mistake."

I definitely had an attitude. How did they think they were going to put me on Front Street, like this entire episode was my fault? Monica played just as much of a role as I did. I wanted this portion of my life to be over.

Before Monica or her sister could get in another word, the nurse came in to draw blood for the test. I kept my mouth shut and my eyes on Monica while the nurse tried her best to find a vein. She poked me seven times before she was able to draw blood, reminding me why I hated needles. My heart dropped when she went through the hassle with my son, his small cry echoing in my head long after she put a bandage on him.

"Sir, if you'd like to wait around, the test should be back from the lab within the hour. It doesn't normally take long."

"That's fine, I'll wait."

The nurse walked out, and I took my seat back in the corner. Monica and her sister made a fuss over the baby, and I heard mention of a shopping spree, but decided not to comment.

In a little over an hour the nurse came back with the results. I wasn't sure I wanted to know. A part of me was hoping he belonged to someone else, but another part of me was hoping he was mine. When I held his little body in my arms, it felt right. The nurse gave both me and Monica a copy of the lab results. I couldn't read mine. I was too scared.

"Monica, I have to get going. We'll talk another time."

"James, what are you talking about? Read the damn paper. This is what you wanted, right?"

"I'll read it later. I just need to get some air right now."

"Let me find out you fuckin' with a deadbeat, Moni. For all this trouble you could've stuck it out with Rico," Monica's sister said from the sideline. I wanted to reach over and pop her in her smart ass mouth, but I decided to just keep it moving. It didn't make sense to cause a scene with my son in the room. "Monica, when will you be released? Do you have a ride home?"

"I'll be discharged tomorrow. Why, are you coming to get me?"

"I was, but since you have so much to say you can find a way home. I'll be contacting you shortly to let you know what I've decided concerning the baby."

"How do you know he's yours if you won't even read the damn results?"

"I'll talk to you soon."

"Of course you will. You know what's best for you."

Reserving any comment, I left the room and went to sit in my car for a second. It took me twenty minutes and tons of tears before I unfolded the paper from Quest Diagnostics. It stated that Junior belonged to me—99.9 percent certain. Now all I had to do was break the news to Jazz.

On the way home I rode in silence, trying to decide my approach. She was due soon, too. I didn't need her stressing, but I believed that if I didn't tell her now, it would hurt her more later. I had enough with the lies, so I decided I would come straight out with it.

I got home at around five thirty. Jazz was in the kitchen cooking dinner, and the kids were at the table coloring on construction paper. I walked into the kitchen, and after kissing everyone on the cheek, I asked her to follow me out to the patio. She turned the fire on low and walked out behind me, making sure the kids were okay. I didn't say anything. I just handed her the lab results. She looked at me with teary eyes and rubbed her stomach. I was at a loss for words, and waited patiently for her to say something.

"James, what do we do now?"

"We live, sweetie. That's all we can do. We'll have to talk to Monica eventually, but right now all we can do is wait."

I pulled my wife closer and held her in my arms as though it would be my last time. Our family was just starting to come together, and now this. But I was confident we would be okay, somehow. God didn't put more on you than you could handle, and even the worst situation wasn't as bad as it could be. We would get through this . . . we had to.

Carlos

Breaking Even

I found out from Yoyo that Monica would be in the hospital for at least two days after she had her baby, so the very next day I went to see my man, Sean. He runs a locksmith shop over near Monica, and I knew for sure that every time he made a key for someone, he made one for himself, just in case.

I was almost sure he told me a while ago he had keys to Monica's crib, because he had been hitting her off for a while before she started fooling with Rico. Arturo would be getting out of the hospital in a day or so, so if I was going to do something I had to make it quick. I broke Yoyo off already because she wouldn't shut the fuck up about it, but she knew she owed me some info so I'd get with her later.

My boys told me they saw Monica and Stenton having lunch in the city and they looked like they were in a heavy debate. That scandalous bitch was probably trying to get some dick, with her ignorant ass.

I parked my car on the little island across the street from the shop, just in case I had to make a quick getaway from the feds, who seemed to constantly be on my back. I checked my surroundings in my mirrors before exiting my vehicle, making a quick exit and practically running across the street. I looked behind me once more before entering the shop.

"Yo, Sean. What's up, my nigga?" We exchanged handshakes across the desk.

"Nothing much, man. Just making this money. What brings you to the 'hood today?"

"I came to holler at you about getting a key."

"Say word? To your crib?"

"Now you know I know how you get down, man. You'll never have that much access to my shit." I laughed. I'd hate to put a bullet in his peanut head if my shit ever came up missing.

"So, what can I do for you, man? You know I got the business."

"And that's why I fuck with you. You remember that chick you was hitting over there on Lincoln Drive? The jawn that be having everybody sprung. She was messing with my boy Rico before he got set up."

"Oh, you're talking about Monica. You trying to get at that? The shot is fantabulous."

"Nah. Yo, you a wild boy." I had to laugh to myself because you just never knew what to expect Sean to say. He hit nearly every dame that came through those doors, and I ain't mad at him. A brother got to pay his rent somehow.

"You sure? I can set that up for you."

"Man, I am positive. What I need is access to her crib, if you get my drift."

"Oh, you want me to do some illegal shit."

"Nigga," I had to step back and look at him for a second. I couldn't believe the shit that had just come out of his mouth. "You already doing illegal shit. I'm sure keeping a copy of everyone's keys can't be lawful, right?"

"Okay, you got me on that one. I feel you, but that comes at a price."

"Name it, but I need them today."

"You can have all three keys and the pass code to her alarm within minutes for five thousand a pop."

"You telling me you want twenty thousand for me to get in the crib?"

"Cash money up front. And keep my name out ya mouth. I don't need the jakes coming down on my shit. I got a family to provide for."

"Damn, you straight robbing me with my eyes open on that one, Sean. Who you know carry around that kind of money?"

"That's none of my concern. I just need five thousand to get started, and you pay by the key. Do we have a deal?"

"Hold on, man, let me go to my car." I was pissed that this dude was straight raping me for the keys to Monica's house, but that was a small price to pay to get some dirt on her and Stenton and to get him off my ass.

I checked the perimeter and made a mad dash to my car, pushing a few buttons once I got inside to slide out my secret compartment. Taking the eight thousand I had, I made sure everything was back in order before I stuffed the cash in an old McDonald's bag from the backseat and dashed back across the street. I got a little paranoid when I saw a cop car pull up behind me, but my heart returned to a regular pace when they kept going.

"Look, I don't have twenty thousand on me, but I do have eight. I'll send one of my men down here with the rest of the money in the morning. My word is my bond."

"Look, I don't be doing no favors and shit, but I'll do it for you this one time. Next time come correct or step."

"Okay, Sean. I feel you. You the man today."

I stood by while Sean counted his money, afterward tucking it safely away in a safe under the desk. I made sure to peep the location on the low just in case I ever had to come back and get this nigga. Ten minutes later I was out the door with three keys and the password to the alarm in my right pocket. I called Hector and told him to send the dough over to Sean, and for him and Jesus to meet me at Monica's crib in an hour. This chick needed to know who she was fucking with. This wasn't a game.

Within the hour we pulled up on Monica's block, opting to park down the street from her house just in case one of her nosey-ass neighbors stayed home from work and was watching her house. With our baseball caps pulled low over our faces, we walked slowly up to her crib like we lived there, and let ourselves in. I was mad after we finally got in because her alarm wasn't even on. That was money I didn't have to spend.

Now, I have to say, her crib was on point. We took our time looking around the crib just to see if something would jump out at us that we could use.

"Yo, C Dogg! Hector! Come up here. You guys got to see this."

Both me and Hector ran up the steps to see what Jesus had found. We found him in what I assumed to be the master bedroom. Entering the room, I turned my attention to the television to see what all the hoopla was about. That shit on the screen made me want to fuck just walking in there and seeing Monica's naked body.

Apparently, little Miss Monica was very busy. The recording was on fast forward but I could see that Monica was a beast when it came to sex. She had just about everyone in town who was of any importance in a compromising position on that tape. No wonder she walked around like she had shit on lock. She was able to fuck up the lives of politicians, judges, and dudes on the police force. I just shook my head and stopped the tape. I popped it out of the VCR and stuffed it in my inside jacket pocket for later use. I was sure it would come in handy later.

We looked around a little more, just to see what was what. But all I saw were some jewels I didn't need, and a couple of dollars on the dresser. A drawer full of dildos made all of us take a step back. I decided I had what I needed, so we bounced.

On the way back down the street Shaneka and this fly-ass chick pulled up to me. Even if I wanted to, I couldn't have kept on walking, because Shaneka would have caused a scene and that was the last thing I needed. I told Hector and Jesus that I would meet them at the car. Stooping down so we were face to face, I paid respect to the driver, then asked Shaneka what was up.

"What you doing around this way? I'm shocked to see you outside of West Philly."

"I had to come check on a few things. What you up to?"

"We about to go see what Monica is up to. I heard she had the baby, but I'm not sure if she's home yet. She got an ass whipping coming to her."

"She ain't home yet. Yoyo told me she just had the baby yesterday. That baby ain't Rico's. It's by some married dude she was fucking with."

"How you know all that?"

"Didn't I just tell you I was talking to her sister?"

"Well, Tanya still owe her, so it's a done deal. I'm on my way through the window."

"Now, Shankea, let's not get stupid. You don't think her neighbors are watching? The moment you climb through that window the cops are called. Here, I got one better for you."

"Carlos, you act like shit is sweet. I owe that bitch. She setup my man."

"Girl, calm the fuck down. She just put him in a bad position. Rico was going to get it regardless. It was just a matter of time."

"Look, I really don't need to hear this right now, Carlos," she said through the window with tears streaming down her face. For the first time I could honestly see that Shaneka did care about Rico. Yeah, she did him dirty, but the love was there.

"Look, here are her house keys, and the alarm is off. I got them from . . . well, that's not important. Go get your shit off, but make it quick. I'm sure someone has seen us coming and going by now."

"Thanks, C Dogg. I owe you one."

"Don't mention it. Just be safe."

Feeling like my work was done, I met up with my boys at the corner and we jetted. I had to make a couple copies of the tape while it was fresh on my mind. I had a feeling life was going to be cool from here on out. I had a couple of officials I needed to see about some things.

Sheneka

Payback Is a Mutha

Tanya and I pulled up in Monica's driveway, not giving a damn who saw us. After fumbling with the locks we finally got in and started tearing the place up. I snatched all the paintings off the walls, afterward cutting them to shreds with a knife from the kitchen. Tanya found cans of paint in what looked like the baby's room upstairs. She started to wreck the mural, but I talked her out of it. That would be the one room we didn't touch. Instead, we took the paint and splashed it all over the house, ruining the carpets and drapes. Tanya cut up the couches and chairs. For a second I felt bad for Monica because I knew this shit cost her a grip. Her house was laid like you wouldn't believe, but by the time we got done you would have thought we had a frat party in there.

Tanya took a can of spray paint and painted obscenities all over the walls. After a while I took a seat in the corner and watched her work. It was obvious she had some shit to get off her chest, so I let her handle her business. Before we left I ran to the car and grabbed the baby doll from the backseat.

Going back into the nursery, I folded the cover down in the crib and sat the baby doll under it like it was a real child. On the way up I got the biggest knife I could find out of the kitchen and used it to stab a whole straight through the doll, impaling it to the crib. Then I took some of the red paint that was left over and poured it on the doll, giving it the appearance that it was bleeding. I would never kill her child, but that was a hell of a message to leave behind. After bashing in the television screens I was finally able to pull Tanya away from the house. Our work was done.

Monica

Home Sweet Home?

Sheila came to the hospital to see the baby a few hours before I was to be released. We didn't really have anything to say to each other after the restaurant incident. I said nothing to her the entire time. She held the baby for a second, and after she commented that the baby looked like James, I called security to make her ass leave. Like I needed the constant reminder.

Surprisingly, my sister kept her promise and was at the hospital to take me home. I was so nervous about leaving because I knew once I got home it was all on me. There wouldn't be any nurses to take the child when I didn't feel like being bothered. I knew for sure the first thing I would do was start interviewing nannies. I didn't have the time to be getting my nails messed up changing nasty diapers. When I pulled up on my block there were several police cars around my house. I started to panic. Did I accidentally leave the stove or the iron on in my haste to leave the house? Or did someone break into my shit while I was gone? Damn, I was only gone for a few days.

I didn't see any flames or fire trucks, so it was safe to assume my shit wasn't burning. The amount of cops on the premises made me nervous. I was clueless as to what was going on. The first officer I recognized was Officer Hill. I approached him after Yolanda stopped the car. I needed answers now.

"Can someone tell me what's going on here?" There had to be at least thirty cops on my property. Some were standing around talking, others were bringing out pieces of my furniture. For the first time in my life I was scared to death.

"Are you the owner of this house?" Officer Hill asked as though he didn't know who I was. I decided to play along until I knew what was going on.

"Yes, I am. What seems to be a problem?"

"One of your neighbors called and reported suspicious activity on the property. She said it might be a possible break in. When we arrived we found your house ransacked. There were no signs of forced entry, so we are assuming the perps had a key. Right now . . ."

I didn't want to hear shit else he had to say. I needed to see for myself what was going on with my house. When I walked in, nothing could have prepared me for what I saw. My house looked like a tornado had blown threw it. My paintings, furniture, everything was torn up. I saw nothing that could be salvaged. I ran through the house like a mad woman, not believing the damage I saw. What broke my heart was what I saw in my son's room.

At first I was happy that whoever did this had spared his room, but what I saw in the crib took my breath away, and all I remember seeing was a bird land on the windowsill before I blacked out. I came to with my sister and half the police force standing over me. All I could do was curl up in a ball and cry. Officer Hill took the report. They said all they could do was investigate and get back to me. Everyone except Officer Hill cleared out. I couldn't call the judge because all the phone lines were cut, and my cell phone was still in Yolanda's car.

"Well, Monica, we'll be getting back to you with a full investigation. Just thank God you have neighbors who care."

"Thanks for your help. Now can you please leave? I need to get my head together."

"I'm gone, but be careful. Things like this aren't random. I guess your time is up in this town, huh?"

"She said leave, nigga. Damn. What, you don't understand English or something?"

I sat down in a fairly clean corner and tried to understand what had happened. I didn't want to say too much around the cops, but now that they were gone, I could get to the bottom of all this.

Yolanda and I, after finally finding two glasses that weren't broken or chipped, got something to drink. I had her grab the baby and follow me upstairs to my room. I pulled all the ruined linen off so we could sit down, then I grabbed the remote off the side of the bed. After pushing a few buttons, the fake bookshelf on the right wall moved to the side, revealing an entire surveillance system.

"Damn, bitch. You like inch high private eye up in this joint. What the hell do you need with that many TVs?"

"You'll see in a minute. Just let me rewind this tape."

We sat in silence as I began to rewind the tape. Yolanda fed the baby in the process. After the tape stopped, I pushed play and fast-forwarded through the day.

At around five, Carlos and two of his men came in snooping around my spot in search of something. I saw them take a tape out of the VCR after they watched it for a while. Carlos stuck the tape in his top pocket, and they searched around a little more before they left. I never turned the alarm on, but I clearly saw him pull keys out his pocket from the camera I had set up at my door. The tag looked like it came from Sean's shop. I made a mental note to go see him.

After they left, Tanya and the woman I met up at the prison showed up and started tearing up the place. Watching that woman in my son's room and seeing what she did burned me up inside, but I held it down. It didn't make sense to be mad now. Later on in the tape I saw the cops come in. Some of them pocketed my money and jewels. I shook my head in disgust at what was playing out in front of me. Hell, if you couldn't count on the law to have your back, then who could you count on?

Taking the tape from the VCR, I gathered all of my son's clothes into plastic bags, leaving everything I owned minus a few pairs of underclothes and some jeans. There would be a for sale sign out front tomorrow. I would hire someone to come and clean up this mess. Hill was right, I was done with this town.

I stayed with my sister for the time being, giving her a couple thousand for the inconvenience. Carlos acted innocent when he came around, and I told Yoyo not to worry about saying anything to him, just get him for all she could before we left. Within a month's time the house was cleaned out, and all of the damage restored. I left the mural up in the nursery, but painted the rest of the house neutral colors to satisfy the buyer. I was practically giving the house away, so it didn't take any time to get it off the market.

On our last day in Yolanda's apartment I sat alone and contemplated my life. I had to honestly admit to myself that I had caused a lot of the drama, but was I really that bad? Furthermore, did my son deserve to grow up without a fair chance? It didn't take me long to decide, I knew what I had to do.

"Come on, Yolanda. We have a plane to catch, but I have to make one stop first."

"Monica, do you have to do this? Things will be better once we leave here."

"Yoyo, I've already made up my mind. Now let's go. We have to have the cars over there two hours before lift off, and you know how long the lines get." I took one last look at my sister's apartment, the place I had called home for the last two months. We would be making a new home in Atlanta, Georgia and I couldn't wait to get there. I had worn Philly out, and there would never be another like me around these parts for a long time.

I took in the city on my ride across town, burning certain landmarks into my mind. I was sad to go, but I knew I had to. There was nothing left here for me except for Jasmine and I had an ace in the hole that I was sure would end her relationship with James if things panned out as I suspected. I had to start over. I deserved a second chance at life and the baby deserved a fair chance at life, and that was what I was determined to provide, all while I waited to reel Jasmine in.

James

The Aftermath

I heard one of the twins crying, so I decided to let Jazz sleep in, and I tended to them myself. Jaden had been having nightmares lately, so I knew it would be a while before I went back to sleep.

As I was coming down the steps I thought I heard someone in my kitchen, and I ran to see what was what. It was three o'clock in the morning, and no one should be downstairs but me. Dashing through the dining room I almost slipped on the hardwood floor as I came to a screeching halt. On my dining room table was a baby in a car seat.

I tiptoed toward the baby, not sure why I was scared. It was only a baby, not a bomb. As I got a closer look, I realized this wasn't just any baby, it was Monica's. I briefly wondered how she got in, but then I saw the note and the house key sitting on the table behind the car seat. Not really knowing what to do, I quickly got the twins a drink before grabbing Monica's child and making my way back upstairs. I made sure the twins drank their water and put them to sleep before I took Monica's baby in to Jazz.

I walked in the room quietly and took the baby out of the car seat. After grabbing the note I sat down on the bed to gather my thoughts. I looked at the baby for a while, then decided to wake up Jazz. She would know what to do.

"Baby, wake up. I need you to see this."

"See what, James? I gotta get up in a few hours."

"I know, baby, but this can't wait until the morning."

When Jazz turned over and opened her eyes, her entire face showed shock. "James, how the . . . where did . . ."

"She left this note."

Jazz continued to stare at James, Jr. before she began reading the letter out loud. I sat in silence and listened to what Monica had to say.

> *Jasmine and James,*
>
> *I know this comes at an awkward moment, but I had no choice. What am I going to do with a baby? For the last two months I tried to be a good mother, but I can't. I fear I'll be just like my mother, and I don't want to take my child through that. I knew if I brought my child to you that he would be where he belonged—with his family.*
>
> *Jazz, if you don't believe anything else I tell you, believe that I loved you with all my heart. I thought if I had James's baby we could be one. Now I realize it would have never worked. Know that you will always be my woman, but you're James's wife, and I'm cool with that. James, it wasn't all in vain, sweetie. You served your purpose. Take care of your family the way you have been, and know that you will not get any trouble from me in the future.*
>
> *I gave up total custody of Junior to you and Jazz, and you'll find all of the paperwork in the boxes in your living room. I also returned the house key so you won't have to worry. It's been real. Stay blessed.*
>
> *Monica*
>
> *P.S. Jasmine, sweetie, don't you think now more than ever is the time to come clean about your little secret rendezvous with the twin brothers from Bally's gym? I mean, word on the street is that they both fucked you in the same bed you and James sleep in! Talk about trifling. At least I had the decency to fuck your husband on the kitchen table and not in the same bed that the two of you sleep on. But to each his own. I think that if you truly love James that you owe it to him to at least tell him the truth. And the truth is you're probably not even pregnant with his kid right now. You know in your heart what I am saying is right. And if I'm wrong then I'm wrong but if I'm*

right . . . Well . . . James you know about blood tests, so
when Jazz delivers why don't you take a blood test to see
if what I am saying is wrong? What do you have to lose?

Jazz and I looked at each other with tears in our eyes. I had
tears and Jazz had a look of shock in her eyes more than anything else. I walked over to the window in silence, not sure
what to think or say but for some sick strange reason I could
sense that Monica had actually won in her vindictive selfish
war she was waging on the marriage that we were desperately
trying to save.

I looked out the window in time to see Monica looking up at
me from across the street. Our eyes met briefly before she got
into her car and slowly drove away. I didn't know how to feel
at that moment. Because although Monica was driving away, I
knew that it was only symbolic. She would resurface and I had
a deep intuition that when and if she resurfaced that Jazz and
I probably wouldn't be together anymore . . .

Monica L. Tyler

I'm rich in love. I'm rich in peace. I'm rich in hope. I'm rich indeed. I'm read y. This is my time. All that I hope for is mine. It's mine, it's mine . . .

I never thought I would leave Philly, but that just goes to show how life can change when you least expect it. Yolanda wasted no time meeting the abundance of men the ATL had to offer. I got her a condo not far from mine so I could keep an eye on her. She was grown, but if I knew Yoyo, she'd be in trouble in no time, and someone had to bail her out, right?

As for me, I was taking it one day at a time. I will say that the first year here I missed my son so much that on a few occasions I packed a bag and was almost on the first thing smoking back to Philly to get him. Each time I got close to the airport or train station I turned my car around at the last minute. I had caused enough pain in James's and Jasmine's lives. I knew my son was in good hands, so there wasn't any need to interrupt a good thing. One day, maybe, we'd meet. I just wondered if I'd recognize him. Would he hate me forever?

It was almost six o'clock. I could finish this painting later. I had an appointment with my therapist and couldn't be late. Dr. Washington has helped me so much since I've been here, and it doesn't hurt that she's easy on the eyes either. But, I'm behaving myself and not going there.

I just wished for the best for my baby, James, and Jasmine. Hopefully, I would continue on with the therapy and if so I knew that I would be all right.

Plus I had bigger fish to fry. After my appointment I had a date with a certain Philadelphia Eagle who was in town for the weekend, and I didn't want to disappoint him.

I said I wasn't going back to Philly. I didn't say Philly couldn't come to me . . .

Jasmine D. Cinque

I look in the mirror and so much has changed. Ever since I had the babies, I just don't feel the same. Every day I'm working or nursing, not sleeping or eating. And my love life is slipping and I feel to blame. . . .

It seemed like overnight my family grew from four to seven. I've been shocked before, but not like I was when Monica left her child and that fucking note! How do you walk away from your own? But then again, who was I to judge her? I needed to be asking myself how could I continue to mislead James into thinking those babies were his?

Nothing is promised to you. You could be a wife today, divorced tomorrow. Your mother could leave and your family could disown you, but your children belonged to you forever. At first, I was against Monica's baby being with us, and told James to take the baby to the police, but then I realized that it wasn't just Monica's baby, it was also James's baby, and the second I laid eyes on him I knew he'd be a soft spot in my heart forever. Apparently Monica and her judge friends worked all of the kinks out, because once we signed the papers, James, Jr. was officially our son.

Monica never contacted us, and although we didn't need her money, a check for three thousand dollars came like clockwork every month. Some of it we used to buy him stuff, but most went toward his college fund. I guess that was pretty decent of Monica. After all, she did drop her child off on us.

Not too long after that Janice and Jordan made an entrance into the world, and we'd just been one big, "sometimes" happy, family since then. I'm seeing a therapist because I am determined not to let this depression get the best of me. James has been wonderful through it all, and I couldn't ask for a better husband.

Thank God he never actually pressured me into taking a paternity test. He apparently believed me when I simply dismissed Monica's words in the note as a boldfaced, cunning lie on her part. It tore me up inside to know that she was more than likely right. I reasoned that if I unconditionally loved and accepted the baby that James had fathered with Monica, then that would clear my conscience and it would serve as more than enough reason to have James forever believe that the new set of twins were his, and therefore, he would have no choice but to unconditionally love and nurture the lives of the two new babies . . .

James D. Cinque

And if there's anything I can do, let me know. I promise you I'll get it done, my pleasure. 'Cause I don't wanna see you struggling no more . . .

Life lessons. Some are easier to swallow than others, but all are worthwhile. If I had it to do all over again I'm sure there are things I'd do differently. In some respects, I'm glad I made the mistakes when I did. I've learned that the power of God is irreplaceable, and no matter how many times you fall, he'll take you back. He's forgiving, and always has his eye on you. I've also learned that vows of marriage are not to be taken lightly, and I cherish every day my wife and I have together. It's not every day you find your soul mate, and Jasmine is that in every aspect.

I felt bad when Jasmine suggested we take Junior to the police, especially when I didn't request a paternity test to see if what Monica was saying was indeed true. I'm a man, and I take care of mine. I started going through the baby's things and I found instructions from Monica to contact a guy named Judge Stenton and he would take care of everything. Soon after that, the newest additions to our family arrived. Sheila, surprisingly, helped us. She set Jasmine up with a wonderful therapist to help her with post-partum depression. She's doing better every day.

I'm steadily climbing the corporate ladder. I keep running into this fly honey from marketing on the elevator, but every time I think of dipping out, I think of Monica, and my ass is right back in place. I have a loving wife, wonderful kids, and a great job. Who could ask for anything more?

Jasmine Cinque
(Four Years Later)

All I asked James to do was pick up the kids from the after-school program. I mean, how hard was it to take responsibility for your own damn kids? It made no sense to me that I was called out of a business meeting because it was after six and no one had gone to claim my children yet. I say *my* children because it'd been years since James acted like they were *ours*. How embarrassing is that? This wasn't the first time this had happened either. Another reason why I was so irritated right now. You could mess with me all you wanted, but do not jeopardize my job or the safety of my children. It would quickly become a sticky situation for the accused.

What worked me the most was that I had to make two stops. Monica's son was a bit of a problem child so I had him in an entirely separate program from Jalil, Jaden, Janice, and Jordan. That meant I had to go get my kids first, and then go and get James's son. Now, I know that sounds harsh, but I really don't give a damn. I refused to take any claim to that boy. He belonged to James and Monica. The rest of these kids were mine.

To make matters worse, it was pouring down rain like we were in the middle of a tsunami, so visibility was down to practically nothing. It was a cold January night, and I hated driving in these types of conditions. When I got to Junior's program the instructor threatened once again to kick him out because he refused to just follow directions from either him or any of the aides who worked there. I wanted to snatch his ass up right quick and check him, but I told James that Junior would be his responsibility, and I was standing by it.

Every time I saw his face in the rearview mirror I wanted to pull over and choke the shit out of him. He looked so much like Monica, and he had her "I don't care" attitude as well. Why didn't she take her bastard son with her? I thought if enough time had gone by I could grow to love him like my own, but I just couldn't feed into the lie. He was conceived by my husband and birthed by a woman I'd once loved . . . still did. I hated myself for missing her, but my heart did what it wanted to do, so what could I do about it?

I hated the fact that I could still picture so vividly everything we'd done sexually. I'd given up on James a long time ago, so all I had was memories of Monica during quick masturbation sessions when I finally got some alone time. Hell, I had five kids to raise, so any "me time" I might have had in the past was a done deal now. I was okay with that sacrifice years ago when I was hype about being married and starting a new life. Now, I wished I would have just stayed the single whore I was. Life was much simpler then. Don't get me wrong, I love my kids, but I didn't sign up to be a single parent. That just wasn't a part of the deal. Now I had James to thank for this bitter-ass attitude. *Thanks, James!*

I'm not even going to go in on Monica's trifling ass. She got to live a carefree life doing whatever, wherever she lived, and I didn't even get to sleep in late on a Saturday morning because I had responsibilities. Then she had the nerve to send us checks like we needed them. Now, I'll be truthful and say that I had no problem cashing the checks she sent monthly like clockwork for her son because that money got me a new Benz that I drove when weather permitted and Jalil and Jaden a new wardrobe. If she thought I was using it for him then shame on her simple ass for leaving him here. I didn't want her son feeling anywhere near comfortable at my house so he got to wear hand-me-down clothes that Jordan could no longer fit into or I no longer wanted him to have, and if you had a problem with that you could feel free to come get him. I'd have his shit packed by the door ready for your arrival.

Time certainly did fly, though. With Jalil and Jaden being the oldest at eight years old, I had some help with my four-year-old twins and Monica's four-year-old, but there was only so much they could do. I refused to bog them down and burden them with the responsibility of taking care of a child at their age when all they wanted to do was have fun and be kids themselves. Janice and Jordan didn't know that Junior had a different mom, and it was really hard to tell considering they all looked like James. I mean, Junior had a lot of Monica in his features, but those were definitely James's kids. Where as the other kids looked like a combination of me and James, it was clear that Junior had a different mother. There was no denying it. So, I just left that bit of information on a need-to-know basis.

I wanted all of this Monica business to stop, and I hated that every time I walked into my house I could still smell her scent. When I walked into my kitchen I could almost see her perched on top of the table while James and Sheila joined her in a twisted orgy that almost got their asses killed. When I went into my bedroom my clit pulsated as I thought about the things she did to me. I could feel her hands touching me in places that James knew nothing about, and when I closed my eyes real tight I could almost feel her warm tongue kissing my nipples and trailing kisses down my stomach. Hell, on a good day in my imagination I would have her and the twins all at the same time. A pure mess, I tell you.

I had to get out of that house or I would've gone crazy, and so we did. We packed up and moved and I threatened James to not tell Monica a damn thing. I promised him I would set up a post office box so that her mail would be directed there, but I never did. We didn't need shit from her. The only reason she would need to know where I lived was to come and get her damn son. You can judge me all you want, but until you've walked in my shoes and lived my life for me there is nothing to discuss. I don't care how you feel about it. Point blank period.

I had been dialing James's cell phone for the past hour and it went from ringing to going straight to voice mail. That just pissed me off even more because that meant he was definitely ignoring my calls. The same damn way he had been ignoring his responsibilities for the last two years, but I had something for his ass though. Payback is a mutha, and when it all came down to it I would be cracking the hell up in the end.

That's exactly why when he got paid I made sure to only leave him enough money in his account to get gas and maybe buy lunch if I felt like being nice that week. Occasionally I would let him go down on me, but as soon as I was pleased and able to release he just ended up beating off in the bathroom to relieve himself. I did that shit to him every time, and his simple-ass constantly fell for it. It would be a cold day in hell before he would warm his dick with my walls again, and the sooner he realized it the better off we would be.

That's not to say that I didn't get it from elsewhere. Best believe I had a lineup if ever I needed a tune-up. I didn't have time to be fooling around with a maybe from James when I could get a definite from any given person on my contact list. Male and female included. My time was precious, and I didn't have a lot of it to be wasting on nonsense.

Most of the time I would get a quickie in my office from the secretary on the second floor in my office building before I left for the day, or I would meet up with any given person at this little hotel I found over in Mount Laurel, New Jersey when I really wanted to dip off and enjoy myself a little before it was time to pick up the kids. James never knew about it, and I just kept all that on the inside, hoping all of my secrets wouldn't just bust out one day. You can't keep everything in the dark for too long. It's just designed to come out in the light eventually. That's just the way of the world.

I had this little issue with those twins from Bally Total Fitness that I couldn't shake as well. They wanted a paternity test to see which one of them was the dad, but I wanted to leave well enough alone. I didn't bother either of them for child support so what was the big deal? It was a one-night stand, for heaven's sake. There was no need to go any further. Anything that happened after that was on me, and those were James's kids. All five of them. I didn't want nor did I need to prove anything otherwise. I thought I had gotten away with it until Monica wrote that letter, and even though James didn't deny Janice or Jordan, he had to think in the back of his mind that there's a possibility that they may have belonged to another man.

He did have a kid outside the marriage, but it's not the same thing as what I did, and my love for him wouldn't allow us to go through that kind of pain. Yeah, I still loved him, although the way we acted toward each other now you wouldn't think so. He just got on my nerves so bad sometimes. We had a lot of work to do, and had strained so far apart that neither of us really knew the first step to bring this thing back together. At this point did I really want to? Did *we* really want to? Was there anything to come back to?

After Monica wrote that letter to James telling him about the twins I had the threesome with to get back at him I wasn't sure where this thing with us was going to go. Dudes run they mouth too much though, and can't never keep nothing to themselves. A woman will cheat forever and never say a word. A man wouldn't even be out the pussy good before he ran running his mouth to anyone who would listen.

James didn't really react as bad as I thought he would. He could have very well just packed his stuff and rolled out, but guys will be miserable just for the sake of not wanting to pay child support. That was exactly why I ate his check up every time. I told him there was no truth to the letter, and at the time he seemed to believe me, but my gut told me that he really didn't. I guess he figured since he had done so much dirt himself he couldn't rightly crucify me for my shit, but he just never let it go. That's part of the reason why we were where we were in our marriage now, and another thing added to the list of why I hated Monica's simple ass.

The rain was coming down harder and I felt myself hydroplaning as I cut through small streets to avoid the end of rush-hour traffic on the expressway. My wiper blades weren't doing shit against the amounts of water that were beating down on my car, like the elements were angry at the decisions I'd made. I told myself to slow down when I slid through a stop sign and almost caused a major pileup a few blocks back. The kids looked scared and helpless, and I knew I would have to deal with my issue with James at a later date. The first thing I needed to do was get everyone home safely.

I called his phone again and this time he answered, but all I could hear was loud music in the background. I was steadily saying hello, but all I heard was a bunch of females laughing, and then the phone call disconnected. When I called back again the phone went straight to voice mail once again.

I was beyond pissed, and it took everything in me not to drive around the city and look for him so that I could string him up by his testicles and dangle him from a utility pole. He made me so sick! This weather was unbearable, and this twenty-three-degree temperature did not make January feel inviting, letting me know that 2008 just may be a difficult year to get through. I needed to make it home because the wind was starting to whip up something serious, and the rain started turning into sleet as we drove. I could see the fear in their eyes, and I knew it was time to wrap it up until I got to a safe place. The combination of the horrible weather and my reckless driving wasn't a comfort to anyone, considering that the car had already almost failed to stop and I even fishtailed a little a few times. Normally the car would be full of chatter from the kids talking among each other about their day, but on this day there was a deathly silence surrounding us.

I tried getting through to James a few more times as I half watched the road and typed him a misspelled text message at the same time. The angrier I got, the harder I pressed on the gas. I wanted him dead, and just as I sent him the message I looked up to see through the rearview Junior pulling at Janice's ponytail.

"Sit y'all asses back or I'll—"

Before I could finish my sentence I realized that I had pressed the brake, but the car was still moving. Everything seemed like slow motion as I slid out into the intersection and my Jeep was hit first on the passenger's side by a Hummer that was taking its turn at the stop sign, and then by another Jeep that collided into my driver's side in the back, causing us to spin out of control. I couldn't control the wheel.

The Jeep did a few quick spins, and all I remembered hearing was the collective scream from my kids as we crashed against the telephone pole. I hit my head so hard on the steering wheel right before it crushed me in, and I was seeing stars. My legs felt jammed under the dashboard, and the wheel was pressed so tight against my chest I could barely breathe. I heard the kids crying loudly, but then everything started to sound muted and all I saw was black.

James Cinque

This chick looked just like Monica. Chocolate-brown skin, kissable nipples, and all. She'd been gyrating and popping her pussy in my face for the last five minutes . . . working hard for this twenty I was holding in my hand. I was contemplating how long I should make her sweat, because if I added just ten more dollars I could get me a VIP session that would mean more than a mere lap dance. The J Spot had some of the best girls in the tri-state area doing a lot of strange shit for some change, and I contributed to their bills more often than I wanted to admit. Fuck it, I was a man after all. What did she expect me to do if I wasn't getting it at home? Keep stroking one out? There wasn't an ice cube's chance in hell that I was going to keep going out like that.

Jazz was messing up my groove though, just like she messed up everything else. I could hear my phone vibrating on the bar next to my shot of Hennessy, but I refused to answer it. I didn't feel like hearing her bitch because I didn't go and pick the kids up. I didn't feel like it. She was being a smart ass claiming she had to stay at work late, but I was sure she'd figure it out when the afterschool program called her because she was late. There was a fee to pay of five dollars for every five minutes you were late, but she had the money. Shit, she practically had my entire check so she'd just have to handle it. I knew she would be at least forty-five minutes late, so she could just spend some of my hard-earned money on something other than shoes and overpriced handbags.

Mocha, the Monica body double who was dancing in front of me, was a snake charmer. The way she moved her body made me sway with her. I couldn't help it. I knew she had to have a juicy pussy, too, and the more I sat there and thought about it the more I knew I had to get at it before I rolled out tonight. It was only right. She entertained me relentlessly every time I came here, so why not test the goods to see if it's worth it? I'd have been a fool not to.

There were two other girls dancing on either side of me, and the one girl picked up my phone while it was vibrating and pushed the talk button. I wasn't even fazed by the shit. I gently took the phone out of her hand, and when I saw that she had answered Jazz's call I just hung the phone back up. Fuck it. Shit was going to be off the chain when I got home anyway, so I might as well have enjoyed myself now. Only God knew when the next time would be that I would be able to get out and have fun after the all-night argument that would go down tonight, so there was no use in rushing home to the bullshit. Feel me?

Mocha bent down and took my phone out of my hand and inserted it in her juicy pussy. Climbing down from the bar she made her way over to the VIP room, and I had no choice but to follow her. After all, she did have my phone. The right thing to do would be to get it out before it started ringing again. My dick was straining against my Sean John slacks, and I couldn't wait for Mocha to release it. She had a wicked smile on her face that let me know I was in for a treat. I paid at the window and was escorted back to one of the many used rooms where I had a ball fishing my now dripping-wet phone from out of Mocha and filling the void with my stiffness. I wore her ass out for the entire thirty minutes I paid for because I knew once I got home it would be awhile before I could come back this way again.

It took me a little longer than it should have to get home because there was a real bad accident blocking Ford Road. The expressway was still a little backed up from the rush-hour traffic, so I had to sit in traffic either way until I found a street I could turn off on. The accident was indeed horrible. A utility pole was knocked down almost completely, causing downed wires on that block. You could see the medics working to get out whoever it was who was trapped inside of the wreck, and it didn't look like there would be any survivors. That just made me wish these people would move so I could get home a little quicker. That was someone's family in that Jeep: a loss no one was ever ready for.

It took me an hour and a half to get home, a trip that would normally only take me about thirty-five minutes. I didn't see Jazz's Jeep in the driveway, so I figured she might have gone to her mom's house before coming home. It was slushy and hailing outside, and I knew how she hated to drive in this kind of weather. I was still feeling a little tipsy from all the drinks I downed at the strip joint so I mellowed out on the couch for a minute before I went upstairs. I knew Jazz wouldn't be out too late so I at least wanted to be in comfortable clothes because I was sure we would be up for a couple of hours arguing.

I must have dozed off on the couch because when I woke up the nightly news was on, and someone was banging on my door. Jazz still hadn't come home, and I got an instant attitude because now she was taking shit too far. She was probably going to stay the night at her mom's, but the least she could have done was called. It was just like Jazz to be on some self-centered bullshit, so I wasn't surprised.

The banging on the door was persistent and I figured maybe she decided to show up after all, and needed help bringing the kids in. I took my sweet old time getting to the door just to piss her off even further. That accident that I went past earlier was being discussed on the news, but I had the television on mute so I couldn't hear what they were saying.

I had my screw face on when I opened the door, only to be greeted by Jazz's brother punching me in my face. He, along with a few of her uncles and her dad, took time to beat the shit out of me in front of my own house. I couldn't swing back if I tried because they were swooping down on me. The cold numbed my body just as fast as the blows from their fists and Tims, so I balled up in a fetal position until they were done.

Her father grabbed me by my bloody collar and pulled me up to a wobbly standing position. *I don't know what I did to deserve this, but Jazz has a lot of explaining to do. Damn, is not picking up the kids worth all this?*

"It's because of your stupidity that my baby girl is in the hospital," her father yelled at me before tossing me into the living room like a rag doll.

"What are you talking about?" I asked as I wiped blood from my mouth with my shirt. I was thinking I might have lost a tooth in the scuffle; I just couldn't tell at this moment.

Instead of answering, Jazz's brother picked up the remote and unmuted the television. I watched in horror as the accident I couldn't get by earlier was played again. I could see what I now recognized as Jazz's truck smashed up against the pole as the newscaster warned us that the scene would be graphic. They showed the Jaws of Life trying to pry open the roof of the car. Even though her license plate was scrambled I knew it was her car. I instantly felt like shit. *Why didn't I just go and get the kids?*

"Where are my kids?" I asked, my stomach feeling weak like I was about to vomit. Here I was out having sex with strippers and my wife was wrapped around a damn telephone pole. The look on their faces said it all. *Did my kids die? What happened with Jazz?* I broke down and cried like a baby. Was I such a horrible person that I would be punished like this?

"Save all those bullshit tears and go clean yourself up. We need to get down to the hospital as soon as possible," Jazz's brother barked at me as he watched the news play back the accident for what seemed like the hundredth time within minutes. I dragged my sore body from the couch, and went upstairs to get myself together. They really did a number on me, but I wasn't concerned with that right now. I needed to see what was up with my family.

When I got back downstairs I could see Jazz's uncles trying to console her father, and I didn't think I was ready to face the situation just yet. What if Jazz had died and they didn't want to say it right now? I felt myself hyperventilating as I was squeezed between the other men in the car. All kinds of crazy thoughts ran through my head as the drive to the hospital seemed to take forever.

"You better hope for your sake that everything is okay when we get there," her father warned from the passenger's seat. I couldn't say a word; I just closed my eyes and tried like hell to rewind the day so that I could do things differently. I knew we were going through shit, but my wife was all I had. Furthermore, and what seemed a whole lot worse, if something was indeed wrong how was I going to explain it to Monica?

Okay, so she rolled out on her son years ago, but that didn't mean that she didn't have the right to know that he had been harmed or even killed. No one could consciously deny anyone that right. I was a lot of things, but heartless wasn't one of them. If something happened to this woman's child then I would have to call and let her know. Simple as that.

Monica Tyler

Philly was a mess. Even more so was the flight over. There was so much turbulence I thought for sure we were goners a few times. I was so tense the entire ride, and as I looked around and saw people sleeping I couldn't understand how they could be. Were they at peace with God to the point that if they died it didn't matter? I had years of praying to catch up on, and I wasn't ready to go just yet. When the plane finally landed at Philadelphia International Airport and we had clearance to exit I was one of the first people off that joint, almost forgetting my carry-on.

I was glad to be back for a few reasons. For one, there was nothing like Philly. The air was different down here. The people were different, and the atmosphere just screamed pride. I loved it, and was seriously contemplating moving back. It'd been four years since I'd been home, and I couldn't wait to get back into the scene. The few times I did come back were to do exhibits, but that was work and I didn't get a chance to chill. I did meet this chic though, Jaydah B, and letting her come to Atlanta and stay at my place was a huge mistake.

Who knew she would be so clingy? She's this famous author right here from Philly who was killing the charts with her erotic novels. She was nasty too, and proved to be a bit of competition in the bedroom. Oh, some of the things she did to me had me like damn! I was giving her all I had and she was giving that shit right back like she knew what she was doing.

For some reason she thought we would just be laid up for two weeks, and that I didn't have a company to run. Besides, the Safe Haven and my art gallery didn't run themselves. Who did she think did all the leg work? Robots? In addition to that, I still photographed for several well-known magazine publications, and they paid me well so there was no way I was missing out on any of that money. When she wasn't out doing book signings she was on my damn phone wanting to talk and have phone sex. I had the lives of damaged teens in my hands that needed my attention, and possible buyers of my art so that I could make money. I didn't have time to fuck all day whether it was by phone or otherwise. She was on fire, and for the first time in never I didn't think I had what it took to turn her out. She wasn't shit like Jazz and Sheila; she knew what to do in the bedroom. She was just a tad bit annoying though so we cut that trip short. It was time for homegirl to go on home and write another book or something. Anything was better than her being in my damn face.

Needless to say, I was not happy when we arrived in Philly and the city was practically shut down. There were normally cabs lined up outside of baggage claim waiting for people, but today they were few and far between, and the line was extra long. I just needed to get to the Embassy Suites so that I could fall back for a second. Jaydah invited me to stay at her condo, but I declined. I had enough of her for the last week and a half to last a lifetime. Sexually, I would definitely hook up with her again, but right now she was riding hard on my nerves and I just needed some space. This was just a chill thing, but she was already acting like we were in a relationship.

The crowds of people who were stranded at the airport were nothing but a huge ball of frustration. People were ready to go home, and from the looks of it they would be sleeping in these hard-ass chairs at least until the morning. I barely made it here myself, and for a lot of people who were on the same plane I was, it was a connecting flight. All the boards had delayed signs coming in and going out, and the chatter of cell phone calls being made to loved ones was almost deafening.

I had no loved ones to call. My sister was out in Atlanta, partying hard as shit, and I'd been having trouble catching up with her for the last few weeks. I thought she would be cool once she made the Falcons cheerleading squad, but all she seemed to do was step her party game way up, and I knew she was sleeping with a number of the players on the team. Those eight balls she loved didn't seem to be enough for her anymore either, and her habit was out of control. I offered help, but she didn't think she needed it so there was nothing I could do but wait and see what happened.

My sister was the truth, too. I'd even have gone so far as to admit she was even prettier than me. Where I was dark chocolate, Yolanda was a smooth, flawless butterscotch. I had a nice ass, but Yolanda had a donkey that many a video chicks was jealous over. She had a nice full D cup that could go braless, and her jet-black hair reached damn near to the top of her ass, and it was all hers. She was the shit, but you could almost see the effects of her lifestyle wearing away at her face . . . almost. Yolanda stayed on point and you would never catch her half ass, and I just hoped she stayed that way.

After standing in line for more than an hour, pissed that I let Jaydah leave, not taking her offer to drive me to the hotel, I finally got a cab. The gypsy driver couldn't stop staring at my ass long enough to put my shit in the trunk, and I let him stare, too, because I knew this ride would be on him.

"Where are you going?" he asked me in a thick Indian accent, and I flirted shamelessly as I gave him directions. His cab smelled like a mixture of Old Spice and an Italian hoagie with all the fixings, but I thugged it out until I got to my destination. I didn't have a choice, being as cabs were scarce at the moment, and I didn't feel like waiting on another one after the rough flight I just had.

"I'm staying at the Embassy Suites on Bartram Avenue," I flirted shamelessly with the cab driver. He looked like he wanted to climb in the back seat and fuck me against the glass, and in my earlier days I probably would have let him. The Embassy was literally only about five minutes from the airport, and would cost no more than ten dollars to get there, but I didn't pay for anything I didn't have to.

This was going to be a quick ride, so I knew whatever I was going to do had to be done if I was riding for free. Searching the outside pocket of my carry-on, I pulled out my trusty pink vibrator. It looked like a thick plastic spoon that had a little dip in the middle of the circle for lubrication. It wasn't shaped like a dick or anything, so unless a person owned one, you wouldn't know what it was.

I turned the tip of it to the left, hoping my battery hadn't died. The buzz coming from my little toy indicated that I would be cool at least from here to the hotel, but I would need some batteries soon. The sound caught the driver's ear, and I saw him through the rearview mirror as we sat at the red light waiting our turn to go. Moving swiftly yet elegantly, I pulled my long dress up around my hips, and slipped one leg out of the tights I wore underneath to cover my bare bottom from the cold. The look on the cab driver's face showed that he was happy to see I didn't have any panties on.

After placing a small drop of KY Warming Liquid directly on my clit, I gave the driver a show as I slowly ground against the pulse of the vibrator. I used my free hand to spread my lips open so that he could get a good view, and I closed my eyes and leaned back as I worked magic on my quickly approaching orgasm. I moaned and licked my lips as thoughts of James, Jasmine, and Sheila took turns licking my pussy and fingering me. It was weird because I hadn't thought much about them in a while, and I guessed being back in Philly conjured up those feelings.

I was so lost in thought, I didn't even realize that we had already reached the hotel and the cab driver had pulled up behind the building instead of at the door. I could see slight drool form on the side of his mouth through the mirror as his right hand moved in a quick up and down motion indicating that he was jerking off. This was going to be easier than I thought. I noticed that the meter was still running, and he had to know I wasn't paying a dime if he got one off too.

"Miss Lady, your pussy sure looks like it tastes good. How can I find out?" the cab driver asked, his accent not as evident as when I first got in. That led me to believe that he only used it when necessary, and that this might not be his first time witnessing a masturbation session in the back of his cab. Eyeing the meter, I saw that it was now up to about fifteen dollars. Now, I was willing to pay ten if I necessarily had to, but anything more than that was not going to happen.

I let the thought spin around in my head for a second as my orgasm approached, and figured what harm could it be to let the man taste the best pussy in the world. After all, he probably never had anything like it before and wouldn't ever get the opportunity again. The look on his face said that he might tear it up, too. Shit, if he was any good I might have had to get his number before he pulled off.

"Okay, I'll let you taste it," I answered seductively while I removed my tights completely and slid my feet back into my Ugg boots so they wouldn't touch the dirty floor. "But this ride is on you. Understand?"

He simply smiled and got out of the car, exposing his rock-hard dick to the rain and sleet that was beating Philly to death. I turned sideways in the chair, and opened my legs wide for him to eat, lifting my dress up over my hips so that only my ass touched the seat. I didn't want to have to get out with a wet spot on my ass. He opened the back door of the cab, and his smile got wider when he saw I wasn't playing. He was working with some shit himself, and if it weren't for his foul body odor I might have entertained the thought of finishing this up in my room. Depending on how he handled his business I just might . . . after he showered of course.

The cab driver scrunched his tall frame into the back seat, and wasted no time placing my legs on his shoulders and devouring me. He practically sucked my entire pussy into his mouth, and I must say I wasn't ready for a beat down like that. If there were walls in the cab I definitely would have been climbing them.

He used his entire tongue to massage my clit, and took the liberty of inserting three of his huge fingers into my tight walls. I flinched a little because I didn't get a chance to see if his fingernails were clean, and I doubted if he had washed his hands at all today. My body paid my thoughts no mind as I bounced up and down on his hand uncontrollably, my pussy begging for release.

"Yeah, just like that," I moaned as I tried unsuccessfully to hold my orgasm a little longer. My walls began to clinch and I could feel my clit pulsate against his tongue as my honey ran out of me and soaked the back seat. The cab driver dove deeper between my legs, lapping up all of my juices from the inside of my thighs, and afterward his fingertips.

"Damn, that was good," he said right before his body stiffened, and he released all over the back of the front seat. The

sight of his babies sliding down the faux leather backing
and onto the floor made my stomach do a flip, but I kept my
composure.

He took a minute to catch his breath, then without a word
climbed out of the back, and took his position back in the front
seat like he was a limo driver, and I was a high-profile client. I
smiled as I watched him use his tongue to taste what was left
of me on the corner of his mouth. When we pulled around to
the front of the hotel, he jumped out and got my bags out of
the trunk while I gathered my stuff in the back seat. He even
insisted on taking my bags all the way inside.

"How much do I owe you?" I asked him with a sly smile on
my face, needing to make this quick because I could still feel
my honey running down the inside of my legs.

"Just take my number, Miss Lady," he said as he gave me
a business card to the cab company he worked for with his
number written on the back. "You can pay me back another
time."

I just smiled, and waited for him to leave before I gave
the receptionist my room information. I didn't need him
trying to creep back up here later on for payment. The bellhop
looked rather tasty, and I could feel him watching my ass
as I sashayed to the elevator. He never took his eyes from my
behind as we made our way to the top floor of the hotel, and I
made sure he knew to come back after his shift was over once
I was situated.

After I got comfortable in the room I looked out at the
snow that coated the city, and the mess that it was creating
for everyone. The real purpose of my being here reminded
me that I had to get on the horn and make some calls. I had
some business that I needed to handle, and first on the list was
finding out where my son was.

James

A World Apart

I can't breathe. I feel like the oxygen was taken out of this car, leaving me to suffocate in silence. I mean, I know there is air in here because the people surrounding me are breathing like it's nothing to it. For me, anxiety has my heart in a death grip and I can't . . . breathe. I'm spiraling out of control right now with madness, not knowing what to expect and how I'll react once I get to the hospital. What if Jazz and the kids are dead, or on their way to dying? What will I do without my family?

It's funny how they say in your last moments of life you see your entire existence flash before your eyes. I didn't think these were my last moments, but the past ten years ran in front of my eyes like a Lifetime movie. All of the ups and downs, and everything in between. The good, the bad, and the ugly. The most joyful times of my life, and the times when I didn't think I would make it through. I really wasn't that bad of a husband and dad, was I? Shit had been crazy at home and I needed a minute to regroup; I deserved that, right?

Okay, so I didn't need to unwind with a stripper, but when I couldn't even get some in-house ass what was I supposed to do?

Let it be known that I never stopped loving my wife regardless of whose mouth was on my dick. Jasmine gave me the gift of children, and a loving marriage at least for a few years. We had chemistry, and a genuine feeling of peace with each other. We could talk about anything, and our dreams were that much easier to achieve because we had each other. The key word was *had,* just in case you didn't catch that. We just lost our way kind of, and I was hoping God was as merciful as everyone kept saying He was because I needed her. I had been wilding out, and acting a fool, but I was done with all that now. I was ready to be a good husband, and bring all this mess to a standstill. I wanted our lives to go back to when shit was good and we had no worries. *I swear if Jasmine makes it through this I'll stop fucking other bitches . . . I think.*

Hell, who was I kidding? I thought I'd definitely need me a good therapy session to get rid of some of these demons. I was not on no Eric Benet shit with a sex addiction, but I liked me a fine-ass woman who was willing to fuck the shit out of me until I didn't have an ounce of cum left in my body. I couldn't help it, and I didn't think I really wanted to fix it. Shit, Jazz used to be that woman, but all the fussing and the cheating and the nonsense just got to be too stressful. She didn't desire me, and I no longer wanted her . . . it was bound to get crazy eventually. I just never thought we would be here at this point like this.

I couldn't think right now. It looked like we were heading toward University of Pennsylvania Hospital, judging by the houses that we were passing, but I couldn't concentrate on anything but breathing at the moment. *What if this is it? For real this time. Like what if this is the fucking end? I need space, but these goons ain't budging. I feel like I want to make a mad dash for it, and I'm feeling antsy.* The ride over to the hospital was the most agonizing ever. I felt like a piece of me faded away with every block we went by. This could really be the end for us. I mean, what if Jazz didn't make it through? What was I going to do without her?

On the way there we passed by the accident scene, and at that moment I wasn't so sure about my family making it out alive. The car was moved from the pole, but was almost folded in half where the middle seats were crushed in and things didn't look good from here. The tension in the car smothered me, and I wanted to break free but I couldn't. I was stuck between Jazz's uncle and brother, and they already warned me that if I cut up they would cut me up into little pieces. I had no reason not to believe them, because they were very protective of Jazz, and had warned me of that early on.

Honestly, I felt sorry for the kids. Anything that happened to me I probably deserved it, but the kids were innocent in this situation. *Speaking of the kids, how do I explain this to Monica if something happened to our son? She's going to wild all the way the hell out. I already know it.* I often wondered why she just never took the boy with her, but Monica was not the mothering type so I understood her motive. It was a bullshit move, but probably for the best in the long run for the kid.

From my position in the back seat I could see Jazz's dad in tears, the sobs racking his body as he tried to control the pain he felt. What did I do? Why didn't I just bring my ass home and deal with my family like a real man? The honest answer would be because I didn't feel like it. I felt like we'd been beyond repair for years. All because I let my lust come before the love I had for my wife. Dealing with Monica was a bad move, but I couldn't honestly say I wouldn't have done it again if I'd had the chance. I had yet to meet a woman who could satisfy me like her, even Jazz. I might have done things differently, but I wouldn't *not* try it again. That opportunity would be too good to pass up.

We pulled up to the hospital after what felt like days later, but we could only drive but so fast due to the nasty weather outside. I felt myself hyperventilating, but Jazz's brother gave me a look warning me to pull it together. I took a deep breath, and straightened my shirt after rubbing my temples. I didn't know what I was about to walk into, and I suddenly didn't want to be here. I was not ready to face the music just yet, but Jazz's father was looking like he was daring me to make a wrong move. Her country-ass uncles looked like they would willingly break every bone in my body on command, and on the real I didn't want it with these dudes by any means.

I could hear the receptionist asking something inaudible because I was in a daze and she sounded like the teacher off of *Charlie Brown* at this moment. My palms were sweating, and I felt overheated despite the cold chill that rushed in every time the automatic doors opened. *I'm not ready for this.* But at this point I knew I had to man up and brace myself for the unknown.

The ride up to the intensive care unit felt like forever, and I was kind of hoping that the elevator would just pick up speed and go straight through the damn roof. I didn't feel like this shit right now, and I was starting to get pissed off. *Why the fuck didn't she just pick up the kids and go the hell home? I've told Jazz time and time again to stop texting and driving, and when I didn't answer the phone the first million times she called she should have just let the shit rest until she at least got everyone home safely. What the fuck? It's like why? Why the hell is this shit happening? Where the hell are my kids?*

"What exactly happened at the accident scene?" I asked everyone, but it was like talking to empty air. No one even bothered to acknowledge that I was even standing there except to ensure that I hadn't run off. I was irked beyond belief, but I didn't feel like these fools jumping on me again so I let it go. Someone would have to answer me eventually.

The dinging of the bell indicating that we reached our floor stirred me from my ranting thoughts for a second. I was actually sizing these dudes up, trying to see who I could knock the hell out first and get away, but I was outnumbered and I really didn't want to make a scene at the hospital. I didn't want to see my wife like this.

I didn't see any kids in the waiting area, and I was scared to ask of their whereabouts so I decided to just wait it out. I would cold snap if my kids weren't alive, and a selfish part of me just didn't want to know that truth if that was the case. Not right now, and not like this. I saw Jazz's dad conversing with a fine-ass nurse at the nurse's station, and my mind wandered to her riding my dick, her huge ass smothering my balls and smacking against my thighs as she comes down on me. *What am I doing? My wife is in ICU . . . Focus, man, stay focused.*

"Let's go," Jazz's father said to me with a straight face, looking like he would hate to have to repeat himself. I struggled from my seat, not even remembering sitting down, the effects of the ass-whipping they gave me earlier starting to show in a small limp and a thumping pain behind my right eye. I was sure this was probably nothing compared to what Jazz was feeling, so I wasn't about to complain.

"Were you in the accident as well?" the nurse asked me as I walked by, but all I could do was shake my head no as I moved toward where I assumed Jazz and the kids were located. I couldn't breathe, for real this time, and I was starting to feel lightheaded as we headed down the hall.

"Are you okay?" the nurse asked as she stopped to prop me against the wall. I didn't answer, instead shaking my head in a quick side to side motion in an attempt to gather myself, and I could see Jazz's uncles looking like they were ready to jump on me if I didn't get it together quick. Taking heed to the threat, I straightened up and got it together.

"I'm fine, just take me to my wife," I managed to squeak out in a low tone as I stood up on wobbly legs and forced one foot to step in front of the other.

The tension in the hallway was so thick you could cut it with a knife, and I was sure both the nurse and the doctor felt it. I was psyching myself up so that I could face the inevitable, trying to make myself believe that it's not that bad even though we're in the intensive care unit. It could just be that they wanted to keep a close eye out on her. All of that went out the window when I got my first glimpse of Jasmine through the glass separating her from the hall traffic. Damn, I wasn't prepared at all for this.

"You're in the right place to die, homeboy," Jazz's uncle said close to my ear to ensure that I heard every word. "Straighten the hell up before you go in."

Nothing could have prepared me for what I was going to see when I approached Jazz's room. I knew she was going to be a mess, but this was nothing like the stuff I saw on television. I was expecting a bandaged head, maybe a little bruising on the jaw line, and even a cast-covered leg being supported by something hanging from the ceiling. I would have even gone for the arm being wrapped up and looking like a chicken wing. Just looking through the glass, all the tubes and bandages brought tears to my eyes. This shit just got serious real quick. With blurry vision I stumbled over to the bed where my wife lay comatose, and cried. Her face was covered with twisted shades of blues and deep purples, and her lips appeared to be sliced to shreds. I held her hand in mine, and kissed every scar from her bandaged fingertips up to where her elbow and hospital gown met. What the hell did I do?

"Jazz, if you wake up I promise to make everything right. I love you, baby. Please don't leave me like this," I whispered in her ear as my tears soaked the material covering her shoulder. This was crazy, and I just couldn't believe it.

I wished I had the power to change places with my wife. Only difference was I would have wanted them to pull the plug on me. She didn't deserve a constant fuck up like me in her life, and I was even considering leaving the marriage once she came through. Jazz deserved someone who would love her unconditionally and would be there for her always. At one time I thought I was that man, but now I was not so sure.

Monica: Bird's-eye View

Standing on the balcony, taking in the sights of the city, I gathered the fluffy terry cloth bathrobe around my shoulders courtesy of the hotel, as I sipped a cup of mint tea from a cute little coffee mug I found at the airport gift shop on my way to Philadelphia. Every so often the wind would pick up, violently swirling the snow around as sleet turned the streets into a humungous ice skating rink. My mom used to always say that when the weather was bad like this, God was angry with us. I could definitely see the truth in that. I personally played a lot into His anger as an adult.

My mind was spinning with all kinds of thoughts, and I didn't know where to start. What if I never found them? What if Jazz decided to try to fight me or something? Furthermore, what if we fell back into the same situation we had before? It was different, kind of, when it was just the two kids, but a five piece? That was a lot to juggle, and I wasn't willing to stretch my time or patience like that no matter how good the orgasm was. Furthermore, I couldn't bear being that close to my son without parenting him either. That was just too much at one time.

It'd been four years since I'd laid eyes on my son, and to be perfectly honest, I was scared of the outcome. Did he even know that I was his mother? He was practically forced on the Cinques, so if they never divulged that information to him it's only right, and there wasn't much I could say about it. They'd been more of a parent to him than I ever could've been then and now. I had the papers drawn up granting sole custody and everything. All they had to do was sign on the dotted line.

When I first split, James would send me picture messages of my boy growing up and walking around. I would cry just looking at them because I should have been there for all of those moments, but I was selfish and scared. What was I going to do with a baby? I was a mover and shaker, and I couldn't do that with a diaper bag on my hip. It got to be too overwhelming watching the videos and looking at the pictures, so without notice to him I changed my number.

I couldn't deal with the constant reminder that I might have made the biggest mistake in my life. The easiest thing to do was ignore it, and so I did. I'd lived my life for the last four years like I didn't have a child. I saw sending out checks to the Cinques for him like a bill I paid monthly. It was nothing to it: write the check, address the envelope, lick the stamp, and drop the shit into the mail. Easy as 1–2–3–4.

Pretty soon he wasn't even a thought and I moved on autopilot. Making sure my sister didn't crash and burn was a job in itself, and with running Safe Haven and my new art gallery my life was pretty full. A child wouldn't have fit in my plans anyway, or so I kept convincing myself. Yeah, leaving him here was the best move possible. Jasmine would love him like her own, and James would show him the ropes. Just the way it should be.

Why did the checks start coming back though? That was like the million dollar question in my head right now. Up until a few months ago the checks were being cashed and everything was good. I sent them more than enough to make sure my boy was properly fed, and clothed. Hell, the Cinques weren't exactly broke so he would have been good regardless of whether I sent a check or not.

I was even more surprised when I called James for the scoop and the number I had for him didn't work. Feeling desperate, I called Jazz already knowing the answer . . . Her number was changed as well. I had a friend of mine—more of a spy than a friend, honestly—go over to the house to see if they even lived there and it was reported back that the property had a for sale sign on it and the house was already empty. That was nothing but Jasmine's doing, but "why?" was the question.

So I called myself, using the voluptuous Jaydah B as a distraction, but she proved to be more of a distraction than I wanted her to be in an annoying way. I really couldn't enjoy her company the way I wanted to because I was trying to decide if I needed to show my face in Philly. She was just interested in achieving multiple orgasms. Rightfully so, after all, that was what she came to the ATL for, but damn. *Who knows, maybe I'll give her another chance when I'm less distracted, but I feel like my son needs me. I've never felt like this before, and I'm not sure why I'm feeling this now. I just hope I won't have to act a fool down here. Right now I come in peace; let's just hope I can leave the same way.*

James

A Midwinter's Night Dream

"James, pull some of it out, baby. I'll let you put it back in," Monica moaned into my ear while I deep stroked her to death. *She wanted me to go deep, and I had no problem meeting her request. The warmth that surrounded us was like we were wrapped in a cocoon near a hot spring, and the shit was driving me crazy. I hadn't had Monica in ages, and I almost melted when I slid into her.*

"James, pull it out, baby. Please, pull it out," she pleaded into my ear, following it up with a low moan that made goose bumps crawl down my back in the same spot where her nails just scratched my skin. I wanted to oblige, but it felt so damn good. Jasmine's pussy never felt like this.

"I'll pull some of it out, but I have to push it back in, understand?" I spoke into her ear as I went deep one more time.

"Yes . . . yes . . . yes. I understand, James."

She tightened her walls around my length, and wrapped her legs around my back, pulling me in deeper in spite of her request for me to pull out. I pushed her legs back so that she could let me go, and after scooting up on my knees I slowly slid my snake from her cave, causing her to shiver all over. With the head of my dick sitting just at her opening, I felt her pulsate as honey oozed from her opening, making the head feel slippery. I had to count sheep to keep my cool, and take control of the situation before we crashed it. She was about to get dicked down something serious, whether she was ready or not.

Monica held on to the headboard for dear life, tapping out because she couldn't handle it. I ignored her taps, slowly inching myself back into her wetness. My dick was brick hard right now, and I swore it felt like it was still growing the closer I got to an orgasm. I would push it in a little more each time, and pull all the way out until just the head was in. The feel of her opening clinching the tip and trying to suck me back in was driving me crazy. She was losing her damn mind, and on the low so was I. I loved a kinky chick in the bedroom, and Monica was all for it. All this shit talking and ass smacking had me feeling some kind of way. Damn, I think I love this girl.

"James, push it deeper, baby," Monica requested in between pulses. She didn't know what the hell she wanted me to do, and from the way she thrashed back and forth, causing her hair to halo around her, I could tell she was in on the verge of an explosion and that shit was turning me all the way the fuck on. I leveled my body above hers and used my feet to brace myself as I pushed into her until it felt like my balls could squeeze in. A gush of warmth coated my dick with a gooey stickiness that made me moan out loud my damn self. Oh, she was playing hardball tonight, but I was ready.

"You like this dick all up in you?" I asked her as I slow stroked her into another orgasm. The light scratching of her nails against my back, and her pleading for me to "take it" was answer enough. I went from an extremely slow pace to almost pounding her brains out, back to a slow crawl. I hadn't gotten fucked good by my wife in years, so I was going to make this shit count.

"James, please . . ."

"Please what?" I asked her, pulling all the way out. I stroked my dick in a lazy up-and-down motion as it pulsated in my hand. This bad boy was about to blow! Rubbing her creamy juices in, I leaned back on my knees so that I could catch my breath. I wasn't ready to bust just yet, but if she kept clinching up on my dick the way she was it was about to be a wrap.

"Please put it back in," she responded, panting loudly, trying to catch her breath as well.

Damn, she still had a gorgeous body, and I still loved her dark-chocolate nipples. She palmed her left breast, and pulled her nipple into her mouth, circling the tight bud with her tongue. I wanted so badly to be her tongue at that moment. *I remembered when Jazz used to be freaky like that. Monica was making it her business for me to forget Jazz, if only for this moment, and I was all for it.*

"What else you want to do with that tongue?" I asked her, pulling my legs from under me, and lying back on the bed, stretching out so that she could see all this dick up close and personal. Oh, I was gonna wear her ass out!

She had a wicked grin on her face as she switched positions in the bed, and rested her body between my legs, taking me all the way into her mouth down to my balls. I loved that she didn't have a gag reflex. Closing my eyes I let Monica enjoy my chocolate stick, pumping slowly into her mouth as she slurped me in. I cupped the back of her head to maintain control, but that shit wasn't working at all.

"Yeah, suck daddy's dick," I said in a low tone as I took hold of the back of her head a little tighter and guided the way. She ran a finger up the crack of my ass and pressed into the space under my balls, causing me to practically jump up from the bed. Damn, that shit felt good. Yeah, she's definitely a keeper.

Releasing the vacuum-like suction from the head of my dick, Monica stood up on the bed with her legs on both sides of me. Squatting down, she took me into her tightness, accepting my girth on the way in and juicing my dick with her walls on the way out. Lawd, how did I luck up on this?

"You gonna cum on daddy's dick?" I asked her while lightly pinching her nipples with one hand, and fingering her clit with my other. She was sloppy wet, and the friction from me smearing her juices across her clit was causing her body to tremor slightly. Seemed as if Miss Lady was losing her composure.

"Yes . . . yes . . . yes," she moaned as she swirled slowly on my pole. The heat emanating from her core had my dick like ten degrees warmer than the rest of my body.

"Yeah? Am I the best?" I asked her, taking full advantage of her weak state. She was grinding down hard, and I could feel my cream slowly rising to the top. She would rise up off of it, and then grind down onto it in a beat that was probably in her head.

"Yes, James, you're the best," she responded in a low tone that sounded extra deep for some reason.

"The neighbors can't hear you," I threw out there as I pinched her clit between my thumb and forefinger, causing her body to convulse uncontrollably until I let it go.

"James, you're the best, baby," Monica moaned out, trying to catch her breath in the process.

"Damn, girl, take that dick," I responded as I tried to keep my nut in my sac a little longer. I was about to plant a thick nut up in her that would permanently knock the back out her pussy.

"Mr. Cinque, it's time to wake up," Monica spoke to me, but her voice sounded like a man's.

When I opened my eyes everything was a blur, and all I could feel was the warmth of her pussy wrapped around my dick. I didn't know what was going on, but I was still trying to get my nut, fuck that.

I felt a hand on my shoulder and it felt like someone was shaking me, but I refused to open my eyes. I hadn't been stroked like this in ages, and I was going for mine. I could hear a man's voice talking to me, and Monica was steadily slipping away. I tried to hold on to her, but I couldn't.

"Mr. Cinque, wake up."

When I opened my eyes, standing before me was the doctor that was handling Jasmine's case. I was fully clothed with an evident hard-on. Sliding up into the chair, I tried to hide my erection and my embarrassment as he updated me on my wife's status with a look of disdain on his face. I already felt bad about what happened, and this man frowning down on me didn't make me feel any better.

Through the room I could see Jazz's family still sleeping on the uncomfortable set of chairs just outside the room. I guessed we all eventually dozed off some time during the night. Taking a peek at my watch, I saw that it was now seven o'clock in the morning. Looking over at Jasmine as the doctor listed her prognoses, I felt a little better knowing that Jazz had a good chance of survival, and that they were keeping her heavily sedated until the swelling around her brain went down.

"We will have to take her into surgery at the end of the day to wire her left jaw. The bone was dislocated in the accident, and will need to be mended in order to set properly. I do want to make you aware that Mrs. Cinque may be a little out of it when she first awakens because of the impact to her left frontal lobe," the doctor explained as I went into a zone.

As I listened to him tell me how the quality of life for Jasmine may potentially change, all I could do was stare at her. I mean, Jazz could be a real bitch sometimes, but she handled her business almost effortlessly, and I couldn't imagine her operating in any other fashion.

"Because of the head trauma, she will have pain accompanied by the discomfort from wiring of the jaw. We will have to assess her motor skills once she is awake and moving around, but she is responsive to touch in the state that she's in now," the doctor informed me as he continued to write in her chart, periodically making eye contact with me.

"There's a possibility that she may not remember who you are at first. In cases like this we often see some short-term memory issue that may or may not correct itself. Either she will remember you, or most of her memories will be from things that happened years ago."

He droned on and on about what to expect, and what type of help was offered to make the transition smooth. I wanted him to stop talking, but for a second I couldn't form any words.

"There is therapy for people with head injuries that will definitely aid in getting your wife's mind back on track, but as already said, we have to wait for her to wake up to see where she is in her mental state."

"Doc, I just need to know . . ." I said to him in a solemn voice. All of this was too much to handle at one time.

"What is it, Mr. Cinque?"

"Can you tell me where my kids are?"

Monica

Plan A

Morning came all too soon, and I hated that I neglected to pull the shade closed all the way. A sliver of sunlight beamed through the crack, and right into my eyes. I usually slept with a mask covering them, but I had forgotten to pack it in my haste to get Jaydah out of my house, and back in Philly. I decided, since my sleep was disturbed, I might as well get up and get going with my day. I had some investigating to do, and I wouldn't get anything done being laid up in the bed all day.

It was early, but I knew if I made a few phone calls I was bound to get things moving at least. I didn't want to do it, but I knew Judge Stenton would have to be my first call. Not that I planned to disrupt anything at the Cinques on purpose. If I needed to get my son and roll out I knew I would need some paperwork. Was I ready to be a mom? Hell no, but if I had to step up to the plate it was a now-or-never situation.

I had the number to his home, cell, and office, and I wondered briefly if Sheila would answer the phone at the courthouse. Still knowing the number by heart, I dialed the ten digits that could possibly connect me to the answers I needed. To my dismay the phone continued to ring, and I really hoped that maybe I had dialed the wrong number by accident. When the district court answering machine finally picked up, I hung up in disgust. After all, it was a week day; why wasn't anyone picking up?

Chancing a look outside, I immediately got my answer. Overnight the city got covered with snow up to our ears. I couldn't believe the amount that had fallen in that little bit of time. Trust and believe I did not miss all of this mess. Turning on the television to see what was going on in the world, I didn't need *Fox News* to tell me that the city was shut down. Such an inconvenience.

As I listened to the television, I gazed through the menu to see what was offered for breakfast. I contemplated whether I want to hit the judge on his cell phone, but I really didn't have a choice. I wasn't sure if he was with his wife and kids, or if he would throw shade since I didn't make it to the city the last time he wanted to see me. I also didn't know how much access he had to city business from home, but it was worth a shot. Just as I was going to pick up the phone, something on the news definitely got my attention. A car wreck flashed across the screen, followed by a picture of Jasmine. Grabbing the remote, I turned the volume to the max:

"Prominent Philly lawyer Jasmine Cinque has been reported to have been in an accident that has her in the ICU. Due to the quick dropping of the temperature last night, it appears that her car spun out of control and smashed into a utility pole in the Bala Cynwyd section of Philadelphia after slipping on an ice-covered roadway. The medics had a hard time getting to her due to the inclement weather, and had to use the Jaws of Life to extract her and her five children from the wreck. It has been said . . ."

At that moment my mind went numb. *Jazz almost died? Or did she die? Wait, the newscaster didn't say she was dead, so she's still breathing somewhere. What happened to the kids?* They didn't say anything about the children, and when I opened my eyes to look at the TV they were showing footage of her car wrapped around a pole, and you could see the medics trying to open her car like a can of tuna.

I was instantly sick, and had to rush to the bathroom before I vomited all over my nightgown. What happened? Furthermore, why was she out in that mess yesterday? Jazz hated driving when the ground was wet, so I needed to know what or who forced her out yesterday in the midst of a storm. My eyes burned from the tears that I refused to let roll down my face. *Damn, did I still love this chick? And where the hell is James?* They didn't say anything about his whereabouts. Did they divorce? Maybe that was the reason why I couldn't get in touch with either of them.

Pacing back and forth, I knew I had to get out of this hotel and on the street. I needed to see about renting a car, and I needed to call the hospitals to see where they were. *Wait a minute . . . let me slow down and think rationally.* I needed answers, and being in a panic was not going to help.

The ringing from my cell phone startled me out of my thoughts, and I dived across the bed to catch it before it stopped, wondering who it was. The only other person who knew I would be in Philly was my sister, and I hadn't spoken with her since I landed so I hoped nothing happened. I wrapped up business before I left Atlanta so I knew the call wouldn't be directly related to that either.

"Hello?" I answered without looking at the screen. My heart was racing a mile a minute. Did something happen to my sister? Was it a company issue? Did someone break into my house and the alarm company was contacting me? All kinds of bad thoughts ran through my head as I waited for the caller to respond.

"Hello, stranger." The voice came through the other end and I couldn't help but smile.

"What a pleasant surprise. I was just thinking about calling you."

"Is that so? My wife told me she saw you in the hotel lobby checking in yesterday, and it made me wonder what brought you back home."

Was it coincidental that just the person I needed to talk to was calling me? When I changed my number I made sure Judge Stenton, among others, knew how to reach me for whatever reason. Hell, he was a very influential man to keep around. Aside from spectacular sex, he donated a lot of money to both my art gallery and Safe Haven, a girls' home for teenagers who had been sexually molested.

"And she didn't say hello? That's odd."

"So what are you doing back here?" he asked, cutting the small talk short.

"Well, for some reason I've been getting the checks back that I send out to the Cinques, and . . ." I explained everything to the judge, even what I just saw on the news about Jasmine being in the hospital. I needed answers, and I needed to know what was going on.

"As far as your son goes, Monica, you gave him up so I don't know what can be done there unless he's being abused. What exactly do you want from them? They stopped accepting your checks? So what! They just may have needed to move on, and didn't need a constant reminder of the role you played in their past."

"But they were cashing them up until recently. It doesn't make sense," I screamed into the phone. He tried to make it seem like I was the crazy one, but in knowing the people I was dealing with, I knew there was more to the story than that.

"How long are you staying here?" the judge asked in a nonchalant voice like he was done with talking about the issue. We were going to talk about it, but I had to play things cool if I was going to use him later. I had to make him think we were doing things on his terms.

"As long as it takes."

"Okay, you can't possibly stay in a hotel that long so as soon as the streets are cleared and I can get out I'll have a car come to get you. You can stay in the hideaway until you get what you came for. For now, just lay low. The city is shut down, so you can't go anywhere anyway."

"Thanks for everything. I owe you one!" I said into the phone as I calculated what my next move would be.

"You sure do, and I plan to collect on it. We'll talk by the morning."

After I hung up with the judge, I decided to at least put something in my stomach as I continued to watch the news. Jazz's story was top news, and I was just waiting for James to show his face. I knew I would need to speak with him, and I wasn't too sure if I was ready for all that. After all, I did wreck what was left of his marriage and dropped an unwanted baby on him. His reaction to me being here would determine if I kept my cool. Hopefully he would just be cool about it and give me the answers I needed. I had no problem going away quietly like I was never here, provided that everything was in order. Now, if it was not in order, then the circumstances of my visit would not be pleasant.

Ordering breakfast was a breeze, and I was elated to see that fine-ass bellhop when I opened the door. He must have held a couple of jobs at the hotel, but I wasn't mad about his hustle. I opened the door wider to invite him in to set up my food in the kitchen area of the suite. Damn he was fine, and I know you're thinking how I could be thinking about sex at a time like this. Easy, my pussy had a mind of her own and she liked to be fed as well.

"Are you the dessert?" I asked him in a seductive voice as I came out of my robe and stood there naked, allowing him to take in all of my curves. He looked like he had hit the jackpot! His eyes seemed to glaze over, and the way he licked his lips was like he was ready to eat me up.

After securing the door, I sauntered over and climbed up on the counter, putting my pussy at mouth level. All he would have to do was bend at the waist and taste it. He seemed to be in shock, so this had obviously never happened to him before. He would surely tell the entire hood about it later on. Grabbing him by the collar and pulling him closer, I leaned back on my elbows to balance out.

"Eat up," I practically whispered to him. Sparks shot through my body when his tongue connected with my clit, and I knew I was going to wear his ass out before he left. I just had to dig out my condom stash from my luggage and it would be on. That didn't mean I forgot about Jazz and James. I'd most definitely be dealing with them later.

James

Live at Five

Since Jazz was a prominent lawyer in the Philadelphia area, I was asked to speak to the public on her behalf, giving everyone an update of her condition. The conference was scheduled to be held later in the day. The city was snowed in overnight, and I was starting to get cabin fever since we were all stuck in the hospital until the cleanup of the city was over. Between trips to the cafeteria, and avoiding the looks of hatred I was getting from Jazz's family, I was ready to blow this joint. True story. It wasn't until the doctor left that Jazz's father decided to clue me in on my children's whereabouts.

"So where are the rest of my kids?" I asked once again when Jazz's dad walked into the room. After getting over the initial shock of seeing my wife in her condition I needed to do a headcount of everyone else.

"The kids are with their grandmother at your brother-in-law's house. All of them were discharged shortly after they came in, except for Jordan due to his injuries," he explained in a sympathetic voice.

"So why did it take so long to get an answer? I've been asking about my kids since last night!" I came back even more frustrated.

"James, you needed to focus on one thing at a time. Trust me, it was for your benefit."

I looked at him like he was crazy. I was guessing that he had already talked with the doctor about who would break the news to me about my son, but it pissed me off that he waited this long to even say something to me. I could have gotten this info on the ride over here. The look on his face had me holding my breath, and I broke down in tears when he told me that all of the kids were okay, but Jordan was in intensive care in the children's ward of the hospital. Children's Hospital was in the next building, but because of the time they came in and the extent of the injuries they kept both him and my wife in the same facility. He asked the doctor to allow him to tell me because he figured I probably wouldn't be able to handle dealing with both Jasmine and one of my kids being near death at the same time. That was hilarious to me that he all of a sudden was concerned about how much I could handle, considering they tried beating me to a pulp not too long ago.

I fell to the floor in a barrage of tears as I curled up in a fetal position wondering what I had done that was so bad that the karma would come back and destroy my family. I mean, I wasn't a monster. I wasn't molesting little kids, and robbing banks or anything like that. I just stepped out on my wife sometimes to be with other women, but what man didn't? Did I really deserve all of this? I asked God why this was happening, and I needed answers now!

"Mr. Cinque." I heard the doctor's voice as I gathered myself from the floor and sat back down in the chair to catch my breath. "Mr. Cinque, I'm sorry about all of this, but I need to talk to you about your son. I'll need you to come with me."

I didn't have the energy to respond, and on weak legs, I got up and managed to drag my body down the hall after him. It was like my body was numb, and I couldn't form any logical thoughts. I wanted to break loose from this place and go back to the day before yesterday so that I could do it all over again. I thought about making a break for it and jetting from the hospital, but where would I go? Jazz's family would just come find me and beat the shit out of me again. I just wasn't ready to deal with all of this, and although I was sure leaving the situation wouldn't make it better I just didn't want to be around. I needed a do over.

When we got to the doctor's office, I took a seat in one of the leather chairs that sat in front of his desk. Eyeing the photos of his family that were strategically placed around his office made me sad. The smiling faces of his wife and kids made me pray even more that everything with Jazz and Jordan would come out okay. I just couldn't take any more bad news.

Looking through the file, the doctor looked like he was trying to formulate the right words to let me know what was going on with my family. I wondered if he ever cheated on his wife. From the pictures he looked to be in love and living a happy life, but I knew enough to know that a picture didn't tell the entire story. A picture was just a snapshot, a brief moment in time that was captured by chance that we could never get back again. It wasn't real life, it was just a moment.

"Mr. Cinque, your son will need a blood transfusion," the doctor explained in a sympathetic voice. "Since your wife is already in a fragile state I'm suggesting we get the blood donation from you as opposed to getting it from the blood bank and risking your son contracting hepatitis down the line," he explained to me. I could see the sorrow in his eyes, and I wondered briefly if it was genuine or if he was just doing his job.

"That's not a problem. How is my son doing? Can I see him?" I asked, trying to control the tears that made my chest ache all over again.

"You can see him, but I have to warn you that there are a lot of tubes exiting his body. He is on a breathing machine as he cannot breathe on his own from the puncture wound that has been fixed in his right lung. He got the worst of the damage because his side of the car was the side that struck the pole and was wrapped around it.

I felt like I was going to pass out. I wasn't built for this kind of shit, and I knew I had to get some strength from somewhere to deal with it. Accepting a tissue from the box the doctor held in my direction, I got myself together so that I could handle my business. I had to be strong for my family.

"Thank you for everything you've done so far. Can I please see my son now?" I asked in a voice that I didn't recognize.

"Yes, I'll take you out to see your son, but we need to stop past the outpatient lab first to collect your blood so that we can get it ready for him. Do you know your blood type?"

"No, I actually don't," I responded, feeling stupid that I didn't know that information. I didn't regularly donate blood or anything like that, and before now I had no real reason to be up on the kind of thing.

"No problem, we get that a lot. We will get all of that information once we send up the samples."

I followed the doctor into a sterile lab that was on the next floor down, where several tubes of my blood were taken. They could have taken every drop of blood from my body at that moment if it would save my son. I remembered it like it was yesterday when I saw him come into the world. His tiny hands and feet, and those eyes . . . it was something about him that I just couldn't place, but the joy of seeing him replaced all of the questions I had in my head. Our family had grown, and that's all that mattered.

The phlebotomist expertly drew my blood, and I could tell she tried not to stare at the scars on my face. When she inquired if I was in the accident I just told her I was to keep down the confusion. She didn't need to know my business. Once I was bandaged up I was escorted to my son's room, where the doctor waited for me outside. The curtains were drawn so that I couldn't see inside, and I was grateful for that. I wasn't prepared to just walk up on him like I had been forced to do with Jazz. I needed to get myself together for this one.

"Mr. Cinque—" the doctor began, but I cut him off.

"Please, call me James," I insisted.

"James," the doctor continued with a look of concern on his face, "your son is in critical condition, but he is stabilized. You're going to get emotional, but please be aware that although he is sedated he can still hear you. I'll be standing right out here if you need me."

He gave me a reassuring smile, and backed away from the door, allowing me to enter on my own. I stood at the door, trying to steady my breathing and brace myself for the unknown. I never imagined having to see any of my kids like this and the shit was really tearing me up on the inside.

When I opened the door tears flooded my eyes, and my feet felt stuck to the floor. *If I could only trade places with him.* There were tubes everywhere pumping different colored fluids into his little body. The machine that controlled his lungs made a soft swishing sound and a small beep permeated the air every so often. My baby . . . he was only four years old. If he didn't come out of this alive I couldn't possibly keep living.

As I finally crept toward him I wondered what Janice would do without him. They'd been joined at the hip since conception, and moved like synchronized swimmers, often finishing each other's sentences. She was too young to understand death, and I hadn't the slightest clue how to get a four-year-old to understand that her best friend would be gone forever.

Placing those thoughts aside, I went over and took my son's small hand into mine. Looking into his swollen face, I could hardly recognize him beyond the bruises. He had his mother's lips though, and I leaned down to brush my lips against his cheek to let him know I was there. Placing the chair next to his bed, I took a seat and leaned into the bed so that I could whisper into his ear. I needed him to come back to me as soon as possible.

"I love you, son," I began, getting choked up immediately. "And I want you to know that we're all waiting for you."

I held his hand as the tears cascaded down my face and wet the side of the bed. I promised God that if He pulled my wife and my son through this I would be the man He intended me to be. I had promised Him this many times before, but this was the straw that broke the camel's back. I had to get my family unit back together.

"Mr. Cinque." A nurse came to the door, interrupting my racing thoughts. "The news vans just arrived. Do you want to get cleaned up a little bit? One of your associates from T.U.N.N. brought you a change of clothes for the press conference."

Looking down at my son, I gave him a kiss on the cheek, hoping it wouldn't be my last. Letting his hand go, I followed her to a private room where I was able to shower and change my clothes, afterward meeting back up with Jazz's family right outside of her room. There was nothing I could do about the black ring that had formed under my right eye, or the scratches along the side of my face and neck, and at this point I didn't care what the media thought. I just needed to update the world on my wife and keep it moving.

"Is it possible for me to have a minute alone with my wife before I go out?" I asked one of my associates, who came to capture the story among the other news stations that would be present.

"Sure, but we go on in ten."

Nodding my head, I stepped into my wife's room, closing the door behind me. As I looked down at her I remembered our wedding day, and how hype we were about getting back to the hotel to consummate our vows only for us to fall asleep when we got there. I remembered how she went from having a flat belly to carrying a huge beach ball that held our first set of twins. I remembered how much I loved her, and how I needed her in my life.

"Jazz, I need you back," I spoke into her ear as I held her hand. "Our kids need you . . . and I need you. Please, make it back to me."

Kissing her on the cheek, I dried my eyes with the back of my hand and straightened my tie in the reflection off the glass. Getting myself together as best I could, I went out and prepared to talk. Jazz's family seemed less angry and more supportive, and I was relieved that they were no longer throwing daggers at me with their eyes. We were all scared, and concerned, and I understood how they felt.

When I stepped up to the podium in the hospital's conference room I trained my eyes on the camera and tried to check my emotions. The tape hadn't even started rolling good, and I was already in tears.

"I regret to inform you that my wife and son are both in intensive care from the accident. From what I understand, the car slid out of control on an icy street in last night's storm, causing the accident," I explained to the media, getting choked up and having to stop several times. I tried my best to continue, but it got extremely hot all of a sudden and I felt like the room was closing in. All I heard next was somebody call for a doctor as I hit the floor, and the room went black.

Monica

Let the Truth Be Told

My eyes were glued to the TV as I stopped mid-pack to listen to the press conference that James was giving on Jasmine's status. My heart sank when he said that his son was hurt as well, but he passed out before everyone could get the rest of the scoop. Was that my son he was talking about? They had three boys; which one was it?

I sat on the bed and waited for them to come back with the broadcast, but it seemed as though that fool might be out for the count for a while. The accident site from the previous night was shown again, and I cringed on the inside at the sight of the Jeep wrapped around the pole and the medics working the Jaws of Life to get them out. They all could have died, and from the looks of the tragedy many people might have thought they already were dead if they hadn't seen the news coverage.

Just as I grabbed my phone to call the judge it rang, flashing the judge's name and picture across the screen. The car he sent for me must have arrived, and I wasn't even halfway packed because I was distracted by the breaking news. The judge didn't like to be kept waiting, and I knew I had to get moving or he would get an attitude.

"Hey, baby," I spoke into the phone in my sweetest voice.

"Monica, the car is outside. Time is money, and I've been sitting here with a brick-hard dick for way too long."

My smile was wiped away immediately, and I started to give it to his arrogant ass and read him his rights, but I still needed him. *This one I'll let slide, but I can't say I'll be that nice the next time.* The judge knew who was really running this show, but I let him feel like he had the upper hand so that I could keep getting my way. It was so much easier and stress free.

"I'm walking out the door now," I responded through a forced smile.

"That's what I like to hear," he said in a deep voice, sounding like he might have been stroking himself in anticipation. "Oh, and Monica?"

"Yes, Judge?" I responded as I threw the last few things I owned in my bag.

"Wear a trench coat and red heels . . . nothing else."

"Yes, Judge," I responded flirtatiously and began removing my Ugg boots from my feet. The judge had long money, and for him nothing was off-limits. Never mind it was dead winter and about five whole degrees on the outside. He always got what he wanted . . . and I got whatever it was I wanted. *This time, it's for my son.*

After quickly changing my clothes, I called to have my bags taken down to the car. Of course my sexy little bellhop friend showed up looking sad because I was checking out, and I wished I had a few extra minutes to break him off before I left, but money called.

Once my bags were stacked neatly into the trunk I was whisked off to what would be my home while I was here in the city. I tried to bring up the news on my phone just in case James came back to finish out the report, but I couldn't get a live stream. While I was riding, I couldn't help but wonder what my son looked like now. He probably looked like James, as the rest of his kids did.

Honestly, I wondered if I was doing the right thing. Who was I to come and disrupt this boy's life after I abandoned him like last season's Louis Vuitton? Did I even have the right to be here preparing to wreck shop? I entertained the thought of just spending the week with the judge until the coast was clear and I got enough money from him, but that tight feeling in my gut told me I needed to be here. Something was about to pop off, and I felt like my boy needed me. Pulling out my iPod to sooth my nerves, I connected it to the USB port in the stereo system, and turned up my Floetry CD. I needed to get my mind off of the problems I was having because I knew once I got to the judge I would need to focus all of my attention on him.

I must have nodded off, because when I opened my eyes again the car was pulling up into the circular driveway of the judge's getaway spot.

The driver came to a gentle, rolling stop, and jumped out to assist me in getting out. Gathering my trench coat around me to protect me from the wind, after checking that my face was still intact, I slipped a Tic Tac in my mouth and strutted up the walkway to the door like I was on a runway in Paris during Fashion Week.

Taking the steps one at a time, I knew I looked scrumptious, and felt sexy as the crisp air caressed my moist clit when my legs parted to take a step up. Before I could touch the knob, the judge had swung the door open and was standing there himself in a house robe and slippers with a tobacco pipe dangling from his mouth. Damn he looked good.

Forever the distinguished gentleman, he smiled as he stepped back and removed my bag from my hand. I sauntered past him, knowing his eyes were traveling the length of my body, and he was removing my trench coat in his mind. I turned to face him just as he was giving the butler orders to take my belongings up to the master bedroom, and to leave out of the back door. Finally facing me, I did just as he did and took all of him in.

He was still extremely sexy. Smooth skin, thick lips to match his even thicker dick, and a fresh cut. He looked a little older . . . wiser, most would say, and I could see a little more gray peeking up at his temples and throughout his beard. Yeah, he still had it. He walked over to me with a confident swagger like he already knew he had me dripping wet. Once he got over to me, he took my hand in his and raised it above my head, turning my body in a small circle. Stopping me when I was facing him, he planted a sensual kiss on my lips, stepping back only to untie the sash on my coat.

He looked pleased as he slowly opened my coat to reveal the surprise inside like he was unwrapping a Hershey's Kiss. Of course I kept a flawless body, and the look in his eyes let me know that I was indeed the truth. He ran his tongue across his lips, tasting the corners like he was hungry and ready to eat. Leaning forward he took one chocolate nipple into his mouth, moaning out loud, and then took the other doing the same. I kept a serious face, thankful for the heat on my back from the fireplace. I didn't want him to know he had me open that fast.

Turning in my heels, I stood still as he removed my coat from my shoulders and allowed it to pool around my feet in a soft puddle of cashmere and silk. Stepping over it, I catwalked toward the chaise longue because it was closest to the fire, making sure he saw my plump ass bounce with each step. He always told me I could have been a model, and I kept a flawless tight body just to keep him guessing.

Stretching out on the chaise with one leg bent at the knee, and the other on the floor, my legs were partly open waiting for him to come and taste me. He circled the chair smoothly, stopping to take in the vision. The flames cast shadows all over my body as I glistened like a shiny new penny. I could tell he was trying to go slow with the flow and not bum-rush me. It had been awhile since he'd had me like this, and he was savoring the moment.

As he got closer he came out of his robe, revealing a tight, muscular chest and flat tummy that I didn't quite remember him having. Somebody had been working out, and I liked it. He had the body of a man in his early thirties, and it was too bad he didn't have the stamina to match. He was usually known for only lasting a good ten minutes; that's why I would always milk the hell out of a foreplay session. *Who knows? Maybe this new body came with new dick control?* I smiled, showing him I was pleased.

He moved toward me, kneeling beside me, spreading my legs wider. My pussy glistened with a sticky wetness that he wasted no time sticking the tip of his tongue in. Catching my clit between his lips, I gasped as he sucked and slurped me into his mouth causing my body to convulse. His huge hands delicately caressed and pinched my nipples sending shock waves through my body. I couldn't control my pelvis from grinding into his face, smearing a glazed layer all over it. I moaned and bucked under him as he lifted my leg up and placed it over his shoulder so that he could get closer.

An orgasm started building up in my gut, and I was trying my best to hold it in, but the judge was steadily dragging it out of me. He fucked my pussy with a stiff tongue that had me ready to pass the hell out, and just when I thought I couldn't take any more the floodgates opened, and I released a river of honey down his throat and all over his neck.

"Please, let it go . . ." I begged as he held my clit captive, forcing wave after wave of orgasmic pleasure to crash against it, making me delirious. I must say I didn't remember the judge being this phenomenal orally, and I silently gave kudos to whoever taught this old dog some new tricks.

His fingers invaded my space, and caused me to jump as he stuffed two of them inside of my tight, wet hole. I bounced up and down on them like I was riding a good stiff dick, bringing myself to another mind-blowing orgasm that almost wiped me out. Somebody was playing for keeps, and I was not mad about it at all.

He licked me slowly from my opening to my clit allowing me to calm down and control my breathing. I swear if he had a close neighbor they would have thought someone was trying to kill me with all the hollering and screaming I just did. I felt like he literally sucked the life out of me, no pun intended. I knew for sure I was going to have to put in some work after that performance.

He rose up from between my legs with a glazed but a happy look on his face. His pajama bottoms tented in the pelvic area letting me know he was ready to go in. I sat up and took hold of it, stroking it through the material of his pants, causing his eyes to close and his head to lean back. A small circle started to form from the pre-cum that I was pulling from him, and I hoped he would last this time.

Using my feet to pull his pants down, I continued to stroke him, taking the liberty of tasting the clear fluid that dripped from the head of his dick. He seemed to have gotten bigger, the mushroom head barely fitting in my hand. Closing my mouth around the head, he moaned as I took him into my mouth an inch at a time until he was balls deep into my throat. I had learned a trick or three myself, and I was more than willing to show him.

Massaging his balls, and inserting a finger into his asshole at the same time, had the judge screaming louder than I was as his legs began to tremble. He tried to back away from me, but the sensation was too good and he leaned toward me instead. Releasing him, and gargling his balls in my mouth had him on opera status and I knew I had him just where I wanted him.

Letting him go completely, I leaned back in the chaise and massaged my swollen clit, palming my breasts with the other hand as I leaned down to take my nipples into my mouth. The judge struggled to get to his knees, and came down into a kneeling position on the chaise right in front of me. Just as he was aiming his dick for the target, I stopped him.

"What's wrong, baby?" he asked between gasps as his dick twitched in his hands. I simply swung my legs around him and stood up.

"We can get back to this in a minute," I told him in a serious tone. "Right now, I need to know what's up with my son."

James

Day-mares and Night Dreams

When I came to I was stretched out in a hospital bed with a bandage on my head. The last thing I remembered was doing the press conference, and everything went black. I couldn't even remember if I got everything out, but I knew for sure that my head was pounding like crazy. When I opened my eyes a nurse was leaning over me taking my vitals, and shining a light in my now open eyes.

"Mr. Cinque, that was a pretty nasty fall you took," she said, smiling down at me while checking my head dressing. My dress shirt was now gone, and all I had on were my slacks and a wife beater. Through the window I could see Jazz's family talking with the doctor.

"What happened? All I remember . . ." I began, but she cut me off.

"Don't talk. I just gave you pain medicine for your headache so let it kick in. The doctor will be in to talk to you shortly."

Taking her advice, I nestled into the pillow and closed my eyes, trying to slow down the drums pounding on my temple. What was going on in my life? I said a quick prayer, hoping some mercy would be thrown my way. When they say "what goes around comes around" they weren't lying.

"How are you feeling?" Jazz's brother asked as he entered the room. My head began to pound more upon seeing him. When were they going to leave?

"I'm okay. Head killing me." I gave a dry response. It was obvious that my damn head hurt considering it was bandaged up. I wasn't sure of what happened but I must have banged it up when I passed out.

"Yeah, that was a pretty nasty hit. They had to wheel you out on a gurney and everything. Of course the media was snapping pictures left and right, but they got you out fairly quickly. Glad to see you awake."

"Thanks, man," I responded before closing my eyes again, hopefully indicating that I was done talking. Too much was happening too fast, and I just needed some quiet. That was short-lived once I heard the doctor enter the room.

"Mr. Cinque, glad to see that you're up. That's a nasty bump you have on your head there, but the CAT scan came back normal, and there are no signs of any internal damage. You just have a pretty nasty gash where your head struck the podium," the doctor spoke to me in a calm tone as he looked over my chart.

"Thanks, Doc," I spoke to him in a groggy voice. "Is the media still here? I need to finish the update."

"What you need to do is rest. You've been through a lot in the past twenty-four hours, and you need to relax yourself. I need you to be on your A game for your wife and son."

"And how are they doing?" I asked, hoping nothing drastic had happened while I was unconscious.

"Your wife and son are still in stable condition. The blood that you gave is in the lab being tested for any trace of disease as well as to identify your blood type since you didn't know that information just as I explained to you earlier. It shouldn't take much longer, and as soon as everything comes back clear we will proceed with your son. I'm thinking everything will come back okay."

"That's great to hear," I said while gingerly touching the side of my head. "When will I get to see them both?"

"In a little while, the medicine you were just given may put you to sleep in a little while depending on how your body reacts to it. Once you awaken I'll allow you to see your family. Also, you're scheduled to do another press conference in the morning, and I don't want you passing out again," he said with a gentle smile.

"Thanks for everything, Doc," I responded, feeling the effects of the medicine kicking in.

"No problem, Mr. Cinque. I'll be here in the morning. If you need anything, my brother will be covering the overnight shift and is aware of your situation. He'll do anything that's needed to make your stay comfortable."

I couldn't keep my eyes open to respond and found myself drifting off. *It felt like I was still awake, because I was sitting next to my wife's bed watching her sleep. She didn't look as beat up as I remembered, and almost all of her scars were gone. The kids, even Jordan, were sitting out in the waiting area outside of the room watching TV, and I wondered when Jordan had gotten out of the ICU. Jasmine's mom and dad were out there, and everyone looked happy.*

Just when I went to get up to use the restroom, Jasmine's hand shot out and grabbed a hold of my wrist. When I looked at her, her eyes were bloodshot and she had a sad look on her face. I was scared, and I knew my face showed it but I couldn't move or speak. All I could do was look her in her eyes.

"James, I'm sorry this happened to us," she spoke in a sad tone as tears streamed from her eyes.

"Honey, it's okay," I responded, finally finding my voice. "Just let me get the doctor, and . . ."

"I have something I need to tell you about the kids," she replied, the tears turning a crimson red as they ran down her face and soaked the sheet that was tucked in around her neck. I wanted to call to get the doctor but she had a death grip on me.

"Jazz, let me go get the doctor. You're bleeding."

"But the kids," she said through her tears. "I need to tell you about the kids. The second set of twins . . ."

Before she could say another word I managed to snatch my wrist from her grip and run to the hall to get the doctor. It felt like the hallway was the length of a football stadium as I ran down it in slow motion to reach the doctor who was standing at a nurse's station. They looked animated as they laughed out loud at something they were reading in a chart. When I finally got close to them, they stopped briefly to look at me, and then burst out laughing again.

"Doctor," I said out of breath as I leaned against the counter. "My wife opened her eyes . . . She's bleeding everywhere!"

The doctor didn't say a word, and simply walked around me and headed down the hallway toward Jazz's room. I followed him, but my feet felt like I was walking through quicksand. I hoped Jasmine didn't bleed to death by the time we got back there because we were moving slow as fuck. Why hadn't anyone called for the EMT or anything yet? I knew for sure that if my wife was dead when I got to her room all hell was going to break loose.

Both the doctor and I arrived to the door at the same time, and I was preparing to see blood everywhere and my wife to look like a shriveled-up prune. To my surprise Jasmine looked like I remembered her: bandaged up with scrapes and bruises with her eyes closed. There was no blood anywhere, and the beep from the life support machine could be heard.

"Mr. Cinque, your wife looks fine, but you look horrible on the other hand," the doctor said in an animated voice like you hear in those scary movies.

"Excuse me?" I asked, wiping the moisture from my eyes only to find blood on my hands.

"Mr. Cinque, you're bleeding all over the place," the doctor said, followed by laughter. As I looked around, everyone, including Jasmine and the kids, was pointing and laughing at me as my blood oozed out of my body and created a puddle on the floor.

The puddle began to swirl around me and create a black hole that I began to sink into. I was calling out for help, but couldn't hear my voice, and everyone was still just pointing and laughing like I didn't need help. I could see Jasmine getting out of the bed and walking toward the door as my body sunk lower into the floor. The look she gave me could have killed me alone if looks could kill. She gave me a sinister snarl as flames began to lick at me feet.

"Thanks, Doc, for helping me with this," she said as she smiled down at me. "Now, me and my kids can live our lives with their real father."

I began to scream, and just as the hole was closing over my head I woke up. The nurse was standing next to the bed checking my vitals. My heart had to have been beating a million miles a minute because I was sweating profusely, and my head pounded more than it did earlier.

"Must have been having a bad dream, huh?" the nurse asked as she removed the blood pressure cup from my forearm. "Try to relax, Mr. Cinque. The morning will be here before you know it."

I couldn't form any words as I lay on the bed with my eyes closed trying to figure it all out. I'd had the feeling before that the second set of twins were possibly not mine, but I never brought it up because of my own dirt. Was the dream revealing something to me that I knew all along? This was just too much for one person to deal with, and I just needed to rest. After the nurse left I twisted around in the bed until I found a comfortable position and willed myself to go back to sleep, hoping my dream didn't pick back up where it left off or got worse off than it was before. Too many skeletons in the closet lead to nightmares, and I knew eventually once things got back to normal that Jazz and I would have to hash it out. That was if we both wanted to sleep peaceful at night. I knew I did.

Monica

Taking Care of Business

"Monica, do we have to talk about this now?" the judge asked me as he sat with a look of disbelief. His once erect penis was now starting to shrivel back down to a soft lump in his lap. I knew he wanted to hurt me at the moment, but he was a smart man. He still had some pussy to get.

"Not in its entirety, but I do need you to understand a few things," I responded as I turned and moved back closer to him. "I'm certain that the city will be up and operating by the morning, so I'll need you to get on it with info about my son."

"Okay, but that's in the morning. What does that have to do with what's happening right now?" he asked in a desperate voice as he began to grow again.

"Just in case I have to take my son back with me, I need things to be handled properly," I said as I kneeled down in front of him, and began to stroke his erection. I was really rooting for the Cinques and hoping that everything was on point so that I could just go back home. I was in no way, shape, or form ready to be on mommy duty, and the sooner I found out that everything was good the faster I could roll out from this dreaded city. Watching his eyes roll up into the back of his head made me smile a little. Yeah, I definitely still had it.

"Monica," he said through deep breaths as he grew longer and began to pulsate, "you have to keep in mind that you gave up all rights when you left four years ago. You can't just swoop back in and take him away from the only family he's ever known."

"But he's my son," I argued as I cupped his balls in my warm hands and continued to stroke him.

"But he doesn't know that."

It felt like all the sound in the house went mute. I could no longer here the logs crackling in the fireplace, or the desperate pants coming from the judge's mouth. The truth of the situation hit harder now than I thought it would after hearing someone else say it out loud, and he was right. My son thought Jasmine was his mother. It was different when I said it to myself a hundred times a day for four years straight, but from out of the mouth of someone else sealed the deal and brought it all into perspective. Sensing the change of the mood, the judge looked down at me with a confused look on his face.

"Monica, come on. You knew all of this would happen. The bigger question is, why after all this time have you shown up? Why are you trying to disrupt everyone's lives?"

"Because I feel like something is going on," I responded as I let go of him and brushed tears from my eyes.

"And why do you feel that way? The Cinques are a good family."

"Well, if they are a good family, why did my checks started coming back with no forwarding address?" I questioned, getting more upset by the second.

"They probably felt it was time to move on, Monica. Damn, did you forget all of the nonsense and headaches? The real reason you are here is not for your son, anyway," he said, standing and grabbing his pajama pants from the floor. Stepping into them hastily, he reached for his robe and slipped it on, leaving me naked and frazzled.

"What other reason would I have to be here?" I asked, confusion lacing my voice. I was not ready to be a mom, I had to admit that, but I felt like my son needed me.

"You're here," he said in a matter-of-fact tone, "because you're hoping that Jasmine still loves you."

Boom!

That shit felt like a slap in the face, but was it truth to that? I did still love Jazz. I'll admit that, because you don't just stop loving someone. I dreamed about her plenty of nights, and I could still remember how her body felt in my hands. I closed my eyes and pictured my tongue exploring her body, and my pussy got wet all over again.

"That's not why I'm here," I responded weakly.

"Listen, I'm going to have a cigar and a little bite to eat. Go ahead and get yourself together and meet me back here in an hour. I'll have some food sent up to you to get your strength back up. When you come back I don't want to hear anything more about the kid or the family he's with. There is nothing that we can do about that today. We will handle it in the morning. Understand?" he asked with a stern look on his face that said he meant business.

I didn't bother to respond because he had already set the rules. Grabbing my bag from the couch, and my trench coat from the floor, I made my way to the master suite where I would be spending the week, permitting I found out what I needed to know about my son in that amount of time. After I got myself situated I took a quick shower, where I allowed myself to cry for the first time in years. I felt so confused about being back home in Philly, but I knew there was a reason why I had to be here. It was hard to explain, and I didn't expect the judge to understand, but I needed his help.

A mother, regardless of any situation unless she really doesn't care, has a connection with her child. Even more so when she has to get rid of the child for whatever reason she has. Although the child isn't in your possession, you can still feel if the child needs you. It's a gut feeling that can't be ignored. I believed it may have been different had I never held him, or if I had cut all ties and just rolled out, but because James kept in contact with me up until I changed my number, I saw all of the things that I would have otherwise missed out on. No, I didn't see him take his first steps in person, but a hundred times I played the video that James sent me as I cried myself to sleep feeling bad about what I had done.

That was only to get up in the morning with puffy eyes, convincing myself that I had done the right thing. No, I wasn't there during the teething process, but when that first little Tic Tac–shaped tooth showed up in his mouth, I got the picture message of my smiling baby showing off his new tooth. On his first day going to daycare I got the picture of him with his cute little outfit, and matching book bag. All of these things took a toll on me, and I just couldn't keep torturing myself. I had to move on, and I needed closure. I was doing good, too, up until that first check came back with no return address and I found out that the numbers I had for James didn't work. That feeling in my gut told me I needed to be here, and I didn't regret the decision I made at all.

By the time I got out of the shower, there was a tray resting on the side of the bed with food on it just as the judge said. I took the time to dry off and moisturize, tucking the towel under my arms. Taking a second, I enjoyed the fruit and cheese and spiced meats that were there for me. I knew I would have to come correct when I got back downstairs so that the judge would cooperate.

Going into my stash, I dusted honeydew powder all over my body. It added a nice shimmer, and tasted sweet. So wherever the judge kissed me he would taste it. I slipped into a lace red boy short with matching bra, and blood-red pumps to match. Checking my hair in the mirror, I was satisfied as I applied a neutral coat of lip gloss to my plump lips. I had pissed the judge off, so I had to bring my A game this time around.

As I walked through the house back toward the chimney, I found the judge sitting in a cushioned chair by the fire smoking a cigar. I would have to work through the wall he undoubtedly had up, but the judge couldn't resist me so it shouldn't have been too hard. As I rounded the chair I stood posed in front of him with my back facing him so that he could take it all in. I could feel the heat from his eyes as they traveled my body from head to toe. Doing a slow spin, I faced him with a mischievous look on my face, ready to handle my business.

He didn't crack a smile, and actually looked disinterested, but that didn't discourage me. He was playing hardball, and I was cool with that since it wouldn't last long. Stepping toward him, I leaned down and kissed him on the mouth where we intertwined our tongues in a seductive dance. Continuing my kisses down the side of his neck, I made sure to pay special attention to his nipples because that would definitely start the melting process. I could feel his erection press against my stomach as I drew circles around his nipples with my fingertips, lightly scratching his chest as I continued to travel south.

Caressing him through his silk pajamas turned me the hell on, and I had to catch myself from drooling on them. When the head peeked through the slit in his pants, I didn't hesitate to put my mouth around it, and take as much of him in as I could. I convinced myself that I just needed to enjoy this and not think about anything else. The anxious feeling in my stomach started to subside as I worked the judge into a frenzy.

Standing up, I allowed him to remove my bra and panties, and I took a seat on the lounge chair so that we could pick up where we left off. He came over behind me and took his time tasting my body. He licked and nibbled on me like he was starving, and I could tell he was enjoying the taste of the honeydew dust that covered me. Pushing my legs back, he captured my clit and slurped all of me into his mouth. I could feel my body reacting, and an orgasm quickly approaching, but I couldn't stop it. I wanted to make him work for it, but that plan didn't seem to be going so well.

By the time he got done with me I was begging him for the dick, and he was more than happy to oblige. Placing my legs on his shoulders, he took his place in between my legs, transfixed on the bull's eye just as he was earlier. My juices were steadily gushing out in anticipation, and he looked like he couldn't wait to get wet.

"Don't think you're going to stop me this time. Once I get in there I'm in it until it's over. Understand?" He spoke in a husky voice that meant business. I didn't even get a chance to answer before he shoved himself inside of me.

I was sloppy wet as he pushed and pulled in and out of me. I was sure my moans could be heard for miles as I stroked his ego with my words and tight pussy. He was killing it though, and for a second there I couldn't handle him pounding into me. He took my legs and positioned them at his side, and flipped me over on my side. I was nervous about falling off of the chaise, but he held on to me as he positioned himself under me so that I could ride him backward. I had to steady myself on my knees, and once I got my shoes off I was ready to go in.

"You miss this pussy?" I asked him as I slammed down onto him, making my ass bounce around for his viewing pleasure.

"You miss this dick?" he countered as he met me thrust for thrust. We were playing a wicked game, and I was betting that I would get him to bust first.

"Yes, baby, I missed it," I responded as I tried to control my orgasm. I couldn't let him win, but he got me when he reached around and circled my clit with his fingertip. That shit sent me over the edge, and I almost lost it.

"See, your problem is you're always trying to control every-thing," he spoke as he forced my body to lean back and connect with his. "You never want to let go and enjoy the moment, do you, Monica?" he asked as he pulled on my clit, and palmed my breasts.

I couldn't answer if I wanted to because my body was feeling something I never felt before. He had me stretched out on his legs, but he was still penetrating me to the fullest, slow grinding me into convulsions. I was also surprised that he hadn't crashed it yet, and was thoroughly enjoying the ride.

He lifted my body up and bent me over, standing behind me on the side of the chaise. Easing himself back inside of me, he went at a steady rhythm, speeding up a little more as he got closer to exploding.

"I've been waiting for too long to have you like this. You ready for me to explode, baby?"

"Yes, I'm ready," I replied as I braced myself for him. I was spent, and really couldn't take any more of the pounding he was putting on me. Hell, maybe he was taking vitamins or even Viagra, but whatever it was I was happy that he was doing it. The judge I knew from back then would have been crashed. Even when we hooked up after one of my benefits not too long ago, it wasn't this good.

"Yeah, take that shit," I moaned out, causing the scene to intensify. He grabbed my hips, and zoned in causing another explosion to build up in me in the process. We were both gasping for air, and I could hardly contain myself. Just as I was reaching up, I turned in time to see the judge grab his chest and fall back. Was this man having a heart attack?

"Call . . . call the butler. Tell him to get help," he gasped as he held his chest. The look on his face was excruciating, and I started to panic. I knew I had a killer pussy, but damn.

Running toward the kitchen, I grabbed the phone and dialed the numbers next to the word "butler" on the call log. Once I informed him of what was happening, I raced back to the judge to check on him. He was in the same spot I found him, barely breathing and still holding his chest. I did my best to get his pants back on him, and even once the butler showed up a few minutes later I was still naked. There was a separate smaller structure on the side of the house, so I assumed that was where the butler stayed on the property. He didn't seem to notice as he dressed the judge in sweats and sneakers. I took the liberty of jetting upstairs and throwing on sweats and my Uggs so that I could travel along.

I found it weird that an ambulance wasn't called, but I didn't say a word as I held his head in my lap all the way to the hospital. I assumed his wife wasn't called, and I didn't ask. I wasn't even sure where we were going, but as luck would have it we pulled up to the University of Pennsylvania Hospital, the same hospital where the Cinques were. *Let the games begin . . .*

James

Ghost of Ménage à Trois Past

I had a splitting headache. It seemed worse now than it did before I went to sleep. It could be from not eating or the bump I got on my head, but whatever it was drained the hell out of me. I sat up on the side of the bed just as the nurse was coming in to take my vitals. Too many events happened within the matter of a day and a half, and I was over it.

"Good morning, Mr. Cinque," the jolly nurse said as she scanned my chart. This nurse was different from the one who was taking care of me last night. She was cuter, too. My eyes traveled her curves, but I forced my mind to go in another direction.

"Good morning," I managed to mumble as I held the side of my head.

"Seems like you still have a headache, huh?" she replied, finally looking me in the face. "I'll get you something for that to go along with your breakfast. Sit back on the bed for me so that I can take your vitals."

Scooting back on the bed, I chanced a glance out the door, hoping Jasmine's family was gone. I was contemplating making a dash for it, but to my dismay her brothers were resting in chairs just outside the door. This shit was like a never-ending nightmare. I felt like I was in jail, and her family were the guards making sure I stayed in place.

I closed my eyes for a split second just as a "code thirty" was announced over the loudspeaker. I could see the nurses rushing, and I wondered if it had anything to do with my wife or my son.

"What does that code mean?" I asked as she quickly took notes in my chart.

"Someone came in under cardiac arrest," she replied nonchalantly as she continued to write in my chart. Soon after I could hear the commotion in the hallway as people started running by. I got a glimpse of a person on a stretcher, but what caught my eye was the woman running beside it. *Was that Monica who just ran past?* I shook my head and rubbed my eyes. The crowd had already passed, but I was still stunned. If it was her, what was she doing in Philly? When did she get here?

"Mr. Cinque, your tray should be arriving soon. I'll put in an order for your pain meds as well. Continue to rest, and I'll be back in a little while."

I shook my head, acknowledging that I heard her, but my mind was gone. Was that really Monica? I had to get a look, but I knew I would have to wait. Everyone would want to know why I was looking around the hospital for a strange person.

Just as I settled back into the bed my breakfast was brought in by a dietary aide. She was even cuter than the nurse who was there, and I had to keep myself from staring at her as well. *What's wrong with me?*

"Good morning," she said with a smile. "Fill out this menu card for your lunch and dinner and I will collect it from you when I come back for your tray."

I gave her a warm smile as she positioned my tray in front of me and made sure my bed was adjusted. I wanted to see my son, and my wife. Did I have to wait for the doctor to see them? Just as I was going to buzz the nurse she came in with a woman from venipuncture.

"Mr. Cinque, she's going to draw some blood from you this morning," the nurse replied as she looked through my chart.

"What for?" I asked her as I held my arm out to be punctured.

"The doctor will be in shortly to discuss that with you."

I tried not to watch because I hated needles, but I couldn't help it. The phlebotomist was quick with drawing the seven or eight tubes of blood that she was instructed to get from me. I didn't think anything of it. I always protected myself whenever I stepped out on Jazz so I wasn't worried about any disease. Once the young lady was done, I went back to eating my food, totally forgetting to ask the questions I intended. I still had to report the news on my wife, and T.U.N.N. was giving me another chance to do so, considering I didn't pass out again in the process. My wife's family, or even the doctor for that matter, could have done it but I wanted to be the one to deliver the news. She was my wife, and as her husband I felt like that was my responsibility. That's what she would have wanted.

I was done with my breakfast and watching the news by the time the doctor came in to talk to me. He had a look of concern on his face that got my attention. Pushing the tray to the side, I sat up on the side of the bed to brace myself for whatever he had to say. Maybe something slipped by that I didn't know about. I had a few wild nights, and a few broken condoms along the way. Although I'd never been burned with a sexually transmitted disease, I know enough to know that some diseases lie dormant and can show up at any time. What if now was the time? How would I explain it to everyone? I was nervous instantly, and needed the doctor to get to the point ASAP.

"Good morning, Mr. Cinque. How is the headache coming along?"

"Pretty good. Hurts less now that I've eaten," I responded as I looked around the room. "Ummm . . . there was more blood drawn this morning. What's wrong?"

"Nothing's wrong. I just want to make sure that everything was drawn correctly. There was a mishap with your blood in the lab yesterday, and the results were tainted. In order to give your blood to your son we have to ensure that everything is on point or it could prove fatal for him," the doctor responded as he made notes in my chart.

"Okay," I responded in confusion. "So, how long will it take for the results to come in? Did I test positive for a disease?" I asked on the verge of panic.

"I sent your blood up stat so it shouldn't take long being they messed up in the lab yesterday. The ABO blood group typing test, which is a type of paternity/DNA test to determine your blood type and to ensure you are a match for your son, was compromised and that's an important factor to ensure that your blood type matches your son's for the transfusion process. If you are an O blood type, you are a universal donor and can donate to anyone, but only A types can go with other As and Bs can only go with other Bs, et cetera. If the blood type is not compatible very dangerous results will occur," he responded with a gentle look on his face. "In the meantime, you should prepare for the announcement. The news team is gathering in the auditorium, and the public is being let in. Your clothes are behind the door and toiletries have been set aside. If you need anything else the nurse will get it for you."

"Can I see my son and my wife before I do all of that?" I asked desperately.

"Sure you can. I'll have transport take you to both rooms."

After pushing my now empty tray to the side, I made use of the facilities and got myself prepared to stand in front of the camera again. Although I wasn't being released from the hospital just yet, the doctor gave me permission to make the announcement; then I would be right back in bed. By the time I finished getting dressed, transport was there to take me to see my family. I protested about the wheelchair, but was quickly reminded that it was hospital policy, so I gave up the fight and let them wheel me around.

We went to see my wife first, and I was sad to see that she looked exactly the same, but I guess I was hoping for her to be a little better than the last time I saw her.

Bending down next to her ear I told her that I loved her, and I couldn't wait for her to wake up. Her fingers flinched a little, but her eyes remained closed. That was enough for me to know that she heard me. What if she didn't recognize me or the kids when she woke up? That was a possibility that the doctor discussed with me regarding her condition. How would the kids handle it? Especially the younger ones? How much different would Jazz be? After taking my seat back in the chair, I hung my head deep in thought and with a heavy heart as an escort wheeled me down to see my son.

The results were just the same with him. Nothing had changed since the last time I was here. I held his little hand in mine, and rubbed my thumb across the back of his hand. This was so unfair! Why didn't God just take me instead of taking my family through all this turmoil? I kissed him on his forehead and stared at him for a few more minutes with no response from him indicating that he knew I was there. Not a twitch or anything.

Taking a seat back in the wheelchair, I prepared myself for the update. It still didn't make sense to me to have to be wheeled around, and I figured I would have to get up and walk to the podium anyway. Once I got to the auditorium I could see a crowd gathering of news reporters and spectators, and I noticed that the podium was more wheelchair accessible and I wouldn't have to stand. In my eyes that painted a picture that I was more hurt than I was, but I guessed they were being cautious of my possibly fainting again.

The escort wheeled me up to the podium, and quietness went across the room as all eyes fell on me. Scanning the crowd, I saw the faces of my fellow coworkers from T.U.N.N., and the good doctor was standing in the back. As I prepared to address the crowd, I could see the reporters from surrounding news stations getting their notepads together, scribbling down questions for me to answer. I was a nervous wreck, but I took a deep breath and pushed forward. Once I got through this I wouldn't have to do it again.

"I would like to thank you all for coming back out," I began in a shaky voice. All of a sudden this was too much to bear, and I didn't think I could do it.

"Take your time, son, and get it out," I heard Jazz's father say from behind me, and I wondered briefly when they had all appeared.

"Thank you for coming out," I said again in a clearer voice. "My wife, Jasmine Cinque, is a prominent lawyer here in the Philadelphia region, and I am sad to report that some time during the night a day ago she was in a really bad car accident that may have caused a bad brain injury. She is being kept asleep until the swelling in her brain goes down, and it will not be until the point that she wakes up that the doctors will be able to determine the true extent of the injuries."

A collective gasp filled the room as pens and pads connected and my every word was recorded.

"Although she is on life support, she is in stable condition and the doctors believe that she will pull through just fine once the swelling goes down," I continued as I held back my tears. Simply saying out loud the state of my wife's condition brought me to tears. What if she didn't make it out? What would I do with all of these kids by myself?

"Was your wife speeding?" came the first question from the audience. I immediately got on the defensive. Even if she was, that didn't mean she deserved to be where she was now.

"I can't say for sure because I was not there when the accident took place. I met my wife and son here after the fact."

"Why was she out traveling in such horrible conditions?" Question number two came from the audience, and I zeroed in on the person who asked. He looked rather young, and may have been fresh to the reporting business. His goal, I was sure, was to get the "drama" aspect of the story to print scandal. I refused to aid in the tainting of my wife's name.

"She was picking up our kids from afterschool care."

"Well, from my research here, it was understood that she was called out of a meeting because you hadn't gone to get them yet. Do you agree that all of this could have been avoided had you just stepped up to the plate?" the fresh-faced reporter responded as he flipped through a few pages of notes. Stunned, the audience turned from him back to me like we were in a tennis match. He caught me off guard with that one and I was sure it showed.

"I'm not too sure of your sources, nor are we here to discuss this in detail. The point of the fact is my wife is upstairs in a room fighting for her life. Those who know and love her deserve to know at least that much, and any scandal you are trying to dig up won't be addressed at this time," I responded in an even tone, although I was ready to come up out of this wheelchair and toss it at his big-headed ass.

"Which son is it? The adopted son or the biological?" came a feminine voice that I recognized immediately. Everyone's eyes, including mine, raced to the back of the room and landed on Monica. I thought I'd seen her fly past my room earlier right after a man came by on a stretcher. Now my suspicions were confirmed, but I did not feel like dealing with her right now. What in the hell was she doing here?

I could see the pens scratching across pages, and a slight buzz could be heard as the element of surprise died down and more questions were thought up. Gripping the side of the wheelchair, I cleared my throat before answering. I had to keep my cool before I ended up doing this interview via satellite from prison.

Monica

Answer That!

The look on his face was priceless, and I'd be lying if I said I wasn't enjoying it a little. Hell, the news weren't the only people in the world who needed answers. Did my son need me as much as my gut was telling me he did? I needed to know, and when I saw people gathering up in here, I was just being nosey while I was waiting on the verdict from the judge. Who knew I would walk in on the Cinque press conference? This was supposed to happen, and I wanted answers . . . now!

"It's my biological son," he responded in an even voice. "One last question and the interview will be closed."

He was pissed!

I was loving it!

Let the games begin!

I heard some reporter present him with another question, but I dipped out the back. I got my answer. It wasn't my son on his last leg, so I was okay for now. I would just need to find out where they lived so that I could make my next move. I would need the judge for that, and he needed to come out of this mess alive and alert.

After grabbing a cup of coffee from the cafeteria, I circled back around to the judge's room. I figured James would be awhile wrapping up the news conference after the last of the questions were answered, considering when it came to interviews one last question could turn into ten more, so I decided to stop past the patient information booth to see what I could find out. When I walked up I was greeted by an extremely attractive woman who looked to be in her thirties. Judging from her appearance, she definitely took pride in how she looked, even though she was sitting at a desk. She showed a bright smile through thick lips, and I briefly wondered how they would feel on my body. Deciding to test the waters, I stepped up next in line. Just in case I needed to use her later, I wanted to get her in my pocket now.

"How may I help you?" she asked with a wide smile and bright eyes. A closer look revealed a nice pair of kissable breasts. A little more than a handful . . . Made me wonder what color her nipples were.

"Hi, I'm here to see my brother. I believe he checked in yesterday. I can't remember what my mom said on the phone," I responded with slight embarrassment in my voice, the actress in me in full motion.

"That's not a problem. What's your brother's name?" she asked as she flipped through a few screens on her computer.

"James Cinque," I answered with confidence.

She took a few minutes to search the system, and after a second or two came up with his room number. Taking a piece of paper from a stack, she wrote down his info and passed it across the desk to me.

"Here you go," she said with a jolly tone in her voice. "Do you have a parking ticket? If so, I can validate it for you to get a discount on your parking. It's not a lot, but every little bit helps."

"No, I was dropped off," I lied, "but thanks for letting me know. I love your lip gloss by the way."

"Oh, thanks." She smiled at me.

"Thank you."

After tucking the info in my back pocket, I backed away from the station, deciding to leave her be. I wasn't certain about her, but if I ran into her again I would definitely give her another try. What *did* disturb me a little was that anyone could walk up and get info on you, and the people at the desk didn't ask for identification or anything. I knew not to check into U of P if I was ever hiding out.

On my way back upstairs I got off of the elevator, and took in the scenery as I walked down the hall to the judge's room. Halfway down the hall I came upon the section where the seating area for families was, and there were a group of kids sitting with an older woman who looked just like Jasmine. I almost tripped over my own feet when my eyes landed on the children. I mean, there they were . . . all of them. They were just sitting there in their own little worlds looking just as exhausted as everyone else. The scene tugged on my heartstrings something serious, and made me sad.

The last time I saw the Cinques' older two they were just toddlers. I couldn't believe how much they had grown. Just the daughter of the second set of twins was sitting there, which meant her twin brother was the one in the ICU. I couldn't believe how much they all looked like James. There were two younger children sitting there, and they didn't exactly look alike, which meant the other one could be none other than my son.

I was face to face with him and I couldn't believe it. I tried to point out features of mine, and I noticed immediately that although he looked like the rest of the kids he had my mouth and nose. He had the same complexion as James, and he and the other little boy definitely looked like brothers. I resisted the urge to scoop down and take him into my arms. My eyes misted up, and I had to get it together considering Jasmine's mother was staring at me strange.

"I'm sorry," I apologized as I willed my feet to move forward again. "I thought I recognized these kids," I said to her.

"It's not a problem," she offered with a kind smile.

"It's just that," I added with dramatic flair, "this little girl looks like the daughter of a friend of mine from a few years ago, but she had a twin brother. My friend's name is Jasmine, and I haven't seen her in years."

"Well, if you are speaking of Jasmine Cinque, these would be her kids," the woman offered with a sad smile.

"For real? Oh, my goodness, where is she? I haven't seen her in so long," I gushed as I played into the vulnerability of the woman. I was going to juice her for as much information as I could before James popped up.

"Well, unfortunately she's in the ICU. I'm surprised you haven't heard because it's been all over the news. She was in . . . Well, that's not really a conversation to have in front of the children," she stopped herself, and then looked around at their sad faces.

"I totally understand," I offered with an equally sad look on my face. "I'm here visiting a friend as well, but if I could leave my number with you could you text me or call me later with the information so that I can maybe stop by and see her at a better time?"

"Sure, I don't see that being a problem. I'll give it to James whenever he comes back from downstairs."

"Thank you so much," I responded as I scribbled my phone number on an old Michael Kors receipt from my purse. This was working out better than I thought it would. James would be upset, but he would call me if for nothing else but to tell me to back off.

I thanked her again as I handed her the slip of paper, and watched as she secured it in her pocketbook. Turning on my heels, I chanced a glance at the little boy once more, taking in his face for memory one last time. A smile spread across my face as just a tear slipped from the inside corner of my eye. How could I have given up such a precious little thing? Seeing him made me happy, but I was so confused at the same time. Would I have been a good mom to him, and how different would my life have been if I had kept him? I wasn't the type of woman who could take care of someone else by myself, and I just wasn't confident that it would have been a fairytale setup.

Kids need a lot of love and attention, something I just didn't think I was capable of giving. Especially considering I never got it. I came from a broken home. We always had to be quiet and stay out of the way of our drunken father's rage. My mother was too busy trying to survive to give us hugs and kisses, and shit just got worse as I got older and other family members got a hold of me. I was damaged goods, and I felt like my son needed at least a fair chance at a good life with a loving family. Something I just couldn't give him.

Stopping in the restroom just past the judge's room, I sat down in a stall and bawled my eyes out. It caught me by surprise because I didn't think I would be so emotional upon seeing him. The last time I looked at him face to face he had a little round face that looked like James's . . . Still did, and now he was inches taller and into his features. Seeing him instantly took me back to the videos that James would send me of him crawling and eventually walking. I erased the voice recording of his first words because I couldn't handle not being there. My thought process: *he's not my responsibility now. He's with his father, where he belongs.*

My question now was did he belong there, and if I did indeed have to take him how would it work out for both of us? My place wasn't exactly kid friendly, and I wasn't 100 percent sure that I was ready to make the necessary changes for him. What if he hated me, and despised me for giving him up? Did he know that he was adopted, better yet thrown on the Cinque's because his real mother was a selfish bitch who didn't want the assumed inconvenience of having a kid around? This was too much at one time, and I couldn't control my sobbing. It took me about ten minutes before I was able to control the tears that were invading my face and racking my body with grief. I had to play this the right way, and I needed to get back to business.

Coming out of the stall, I took a few minutes to wash my face and get myself together at the sink before I went into the judge's room. Just in case he was up and noticed I was crying, I would just tell him I was concerned about him and thought that I had lost him. He was so self-centered his egotistical ass would believe it.

After applying a fresh coat of lip gloss, I stepped out into the hall just in time to see James reunite with his family. From what I gathered, he must not have seen his kids since the accident. The group hug and the way all of the kids screamed out "Daddy" when they saw him was a touching moment. He looked drained and pissed at the same time when he exited the elevator, but when he laid eyes on his kids the expression changed to one of love and relief. I got misty-eyed again, but kept it moving before Jasmine's mom pointed me out to him. I wasn't ready to meet him up close and personal right now, especially considering I crashed his press conference. I knew I wasn't his favorite person in the world at this moment in time.

Stepping into the judge's room, I could see that he was still asleep. The nurse informed me that he was on private status in the system so no one would be popping up unexpectedly. She addressed me as his wife, but I didn't bother to correct her. I didn't need a scandal breaking out at this time. I needed him to do some shit for me, and I needed everything to run smoothly. There was a bodyguard at the door twenty-four/ seven, and I was simply waiting for him to wake up.

"So . . . ummm . . . how long will he be down for?" I asked the nurse to gauge how much time I had to sit in this dreadful place. Maybe I could go shopping in the meantime and check back.

"He should be waking up by tomorrow morning, Mrs. Stenton. We gave him drugs to keep him asleep until the test results come back, and to keep him comfortable. The doctor will be making rounds soon, and should be able to explain everything better," she responded as she read from his chart.

"That sounds like a plan," I responded as I pulled my Kindle from my bag and got comfortable. I was going to have his driver take me back to the hideout, but I didn't want to risk leaving and on my return not be able to get back in for any reason.

The image of my son's face popped back in my head and brought a small smile to my face. I was happy and nervous at the same time because I didn't know what the outcome would be.

James

Picking Up the Pieces

I swear she's just as messy now as she was back then. I knew I saw Monica fly past my room earlier, but did I think that she would show up at my press conference? Hell no! Then she came in there asking questions, and stirring up shit for no reason. *Why is this woman constantly trying to wreck my flow?* If I would have known that a night of great sex with a sexy-ass woman would lead to all of this mess years later, I would have stayed faithful to my damn wife, or at least used a condom. Maybe we wouldn't have been in this shit now. As a matter of fact, I know we wouldn't. Hindsight is a bitch in a sexy dress and heels, and whatever lesson she intended to teach had been well learned. Trust me on that one. After all of these trials and tribulations I couldn't even be sure that I would even want to touch my wife.

I left the press conference feeling defeated, but I was glad that it was over. Now that the deed was done I could concentrate on my family. I was wheeled out of the room before things got too heated, and held my head down as various reporters from the news took pictures to no doubt post as headline news. When I got up to my floor, I removed myself from the wheelchair and began walking down the hall. I just needed to stand up because the wheelchair made me feel more helpless than I already was.

Halfway down the hall I looked up and made eye contact with my oldest daughter. It was like everything started moving in slow motion as tears made my vision cloudy and I started running toward her.

"Daddy!" my daughter screamed out as we collided in a tight embrace in the middle of the hall. Pretty soon, I could feel the arms of all of my children wrapped around me in a tearful embrace. I didn't think this day would ever come. Every time I asked about my kids I got the grizzly.

When I stood up, picking up my youngest daughter and Monica's son, my mother-in-law walked up to me with tears in her eyes. I knew she would be in my corner regardless of the mess that was going on now. When I reached her, I sat the kids down, and she gave me the tightest hug her small frame could manage, letting me know everything would be okay. Taking a seat in the waiting area, the kids continued to cling to me for dear life as we discussed the goings-on of my wife and son. This was a major stressor for all of us, and we were all waiting for one of them to wake up.

"So what did the doctor say about Jordan?" she asked just as Jazz's dad, brothers, and uncles walked up. Everyone stopped to give out quick hugs before I updated them on what I knew.

"I gave blood this morning because Jordan will need a transfusion," I replied, not letting on that an error had occurred with the previous sample. I didn't want any cause for alarm to upset anyone.

"And what about Jasmine?" she asked as she blinked back tears.

"Jazz is the more stable of the two. They give her meds to keep her asleep until the swelling goes down. She whacked her forehead on the steering wheel pretty hard, and although it doesn't look like a lot is wrong, they just want to be sure," I responded as Jaden cuddled up closer to me. We sat and conversed for a while, and just as Jazz's father offered to take the kids for something to eat in the cafeteria the doctor walked up and greeted us.

"It's nice to see everyone here." He spoke with a gentle smile that one couldn't help but return. "Despite the circumstances, how is everyone holding up?"

"Pretty good so far, Doc," I responded for everyone. "These are my children, and this is my mother-in-law."

"Nice to meet everyone," he responded. "James, I need you in your room so that I can check you out, and discuss some things."

"No problem, the kids were just going to get something to eat."

After they all left, Jazz's mom slipped me a piece of paper that I stuck in my pocket on the low. I knew she didn't want the others to see it by how she handed it to me in a hug, and winked her eye at me afterward. Following the doctor into the room, I took a seat on the side of the bed, preparing myself to be checked out so that I could sit next to my wife and son.

"So how are you feeling now that the press is done with you?" he asked as he checked my vitals.

"Pretty good, considering the circumstances."

"That's good to hear," he said as he scribbled something in my chart. "You will be free to check out today, but I need to talk to you about your blood test, and your son."

"Ummm . . . okay? Is everything all right? Do I have a disease?" I asked, borderline panicking.

"No, you don't have a disease," he responded with a kind smile as he pulled up a chair. *This shit must be about to get deep.*

"Okay, so what is it? Just give it to me straight."

"Well, after sending your blood up to be tested yesterday I thought it was weird that your paternity type didn't match your son. That was the reason why I had it redrawn this morning, but when I got the same results I knew then we had a major problem."

"What are you saying, Doc?" I asked, already knowing the answer.

"I'm saying that Jordan is not yours, and if we are going to do the blood transfusion using a family member's blood we have to act fast. I can take it from your wife, or the child's twin. I just need to know what you want to do."

Boom!

The other shoe had fallen, and it's safe to say a bomb was just dropped on me. Did this man just tell me Jordan wasn't my son? I felt myself hyperventilating, and the last thing I heard before I blacked out was the doctor calling for a nurse. Why was this happening to me?

When I finally came to I was stretched out on the bed with my family surrounding me. This was all just a bad dream . . . it had to be. I knew it wasn't when the sad look on my mother-in-law's face came into view. So it was true. Jordan wasn't my son. And if Jordan wasn't my son, that meant that Janice wasn't my daughter. It didn't make any logical sense because they looked just like me, just like my other kids did. If I wasn't the father, then who was?

I was pissed, confused, hurt . . . hell, all of the above! Did Jazz really do this to me? To us? To our family? Yeah, I did my shit too, but nothing of the magnitude of this. Some would think that I was justifying my wrongdoings, but in *my* head our situations were *not* the same. She knew I was sleeping with Monica except for the times that I crept out, and when Monica turned up pregnant there was no way it belonged to anyone else but me. Jasmine, on the other hand, had sex with someone I didn't know about, passed the kids off as mine for years, and never admitted to it. That, in my opinion, was hardly the same thing. Call it biased, a double standard, an excuse . . . I don't care. I needed her to wake up *now!*

"Mr. Cinque, I'm glad you're awake," the doctor spoke from the door as the nurse took my vitals. It was kind of hard to do with my oldest daughter wrapped around me, but she managed. Hopefully they didn't tell the kids the God-awful news I just heard.

"Do you guys mind if I speak with him alone?" the doctor asked. Jaden protested at first in a tearful fit, but I promised her it wouldn't take long before she was right back in my arms again. She was comforted by Jalil, and it made me proud to see my son step up to the plate at such a difficult time. Once everyone was out, he took a seat on the side of my bed to talk to me. Tears flooded my eyes instantly.

"Mr. Cinque, I'm sorry I had to give you that type of news at a time like this, but we need to make a move if we are going to save your son. Do we take the blood from your wife or the twin? I know it's a lot to digest right now, but I need an answer or your son may die."

I was still speechless. He just told me that Jordan wasn't mine, but he still referred to him as my son, and honestly I didn't know how to feel. Betrayed. Confused. Hurt. Uneasy . . .

the list just went on and on. I had so many questions, but I knew I needed to sort my thoughts out, and now wasn't a good time.

"Whose blood would be better?" I asked as my thoughts swam around in my head, colliding into each other. Jordan wasn't mine . . . and the thought echoed in my head over and over again.

"The twin's blood would be an excellent choice since they share everything already, and we would only need three pints. The procedure for testing is the same to make sure they will be compatible, just as a precaution."

"Will it hurt her?" I asked, concerned about my baby girl. I had the overwhelming urge to hold her in my arms and look at her face. The needle that was used to collect the blood was huge, and hurt me, so I could imagine the pain in the arm of a toddler.

"Since she's so young we will put her to sleep, because I doubt she will sit there for the procedure," the doctor stated truthfully as he looked me in my face. I must have looked a mess.

"And what if you got it from Jasmine? Will it put her at risk?" I wondered. I was seeing her in a totally different light at this moment, and I needed answers from her.

"She's already out, so it's just a matter of obtaining permission from you and we can get the blood from her now."

I thought about it for a second, and I knew I didn't want to put my daughter through that kind of mess. My daughter . . . or whoever she belonged to. This shit was crazy, and I found myself getting more pissed off by the second. How was I supposed to be acting now?

"Let's get it from Jasmine. I can't take my baby girl through that kind of pain if it's not necessary," I responded, trying to sound sure. "When will the surgery take place?"

"I'm going to send someone in now to get the blood, and as soon as the blood is run for testing we will begin. Everything is being done stat so that we can move quickly."

"Do what you have to do to save my son."

The doctor nodded in understanding, and exited the room to start the process. In the meantime my head was spinning, and I was confused. Almost immediately after the doctor was gone, my children busted into the room and surrounded me. I grabbed Janice into my arms and stared into her face, trying to see something different. All I saw were my eyes looking back at me. Cuddling her to my chest, I placed my free arm around Jaden, and made room for Jalil and Junior to embrace me as well. I didn't know what Jasmine did, but this was my family, and I was not going to trip.

If nothing else, I knew I needed to have a talk with some twin trainers from Bally Total Fitness. Monica warned me of this in a letter years ago, and I didn't have cause to believe her until now. I guessed it was time for me to investigate the truth.

Monica

If It Ain't One Thing It's Another

It felt like I'd been at the hospital forever waiting for the judge to wake up. This was some bullshit! I'd never had to sit in on a heart attack victim before, so I didn't know exactly what it was I was supposed to be doing at this moment. I found myself staring at him, and he looked a hundred years older than he did hours ago. I still hadn't found out the cause of the cardiac arrest, and the beeps from the monitor he was hooked to were driving me crazy.

The time on my watch read 4:00 p.m., and I was wondering if the Cinques were still gathered in the hall. I needed to get out of this room before they would have to check me into the psych ward. Deciding that maybe I could go out for a little while and come back, I gathered up my things and kissed the judge on the forehead, whispering in his ear that I would be back. I couldn't really go far since I didn't have a vehicle, so my first stop would be to hail a cab to the Enterprise center located on Market Street so that I could get some wheels. I had to be able to move around.

What I loved about University City was that at any given time of the day there was a Yellow Cab waiting to make money. Upon leaving the hospital, I was able to walk right out the door and into the back of the cab. To my surprise, it was the same cabby from the airport. Looking at my watch again, I knew I wouldn't have time today to let him hook me up, but maybe he would go for an IOU. He smiled immediately when I closed the door, asking me where I wanted to go.

"Where to, pretty lady?" he asked, minus the accent that I was sure he used with other customers. Surprisingly, he smelled like he might have actually showered today, and the Old Spice and bologna stench in the cab itself was faint.

"Enterprise," I spoke with a smile on my face as well; afterward confirming my rental on my iPhone. I figured I'd hit the mall, find something good to eat, and check back to see what the judge was up to before deciding where I would lay my head for the evening. I'd be damned if I was staying in this hospital all night. Since his condition had changed, I wasn't 100 percent sure that staying at his place was the best thing to do. As far as I knew, his wife didn't know about that piece of property, but somehow she found out he was in the hospital, so who knew how much information she was able to gather up? I just wasn't in the mood to figure it out, and would rather just play it safe in the comfort of a hotel. I would just get the cash I spent for it from the judge at a later date.

He must have taken other patients there because he didn't even bother to ask which location as he drove a few blocks down and over. The meter didn't even reach twenty, but I held the bill in my hand to see what he would do. To my surprise he didn't take it.

"You still have my number, right?" he asked, looking at me through the rearview mirror.

"Yes, I do," I replied.

"Good, this ride is on me. The next *ride* is on you."

The cabby definitely had me intrigued, and once again I thought about giving him a chance to prove what he could do. If his head game was any indication of what else he had in store, it might just be worth a try. Shaking my head, I exited the car and made my way inside the building to pick up my reservation. The more I moved about the more I started thinking about moving back to Philly. It didn't take long for my car to be brought around, and once we did the visual inspection, I was behind the wheel and on my way to find something to get into.

Deciding to take a ride through the old neighborhood, I first went through my block to see if it still looked the same. What I thought would be happy memories were shut down as soon as I pulled up the front of the house.

I took a look at the place I once called home and was dissapointed to see that the color of the house and the driveway had been changed. I guess I couldn't get too upset about changes done to a house that no longer belonged to me though.

Anna J.

Pulling off, I made my way to the Cinques' old house to see what was going on over there. Seemed to me Philly hadn't changed a bit. As I drove I noticed a black car following me, and at first I paid it no mind. No one knew I was in Philly, so I wasn't too concerned. However, I did become more concerned when every corner I turned the car turned. I even went around a block twice just to see if they would follow and they did. Whoever had a tail on me wasn't doing a good job being inconspicuous. I didn't panic though; I was too smooth for that. Instead, when I got to the Cinques' old house I pulled over into their garage like I lived there and shortly after I could see the car pass me by in my rearview. Whoever that was, they were on my ass, but I was ready. Philly didn't know what it was about to get itself into. *Monica's back, and holding no punches.*

James

For Better or Worse

The surgery started exactly two hours later. I sat by my son's bed the entire time leading up to it, wondering who his real daddy was. I mean, I'd been there since the beginning, so I was technically his dad, but who created him was the real question. Me and dude must have looked alike because Jordan had all of my features, from my thick eyebrows to my full lips. Jasmine hated that none of the kids looked like her, and I often teased her that I did all the work and it showed. Those were the days when we were in love, and nothing could have come between us. Before Monica came and poisoned everything we worked so hard to achieve. That bitch! Honestly, the poison had to have already been in the works for her to come and mess everything up so bad, but I didn't have the energy to contemplate all of that at the moment.

What was she doing back in Philly was the next question. I hadn't heard from her in months. Even after we moved and I tried to get in contact with her I couldn't. The cell number I had for her changed and she never responded to the letters I wrote and sent to the return address on the checks she sent us. I used to send her pictures and videos of Junior all the time and I guessed it got to be too much for her. I just felt like although she wasn't physically a part of her son's life that didn't mean that she shouldn't know about it or him. He was just as much a part of her as he was a part of me.

It wasn't lost on me either that Jasmine didn't really care for the boy being around. She wasn't beating the shit out of him, or locking him in closets or no shit like that. Her temperament with him was noticeably different from the other kids though.

Just because you hate the boy's mom doesn't give you just cause to treat him different. He didn't ask to be here. What pissed me off now though was that she was doing all this crazy shit and acting all crazy with Junior, and here we were four years in and come to find out there are two children who ain't even mine. Two! Like, for real? I swore if she wasn't already down for the count I'd have put her ass there for this scandalous shit.

Lord, I can't wait until she wakes up. Oh, I'll make sure she's cool in the gang first, but then it's her ass. Ain't no way to worm out of this one. The only thing I ever did wrong was bring another woman and a kid home. Shit, I guess that makes us two for two. My shit was up and out in the open though . . . Secrets definitely hold more sting.

When the nurse came in to wheel Jordan up to the surgical unit I broke down in my mother-in-law's arms. Kids are not supposed to go through these types of ordeals. Yeah, the occasional bruised knee or broken arm from climbing a tree, but near-death experiences? Naw, that wasn't natural. On the flip side, we would have still had all of these secrets. The entire thing was a mess, but it's always been said that what goes on in the dark comes to light, and right now the light was shining bright as hell.

The doctor said things wouldn't take long; they just had to operate on one of his lungs to get everything moving and he would be good to go. The rejection rate wouldn't be high because the blood was coming right from Jazz, who shared the same blood type.

About an hour and a half into the surgery the doctor came out to talk to us. As soon as I saw him I sprinted over to him, wanting to be the first to hear the news. Jasmine's mom had long ago taken the kids home, and the only one left here with me was Jasmine's dad. I guessed to ensure I wasn't a flight risk. I was past that feeling of wanting to leave though. Now, I just wanted to be sure that everything was going smooth with my wife and son. I wanted to crack Jazz's skull most of all, but there was a time and place for everything. I just needed everyone to come out of this alive.

"Mr. Cinque, everything is looking good, but we are not out of the danger zone yet," the doctor began with a straight face.

"What do you mean, Doc? I don't think I can take much more of this."

"Well, the lung issue is fixed, and the blood transfusion went well. He's just being closed up as we speak. We just need to ensure that there will be no setbacks with the blood transfusion after the fact. Although the blood came from your wife, and everything looks good now, we just want to make sure everything stays good."

"Okay, that's understandable. When will I be able to see him?"

"In about a half hour or so. Once we have him stabilized and in recovery I'll have one of the nurses come to get you and your family. Don't worry, Mr. Cinque, everything will be fine," he answered in a reassuring tone.

"And if it's not?" I questioned back, feeling uncertain.

"Then I will do everything in my power to make it right. I know you want your son home, and he will be soon."

My son. Not the dumb-ass man Jazz was foolish enough to have unprotected sex with, but *my* son. The doctor reached over and gave me a hug, and I had to gather myself before I broke down again. As he walked away, I went and took a seat next to my father-in-law. I wanted to have a heart-to-heart with the man, maybe get some words of wisdom from someone who'd been doing this marriage thing for years. I had questions, and I needed guidance to get through this mess that was my life.

"I know I messed up this time," I began in an apologetic voice. He turned his head to look my way, but didn't say a word. I took that as my cue to continue.

"I just need to know what to do to get back on track. You've been with Jazz's mom since forever. You telling me you never messed up?" I asked him, getting all emotional and shit. I was just so tired of things being the way they were now.

"Of course I've messed up, son. Of course I have," he responded, shaking his head back and forth. "And I know what kind of pain the mess-ups caused to my wife and kids. I promised my wife years ago that I would never do anything else to disrupt our unit. My kids will never see us go through anything damaging again," he said in a sad voice.

"What do I need to do to get back on track?" I asked him in a desperate voice. I needed help . . . I needed answers.

"You get out what you need to discuss and you let it go. Move forward and don't look back. I know you're hurting, son. I know you feel confused because a huge lie was brought to light. Both of y'all did some crazy shit to each other. Discuss it and let it go. Move forward, and create a better atmosphere for your children. All you and Jazz have in the world are each other, outside of family of course, but we can't be or stay married for y'all. It's all on you."

I understood exactly what he meant, and no more words were needed. I had to stand up, and bring us all back together. It was time for me to step my game up, and get everything back on track. Jazz and I needed to discuss how we were going to move forward, whether it was with each other or solo. However it was going down, it needed to be discussed as soon as possible.

I sat back in the chair and closed my eyes, thankful for Jazz's father. Even her brothers. I didn't even have any hard feelings about what they did to me because if I had a sister I would have done the same, if not worse, for her. At the end of the day all we had was family, and we had to stick together through the thick and the thin, no matter how thin shit got.

Lord, I just wanted it to be over. I knew my son would be coming out of surgery soon, and we would be able to meet him in recovery. I wanted to be ready, so I told my father-in-law that I was going to use the restroom right quick so that I could be ready to go down to recovery when it was time.

It didn't take long to relieve myself, and as I stood in the bathroom mirror, I could see the toll the last few days were taking written all over my face. Cupping my hands under the faucet, I took some water and splashed it on my face in order to wake up. That helped a little, but what I really needed was a soft bed. After drying my hands, I dug into my pockets for a piece of gum to get this stale taste out of my mouth.

I felt the piece of paper, and when I unfolded it I recognized the handwriting before I even saw the name. *Monica . . . that bitch! I swear, she always found a way to worm her ass in where she's not wanted.* Jazz's mom didn't know about all the nonsense we went through with her, and I was sure when she approached her she played it innocent. And if she saw Jazz's mom that meant she saw her son. Once again, this was all too much! I simply folded the paper and stuck it in my wallet. I wasn't sure if I was going to contact her or let her find me. Monica always got what she wanted, but what, in fact, that thing was I was unsure about at the moment.

This woman was going to drive me crazy, but I didn't have time to think about that at the moment. Tucking my wallet back in my pocket, I went out and sat down next to Jazz's dad. He gave me a comforting smile, letting me know he understood and he was there for me. I felt a little better knowing that things could get better if we worked on it. The kind of love that Jazz's parents had was undeniable, and I felt like me and Jazz could have the same happiness if we worked hard enough for it.

I remembered on our wedding day Jazz's father told me that marriage wasn't easy, but worth fighting for. There would be plenty of ups and downs over the years, and sometimes it would feel like we would never make it through.

"Son, just hang in there," he said to me over a glass of champagne. "It's a rough road, and when you think you can't take it, look back on what you've already made it through. Those are the times that will remind you that it's worthwhile."

That statement never meant much to me before, but as I sat here and reminisced about how things used to be, I couldn't help but wonder how much work it would take to get it back. Was getting it back even the way to go? *Will Jazz even want to? I'm angry about a lot of shit, and I know she is to, but for the moment we'll just have to see where this road takes us. For better or worse, through sickness and health was what we vowed to one another.* There was no turning back now, and I was ready to fight for mine . . . whatever that is.

Carlos

Tailgating

"Was it her?" I asked the person on the other end of the phone. I thought Sheneka was lying when she said she saw Monica at the airport. Was the bitch serious? It'd been years since she stepped foot back in Philly, and I wondered for a second what she was doing back here. I still had an unsettled beef with her regarding Rico, and Sheneka had some shit to get off her chest as well.

I had one of my top lieutenants follow her just to make sure. Sheneka had an undying vendetta against Monica, and I had to make sure she wasn't sending me on a wild goose chase like she'd done in the past. Every dark chocolate woman she saw with curves reminded her of Monica, and at one point over the years I had to check her into a mental facility so that she could get her head on right. Hell, she was in one now, and they allowed her to hold a little part-time job during the week, so she worked at a coffee cart at Philadelphia International. I knew she loved the hell out of Rico, in her own way, but was it cause for her to go crazy? She was cool for a while, but it seemed like old crazy and deranged was showing back up, and before any moves were made I had to be sure.

"It was definitely her," the voice responded. "I wasn't too sure myself, but when I saw her getting out of a car at her old crib and talking to some people who lived there I snapped a few pics just to be sure."

"Send them over, and I'll check them out. Who was she talking to?"

"I don't know. Some bitch was outside with her kid. I wasn't sure if she knew the chick, but she went into the house so she had to. I followed her after she came out, and got flicks of the car she's pushing also. Sheneka might actually be on point this time."

"Okay. We won't make any moves yet, just be ready when I give the word."

"No problem."

And the call was disconnected. A minute or so later my phone buzzed, indicating I had a picture message, and sure enough Monica's ass was back in Philly. She was still fine as hell, too. Even better than I last remembered. Wherever she went to must have been a good move because she was on point. I scrolled through the shots of her and the car, quickly realizing that she had a rental. She definitely wasn't here to stay, so what brought her back?

I also noticed that she was by herself, and last I remembered she had just pushed out a kid. Where was the baby? And where was that fine-ass sister of hers? I had plenty of questions, and I knew Sheneka would have plenty more, so I held off on hitting her up right now. I didn't feel like the bullshit with her today.

Rolling over, I signaled for the young buck I had lying next to me to handle her business. Without having to say a word, she gave up the best head service ever. I almost couldn't concentrate, but ol' girl was handling her business. I knew I had to get some answers from Monica, because I was still not convinced that Rico killed himself. He definitely wouldn't have gone out like that, but who did it and why? Questions, and more confusion . . . First thing I needed to do was find out where she was resting her head, and then I would find out why she was here.

I didn't really feel like dealing with the shit right now though, but my head was definitely spinning, and Monica was going to get hers. For right now . . . I'd just enjoy this blessing, and as I gripped the back of the young girl's head I let my mind relax and my body surrender to the feeling of excellent head service.

Sheneka

Don't Take It Personal

I told that fool that I saw Monica's trick ass. I was pissed that I even had to go through all the hoops to get Carlos's dumb ass on board. Okay, so a few times I was off the mark, but I was sure this time. I was just waiting on him to call me back to confirm. I wished for a second I was allowed to carry a cell phone because I could have taken a picture of her. The program I was in didn't allow us to have phones, and we had a curfew on top of that! I didn't want to get fired for abandoning my job, so I couldn't follow her out of the building. It's cool though, because I straight used the job phone to hit Carlos on his jack. I wanted Monica's head, and I wasn't stopping until I had it.

Yeah, after all this time I was still upset about Rico's death. Who are you to judge me? I really loved him, in spite of what everyone chose to believe. Yeah, I let Carlos and a few of his other homeboys sample the goods a few times, but that was just revenge when Rico pissed me off. It wasn't that serious for me. I thought we were good, me and Rico. We had a really bad argument and I told that fool to step, but I didn't know Monica was going to swoop in like she did. Put me on ten every time I thought about it!

What pissed me off the most was how fast she had this fool open! *Like, for real, Rico?* I knew that bitch pussy wasn't better than mine, and he was out here acting like he just hit the fucking jackpot! Holding hands in public and everything! Oooohhhh, I was pissed! This dizzy bitch had the stash spot on lock and everything. By the time we got there it wasn't a damn dime or jewel left, and since it was all drug money it wasn't like we could report the shit stolen. Oh, how I hate a bitch more scandalous than me.

Before I could even visit him word on the street was somebody got the drop on Rico. The word was that he was found dangling from the top bunk with a broken neck or some shit like that, but Rico would have never just killed himself. That wasn't how he got down, and I wasn't even believing that shit. That bitch got him murked . . . That's my story and I'm sticking to it.

I wanted to kick that bastard of a child out her gut through her damn nose, but I could never catch up with her slick ass. Besides, regardless of how crazy my ass was, the baby had nothing to do with it. I just wanted her. Before I could get a hold of her she had jumped ship, and I didn't know where to find her. I was patient though, and I knew she would show her face eventually. A few false alarms had me ready to get shit poppin' on complete strangers, and that's when I knew I needed to lay my ass down on a couch somewhere and talk to a shrink. Yeah, they tried to convince me that what I was feeling was connected to some random childhood incident, but I wasn't buying that bullshit with the last dollar to my name. She fucked up my life, I wanted revenge, and no matter how long it took I was going to be on her ass. *Oh, it took about four years, but lo and behold the bitch is back . . . and I'm ready for her ass!*

James

A Brighter Side of Darkness

My boy made it through safe. I was so relieved when I got down to the recovery room and saw him breathing. He was out like a light, and had tubes coming out of his body, but he was alive. I'd take that over dead any day of the week. Jazz's father looked relieved as well. I wanted to ask him how he felt about the news of the second set of twins not being mine, but I figured I'd already asked enough questions for the day, and I would ask once the coast was clear.

The doctor said that Jordan would have to stay for observation, but should be able to go home in a few days. The injuries that he sustained from the accident were healing well and it was just a matter of time before he was back to his normal self. He would still be on bed rest, and it may take a few more days before he was up and moving around, but each day would get better. That was music to my ears. The doctor was also talking about waking Jazz from her medically induced coma, depending on how the swelling around her brain was looking. It could be a few more days or a few more weeks; they would just have to chart the progress and keep an eye on her. Hell, it'd only been a few days since all this dumb shit went down, it just felt like we'd been here forever.

I stayed with my son overnight, and after putting in for a short family medical leave at work the next morning, I was up at the hospital visiting both my wife and son, waiting for them to wake up. He was really tired, but when Jordan finally opened his eyes and saw me sitting next to him a small smile spread across his face. I called the nurse immediately because he was strapped into the bed. They did this as a precaution so that he wouldn't wake up and yank all of the tubes out. My eyes welled up with tears instantly, and for the first time in about a week things were starting to look up.

He was on pain meds from the rib injury, and he was out instantly when the nurse gave him another dose. I wanted to hold him, but he seemed so fragile. I didn't want to cause him more pain than he was already in, but I did kiss him gently on his cheek and I held his little hand in mine, keeping him close. I was informed that his lung injury was doing great as well and that definitely helped me breathe easier.

I spent a little time with Jazz as well, but the atmosphere in her room was different. I spent most of my time just staring at her, wondering when shit got this bad. We both did things that I was sure we regretted now, and I wondered how she would be once she was finally allowed to wake up. Periodically I would reach over and touch her, but she felt so cold and clammy. I wondered where the love was that I had for her when we first met. Where did that feeling go? I mean, I loved my wife, but it wasn't the same kind of love that we had pre-children. Did she still love me? All of these thoughts swam around in an angry sea of emotions in my head that I just couldn't shake, and to be totally honest . . . it made me nervous.

On my way out of Jazz's room to go grab a bite from the café I was thankful to finally have some time to myself. As I was passing the rooms I saw transport bringing out the judge's body and everything clicked instantly. *That's why Monica was at the hospital.* I remembered what he looked like from the court-issued papers we got for Junior.

"Monica probably gave that man a heart attack," I said more to myself as I kept stride right past him and made my way to the elevator. I knew I shouldn't call her crazy ass, but I knew I had to. I reasoned in my head that she probably just wanted to see her son.

I made my trip quick to the café, and by the time I got back up to Jordan's room, Jazz's mom was there. I stood outside the door to let her have her moment. I could see the tears glistening in her eyes and running down her cheeks. At the moment she reminded me so much of Jazz, and I knew that's exactly how Jazz would look when she reached her mom's age. After a few more minutes I walked into the room and gave her a hug. She leaned into my shoulder and accepted it, and I knew in that moment that regardless of how raggedy this situation was between me and her daughter, she still loved me like her son.

"James, you're doing a good job with these children," she began in a sad voice. "I know you were caught off guard by the discovery, but these are your kids. Just promise me you will continue to do right by them."

"I will . . . I definitely will," I reassured her as I held her tight. Didn't she know that these kids were my everything? I'd been beating myself up every day about this horrible accident, and I promised myself that I would be more active in their lives and help Jazz out more.

"That's your son, James, that test doesn't mean a thing."

I didn't even bother to respond because I already felt that in my heart. We were a unit, and nothing would break us. I was just ready to get my family back together so that we could have a clean slate and start fresh.

"Mr. Cinque, glad I was able to catch up with you." The doctor greeted us both as he walked into the room. "Your son is doing well, and I'm thinking he may be released early next week. He hasn't shown any sign of rejection, and his vitals are looking good. Right now he is doing pretty good sleeping on his own, and as you can see, he's just on a drip to keep him hydrated and asleep for now. This will keep him down during the night, and once he wakes up in the morning he should be okay."

"Wow, that's great, Doc! I wasn't expecting it to be that quickly," I responded as I looked from the doctor to my son's sleeping form in the bed.

"Well, the transfusion portion only takes about an hour or so, and his ribs are positioned and bonded. He will definitely be sore, and we will give you pain medication to manage that. Expect him to sleep a lot the first few days home, which is probably better for him to deal with the pain. As long as he isn't developing any fever or hives he should be okay. The tenderness in his ribs will subside over time as well."

I was elated to hear this news, and so was Jazz's mom. She was just telling me how much the kids missed their brother, so

I knew they would be hype that he was finally coming home. I knew I would put him in the bed with me where I could keep an eye on him just in case he needed to go the bathroom, or needed more medicine. This was going to be a journey, but I was more than ready to take on the challenge.

"And what about Jasmine?" my mother-in-law asked. I was wondering the same thing.

"We are going to keep her under for a little while longer just to be sure that the pressure in her skull is going down the way it's supposed to. That way it would hopefully lessen any brain damage that may have occurred. With the drilling we performed on her skull, the pressure will subside fairly quickly if everything continues to go as planned. "

"Brain damage?" she said more in disbelief than shock. We were informed of the possibility of such things on the night of the accident, and I guessed we were all just hoping for the best.

"How would we know the severity of it?" she asked again, fear creeping up in her voice.

"We won't know until she wakes up. She may be perfectly fine, or it may be severe. As of right now she's having normal brain activity, but it's hard to tell."

"Okay, thank you for everything you are doing," I finally intervened to keep her from getting even more upset. This entire situation was depressing, and I just wanted it to be over.

"No problem. If you have any other questions I'm on call."

After he left the room, we both sort of breathed a sigh of relief. We had one out of the woods, and if Jazz would pull through soon everything would be on track.

Later in the evening Jazz's mom followed me over to the house so that we could prepare for Jordan and the rest of the kids coming home.

We got to work with changing the linen on all the beds, and picking up around the house. Jazz's parents were staying at her brother's house not too far from here, so once we were done she called Jazz's father to let him know she was on her way. I sat by the window with the phone in my hand and waited until she was safely pulled off, and I didn't move until she called to let me know she had arrived safely. It wasn't until then that I was able to kick back and grab me a beer. I needed to get my head on right, and I knew once the kids got back I would have to focus on them. I reminisced about my life over the last four years, and I knew I would do whatever I had to do to get us back.

All of it wasn't a total bust. There were those times over the years when Jazz and I were able to come together as a unit and operate like a normal family. Especially when it came to supporting the kids with school. Even when a morning was hectic, we always showed up to any function, parent-teacher conference, school play, or whatever else was going on the way we were supposed to. I must say, when things were good with me and Jazz, it was amazing. When things got bad though, oh, my goodness it was the worst ever.

Rising early the next morning, I made my way up to the hospital to check on my family. Monica had been on my mind all night, but I was able to refrain from calling the number that I got from Jazz's mom. I didn't feel like playing with fire.

When I got to my son's room, he was up being fed breakfast by the nurse in between talk about *SpongeBob SquarePants*. I was so happy to see him up. He still looked tired, but he was alive. At that moment that was all that mattered in the world.

"Daddy!" he yelped out in a weak, scratchy voice that almost brought me to tears. There was no way in the world I was going to be able to tell this boy that he wasn't my flesh and blood.

"I'm here, son. How are you feeling?" I asked as I kept my tears in check, and resisted the urge to scoop him up into my arms.

"Everything hurts, Daddy," he spoke in a tiny voice that pulled at my heart.

"We had just gave him some pain medicine, Mr. Cinque, and it should be kicking in soon."

I thanked her, and told her that I would feed him the rest of his breakfast. Switching places, I sat close to the bed after kissing him on the forehead. Studying his slightly swollen face, I couldn't help but try to place it. Whose face did he have? Banishing the thought immediately, I smiled as I fed him a little more food. The medicine was starting to take effect, and I could see him trying to fight to keep his eyes open.

"Daddy, will you be here when I wake up?" he asked right before drifting off.

"I sure will, son," I responded as I laid the back of the bed down, and positioned the pillows so that he could be comfortable. He would be going home pretty soon, and I couldn't wait.

Monica

All's Fair in War and War

I waited a little while longer before backing out of the driveway just to make sure my little follower wasn't creeping back up on me. Well, that and I saw the shades move in the old Cinque house, and I didn't want the resident to think I was lost or crazy. It puzzled me what all of that was about, and I didn't have a clue as to who would want me trailed. Yeah, I had tons of enemies in Philly, but there were too many to pinpoint at the moment. Besides, I still had to figure out where I was going to stay.

It had been a few hours since I'd been back to the hospital, and I had yet to make it to the mall. I didn't even feel like going at this point. Turning the car onto the street, I decided to just go back to the hospital, and figure it all out from there.

When I entered the building, the cute little receptionist was back at the desk with her sunny disposition, but I didn't even feel like trying to figure her out today. I did wave hello on the walk by though, and hopped in the first elevator available going up to the room. As I was walking down the hall, I was relieved that none of the Cinques were out and about. Their son was on a different floor, so I was sure someone was there, just not down here right now.

As I strolled the hall, I could see into the patients' rooms. The rooms in the intensive care unit were different, and a shaded window was there as opposed to a solid wall. This entire floor was depressing, and gave me goose bumps.

Making my way down the hall I almost tripped over my own feet when I came across Jasmine's room. Now, when the judge was admitted to ICU I didn't think the possibility of running into Jasmine was high because the ICU was huge and there were a ton of rooms on this floor, and when we got here everything was a blur so I wasn't really thinking about it. To see her now was crazy. My goodness, she looked horrible! I mean, her car was wrapped around a utility pole just a few days ago, but I wasn't prepared for what I saw. Her entire face was black and blue, and she had all kinds of tubes coming from her body. I couldn't believe my damn eyes, and had to get a closer look.

Checking my surroundings to make sure the coast was clear, I dipped into her room and stood beside her bed. She had tight, angry-looking stitches across her left eyebrow, wrapping around her jaw, and stopping just at her perfect lips. Dark purple to almost black bruises covered her swollen face, making her look like an alien. A small patch of hair near her ear was shaved off, and I assumed it was from having to have her jaw wired shut. I found myself having to get wired down once years ago, but that's a story for another time.

The dull beep of the machines that she was hooked to in combination with a slight swooshing sound let me know that she was still alive, but the machines were probably what was keeping her here. I reached out hesitantly to touch her hand, and it felt cold and clammy. Snatching my hand back, I was shocked to find a lone tear traveling down the side of my face. I knew the accident was bad, but I didn't know it was this serious.

"Jazz, what were you doing out in a storm?" I asked the dead air, not really expecting a response. I stood there for a little while longer just taking it all in, deciding to leave before I was caught. Just as I was turning around, I could hear someone clearing his throat. Spinning around completely I was greeted by a handsome doctor who held an amused yet puzzled look on his face.

"She's been down for a few days now, but I don't remember meeting you. Are you a friend of the family?" the doctor asked in a deep voice as he entered the room. Taking a second to wipe the tear from my face, I got myself together before answering.

"Yes, Jasmine and James are . . ." I trailed off, not sure of how much to reveal. He didn't need to know that I was a home wrecker who left my baby because I was selfish, and just now decided to pop up and check on him. I also didn't want to say too much because I was sure the doctor would mention it to James whenever he came back up to visit. "They are good friends of mine. I'm here visiting another friend, and I just happened to see Jasmine in here."

"Oh, okay, well, Mrs. Cinque is unresponsive at the moment, and since there isn't a visitor restriction list I guess it's okay, but I want you to make this visit quick so that she can rest peacefully, Mrs. . . . " He trailed off, waiting for a name.

"Stone . . . Sheila Stone," I replied, giving him the judge's secretary's name instead of my own. In fact, I needed to see what was going on with old Sheila anyway. *It's been years, and I'm sure she misses me. Not!*

"Okay, Mrs. Stone. Wrap this visit up quick, and have a great night."

"Okay, I will."

Once the doctor was gone I turned and stared at Jazz for a few more minutes. What was going on in the Cinque household that shit got this bad between them? This was how I was able to get back in before, and something told me I needed to use this down time between them to get next to my son while I still could. James, I was sure, wouldn't have a problem, but if Jazz was anything like I remembered, she would definitely make this shit an issue beyond what it really was.

Pulling out my cell phone, I focused in on her bruised face and snapped a few pictures of her. Securing my phone back in my bag, I walked off to find the judge, contemplating if I would sell the pictures, and to what news station. I was sure they were worth some type of money, but for now I would sit on them. Just in case I had to use them to my advantage. *You just never know these days.*

Making my way down the hall, I was stopped by two bodyguards who were blocking the judge's door. Before I could go clean off, I was given an envelope and a menacing look as I was instructed to leave the premises. One of the guards took the liberty of escorting me to the elevator, and warned me not to spazz out and to just read the letter. I saw a woman sitting next to the judge's bed, but I couldn't really make out her face from the door. It was probably his miserable-ass wife. I saw her at the airport, so she knew I was here. I was just wondering if she knew we were hooking up while I was here. Still shocked, I got into the elevator, and stepped back as he pushed the button for the ground floor and stepped back out, giving me one last evil look as the doors closed.

I was numb as I walked through the hospital and out to my car, seemingly not breathing until I was safely inside with the doors locked. I sat in silence for a long while before realizing I still had not opened the envelope. Hurriedly, I tore open the sealed envelope. Inside was the key to the hideaway, a note, and the address with directions on how to get back there. The butler instructed me to stay there until the judge was able to communicate. What kind of backyard barnigan's bullshit was this?

Feeling like I didn't really have a choice—after all, all of my shit was at the judge's spot—I started the car and got myself together so that I could take the drive out. This was some bullshit if I'd never been involved in any before, and I knew I needed to make my stay in Philly short and sweet.

The directions were precise, citing landmarks and all as I carefully drove out to the outskirts of the city. A dusting of snow fell as I drove, and I took my sweet old time, not wanting to end up wrapped around a pole like Jazz had been just days ago. The only difference between us two was that she had family who cared enough to visit and rush up there to make sure she was okay. If my car skidded out of control and crashed who did I have to call? My sister? If anything she would only care long enough to get a hold of my money and any policy info that I had to collect on. My brother had been MIA for as long as I could remember, and most of the time I forgot that he even existed.

These thoughts made me sad as I drove, knowing that I was really in the world all by myself. Pulling the car to the side of the road to avoid a potential collision, I put my head on the steering wheel once I was safely in park and cried my little eyes out. One would think that I would be immune to these feelings by now, but every so often they crept up on me and broke me down. For a second I thought about calling Jaydah up for company and comfort, but she worked my nerves so bad in Atlanta that I couldn't even be bothered.

Shaking off the sad feelings as best as I could, I eased the car back on the road and kept moving toward the judge's spot. When I finally got there, the butler greeted me at the door, and came to help me inside. Once the door was locked for the night, I barricaded myself in the room, and hopped in the shower to wash the day off. I made sure the door was locked because I didn't want the butler's creepy ass to be masturbating to my naked body while I was in the shower. I mean, he didn't look creepy as far as description, but there was a quiet creepiness about him that I just couldn't put my finger on at the moment. On top of all of this, I was horny as hell, and I didn't want him to catch me at a weak moment. I saw the way he looked at me, and if he kept it up my pussy would be sitting on his lips before he could hum a tune.

Taking the time to dry off and moisturize, I slipped into some boring pajamas, afterward popping out my laptop to download the pictures of Jasmine onto my flash drive. Looking at the pictures, the scarring looked even more brutal as I studied her face up close. Shaking my head, I couldn't believe what had happened to her. It made me rethink selling the pictures, but I knew I would keep them just in case shit got crazy when it came to my son. It was a shame, but it wasn't my fault so I wasn't about to feel guilty.

I downloaded the pictures quick, then made myself comfortable on the bed. My stomach was growling something serious, reminding me that I hadn't eaten all day. I wanted to call the butler, but I didn't want him to have a reason to come up to the room. Taking the chance, I slipped on my Ugg slippers and crept through the house. When I made my way to the kitchen, I found a tray of food set up for me. Creep factor number five! How could he just assume I was hungry? Dismissing the fact, I looked to see what he made me. I had a thing about eating in the room and I already did it once, so I opted to eat at the kitchen bar instead. Searching through my phone, I looked at some e-mails from potential buyers from my art gallery listing as I noshed.

Out of the corner of my eye I saw movement, and I turned to find the butler preparing a sandwich for himself. Damn, he was light on his feet. I stared at the man as he moved about in the massive kitchen like I wasn't even there. Sizing him up I concluded that he had to be gay. Okay, so it wasn't like I was sitting here in lingerie, but I still looked damn good in my Victoria's Secret pajama pants and wife beater. No bra or panties underneath by the way, and I smelled delicious! A sultry mix of pineapple and coconut radiated from my skin in tantalizing waves that even turned me on, so I knew he had to be on it. This man would be a fool and gay, both at the same time, not to want this.

Deciding to test the waters just to see what he would do, I sauntered over to start some shit. He was busy spreading mustard on his bread and pretending like he didn't notice my sexy ass in this room. Stepping out of my clothes, I kindly slid the platter he was working on to the side, and hopped up on the counter, him still standing there holding the knife and the bread. Spreading my legs wide, I leaned back on my elbows, giving him full access to my pierced clit and juicy hole. My nipples were standing at attention, and I had an "I dare you" look on my face. He looked like he was contemplating taking the risk, and I counted down from ten in my head giving him even less time than that to make up his mind. As I approached "six" and prepared to close my legs, he leaned in and swirled his tongue around my clit.

Good boy, I thought as I took the liberty of placing my legs on his shoulders and scooting to the edge so that he could have full access. After this stressful ass day I needed some release, even if it was from the damn butler.

James

Welcome Back, Jordan

My son was coming home today. After about two weeks, and a major setback, he was finally getting out of the hospital. The puncture in his lung was giving him more trouble than the doctors anticipated and he had to go back into surgery because there was a small leak near the inside suture site, but he pulled through just fine. The kids were so glad he was coming to the house, but it was a bittersweet moment because their mom was still down for the count. Splitting my time between home and the hospital was draining, but I didn't have a choice. Yes, Jazz's family was there to help, but I had to step up to the plate and take care of my business. The doctor said that the swelling in her brain was making progress and going down as scheduled, and they didn't want to chance waking her up too early and making matters worse. She responded to the touching of her feet, and hands, and displayed normal brain activity for someone in a dream state. I was relieved to hear that, and was happy to know that there was still a chance.

The kids and I spent the entire morning decorating the house for Jordan's welcome home party. After baking cupcakes and hanging streamers and balloons, we cleaned up and were ready to go. I warned the kids before I left that Jordan wouldn't be able to run around with them because of the type of surgery he had, and he might be asleep well before the party was over, and they appeared to understand. Janice was super excited because her other half was finally back. She was lost without him, and I could see it all in her actions. She wasn't as energetic as the other kids, and was sad all the time. When I told her that he was coming home, her entire mood changed.

Thank you, Jesus! There were other family members there as well to great him, and everything was going as planned for the first time in never.

Jasmine's mom and dad stayed with the kids at home and her brother rode with me up to the hospital to help me with Jordan. I didn't want Jordan to see his mom in the ICU, so we stopped there first to see Jasmine before going up. I knew I would have to bring the kids up eventually, but not in her current state. They would have tons of questions that the younger ones wouldn't comprehend and it was just too much at once.

When we got to the room, the doctor was there charting observations, and instructing one of the nurses on doses of medication for Jasmine. We stood back to let him conduct business, waiting patiently for him to finish. I knew he would fill me in on everything afterward. It didn't take him long to finish up, and pretty soon he was ready for us.

"Mr. Cinque, it's homegoing day for young Jordan, right?" he asked as he shook my and my brother-in-law's hands.

"Yes, sir, it is." I smiled at him. "The kids and I are excited."

"That's good. He's been waiting for you guys since early this morning," he responded as he scribbled something else in Jasmine's chart. "As for your wife, I pushed up her dosage of pain medication due to her response to the pain overnight. She hasn't woken up yet, but her blood pressure did shoot up a little, and the nurse charted some incoherent moans, indicating discomfort. She was taken off of the drugs that put her in the coma-like state so that she could wake up slowly."

I nodded as he talked, not really sure on how to respond. I had so many mixed emotions, and I wasn't really sure how I was going to be able to deal with Jasmine once she was finally allowed to wake up. How would she respond to her scars? So many emotions and questions were swirling around in my head, and I had to take a seat to digest it all.

"So, for now, I want you to enjoy your time with your son. The hard part hasn't begun yet, James. Once Jasmine comes through, it's going to take a lot of work and determination. There's a possibility that she will be angry at first, and maybe for a long while. We have therapy and everything here to help you through. For now, concentrate on your son, and everything else will fall into place."

I nodded my head as he talked, going into my own thoughts. Were we going to need therapy? I was certain that she was going to be angry because it was my fault that she was in here in the first place. Shit just got real, and I would be the first to admit that I wasn't handling it too well. It just sunk in that it was going to be a long time before there would be some kind of normalcy in our family. *Lord, just help me get through it.*

"So, take a few minutes to let your wife know that you are here. She can hear you, she just can't respond right now. The nurses are here if you need anything, and I know Jordan is excited, so enjoy your ride home," the doctor concluded, shaking our hands and giving the nurse further instructions before leaving.

I was stuck on stupid for a minute just standing there staring at Jazz. Her brother excused himself to give me a little privacy, letting me know that he would be waiting outside the room. There was an awkward silence in the room. It was funny how since she'd been here I never bothered to say too many words to her. The majority of the time I just sat and stared at her and wished that things were different. What was I supposed to say? I was sorry that things turned out like this? I'd already said that a million times. I guessed she would want to know if the kids were okay, but after telling her that what else was there to talk about? It was too early to talk about the "who's your daddy" issue with the twins, and we would just have to cross that road when we get there.

Taking a seat next to her bed, I took her hand into mine and just stared at her. At that moment I didn't see the banged and bruised Jasmine lying in a hospital bed. At this moment it was on our honeymoon, and we had just finished making love for the third time. Even then I couldn't believe I lucked up, and got to marry her. Tracing a finger along her bruise, I saw her at a time when she was taking a quick nap and exhausted from carrying our first set of twins, and not in a medically induced coma. We were so excited and cautious at the same time because she had already miscarried twice before. She had made it to almost seven months, and the twins were doing good.

"Jazz . . ." I began in a hesitant voice, trying to unscramble my words and my thoughts. "Jazz . . . I'm sorry this happened to you. I know I've already apologized a million times, and if I need to I'll do it a million more. I love you, and I'll be here for you when they wake you up."

Her fingers tightened a little around my hand, and a tear slipped from my eyes. She heard me, and that's all that mattered. I sat there a moment longer, taking her in and remembering the times we had. Even the dumb shit that happened over the years, and I knew for certain I wasn't meant to spend my life with anyone else but her. As I prepared to leave, the doctor stepped back into the room.

"James, I'm glad I was able to catch you before I left for the day," the doctor began as he walked closer to us. "A young lady stopped by earlier to see your wife. I believe her name was Sheila. She said she didn't know your wife was here and that you guys are good friends. Just wanted to tell you that just in case she called."

"Oh, okay, thanks a lot," I responded. Monica was a slick bitch indeed, and I knew I needed to stop her in her tracks before she started some shit. That was clever of her to give the doctor a different name, but I knew the game and was already five steps ahead of her conniving ass.

"No problem, I'm on call if you need me."

After giving Jazz a kiss on her forehead, I met up with her brother in the hallway, and we made our way up to Jordan's room. I felt for my wallet, remembering that was where I stuck Monica's number, and I decided that I would call her once I got settled later in the day and all of the kids were asleep. This bitch always showed up at the most inopportune times, and I had to get her straight before Jazz came back into the picture. My wife didn't need to be stressed out with her antics; we already had enough drama going on.

When we approached Jordan's room I could hear his laughter before I even got to the door. He sounded stronger today, and that just warmed my heart to know he was recovering in a timely fashion. I hated to see my son all strapped up and taped up with tubes coming out of everywhere, and I was glad to see them removed. It was just too damn emotional. He was cracking up watching a cartoon, and his little voice spoke volumes of how he was feeling.

When I and his uncle walked into the room, his face lit up, and my heart broke when he tried to move in the bed and realized he couldn't. Quickly moving to his bedside, I took him into my arms as gently as I could, and gave him a hug. He looked so happy to see us, and I was definitely glad that he was well on his way to getting better. Just thinking that he could have easily died in that car crash brought me to tears every time, but I had to be strong for him.

"I'm going home today!" my son shouted as he jumped around a little too much for my liking. The pain medicine that they had him on must have really been on point because he was acting like he didn't feel a thing.

"Yes, you are. Are you ready to see your brothers and sisters?" I asked him as I helped his uncle change him into an outfit to go home in. The streets were a little better today, but it was still really cold outside, so we made sure to bundle him up as best we could with keeping him comfortable at the same time.

"Yes, I miss everybody," he said in an excited voice.

"That's good. They all missed you too," I spoke to him as I blinked back tears. "We have a surprise for you when you get home."

"You do?" he asked with that bright smile on his face that almost made me forget that he was conceived by someone else. "Will Mommy be there?"

The room went silent, and I looked to Jazz's brother for help. He busied himself with the packing of Jordan's stuff, but I could see the nervousness in him. How did I answer the question without causing alarm in my young son? He was still fragile from his own shit, so I didn't need him to worry about something that he couldn't fix.

"Mommy won't be home for a while because she's not feeling well," I began, hoping that he understood. "Your grand-mom and your brothers and sisters are waiting for you though. Are you ready to get out of here?"

"Yes, Daddy," he said as his little eyes began to close. The medicine that they had him on was making him sleepy, and at the right time. Lord knows I didn't feel like answering a bunch of questions that I really didn't have the answer to. Jazz's brother looked relieved as well that Jordan was falling asleep, and once I signed the discharge papers, and got the medicine from the pharmacy, we were ready to go.

As I drove back through the city to take my son home, I just hoped that I could do this by myself. Although I had plenty of help from the family, everyone couldn't stay forever, and would have to get back to their own lives pretty soon. I also had to get at Monica before she started acting crazy. It'd been a few years, but I wasn't sure about her mental state. For all I knew she might just try to take her son from us, and that in itself was a whole, entirely different headache that I didn't feel like dealing with. Jazz probably wouldn't mind seeing him go since she never really got attached to him in the first place and he was such a problem child in her eyes, but the kids would be devastated and I wasn't about to let that happen. This was too much going on at one time, but it was happening for a reason. It was just time for me to embrace it, and try to move forward.

Monica

Stirring the Pot

I was getting bored sitting around this house. The judge was still locked down in the hospital surrounded by security, and I wasn't permitted to leave the house without a guard as well. This was some bullshit, and I swore as soon as I checked on my seed I was out of this joint. *Philly can kiss my black ass.* Shit with the butler got real old real quick as well. He had the tools to get things popping; he just didn't know how to use them. That was a shame, too, because his head game was off the hook! I ended up beating off in my room because this fool just wasn't hitting the mark.

So, I found myself not wanting to do shit, and the only time I called the butler was when I wanted something to eat. The streets were clearing up, and the storm had moved on, so it was safe to go outside now. I just didn't have anywhere to go. I wasn't even amused by the Cinque updates on the news any-more, and I was getting pissed because James had yet to call me. What was this fool waiting on? The one time I snuck up to the hospital I found out that their son had been discharged by cutie behind the desk, but Jazz was still there. I attempted to visit Jazz, but as soon as I stepped off the elevator, the judge's bodyguards rushed me and had me escorted back out. They weren't even trying to hear that I was there to see someone else, and that time I was actually threatened not to show my face up there again. That was like a week ago, and I was ready to bounce.

The plan was to dip into Philly, check on my seed, and slide back out undetected, but shit never worked out the way I wanted it to. I had a damn lunatic following me around in a car I didn't recognize, but it had me nervous about going back out on the street alone. The Cinques were experiencing their own bullshit, and I was stuck in this gorgeous-ass house with nothing to do but play with my pussy all day. For some that may have been the bomb, but for me this was not the move. I wanted out now!

I just couldn't bring myself to leave for some reason. There was no one or nothing keeping me from driving to the Philadelphia International Airport, turning in my rental, checking my bags, and getting the hell out of dodge. Not one thing that I could think of really. My assistant kept me abreast on business, and everything was running smoothly. She even checked the condo while I was away, and there was nothing to report, so what was really keeping me here?

Even though I gave up my son it was my responsibility to make sure that he was safe and being taken care of properly. This feeling I was getting in my gut wasn't merely a case of bad gas; my son needed me. Or so I led myself to believe. From what I'd seen so far he didn't seem to be in harm's way. His hair was cut and his clothes were clean, he was gathered with the family and not set off by himself, and he looked like he was being fed and not undernourished. There was just something that I couldn't see right now, and I knew if I left before finding out what it was I would regret it, so for now I was staying until I felt like I could go in peace and not have to worry about him.

Deciding to make contact with the outside world, I thumbed through the Rolodex in the judge's office to see who I could get to help me with this kid situation that I was having. I knew there had to be someone out there who could help me, and I didn't want to have to wait on the judge to get better to get to work on this. I was not staying in Philly any longer than necessary. I had businesses to run back in Atlanta, and being here wasn't working in my favor.

A lot of the names I didn't recognize, but from the listing of the Rolodex they appeared to hold prestigious positions so I took the liberty of storing the info in my phone of the ones that I could utilize later on. I made my visit to the office quick, after snagging Sheila's number, because I didn't want to get caught by the butler. After all, Stenton was just asking for someone to be in his business. My office would never just be left open for anyone to walk in and browse around. I had too much at stake.

Once back in my room, I blocked my number and called Sheila to see if she would answer. She was probably at work and wouldn't answer right away, and I decided against leaving a message because I knew she would never call back. Allowing the phone to ring until the voice mail picked up, I hung up and called the courthouse instead. That was a phone she had to answer.

"District Court, how may I direct your call?" Sheila answered the phone in a very professional voice that held a lot more confidence than I remembered. I guessed once I left Philly she was able to do her.

"Sheila, it's Monica. I need your help," I began, ready to run down a list of errands for her. As I was talking I noticed the phone was awfully quiet on the other end. Taking the phone from my ear, my screen read that the call was disconnected. *Did this bitch just hang up on me?* Going to my call log, I hit the number again, waiting for her to answer.

"District Court—"

"Did you hang up on me?" I spat into the phone, ready to get rowdy if necessary.

"Monica, now is not the time—"

"Then when is the time? This is about my son," I said, cutting her off midsentence.

"Look, I get out of here at five. Get a pen and pad to take down my number and we can discuss it then. Right now, I'm working and don't have time for this."

Seems like we got a backbone while I was gone, I thought as I got a piece of paper ready. I already had a number for her, but the judge's Rolodex may not have been up to date, or she may have been operating from a different phone. The number she gave me was the same number I had, and after confirming that I would call her at five fifteen, I hung up. I needed to get in touch with James, but I wasn't really sure how to go about it.

Falling back on the bed, I just stared at the ceiling, trying to sort everything out. My phone ringing scared the shit out of me, and I jumped up to see who it was. The screen read Jaydah's name above the number, and I was not beat for her today. I was surprised that it took her this long to call me. Maybe she had book signings or something that kept her busy because surprisingly she hadn't called me since we touched down in Philly three weeks ago. I wondered to what I owed the pleasure of her call today. I was almost tempted to let her go to voice mail, but I was bored out of my mind and could use some form of entertainment for the time being.

"Hello?" I spoke into the phone in a sleepy voice like I had been awoken from a nap or something. Hopefully she would take that as a hint and not want to talk my head off.

"Monica, how have you been?" She spoke in what I assumed, by the huskiness in her tone, was supposed to be a sexy voice, but I was not moved by it at all. As good as the sex was with her, I didn't need to give this chick any ideas. She was too damn clingy for me, and I just didn't feel like the shenanigans.

"I've been good," I responded, not bothering to give up any detail. She knew what I was here for, but I wasn't about to give up details. We were just fucking, ain't like we were buddies.

"Okay . . ." she said, becoming silent for a while. I just sat on the phone, listening to her breathe. "Well, did you find your son?"

"I never had to look for him. I know who he's with."

"Yeah, but you said they had moved, and—"

"So, what exactly is the purpose of this call? I know you didn't call to get in my business," I responded, rudely cutting her off. This bitch was acting like we knew each other forever.

"Well, I was in fact calling to see if you made progress, but you've made that clear that it's not my business," she answered in a measured tone that indicated I might have struck a nerve and was working her nerves. Ask me if I cared.

"I'm doing okay."

"Cool. So . . . ummm . . . when are you going to let me eat your pussy again?"

Speechless. Direct and right to the point was usually how I liked it, but this one definitely caught me off guard. I must say she had me intrigued. Taking a second to think, I knew I had to meet up with Sheila later in the day, but it was still early. Maybe I did have time to fool around with Jaydah for a second. I could definitely give her something to write about in one of her freaky novels. The butler was out getting food and paying bills for the judge, and I didn't see security anywhere so maybe

I could sneak out undetected for a while. He wouldn't even know I was gone.

"Okay, what's your address? I can't stay long, but I guess I can come and play for a little while."

"Or I can come to you if that would make it easier," she offered, sounding suddenly happier that I agreed.

"No, I'll come to you," I said, looking for a pen to write down her address. I couldn't be that disrespectful and invite her here because I didn't know how the judge would feel about it. I had a feeling that I might be able to talk the butler into a threesome, but Jaydah didn't like to go home when it was time. I found that out the hard way when she came to my house. Basically, the safest bet was to just meet up with her.

Writing her info down, I took a few minutes to refresh and get myself together because if I knew her, she would be on me the moment I walked in the door. The streets looked pretty clear from here, so I made sure I was by myself before jetting out. I didn't feel like being surrounded by bodyguards today, especially since I didn't really need it. Unless the judge had a hit out on me or some shit.

I got down to Jaydah's house in no time, keeping an eye on the rearview mirror to make sure I wasn't being followed. I didn't know who was trying to set me up, and my motto was always to trust no one. When I pulled up to her condo I could hear my phone ringing, and became instantly annoyed. *Is this bitch eyeballing me from the parking lot?* I never told her what kind of car I was driving, so how did she know it was me? Searching my bag for the phone, I pulled it out, ready to go in on her ass, only to see a strange number on my screen. I didn't think nothing of answering, figuring maybe she was calling from a house phone.

"I'm on my way up now," I spoke into the phone as I gathered up my stuff. She must have been extra horny to be stalking me, but it was cool. I was one hell of a catch.

"Monica?" A male voice came across, and I had to pause for a second. Was this who I thought it was?

"James? Is this you?"

James

Moving Forward Looking Back

"Monica, I'm sorry if I caught you at a bad time," I stuttered into the phone nervously. I didn't know if she was going to ram on me and start cursing me out or what, and I just wanted to brace myself for it.

"Oh, no, it's not a bad time," she responded, just as nervous. "What's going on?"

I had to pull the phone back and look at it. Was she serious? Not sure what kind of games Monica was playing, but I just wasn't beat for it. *She gave my mother-in-law the number to contact her for a reason, and if it ain't about her son then we ain't got shit to talk about.*

"Well, you took extreme measures for me to contact you. Is this about your son?"

Again the phone went quiet on the other end. I was starting to lose my cool with her, and this was about to be a wrap before it got started. This was the first time in weeks that I got a moment to myself, outside of Jordan being upstairs sleep, and I needed to get this with Monica—whatever *this* was—done and over with. I just didn't have the energy to go through the motions with her at this point in my life.

"Ummm, yeah. Is there a way I can meet him . . . I mean, meet up with you to discuss the situation?" she asked in a still-nervous voice. I decided to be a little nicer to Monica. I was sure this had to be hard for her, and it took a lot for her to even step foot back in Philly in the first place.

"Well, we definitely need to talk. When can we hook up?"

"Right now."

Now it was my turn to be quiet. I didn't want to get caught up in her web again, so I didn't want to bring her to the house.

I also didn't want being seen out with her in public to be misconstrued, so I knew I had to be discreet. We definitely couldn't meet in Philly, but I couldn't leave my son alone. Maybe getting her to the house real quick was the best move. At least there she could state her purpose and keep it moving.

"Hello?" she spoke into the phone, probably thinking that I hung up.

"Yeah, I'm here. Do you have a pen? I'll give you my address so that you can come by the house."

I regretted it as soon as I spit the numbers out, but it had to be done. Hopefully we could just get this done and over with, and her seeing a few pictures of her son would be enough.

What I needed Monica to understand was that she couldn't just pop back up into this boy's life like everything was cool. As crazy as shit was, Junior thought Jasmine was his mom. Plain and simple. Yeah, she was extra hard on him, but she was all he knew. He grew up with the other kids, and knew us as a family. What if she wanted to take him away? How would the kids react? So many thoughts went through my head, and I could feel myself starting to panic. Monica could act crazy if she wanted to, but if she tried some slick shit it would be on. I needed to restore some type of order before Jazz came home, and getting her out of the way was one of the top things on the list to do.

"How long will it take you to get here?" I asked as I looked around to double check that the house was neat. I didn't want her to think that we weren't on point around these parts.

"Give me thirty minutes."

"Don't be late."

Not even waiting for a response, I just hung up on her. I hated to admit it, but I was nervous. Monica made me weak, and I really hoped that she would be strictly business today. She still looked damn good, and I had to adjust my growing erection in my pants. Just thinking about what those lips and hips were capable of had me ready to get it popping. Shaking my head, I went to check on Jordan. He would definitely get my mind straight for that devil that was about to show up at my front door.

I thought to maybe at least call Jazz's mom to see if she could stop by after her workday was over; that way if things got heated she could possibly show up just in time to stop it. Monica was irresistible, and I knew I would want her. I just had to try my best to stick to the matter at hand.

The clock seemed to be moving in slow motion, being as though only about ten minutes had gone by. A part of me was hoping that she would show up early so that we could get this over with. I already decided that if she showed up even a minute late then she would have to reschedule. I didn't want her to be here when the kids got home from school because there would be too many questions. They would want to know who she was, and I would have to lie because they weren't ready. This was already becoming too much.

At the twenty-three-minute mark I heard a car pulling up to the door. My heart was pounding in my chest, and my palms were sweaty as I walked toward the door. Who was I kidding? I was not ready for this meeting, and I should have just told her that now wasn't a good time. Hell, it was too late now because she was already here.

Approaching the door, I took a deep breath before opening it, only to be greeted by Jazz's mom. Damn, she showed up too early! I thought she had to work, but she either had the day off or only worked a half day. I should have called her when I thought of it. At least I would have known she was on her way and I could have stalled her to show up after Monica got here. Well, it was too late now, and I would just have to wing it. After all, Monica only had about five more minutes to show up, and then it would be her loss.

Of course my luck wasn't that good, and as soon as I took the bags from my mother-in-law's hands to take in the kitchen I heard another car pull up. I kept walking like I didn't hear it, and decided to let her answer the door so that I could feign surprise that Monica actually showed up.

From the kitchen I heard a muted conversation between Monica and Jazz's mom, so I busied myself with putting the groceries away to buy more time before I went into the living room. Just as I was putting the eggs and milk into the fridge, the two women appeared in the kitchen doorway. I was speechless because Monica looked even sexier up close, and once again I had to control a growing erection.

"James," Jazz's mom began, "this is the young lady I saw at the hospital who gave me the number. I didn't know you called her."

"I just got around to calling her today," I responded as my eyes bounced around the room, trying not to make eye contact. It appeared that she was almost wallowing in my discomfort, but she wouldn't win today. "She's an old friend of Jazz's and mine."

"Yes, she told me that at the hospital. I'm going to be heading out soon. I just came to check on Jordan and to make sure the kids had food for breakfast. I have to get home to start dinner for that spoiled husband of mine," she said with laughter in her voice and love in her eyes. I wondered briefly if Jazz would feel that way about me one day.

"He should still be sleeping. I just gave him some pain medicine not too long ago."

"Okay, I'll go check," she said to me before turning away. "Go ahead and catch up with your friend. I'll stop back in before I go. It was nice to meet you again, Monica."

"Nice to meet you as well," she said, extending a sweet smile. She was so damn conniving and came off as sweet and innocent. I had to keep that in mind as I talked to her fine ass.

"Well, have a seat," I offered as I sat down on the opposite side of the kitchen table. This entire experience was just too soon, and I knew I was making a mistake. When was it going to bite me in the ass was my biggest concern. Jasmine would not be happy about Monica being here in this house, around these kids, or anywhere in Philly for that matter. I knew that would be another hurdle to cross, but I couldn't tell this woman she couldn't see her son. I mean, I could, but all that would do was cause problems in the long run, and it was better to just avoid the shit now. Jasmine would be angry but she would just have to get over it.

Staring at her for a moment too long, the first thing I noticed was that she still looked exactly the way she did the last time I saw her. She didn't appear to have aged at all; she just looked more mature. Everything was definitely still on point.

"So what brings you to my neck of the woods?"

"James, you already know what it is. I came to see about my son."

Before I could respond, Jazz's mom came back into the kitchen to let me know she was leaving. I excused myself to lock the door behind her, and to get myself together. I commended her for getting straight to the point, and for the first time since our initial conversation I felt like I could get through this. I just hoped she didn't flip the script on me and try to seduce me . . . She might just end up getting some head out of the deal. Yeah, I was sure her main reason for the visit was to see about her son, but Monica used sex to get results for everything. That wasn't to say that she hadn't changed over the years, but that's the Monica I remembered and it made me nervous.

Monica

Any Way the Wind Blows

The moment James said that I could come to talk about my son, I hopped back in the car and was on the road. I was driving so fast that I forgot to call Jaydah and tell her that I had to make a detour. I left my phone in the car, so I couldn't even call her once I got inside, but it didn't matter. At this moment she was a nonfactor, and I had to handle my business.

We sat quietly at first once he returned to the kitchen. I smelled his cologne before I saw him. I had to squeeze my thighs together to keep my clit from jumping, and to control the splash that would soak my panties. I couldn't believe that this man still turned me on. He looked less bruised and beat up now, and I could tell that a lot of the scars would heal nicely, and not be a permanent fixture on his fine features. He looked more . . . mature. A shy smile crept up on my face as a thought of one of the times we hooked up popped into my head, and I had to make myself stay focused. I was here to get the dibs on my son, and that was it, but if he made a pass I couldn't guarantee that I would resist.

"How is your wife?" I asked, my voice sounding foreign to my own ears, and I didn't recognize the sound coming out. I did a quick scan of the room, taking notice that it was just as laid out as the living area of the house. I wondered briefly what the bedroom looked like, but I knew I could never go anywhere near it. The things that would happen on that bed would be a sin and a shame, and that wasn't the purpose of my visit this time around.

"You're not here to talk about her."

Stung. James was playing hardball, and I knew I needed to bring my A game with him. It was apparent that this wasn't going to be a pleasant meeting, so I might as well get down to business. Now wasn't the time to pull punches.

"Okay, well I'm here because the checks were being returned and I couldn't get in contact with you. What's up with that? Then I get here, and this horrible-ass accident is going on, and I just needed to make sure my son is okay." I came at his neck with way more attitude than needed, but I felt the conver-sation warranted it. No, I didn't come to talk about his damn wife, but asking about her was the polite thing to do. *Damn, I see I can't even be nice to this fool. Every time I think I can get out of "bitch mode," somebody shows me that I can't.*

"Okay, first off, he hasn't been your son since the day you dropped him off on my kitchen table. A check doesn't make him yours."

Boom! And there it is. I guess he told me, huh? I almost didn't have a comeback, but I wasn't about to let this fool chump me. He had the wrong chick for that. I took a second to gather myself, because James's simple ass was about to catch a bad break. I knew he may be angry about some shit, but he really didn't want it with me, and I guessed I needed to remind him of how ignorant I could get.

"James, you're about to take me to a place that I haven't been to in a long time. I did what I had to do at the time for me, and what was best for my son. You think that was easy for me?"

"I'm not saying—"

"And I'm not done," I cut his ass dead off. He was about to put me in my bag, and I had to rein it in before it got ugly in this joint.

"I did what was best for my son because I knew I wasn't going to be able to provide a loving home for him. That shit was not easy, and I knew with you he would get the love he deserved. Who are you to judge me? What did you want me to do with him? Put him in foster care?"

"No, I wanted you to get a damn abortion. I told you that from jump."

Pow! It was like we were in a boxing ring and he kept giving me gut shots. I don't know what made me think that this was going to be a pleasant meeting, but I didn't think it was going to get this real this fast. It was obvious that there was some resentment toward me for jetting out, and it wasn't like I gave him a choice. I got that. I dumped my son on the Cinques and left. It was as simple as that. Maybe I should have at least kept in contact, but in all actuality I was really trying to get past this portion of my life.

I guessed sending the checks was my way of keeping an attachment, and keeping the guilt at bay. Hell, I needed some peace. I couldn't even get a real good sleep in the first year I moved to Atlanta because of the guilt. Rethinking my position, and the position I put him and his family in, I decided to go with a different approach. After all, I wasn't here to start trouble. I just wanted to make sure everything was cool.

"James, listen, I'm not here to disrupt your life. I had a gut feeling that I needed to be here for whatever reason and I followed that instinct and came back. Not because I want to fuck up your marriage, or sleep with you, or take my son away. I just want to be sure that he is okay," I said with a straight face, partially telling the truth. My motive definitely wasn't to bed this man, and if my son was living in safe conditions that would solve my next issue and I could leave peacefully. He just needed to know that I was ready to do whatever it took to ease my mind, and if taking my son back to Atlanta was it, then that's where we would be headed.

The look on his face changed to one of a little less aggression, but the aggravation was still very evident. There were so many things that I could have done differently, because even though Jasmine probably didn't want any dealing with me, James still sent the pictures and the video clips and all of that to me so that I could still watch my son grow up. I owed him at least the courtesy of respecting his feelings.

"Listen, the kids will be getting home from school soon, and I don't want the first meeting to be this abrupt. I will call you in a few days once I've prepped the children for your arrival, and we will further discuss this situation then," he said, wiping his hand down his face. I could see the confusion and questions in his eyes, but I decided against pressing the issue. At this point I was just grateful that he was cooperating, so I would just leave it at that.

Thanking him again for his time, we shared an awkward hug at the front door that we both might have enjoyed a little too much. I almost melted in his arms as he held me close, and it was like we both didn't want to let go. I could feel his growing erection pressing against my stomach, but I gave him a pass because I knew if I pressed the issue it could have easily popped off. That and his son was upstairs. In combination of his kids coming home soon, and not knowing when one of his in-laws would pop their head in, I gave him a break and rolled out. He was definitely still weak for me, and I felt the same way.

Finally stepping back from his embrace, I did a light sprint to the car, making sure the coast was clear before pulling out. It wasn't until I got down about four blocks that I remembered I forgot to call Jaydah when I got back in the car. Of course I had sixty million missed calls and about 8,600 texts from her, but I didn't even care. I was definitely in a good mood, so whatever bad mood she had would change once I got there. I was gonna wear that ass out in more ways than one . . . if she didn't give me too much trouble that was.

Following the GPS directions, I made it to her house quickly and it didn't take long to find a parking spot that was closer to the door. As I was going up to her building she was ringing my phone again, but I sent her straight to voice mail, opting to deal with her face to face. When I approached her floor the phone started ringing again, and I could hear her getting an attitude as I walked up to her door. Oh, she was pissed, but she wouldn't be for long.

She didn't even bother to ask who it was as the door swung open and the attitude that showed in her face changed to a look of concern. I pushed past her, inviting myself into her place. Looking around, I could see she had the potential for good taste. She just needed a few of my paintings in here to seal the deal and she would be in there. Everything had its own neat space, and it didn't look as if she tried to clean up real quick because I was coming. It looked like it naturally stayed in order. Taking a seat on the couch without asking, I called her over to me. She was pouting, and it was too cute, but she came and straddled my lap anyway.

"I had an emergency," I began as I rubbed my hand across the exposed skin of her shoulders. She melted instantly, and I knew I had her exactly where I wanted her. "I got a call about my kid, and I needed to go handle it."

"It's okay, you don't have to explain anything to me. I was just worried," she responded, followed by a moan as I gently took her erect nipple into my mouth through her sheer night top. Homegirl was definitely ready to get it in, and I was about to definitely get in it.

"So, you're not mad at me?" I questioned as I ran a finger over her slit, through the matching thong that barely covered her pussy. My finger smeared the juice that seeped out of the side, up to her covered clit, soaking it a little. This was going to be fun.

"No . . ." She moaned out again. "I'm not mad at you."

"Good. Are you going to show me what I've been missing?" I asked as a finger slipped in between her folds, and was sucked in by her tunnel. Her walls clenched around my finger like she was milking a dick, and that shit had me turned all the way on.

Instead of responding, she lay down on the couch, lifting her legs to remove her thong, and spread her legs wide so that I could see her glistening pearl clearly. My mouth began to water immediately. Scooting down, I positioned myself between her legs, and ran my tongue across her swollen clit, making her jump. Taking my time, I slurped and sucked her into a screaming orgasm that I was sure made the earth move. Homegirl wasn't ready, and we wouldn't be stopping anytime soon. I'd been needing to get one off since I got here, and now was the perfect time. Replacing her face with Jasmine's, I gave her a session that she would never forget.

James

Beautiful Liar

It took me awhile to unglue my feet from the door after Monica left. Just the smell of her had me open again, and I was almost tempted to peek into my checking account to see how much I had available for a night with her. Yeah, I knew now wasn't the time to be thinking about sex, but I was a man after all. Shit, I couldn't remember the last time I got laid properly, and I didn't even know when the next time would be. *Lord, let me just go check on my son, and get a snack ready for the kids.*

Peeking into my room, I saw that Jordan was still asleep. He shared a room with the boys normally, but with him having to heal, and the boys used to being rough I decided it was better to keep him with me during the night. He was moving around a lot better, and was able to go longer in between doses of pain medication, so that was a good thing. When I took him back for his follow-up visit the doctor said he was right on schedule, and would be back to normal real soon. I couldn't wait, and I knew his brothers and sisters were ready for some real playtime.

Janice was so attentive to her brother when he was around them, making sure he didn't try to run too fast and wasn't in any real pain. I could tell that she was happy to have him back. All of the kids were. I also noticed that Junior seemed a lot more at ease, and less troublesome without Jasmine around. He hadn't gotten in trouble in school since they'd been back, actually earning a gold star every day. The teachers were very impressed with that. He also wasn't as distant and mean to the other kids, and they all got along nicely. What was Jazz doing that I wasn't, and vice versa? The kids seemed at peace, and it was odd that none of them really inquired about her whereabouts. That definitely struck me as odd, and I couldn't point any fingers because I was out doing me most of the time, and Jazz would be stuck with the kids. I was sure she was extra stressed out, and was probably in here snapping on them. Things were definitely going to be different once she got back home so that we could maintain a happy household. It was a must for these kids.

From what the doctor had told me, things were looking good and she was having consistent brain activity for someone in her state. He was taking her out of the sleep-induced coma slowly and giving her a chance to wake up naturally, so it would be determined once she was awake when she would be able to come home. The dosage that he was using was being lessened over time to prevent any further complications. It was explained that bringing her from that type of sleep to fully awake wasn't a good idea. The family and I hoped that it would be soon.

I decided that I would talk to Jazz's mom about the situation with Monica. I didn't have anything to lose, so I was going to just run down the entire sordid affair from the beginning so that she could understand everything. The last thing I wanted to do was keep Monica from her son. I just needed her to know that she couldn't have him back. The kids would be devastated, and that would open up a can of worms that no one was ready for.

By the time the kids got home, I had peanut butter and jelly sandwiches and cold milk waiting for them on the table. They were usually hungry when they got in, and that would hold them over until dinner was done. I must admit that I could never be a *Mr. Mom*–type dude. All this cleaning and cooking, ironing and folding clothes, checking homework and doing projects was all too damn much for one person. Yet, Jazz did this and held down a job. Women are truly amazing.

Jordan was just waking up when the kids pulled up to the house in their uncle's truck. He volunteered to pick the kids up from the afterschool program for me so that I wouldn't have to drag Jordan out of the house every day in his condition.

I was helping Jordan out of the bed and into the bathroom when the kids came barreling into the house. They were hyped up, talking about whatever happened in school, and I was sure they talked the entire ride home. Jazz's brother was running around as Junior and Jalil chased him around the living room in a never-ending game of freeze tag. Their laughter reminded me that sticking all of this out was worthwhile.

"Jordan!" the kids screamed in unison as we approached the steps to come downstairs. He smiled as he held on to the railing and took the steps down slowly. He was so excited to see the kids every day, and I knew that he couldn't wait to get back to school. The doctor said that he would only need a few more weeks. Hopefully Jazz would be home by then.

"Kids, there are snacks in the kitchen for you to eat until dinner is done. Everybody wash their hands first!" I yelled after them as they ran toward the kitchen. I couldn't help but smile at my children. Jazz's brother had the same look on his face.

"Thanks a lot for helping me out. Can I please at least give you gas money?" I asked him as I gave him a quick handshake. He refused every time, so I knew this time wouldn't be any different.

"No thanks, James. This is what family does for each other."

"I really appreciate this, man. Thanks for everything."

"No thanks necessary. See you tomorrow," he replied, giving me one last pound. "Bye, kids!" he called out toward the kitchen.

"Bye, Uncle Ronnie!" the kids sang in unison, sounding like their mouths were full. All we could do was smile.

I went to use the phone while the kids chatted about their day, and caught Jordan up on what was going on in school. I had a nagging thought on my mind, and as much as I was trying to get past it I couldn't. Glad to finally have some time to talk, I called Jazz's mom. I needed some understanding and clarity, and I knew she would have the answer for me.

"Hi, Mom," I spoke into the phone the minute she answered.

"James, how are you and the kids?" she responded, and I could hear the smile in her voice.

"Everything is good. Are you busy? I just needed to talk to you about something real quick."

"Sure, just got to my son's house, about to start dinner. What's troubling you?"

"Mom, I'ma need you to grab a seat. This is about to be heavy."

It took me about forty-five minutes to run down the idea of the threesome turning into an actual act, and all that happened before that. I'd spent years blaming Monica solely for the demise of my marriage, when in reality had I not sought her out in the first place it wouldn't have even gotten to this point. Yeah, Monica had an agenda, but so did I. I just wanted a threesome. Who knew that it would turn into all of this?

"And the last time we saw Monica she was driving away from my house after leaving my son on the dining room table," I concluded with a sigh. After revealing to her who exactly the girl was who gave her the number at the hospital, it all clicked for her and she was extra quiet on the phone.

"Well, James . . ." she began, becoming quiet for a second again. "This is a tough decision. The things that you did in the past are just that: the past. Every mother wants to have a connection with her kid. I don't see it being a problem because she appears to come in peace. Let's make it a day over the weekend so that all of the kids can meet her at once, and we can all be there."

"I like that suggestion. Is this weekend too soon?" I asked, not sure if I would go through with it if I waited too long.

"Better now than never. Go ahead and give her a call. I'll come on Friday to help you break the news to the kids."

"Thanks, Mom. I appreciate everything you're doing."

After we hung up I sat for a minute to think about my next move. Something was telling me to just let it go, but I couldn't. Since we were all reconnecting and getting closure from past events, there was just one little matter that needed to be handled. Scrolling through my call log, I hit the number I had used to call Monica earlier, hoping she would answer. Three rings later she picked up, sounding like she was out of breath.

"Monica, I'm sorry to bother you. I just had a question to ask you."

"It's not a problem, James. Can you hold on for one second?"

"Sure."

It took her about a minute or so to return to the line, and she sounded a little clearer. I might have caught her in the middle of something, and the visual in my head caused my dick to jump in my pants. Shaking my head to clear the image, I attempted to focus on the situation at hand.

"Sorry about that. Is everything okay?" she asked in a concerned voice. She probably thought I was calling to tell her she couldn't see her son, but I squashed that immediately.

"Everything is fine. I just wanted to see if we could meet up on Friday to discuss the kid situation. My wife's mother will be here."

"Oh, sure, that's not a problem. Just give me a time and I'll be there."

"Be here by two, so that way we can talk before the kids arrive. It hasn't been decided yet how we will introduce you to the kids, but it will definitely be done," I informed her as my mind raced. I wanted this experience to be as smooth as possible without any backlash if I could help it. The way I figured it, if I gave Monica what she wanted, and that was to see her son, then we could be done with this and move on with our lives.

"James, I'll be there, and I really appreciate this."

"No problem. I'm just doing what I can. Just know that the kids may not be as receptive as you could be expecting them to be. You are a stranger to them, Monica."

"I totally understand that, and once again I appreciate everything you are doing."

After running down the discussion we would have, and how she would be introduced, she sounded a lot more relieved. That nagging thought in my head wouldn't go away, and I just needed to get it out and over with. It was like a now-or-never type of situation. I yelled her name out before she hung up and I lost the courage to dig for more information.

"Monica, I have a question to ask you, and I just need you to be honest with me."

"Sure, James, what do you need to know?"

"Well . . ." I paused before continuing. I was about to open a can of worms that I knew I probably wouldn't be able to close, but I just couldn't help it. "A few years ago when you left that letter on the table you said that Jasmine had an affair with some twins at the gym. How true is that statement, and can you help me find them?"

The line sounded like it went dead, until I heard her breathe on the other end. I needed to know the truth, and she was the only other person who could help me. I left that part out when I talked to Jazz's mom. Although she found out when I did that the twins weren't mine, she didn't know that I had this suspicion for years. I needed to know the truth, by any means necessary.

Monica

No Turning Back

Speechless. Who knew that James would bring that up after all this time? I mean, from what I saw, all of the kids looked like him. Why would he have a reason to believe that they weren't? Unless of course something went down with that twin who was in the hospital, and he found out that way.

"Well, James, I can't promise you anything. I'll have to make a few calls because I haven't seen the twins in years. I overheard them at the gym talking about the threesome they had with Jasmine, and I felt you needed to know. That's why I included it in the letter I left you before I moved out of the city," I responded.

"They were bragging about my wife in public?" he asked, sounding angry and surprised.

Shit, that's what men do: lie and brag about their sexual trysts in public. Why was he so surprised? "Basically. You know how guys are at the gym. They all want to brag about who slept with who, who has the biggest dicks, et cetera. You know the drill. From what I heard, when you guys split up Jazz was going to them for personal training. I guess it got more personal than just working on the machines."

He got quiet for a minute, and I allowed him that time to digest what I just told him. Even though men cheat, it's different somehow when a woman does it. It's like, they can dick down a dog and it be cool, but as soon as we let someone else besides our mate dip in the cookie jar we are tainted, damaged goods. Women obviously do it better. Cheating, that is. Hell, not only did she step out, but she pushed out two babies and still held the secret for years. Jazz was a bad bitch, if I could say so myself. I guessed James had no reason to suspect her of being pregnant by someone else because they already had a set a twins, and twins probably ran in either or both of their families. I never cared enough to find out either way.

"Hello?" I spoke into the receiver to make sure he was still there since I didn't even hear him breathing.

"I'm still here. Could you just do me that solid and get the information for me? I would really appreciate it," he said, sounding weary and defeated.

"Sure, no problem. I'll get the info you need to contact them by Friday. I'll have it when I come over."

"Monica, thanks for everything. I really appreciate this."

"Thank you as well. I'll see you then."

I had to get my head together for a second. From what I gathered, it appeared that everything was really a mess over at the Cinques! It's always been said that what you do in the dark comes to light, but damn. I couldn't say that I blamed him though. If I had been in his situation I would have done the same thing. It's not like Jazz would keep it real with him about it anyway. Knowing her, she probably wouldn't even want to discuss it, and when you got something like that bugging at you, it's hard to let it go.

Looking to my left, I found a pissed-off Jaydah staring back at me. I apologized because we were in the middle of handling business, but I needed to take all calls, and I couldn't afford to miss any. I saw that it was almost five, and I needed to get at Sheila when she got off work. Rolling over I jumped right back into action, knocking that attitude clear off her face. I really didn't feel like any beef with this chick, so I needed to at least let her get a nut before I bounced out, and thankfully it didn't take long.

The minute she was done convulsing and hanging on for dear life, I peeled her naked body from mine and hopped in the shower. I needed to call Sheila, and I didn't want her to have any excuses not to help me. Oh, Jaydah was pissed that I was rolling out and I had to promise her I would come back just to get out of her place. She was still just too damn clingy, so I knew I would have to watch out for her ass. Taking the steps two at a time, I got down to my car as quickly as I could, locking the door before pulling my phone out. It was five thirty, and I was supposed to have called Sheila fifteen minutes ago. *God, please let her answer the phone.*

"You're late," she answered the phone, not even bothering to say hello. I wasn't in the position to snap back because I needed her, so I took a deep breath before responding.

"Sheila, I apologize. I was caught up and—"

"What do you want, Monica?"

For real? I had to pull the phone back and look at the screen to make sure I dialed the right number. The times had definitely changed, because the Sheila I remembered would have never talked to me like that.

"Well, can we meet up somewhere to talk?" I asked hesitantly, not sure of what to expect. I couldn't believe this chick had me nervous.

"Talk about what? I have to pick up my son, and I have things to do before then. I don't have a lot of time right now for your shit."

"Sheila, you might want to bring it down some. I'm not calling to start anything up. I just need your help, and I thought since we were friends—"

"Friends? With who?" She cut me off with even more anger in her voice. "Bitch, you tried to ruin my life, or did you forget that part?"

Speechless once again. Between her and James I didn't know who was worse. You leave your beloved city for a few years, and come back to totally different people. Yeah, it was time for me to get back on my game because it was obvious folks done forgot how I got down. Playing it cool, I put the phone back to my ear, feeling totally in control. *Sheila had better recognize real quick who she is dealing with.*

"Sheila, first of all I don't know who pissed in your coffee today, but you might want to tone that shit down. I just need some info from you, and I was going to pay you for your time, but since you want to be a dizzy bitch—"

"Hold up—"

"No, you hold up. All of this attitude you giving me is really unnecessary. I ain't calling you for your raggedy pussy. I need your help. Now, do you want to make this money or not?"

"Meet me at Ms. Tootsie's in an hour," she said in a defeated tone. I was going to apologize to her, but I changed my mind. Apparently she liked being checked . . . Simple ass.

"I'll see you in forty-five minutes," I responded before hanging up. Starting the car, I backed out of my space and pointed my rental toward Center City. I swear I didn't feel like all of the aggravation that I was experiencing in my hometown, and best believe when all of this was over Philly would never see this face again. It was too much damn work.

As I was driving I noticed a few cars back that same black car that was following me before. But then, I wasn't sure if it was the exact car or just someone with a car like it. Turning off a few blocks down, I noticed the car did the same as before and turned off with me. This went on for like ten minutes. Deciding to drive slow, the cars that were in between us went around me, leaving the car that was following me no choice but to catch up. Stopping at the red light, I put the car in park and prepared to get out. I couldn't see who the other driver was because the windows were covered with dark tinting. My plan was to go tap on the window and see who was inside. This shit was getting ridiculous.

I hoped for a second that maybe they had the wrong person, and maybe they needed to see who I was. Everyone knew that my fellow Philadelphians hated me. That wasn't lost on anyone, but after all this time folks still wanted my head on the chopping block? Really? I hadn't stirred up anything in years, and totally left Philly alone when I rolled out of here. This time, I just needed some information, then I would be gone. No harm, no foul.

Putting my hazards on, I got out of the car, leaving the car running and the door open just in case I had to get back inside and get ghost. I did not feel like dying today, but someone was gunning for me and I wasn't in the mood to run. I popped the trunk like I had to get something out of it, just in case my plan to approach the car didn't work too well and I lost the heart to do it. I wasn't even five steps out of my car before the car behind me rolled back a little and then slammed into the back of the rental. I barely had time to jump out of the way. Landing on the ground near the curb, I saw the car back up once again, and the driver turned toward me. I hopped up off the ground and dodged in between two cars just as he got up on me, and whipped the car the other way. Yep, someone definitely wanted me dead.

Other pedestrians and drivers stopped to gawk at the scene, and a few even came over to help me. I could already hear someone speaking to the police on the phone, repeating the license plate number of the other vehicle to the cops. It was a good thing I did get out of the car because I could have been seriously hurt.

"Ma'am, are you okay?" one of the pedestrians asked me as I stumbled toward the car to get my phone and pocketbook.

"Yes, I'm okay. I just need to call my friend to tell her I will be late," I responded in a daze as I searched under the seat for my phone. I could not believe this shit was happening, but it's cool. I knew I had to call in reinforcements for this one. Wasn't nobody in Philly going to chump me.

"Sheila, is there somewhere else I can meet up with you in about two to three hours? I just got into a car accident, and I'll need to handle this so that I can get another rental."

Surprisingly she cooperated, and gave me the address to her house. My next call was to Enterprise, informing them of the damaged vehicle, and that I would need another one. Thankful that I opted to get their insurance as opposed to using my own, I cleared the car of my belongings once the cops took my statement and the statements from a few witnesses. The tow truck didn't take long at all, and pretty soon I was back at Enterprise in a new vehicle with tinted windows, and the deductible paid on the damaged one. I needed to make this visit with Sheila quick and get back to the judge's spot before anything else happened. I must admit that I was a little shook, but I was too cool to let the enemy see me sweat. If they were going to chase me out of here they would have to try harder than that.

On the ride over to Sheila's place I ran through a list of people who could possibly want to take me out. It wasn't a long list, but a list nonetheless. I mean, there was that situation with Rico that never got resolved. After I cleaned out the spot I knew for sure that his team would want me dead. I didn't take everything; the cops did grab a few items "for evidence," or so they said. Those were the very same cops who wrecked my place down the line. I swear, you can't even trust the law to stay clean nowadays.

There was Rico's girlfriend at the time, Sheneka. Now, she was a crazy bitch, and apparently really loved Rico.

There was Sheila, but I just as quickly dismissed that thought because that wasn't even her type of thing.

The Cinques were a thought as well, but I dismissed that notion too. They had my son, and my money. Why would they want to kill me? There was the judge's wife, and the mayor's wife and daughter, and even that cop I slept with to avoid getting a ticket that time, but none of them seemed like logical candidates. Sheneka didn't even know I was in the city, or did she? I was confused, but out of all of those people someone wanted me dead. The question was who, and I would try to figure that out before I left the city. That was, if I made it out of here in one piece.

I arrived to Sheila's apartment about two hours later, and I could see that she was definitely making more money now. Instead of the little apartment she used to have, she now lived in a split-level layout in Presidential City right off of City Avenue. It made me smile to see that she had come up the way she did. When I got into the building I had to sign in at the desk, and wait for a call to be placed to her apartment to let her know I was there. They had this thing on lock, so I knew there was no way I could come kicking and banging on her door like I did back in the day. After all of the technicalities, and damn near being strip searched, I was granted access to the elevator that led me to her floor. When I got off I could see her door cracked open, waiting for me to come inside. I was a little irritated that I even had to go through all of that, but I didn't even feel like getting into it with her.

Once inside, I took my shoes off because I didn't want to risk scratching the hardwood floors, and as I crossed the room my feet sunk into the area rug, which showcased a beautiful carved coffee table, which looked like a family tree minus the names.

Sheila looked amazing. When she walked out from what I assumed was the kitchen, holding a steaming cup of something, I checked my smile as I took her in. The last few years had been good to her. From the top of her neatly curled head to the tips of her cranberry toes and all the curves in between, homegirl looked good. She sat down on the chaise across from me, tucking her shapely legs under her body. Making eye contact before speaking, she sipped from her cup and set it down on an onyx coaster. Damn, I wanted to kiss her.

"Why are you back here?"

"I just told you over the phone—"

"No, why are you here in Philly? The city was at peace without you."

Taking a deep breath, I ran down the entire story concerning the Cinques and the returned checks and how I was being followed since I arrived. I skipped telling her that I was staying with the judge, but I did remind her of the reason for my visit.

"Although I don't think he will use it against me, or keep me from seeing my son, I know this is important to him and I really need that information."

She sat and stared at me for a long moment, and I thought for a second that maybe she didn't hear what I said. I wasn't in the mood for anything extra, but if I had to I would throw in some extra cash, or whatever it was that she wanted. I just needed to get this over with.

"It appears that today is your lucky day. The twins work out at the same gym I do, and one of them is my personal trainer. I have their number, but you didn't get it from me. I don't want no part of this bullshit." Sheila spoke with venom as she looked at me through slits because her face was in such a scowl.

Going through her phone she scribbled down some information for the twin who was training her, and the location of the gym that she used close to the job. It was an awkward moment because I didn't know that Sheila could be this strong without me, but I was grateful. She was so quiet and mousy years ago, and so easy to control. I had her wrapped around my finger, and she pretty much did whatever I told her to. She wasn't as sexy four years ago either, and she looked like she was slimmed down and toned up nicely. This was definitely a new Sheila I was looking at, and I was happy that she came into herself and took control of her life. She had to once I left because we both knew, had I stayed, she would have still been a damn puppet for me to play with.

I didn't want to waste any more time, and since it was getting late I needed to get back to the judge's house. I was sure by now his butler/bodyguard knew I was gone and I didn't want any shit. Getting up, I headed toward the door, slipping back into my shoes when I got there. When I turned back around to thank her she was still on the chaise, sipping from her cup. She was definitely a totally different person than I remembered, and I was happy that she had gotten stronger.

"Monica, do me a favor," she said to me as I slipped into my coat.

"Anything for you," I responded, waiting for her request.

"Make sure you never contact me again, and feel free to lock the door behind you."

Damn, was it like that? It caught me off guard, but I wasn't about to give her the satisfaction. Taking my cue, I exited stage left and went on about my business, leaving her to her thoughts. When I got outside I made sure to lock the car doors, and I searched the lot for suspicious activity before pulling out. I paid close attention to the road and the rearview as I made my way back to the judge's spot. A million thoughts swam through my head as I drove, mainly on who was trying to off me, and I knew I would need me a good stiff drink once I got inside. I wondered briefly how different my life would be if I had stayed, but I knew going was the best move I could've made in my entire life. If my own child couldn't keep me here, there was nothing else here for me.

I was greeted by the butler when I pulled up, and that shit creeped me out a little because I didn't know how he knew I was even pulling up at the time. I got out of the car and tiptoed through the door, ignoring the scowl on his face. I needed to get my thoughts together before Friday got here. I had something to bring to the table to level the playing field and I was ready to go to war if needed. I was all hype about meeting my son, but what if he wasn't ready to meet me?

Carlos

Let the Games Begin

"You did what?" I barked into the phone. I swear, whenever you want something done right you have to do it yourself. I told this fool to just keep tabs on Monica. How hard was it to follow someone around without being seen?

"It was an accident. She got out of the car like she was about to pull a hammer from the trunk, so I stepped on the gas. I didn't think I was going to hit the bitch."

"Yo, you are so fuckin' stupid. She ain't carrying no hammer, fool!" I yelled into the phone, steaming. Monica with a hammer? She ain't never been that kind of chick. Yeah, she needed to have her ass served for the shit she did to my homie, but she wasn't a known criminal. Damn!

"Dude, I didn't know. I was just trying to—"

"Where did you put the whip?" I cut him off, mad as fuck that he wrecked my damn ride. *That Infinity set me back a nice amount, and this fool goes and bangs it up. Irked!*

"I took it to the garage."

Click! I had to get my head on straight before I blasted this fool. I had a plan set up, and people just didn't know how to follow directions. Simple-ass directions that a toddler could get with ease. I owned several auto body shops and convenience stores in the area, so I wasn't worried about getting it fixed, but the cost was coming out of his cut. Damn that.

Rolling out of the bed, I took a quick second to roll an el before popping a squat on the toilet. Sheneka was on my damn top, and I knew that she was ready to get shit poppin'. Sometimes you just have to slow down, and let things play out the way they are supposed to. Monica was very smart, and at this point I was certain that she knew someone was gunning

for her, even if she couldn't put a name to the face. Now we'd
have to wait it out, because no doubt she would go into hiding.
I swear a boss's job is never done.

After smoking the entire blunt to the head, I did my hygiene
thing, and got myself together for the day. I made a few rounds,
making sure that business, both legal and otherwise, was on
point. I had to keep the legal business to wash the money I
was making on the street, but I had to admit that once Rico
got knocked it took awhile to get my game back up. Niggas
was acting crazy now that the top dog was down, and I had to
make a few examples of some folks to put the word back out on
who was in charge. I hated to even take it there, but some folks
need hands-on experiences to get the picture.

Pulling up to one of the warehouses that we kept merchan-
dise in for the body shops and convenience stores, I made
sure the coast was clear before entering the building, and
locking the door behind me. As I made my way to the back, I
took notice of the inventory in stock, and what I might need
to order more of soon. Heading straight to the back I took the
steps down to the basement toward another door. It was dark
and cold down here, but it served its purpose. When I opened
the door I was greeted by one of my soldiers tied up in a chair,
bloody from head to toe. Several of my other men were seated
around him with menacing looks on their faces. I just shook
my head as I looked at him. He was one of the best I had; too
bad he had to die.

"So, did you get all that you wanted?" I asked him as I leaned
against the wall and stared into his swollen eyes. He had been
caught skimping off the top awhile back, and today was pay
day.

"Yo, C, you gotta believe me. I wouldn't do this to you, man,"
he pleaded through bruised and swollen lips. All of that
bullshit fell on deaf ears. We had solid proof and too many witnesses to even believe the bullshit he was spitting at the time.
As he droned on and on I checked my Myspace account, bored
by what he was saying and needing a distraction. Looking
through my updates, I saw a post from this fool, posted a few
hours before he was snatched off the street, bragging about
stealing my shit and me not finding out. Shaking my head, I

turned the phone so that he could read the screen through his one good eye. *People are so stupid.*

His eye stretched open wide as he read what he typed.

"Carlos, I respect you too much to do that, man! I swear somebody broke into my profile and set me up! I didn't post that! I would never bite the hand that's feeding me. I got kids, man. My baby moms is pregnant right now. I'll get off the block. Just please let me ride," he pleaded for his life. None of that shit fazed me, and I was already over it. The team knew the consequences of stealing, so off with his head it was.

"Wrap this up, guys. You know what to do," I instructed as I turned to walk out. I thought he suffered long enough. By the time they cleaned up the body and the mess it would be ready for Monica's simple ass. I hated to even have to drag her fine ass through the warehouse, but when you crossed the crew those were the consequences. I didn't make the rules, I just reinforced them. Besides, Rico would have wanted it this way.

Leaving the warehouse, I dropped by a few more spots before going to check on Sheneka. This entire Monica situation had pushed her over the edge, and had her tripping. The facility had to put her in isolation, and they had her on meds to calm her down. I knew the sooner this ordeal was over the better, and maybe she could get back to her old self. Either way, it was going down . . . just as I planned it.

James

More Secrets More Lies

I was nervous. I couldn't wait for Friday to get here, and now that it had arrived I was stuck. What if this thing didn't work out the way we all planned it? Jazz's mom came back to the house with me after we visited Jazz, and I was kind of relieved that she was still under. The doctor said that her brain activity was still stable, so I was happy that things were going as planned. I could only deal with one thing at a time, and I needed to get this Monica business out of the way first.

I decided to let her meet the kids, but under certain circumstances. I just hoped she would understand that Junior could not know she was his mom. That would confuse all of the damn kids, and I wasn't even in the mood for it right now. I wasn't 100 percent sure if the older twins knew the deal on Junior, and after all this time they might have forgotten about it since it was never really brought up again and he came into the picture when they were both really young. I had Jazz's mom there, hoping that Monica would have enough respect for her to not flip out in front of her, but you never knew with Monica. She would lose her mind without warning, and there was no stopping her at that point. We decided that she would be introduced as their aunt, and that's how we would roll with it. After all, she just wanted to be sure that he was in good hands. I couldn't knock her for that.

I had her scheduled to arrive before the kids got home, so that way we could just ease into it. I wasn't too sure what the kids' reactions would be, but hopefully everything would go smooth. I was a nervous wreck, and Jazz's mom tried to calm me down by telling me I was doing the right thing, but I wasn't so sure about that. *What would Jazz do in this situation?*

The ringing of the doorbell startled me, and I had to grab my chest. It was about to go down and there was no turning back. I was inviting Monica into my world again, but this time we would be following my rules. I could not invite her to my bed again, and I kept that in mind as I answered the door.

"Hey, Monica, glad you could make it. Please come in." I greeted her at the door with a smile on my face.

She was dressed nice in a pair of fitted jeans that cupped her plump ass just right, and were tucked inside of a pair of riding boots that I knew Jazz would die to have. Her Coach peacoat fit nicely on top of a cowl-neck sweater in a burnt orange that went nicely with her highlights. She had a touch of lip gloss on kissable lips that I had to avert my eyes from. I took her coat to place in the closet, and took a quick whiff of her perfume before hanging it up. Thoughts of her legs wrapped around me tried to invade my mindset, but I pushed them to the side and kept it strictly professional.

"Thanks for having me, James. I really appreciate this," she responded nervously, and I could understand why. She was meeting her son for the first time today officially, and I was sure she was on pins and needles. What if he didn't respond to her the way she thought he would? I wasn't sure what she was expecting to get from the meeting, but if I were in her shoes I would think that she was hoping the situation went smoothly. This entire situation could turn out to be a total mess.

We settled around the kitchen table, and Jasmine's mom joined us after giving her a hug. That made me smile because that's just how Jazz's mom was. She always welcomed every-body regardless of the situation. I offered her a drink, which she declined, so I decided to just get down to business.

"Okay, so after talking this over with Jazz's mom, we decided that you can meet your son under the guise of being intro-duced as his aunt," I began, being sure to keep eye contact.

"His aunt?" she repeated more so than questioned. I knew she was hurt by the revelation, but I figured once I explained it she would better understand.

"The way we figured it, if we told Junior you were his mom it would undo everything we already have set in place. He only knows Jazz as his mom, and although the older twins know the deal, it would just confuse everyone. Do you understand what I'm saying?"

"I totally understand."

Both Jazz's mom and I were shocked. I warned Jazz's mom that Monica had a temper, and might spazz out, so we were prepared. Although I was surprised that she didn't go clean off then, I still needed to stay on guard because you never knew with her.

"Okay," I continued, trying to move this thing along. "The kids will be arriving home soon, so do you want to help us get the snacks ready?"

"Ummm . . . sure. What do you need me to do?"

After setting the table and getting cookies and juice out, I pulled Monica to the side while Jazz's mom was in the restroom. I didn't want her to feel funny about the situation, and I guess I needed her to know that there were no hard feelings.

"Monica, everything is going to work out just fine. The kids are going to love you."

She gave me a nervous smile as she finished up with the snacks. I could see her tense up as we heard the kids burst into the house, followed by their uncle in a never-ending game of freeze tag. I could hear Jazz's mom yelling for the kids to wash their hands and get ready for their snacks. As the kids barreled into the kitchen, they all came to a halt as they entered the kitchen and came face to face with Monica.

She looked frozen as well as they all made eye contact. I stood back to see how the situation would play itself out. Like I warned Monica during our talk, the kids may have clung to you or just the opposite. She was a stranger, and although the kids were pretty easy to get along with, you just never knew.

"Hi, I'm Janice. What's your name?" came a small voice from the crowd of onlookers. I wasn't surprised that she was the first one to speak up. She had always been very inquisitive, and curious about everyone we came across.

"I'm your Aunt Monica. It's nice to meet you, Janice," Monica replied as she got down to eye level with her. She looked a little nervous, but once Janice came rushing toward her and wrapped her little arms around Monica's neck in a loving embrace, the tension left the air immediately. All of the kids followed, and it was just one big hug fest. I certainly felt relieved, and the relief was on Jazz's mom's face as well.

"Okay, kids, wash your hands. We got snacks!" I hollered out. The kids crowded around the sink as I pumped out foam soap into their little hands. The kids engaged the adults about their days as we ate cookies and drank milk. I stepped away from the table to prepare dinner as the conversation went on. They didn't even put up a fight when their grand-mom left because they were all so intrigued by their new aunt.

As they were having fun at the table, I could see Monica staring at her son periodically. It was crazy how much he looked like her. They had the same smile that accentuated deep dimples, and were almost the same complexion, with Junior being a half shade lighter than Monica. It was a great moment, and I was glad that she came by. At least if she never came back, she could say that she got to meet him face to face. Unraveling this white lie would be a mess, I was sure, but for now this was how it had to be.

"So, where do you live?" Jaden asked as she stuffed her face with Oreos. She looked so much like her mom at that moment it was scary.

"I live in Atlanta," Monica replied with a polite smile. I watched just to make sure I didn't have to intervene, because the kids would question you to death. I didn't want her first and possibly only visit to be overwhelming for her.

"Where is that?"

"It's far away," Jalil answered before Monica could. It brought out the prettiest smile on her already gorgeous face, and drew a quick laugh from the crowd. Of course Jaden didn't think that it was funny, and it showed on her frowned-up face.

"Dad." Jaden turned around, ignoring her brother. "How come Mom didn't say who Aunt Monica was when we were at the hospital?"

It got quiet and all eyes were on me, ready for an answer. Monica looked horrified, and ready to jet. I knew this meet and greet was going too smoothly. I came from around the island, and took a seat at the table, ready to tell my trusting children more lies. The only reason I knew I would get away with it was because I was not that close with my family, and once Jazz and I got married I didn't keep in contact with them. The kids spent the majority of the time with Jazz's family, and that's just how it'd always been. I hated to even go there with them, but like the old saying goes, "you tell one lie and end up telling another, and you tell two lies to cover each other" . . . You know the song.

"Well, that is because Grand-mom had never met Monica because I don't see that side of my family a lot. Aren't you glad she's here now?"

"Yes," came tiny voices in unison.

"And what do we do when we're happy about something?"

"Hug fest!" all of the children yelled as they embraced me and Monica.

We barely dodged the bullet on that one, but I was happy I was able to skate through. As the kids continued to chat, I went back to preparing dinner. I couldn't help but wonder, as I watched Monica with the kids, if I was doing the right thing. I mean, things with me and Jazz were on the brink of being over, and I briefly wondered if I could do the family thing with Monica. Just as quickly the thought left my head. My place was with my wife . . . or was it?

Everything just seemed so easy with Monica here today. Normally Jazz and I would be fussing with the kids to get their hands washed and get seated for dinner. Junior would no doubt be fighting with one of the older twins, and the tension between Jazz and me was always thick because we never ever resolved any previous arguments. The shit just piled on from one drawn-out disagreement to the next, to the point where we didn't even know for sure why we were upset with each other at the current moment. Was it some recent shit, were we beefing about something from the past, or a combination of both? It was just a mess, and we didn't hide as many arguments from the kids anymore. It didn't get downright ignorant like it did in the privacy of our bedroom, but the side comments and snide remarks weren't missed, and luckily the kids didn't get it. They knew something was wrong, but exactly what remained to be determined.

There was a sense of calm in the kitchen, and fascination on the kids' behalf. The girls were in awe and wanted to play in her long hair, and the boys just smiled at her openly. The flow of conversation just . . . well, flowed! It was a great night all the way up to dessert, and it just seemed to happen so naturally. Just the way it should have been all the time.

Dinner was amazing, and I marveled at how my and Monica's moves in the kitchen were nearly synchronized. Even during the meal, she served all of us before fixing her own plate, and her interaction with the kids was great. Jazz would fix the kids' plates and hers, cooking just enough for them and maybe some scraps for me, leaving the rest of the food, if any at all, for me to scrape from the bottom of the pans. Even after dinner, we had a good family night as we played Twister and Scrabble with the kids, and even tucked them in at the end of the night. All of the kids went to sleep with smiles on their faces, and Jordan even insisted on sleeping in his own bed. I was hesitant at first because of his injuries, but Monica reassured me that it would be okay. I even stayed back as she kissed each kid good night, and made sure that they were all tucked in. All Jazz ever did was holler at the kids during bath time, threatening them to hurry up and get in bed. There were no bedtime stories, or tucking them in, and if it weren't for me going back to their rooms after they were all done to say good night, and make sure they were okay, the kids would probably think we didn't love them at all. Monica handled this all very differently. *A girl after my own heart.*

After rinsing the dishes and stacking the dishwasher, we sat down to catch our breath from the busy afternoon and evening. Monica still had that bewildered look on her face, and I knew she was probably just taking it all in. I was happy that she got to see and spend time with her son, but at the same time I wondered if that would be enough.

"So, what do you think?" I asked her, directing my question about the evening we just spent as a family.

"It's . . . I don't know. A lot, I guess. I could see myself doing this."

It got quiet again. Those roaming thoughts popped in my head again, but I knew I couldn't go there with her. There was no way I was going to walk out on Jazz and leave her ass out to go live it up with *our* jump off. I gave her a gentle smile, indicating that I understood.

"How long are you in Philly for?" I asked in an attempt to change the subject.

"I'm not sure. Had some things on my to-do list that I needed to get squared away, so once I'm done with that I guess I'll be heading out."

"I hear that," I said, followed by an awkward silence. "Well, let's be sure to get together again before you go so that the kids can get to see you before you head back to the ATL. You know they will ask about you."

"I'll be sure to do that."

We sat there staring at each other, and I could feel the connection. I had to divert my eyes and think about baseball because my boxers were getting tight. Getting up, I went and grabbed her coat out of the closet and walked her to the door. I was afraid that if she didn't leave right then it would definitely go down. Planting a kiss on her cheek, I waited until she was securely in the car and pulling off before I closed the door and locked the house down for the night. I didn't go upstairs until she called to let me know she was home, and once we were done with our brief conversation wishing each other a good night, I was able to get my head on straight.

Later in the shower I couldn't help but fantasize about the things I would have done to her pressed against the shower wall. I had a firm hold on my manhood as I leisurely stroked one out, pretending my hand was her mouth. Lord, that woman still had me open. After toweling dry, and slipping into my PJs, I doubled back to check on the kids, and was happy that everyone was asleep. Slipping into my bed, I willed myself to do the same thing. Saturday mornings in the Cinque household meant fixing breakfast for five hungry bellies, and the kids never let me sleep late.

As I rolled over and got comfortable I came to terms that I did the right thing by letting Monica come by, even though we had to formulate a lie that I was sure would later haunt me. After all, Jazz's mom agreed to it as well so it had to be cool. Hopefully she would just leave because I wasn't too sure that I would be able to stay off of her the next time she came around smelling delicious like she always did. Closing my eyes, I dozed off with a smile on my face as my mind drifted to her chocolate thighs resting on my shoulders while I used my tongue to scoop out her creamy middle. I knew I couldn't have her in real life, but in my dreams anything went.

Monica

On a Brighter Note

I got to see my son. That made me smile from ear to ear. I'd never thought I would see the day, and I couldn't believe how much he looked liked me. I changed my number a little over two years ago, and the pictures I had of him in my phone were erased so that I could attempt to move on. Kids change so much when they are growing and he looked the same but different than the past photo I saw of him. He definitely belonged to me though. Same dimples and everything. I gave all of the kids equal attention, but it took all that I had not to grab him in my arms and just hold him. I wanted to memorize the feel of his hands, and that smile, and his scent so that it would be etched in my mind forever. I caught myself a few times staring at him, and I got choked up, almost busting out in tears in front of everyone. But I held it down, and I felt good about this entire situation. He was obviously loved at the Cinques, and I came to the decision that I wouldn't interrupt their flow. That wouldn't be fair to them. I did decide that I would make more trips to Philly to keep in touch though . . . that was, if I survived this one.

That whole thing with the weirdo who banged into my car earlier was still on my mind. Who sent this fool, and why was he trying to kill me? It wasn't lost on me that people wanted my head in Philly, but was it really that deep? I mean, damn! It'd been years since I'd been here, and stayed longer than it took to handle business, and not too many people knew I had even touched down when I did. I did see the judge's wife when I first arrived in the hotel lobby, but it wasn't that deep. Did she have that kind of pull all of a sudden? This was all too much at one time, and I just needed to think.

Being mindful of my surroundings, I kept watch on the rearview mirror as I drove back to the judge's spot. I was not in the mood for any more surprises, and I really just wanted to think about my day before going to sleep. I noticed that Jaydah had called me a few times while I was in with the Cinques, but I didn't feel like being bothered with her tonight. She served her purpose and it was time to move on. I might hit her up before I rolled out, but I would just have to play it by ear.

When I got to the judge's spot, of course the annoying-ass butler was waiting by the door. This man was wearing me out, and as I stormed past him into the house I felt like I was a teenager being scolded for missing curfew. I mean, damn. I was grown the last time I checked. Making a beeline to my room I was greeted with flowers and a card from the judge. I didn't even bother to read it, and skipped past the flowers as well. This was getting to be a headache, and suddenly I felt like I would be better off in a hotel. At least that way I could come and go as I pleased. I thought I needed the judge to help me, and I guessed in some ways he did. If he would have never had that heart attack I wouldn't have run into the Cinques at the hospital. He didn't help me the way I thought, but I would take it any way it came.

At the same time, there was that little issue with my stalker I didn't really feel safe from, so maybe it was best to stay here. I didn't even feel like thinking about it, and decided to just call it a night. I took a little longer in the shower to sort my thoughts, and I wished for a second that I was more of a family type of girl. I would do great with those kids and Jasmine wouldn't need to be there. She was probably pissed at what happened anyway and wouldn't want to be there. We would be a happy family, and the kids would love their Aunt Monica.

Shaking the thought from my head, I decided I would go up to the hospital to check on Jazz's progress, if it was at all possible, just to be nosey. Maybe she had woken up, and since James made it painfully clear that his wife's well-being wasn't any of my business I had to find out on my own. The judge still had the floor on lock, and I wasn't sure how close I would get. The doctor did what I needed him to do by telling

James I was there, so I didn't anticipate it being an issue if I was caught in there again. I just needed to know what was really good with her. I never really got into the particulars with James, and maybe he would be more open to talk about it. I did well with the kids, so I was sure he didn't see me as a threat anymore. I honestly didn't want any trouble; I just wanted to be up to date.

When I got out of the shower I took out my laptop and sat on the bed naked. Who wanted me dead? That question kept running around in my head like crazy. No one had tried to kill me per se, but that's always how it ended up in the movies so I was sure it wouldn't be different now. The car incident was on purpose, and I just barely missed that. What would be next?

Pulling up some files in my computer I looked at Rico's crew. They definitely had a number on my head, and it was probably them behind the car crash incident. Out of all the people who hated me, they lost the most so it was just the logical guess. I just couldn't picture the rest of my enemies gunning for me that way. The thing that got me was they weren't normally that sloppy. I tried to get a look at the driver. But between the dark, tinted windows and having to dodge the collision, I didn't really have a clue. I knew people in the city, so that would just be a call in the morning to look at the red light tapes. Even if I couldn't see directly in the car, they would have the license plate. At least with that I could find out who owned the car. I didn't even think about getting that info at the time because I was so busy rushing to see Sheila.

This entire situation had me exhausted, so after securing the door and getting comfortable, I took my little bullet from the drawer and tested the battery to make sure there was still some juice left. Being wrapped around James was still on my mind, and I couldn't help but wonder if he was thinking about me too. I thought about calling him for a quick phone sex session. But that would just fuck up everything I worked hard for. Closing my eyes, I let my mind work wonders as I pressed the vibrating bullet to my clit.

Pretending it was James's tongue and fingers, I explored my slippery folds with my toy, pulling my knees back and pushing my legs out as far as they would go for maximum pleasure. A small puddle formed at my opening as I took the tip of the bullet and swirled it around in there before sliding it up to my firm clit. Taking a nipple into my mouth, I drove myself crazy as I fantasized about me and James.

The thoughts quickly turned to me and Jazz, and I could almost feel her soft body pressed against mine, and her mouth greedily slurping and sucking on my body. I could feel her chocolate nipples on my tongue as I kissed and fondled my body. It quickly turned into a threesome as Sheila joined us on the bed, and shit got wild. My imagination was on overload as tongues and fingertips were stuck in every possible pleasurable hole, and the buildup in my body finally erupted in a creamy volcano that created a huge puddle on the sheets under me. The tingling in my body from the tips of my nipples down to my toes caused mini spasms throughout my body, and the moan that escaped my mouth surely woke up the entire neighborhood.

I had to brush my hair from my damp forehead before rolling to my side. That shit was intense, and I was almost embarrassed because I was sure the butler heard me. I didn't really care though, and once I found the strength to pull the covers up over my shoulders, I settled down in my wet spot and went to sleep. I had a lot on my plate for the morning, and I needed to be ready to work. I could see the old Monica had to come back out, and Philly was about to get what it'd been asking for. Revenge.

Jaydah B

Picking Sides

"She's not answering the phone, Sheneka. I told you she was visiting her son today. I may have to try in the morning."

Out of all the women I'd met, of course Monica had to be the bitch who got my sister's boyfriend killed, or so they said. I mean, out of all the women in Philly she had to be the one I met and fell in love with. Can you say *irked?* I just wasn't convinced that how the streets were saying it went down was really the way it happened. Rico was the man . . . with plenty of enemies . . . anyone on the joint could have murked him. He had a price on his head, and for years had been untouchable. It was just his time when he got locked up. He got caught slipping, and I could see how. Monica was that bitch. Period. Everyone she came across probably got lost on the same spell. Even my simple ass.

I didn't think it was going to be that deep. When I met her at the demonstration it was supposed to be just a quick bang thing, but I didn't know homegirl was going to put it down the way she did. When I got to Atlanta she had me in feen mode, and I couldn't get enough. It was almost like every moment that I had free she was in me or wrapped around me, and I found myself falling head over heels for her. Shit, I would have easily picked up my stuff and made the move if she had asked me to. I wasn't sure exactly what happened, but a letter came one day and my trip was cut short. It was cool because I needed to get back on my grind anyway, but she kinda got ghost when we got here so I gave her room to breathe.

Now, when I had the conversation with Sheneka about her I didn't know that *my* Monica was the same chick who had turned her world upside down. When I got back from my trip

I checked on my sister's crazy ass to make sure she hadn't possibly committed suicide while I was gone. We weren't as close as our mother would have liked us to be, but we were at least cordial and would check in every so often. I knew that she was hurt by what happened to Rico and was hell bent on getting revenge on the person who did it. I just never put one and one together, and I didn't discuss my business with her like that for her to have done the same. I really didn't pay much attention to her ramblings during phone conversations because she just repeated the same things over and over again. It was very frustrating, and I just didn't have the energy for it.

Sheneka was in *love* with Rico, you hear me? It was like this dude could do no wrong. Never mind the fact that he had dicked down a few of her girlfriends, and had the tendency to smack her around from time to time. She was doing her thing as well, so I guessed that was the nature of their relationship. Maybe the Gucci and Chanel were enough to forget all of those little mishaps. A pure mess if you ask me, but since you're not I'll just keep it moving.

So now Sheneka wanted me to help set Monica up, but I wasn't really sure that I could. I mean, I really liked her . . . loved her even! Why would I do a crazy thing like that? I was even thinking of exploring the possibility of us being together, on her terms of course. I figured she liked me too, judging by the way she beat my pussy down when she was here a few days ago. She had a lot on her plate though, and I didn't want to crowd her with my shit when she was handling business with her son. It was only right to give her the space she needed.

"Call her again," my overly aggressive sister demanded as she paced back and forth, wearing the carpet down behind my couch. I rolled my eyes in my head as I pretended to call Monica's phone, and actually dialed the number for information. I wasn't about to be blowing this chick's phone up again because that was clearly one of the issues she had with me, and she would jet off because I was on her heels. I loved my sister and all that, but I wasn't about to let her fuck up a good thing again. Now ain't even the time to get into what happened with Nevaeh, but I learned from that lesson. I wanted to hook up with Monica again before she left, possibly to seal the deal.

That way, once she went back home I could spend more time in the "A," and we could work on us.

"Sheneka, she's not answering the phone, and it's getting late. What time do you have to be back at the program?" I asked her as I held the phone to my face. I made a mental note to talk to our mother about possibly switching Sheneka's facility to one that was more controlled. I understood that they were all grown people there, but allowing her to come and go as she pleased wasn't a good idea in her mental state. Unless she dipped out again like she did the last time. I knew they at least let her out to work, and she probably lied just to get out this evening. A damn mess if I'd ever seen one.

"In an hour," she answered as she continued to pace the floor. "What's her number? I'll just call her myself."

"You tripping if you think I'm passing off that kind of info. Just come back in the morning and I'll call her then. I have a book to finish up that I need to get to, and it's getting late," I responded as I stretched and yawned like I was tired. In reality I was a little irked that Monica was back to ignoring me, but I wouldn't spazz right now. She had until tomorrow though; then it would be on. I envisioned that she was probably sitting right there staring at the phone seeing my call come up. The smirk she probably had on her lips made my blood boil, and I had to shake my head to come up out of my daze before I snapped out. If she thought she was sneaking out on me she had another thing coming. I didn't just give me heart to anybody, and she was going to love me whether she was ready or not.

"Listen, I'll be here early—"

"Don't ring my phone before eleven—"

"I'll be here by eight," she cut me off as she gathered up her coat to bundle up in the cold weather. I could see that crazy and deranged look in her eyes that she got when she was about to go off, and tonight her ass would be 302'ed because I was not in the mood. I slipped on a jacket to walk her outside, and I noticed that the car we approached was banged up in the front.

"What happened to this car, and who does it belong to?" I asked as I inspected the damages.

"I borrowed it real quick, don't worry about it. Just go in, and I'll see you in the morning."

I decided to mind my business because you just never knew with Sheneka. She ran with some unsavory characters, and I didn't want any part of the shit. Whoever she got the car from did something dumb to it, no doubt, and her simple ass was probably caught up in it. Shaking my head, I raced back to my building, out of the cold, and into the house. Monica still hadn't called back, but it was cool. It had gotten a little late, and she was probably asleep. I would just call her in the morning.

Busting out my laptop, I worked on my story, incorporating the wild sex I had just had with Monica into my story. Just thinking about it had my walls clenching, and I knew I wouldn't get through the night without stroking one out. As I lay back on my bed, I replayed my time with her like a never-ending porn movie as I satisfied myself. I knew I would have to get back with her because as satisfying as masturbating was, I needed the real thing. Savoring the last moments, I allowed my body to release on my toy as if it were Monica's tongue, willing her to call me back the entire time. As I drifted off to sleep I wondered where Monica was staying, and how I could send her a bouquet letting her know I was thinking about her. I simply couldn't wait to have her all to myself.

I couldn't help but think of the ugly picture that my sister tried to paint of Monica, and I dismissed the thought immediately. There was no way one woman could have that much power over so many people. Somebody had to be on to her game by now, right? As I snuggled up under my covers I thought about my story line, and how I would make Monica the main character.

I was sure she would love the idea, and I couldn't wait to run it past her. After all, I wrote *New York Times* bestsellers. There was no way she wouldn't be down with that. With a smile spread across my face, I dug down a little deeper into the pillow and allowed sleep to take over. I had to be rested to deal with my crazy-ass sister come the morning, and I knew she would come with full force.

Just as I anticipated the morning came too soon, and it was exactly eight on the dot when I heard the banging on my front door. I knew it was my simple-ass sister, but it was really too early for this bullshit. I rolled over, and dug down deeper into the covers, hoping she would get the hint and come back later. Of course she didn't, and when she started hollering my name out and banging on the door like a crazy woman I knew I needed to get up before one of my neighbors called the cops. Haphazardly tossing on my robe, I made sure to tuck my toys away in my top drawer before storming into the living room to answer the door. I didn't need her all in my personal business, and I planned to make this visit quick.

"Sheneka, are you serious?" I forced out as I swung the door open and glared at my sister. I swear I didn't like being up early unless I had to be. That's why I wrote books for a living, and didn't work a nine-to-five like most people I knew.

"Oh, did I wake you up?" she nonchalantly tossed over her shoulder as she glided past me into my space, and made her crazy ass comfortable on the couch. Sighing, I closed the door and locked it, afterward grabbing my phone. I knew she wouldn't leave until I at least tried, and I promise you I just wasn't beat for the bullshit with her today.

"What time do you have to be to work, Sheneka?" I asked with all kinds of attitude in my voice. Her lunatic ass would be late today if she wasn't driving because I was not about to get dressed to drive her anywhere and she worked clear across town.

"I have time. Call up the chick."

Sighing out loud, I dialed Monica's number just for it to go straight to voice mail. My face frowned a little as I hung up and tried it again only to get the same result. It briefly popped in my head that she might have stayed the night with her kid's father, but I quickly dismissed the thought. There was no way she was giving my pussy to someone else.

"Her phone is going to voice mail, Sheneka."

"Well if you just give me her number I could check back later."

"And I already told you I wasn't doing that."

"Then get ready to keep seeing this face because I'll keep popping up until she does."

I didn't even bother to respond. Grabbing her jacket, I watched as she marched out of my condo, slamming the door extra hard behind her. Locking the door, I hurried back to the room and got in the bed, hoping I could fall right back into my sleep. Monica was starting to burn me out as well, but I wasn't about to even take it there. I dialed her phone once more and still got the voice mail, but I kept my cool. I would just catch up with her later in the day. *If Monica knows what is best for her she had better answer the phone soon. She really doesn't want me to get on my bag, and for her sake she better hope that I remain calm.* Her trip to Philly would not be a good one, if you get my drift.

James

Caught Mid Stride

I wasn't surprised that Monica called a few days later wanting to see the kids again. I kind of figured as much. I told her she could come over, and as a surprise I sent the other kids with my mom so that she could have some one-on-one time with her son. I was certain that she understood that he couldn't know the truth, but I knew she needed that time or she would never feel complete.

Her perfume arrived before she did, tickling my nose as the winter wind carried it across the driveway and wrapped it around me in a soft cloud. She looked scrumptious as always, but I kept it in check. I could easily get it poppin' with her, but we were not going there this time. *That's how we ended up in this shit in the first place.* I allowed her scent to linger around my head a little longer before attempting to shut it down. I moved my eyes from watching her hips sway back and forth, and traveled up to delectable breasts that were begging to be held and kissed. It was like she was moving in slow motion.

I hugged her when she got close enough to step into my embrace, and she felt soft like she could just melt into me. We had to stop doing this. I stepped back reluctantly to invite her into the house, and she looked like I had moved away just in time. Yeah, I would be making this a short trip because I didn't trust myself around her.

"Thanks for letting me come back," she responded while removing her coat. I didn't even bother to hang it up, instead draping it over the back of the chair because she wouldn't be here long.

"No problem. Junior is here. I sent the other kids with their grand-mom so that y'all can have some one-on-one time," I told her as I kept a good distance from her. She had a puzzled look on her face that I could clearly read. "She knows the situation involving the kids."

"Oh, okay."

Without saying a word I took to the steps with her following close behind me. Junior was taking a nap, and I decided that I would let her wake him up. I reasoned in my head that it was okay for them to form a bond, as long as it didn't interfere with the other kids, but a nagging little part of me still had doubts. When we got to the room he was knocked out with his mouth open wide, snoring softly. That boy didn't play any games when it was time to sleep.

She hesitated at the door, and I moved to the side, letting her know that it was okay for her to go in. I could see her get a little teary-eyed when she approached him, and she quickly wiped them away as she took a seat on the side of the bed. They looked so much alike it was scary, and she was probably having regrets. Hesitantly, she reached out and rubbed his back, waking him gently. He stirred a little bit, but Junior did not like to be disturbed from his sleep. I smiled a little as I watched them connect, and I knew that I had made the right decision. Giving them some privacy, I went to prepare a light lunch for all of us. I knew Junior would be hungry after his nap, and he would want to play. Monica was definitely in for a treat.

They entered the kitchen right on time as I was putting the food out on the table. I wasn't sure what Monica had planned for the day, but they entered the kitchen laughing about something, and that put me at ease. They were getting along, and I was happy about it. We chatted over soup and sandwiches, and Monica caught us up on her goings-on in Atlanta. Junior had so many questions about why they had never met her before, and I let her take the reins as I watched them interact. They even ate and chewed the same.

"I moved out of the city when you were born, but your dad always sent me pictures and videos when you were a baby," she answered honestly. I was glad she did and didn't makeup an entire story that I would have to remember later. I already had too many lies to remember and keep going as it was.

The questions came back to back, but Monica handled it all pretty well. I was hoping that he didn't bring Jasmine up, and he never did. She didn't really like him, and I didn't need Monica acting up. We made it through lunch unscathed, and ended up in the den playing *Michael Jackson: The Experience* on the Wii. I called to check on the kids throughout the day, and they arrived in time to play with us as well.

The kids were hype, and I wasn't surprised that Monica was able to keep up with the moves required to get points on the game. I even got in there a few times to show them how "Smooth Criminal" was really supposed to be done. We were having a ball, and it actually felt like family. Only this time the kids had a female figure, and didn't have to hear their mom yelling from the other side of the house to be quiet. The girls loved Monica, and were elated that she let them play in her hair. They wanted to bust out their mother's nail polish, but she told them that the next time she came they could all go to get it done professionally.

She tired the kids out, and once again got the opportunity to tuck them all in after bath time and kiss them all good night. When the last door was closed, we took a seat on the couch, exhausted from the day as well. She had her head leaned back on the sofa with her eyes closed. I smiled at the cute little makeshift hairstyle that the girls gave her, and I was so glad to see that she had a human side. Why couldn't Jazz be this chill?

"Want a glass of wine?" I offered as I got up to get myself one.

"Sure, but just half of a glass. I still need to drive home."

Nodding in understanding, I went and got us refreshments. I knew I should have sent her home right the hell now, but I wasn't exactly ready for her to go yet for some reason. I'd been surrounded by nothing but kids and family for weeks, and I needed someone on my level to relate to. When I came back with her glass, our fingers touched as she took hers, and it felt like a spark passed between us. I paused as I resisted the urge, and I sat down all the way on the other end of the couch, adjusting myself in the process. I could feel myself growing and throbbing next to my thigh and I needed to get a grip.

She took notice, but played it cool as a sly grin spread out across her face. I was uncomfortable and it showed on my face as well. We both took a sip of our wine and breathed a sigh. My wife was in the hospital in a coma, but even that thought didn't keep my dick from jumping in my pants. I moved to adjust myself and I swear I somehow ended up on the middle cushion closer to Monica. I needed to release and lie between some warm thighs, but I knew it was the wrong thing to do. Still, the body wants what it wants.

"I'm going to use the restroom," Monica said, setting her glass down on the table. There was a bathroom in the hallway, but she went upstairs. *Lord, why does she have to go near my bedroom?* Downing the rest of my drink for some liquid coverage, I crept up the stairs and checked on the kids. They were all sound asleep, but a part me was hoping that at least one of them would be up. I started to nudge Jordan awake, but it would be hell trying to get them back to sleep.

Walking past the bathroom, I was making my way to my bedroom when Monica opened the door. She had brushed her hair back down to the way it was when she first got here, and her lips looked moisturized with a fresh coat of gloss. I knew I was wrong, but I entered the bedroom anyway hoping that she would follow. She did.

No words were needed as she entered and closed the door behind her, being sure to lock it. I sat down on the edge of the bed and watched as she came out of her clothes one piece at a time. The stripper at the joint I went to was damn close to being Monica, but the real thing was out of this world. She walked . . . no, more like strutted toward me like a lioness ready to eat its prey. My entire body shook as she seemingly slinked over to me, reminiscent of a cobra ready to strike. From her cranberry-colored toes to the honey-blonde-streaked tresses that covered her shoulders, she was gorgeous. And that was putting it mildly. She was a bag of dimes all balled up into one. I licked my lips in anticipation of what was coming next.

Her body wrapped around me, and I could smell her essence when she spread her legs and straddled me. I took the liberty of spreading her lower lips and dipping my finger into her honey pot, giving it a slow stir before I brought it to my lips and sucked it clean. My eyes closed as her sweetness coated my tongue, and I felt like I had died and gone to heaven.

Lying back on the bed I rolled her off of me, and stood to come out of my clothes. My rigidness sprung free from my boxers immediately, and I ripped away at my clothes in wild abandonment, ready to dive in. First placing my wedding picture face down on the nightstand, I rolled back to get in between her thighs. Pre-cum stained the comforter as I made contact with the bed, and the pulse that flowed through my midsection had me about to lose my damn mind, but I had to taste her. I had been waiting, fantasizing, and dreaming about this moment for way too long to just let it slip away.

Monica was still nasty just like I liked her, and I loved that she was ready to go. Opening her legs even wider, she took the liberty of spreading her lips for me causing her clit to pop out. I slurped it up greedily, plunging into her tight hole with my tongue. I dug my fingers into her juicy ass cheeks, loving the firmness of it. I had been fiending for her since her last visit, and I was in too deep to stop now.

Our bodies were on fire as she pushed me out of the way, and placed her body over mine in the sixty-nine position. It felt like I'd submerged my dick in lava when her mouth covered me, and I almost coated her tonsils on contact. She placed her neatly trimmed pussy on my mouth, and I ate up like it was the *Last Supper*. It was like we were in a damn sauna it was so hot in here, and the heat radiating from our bodies had us melting together like candle wax. Damn, she had me open again, and that was never a good thing.

"Monica," I moaned out in between licks, "I'm gonna bust, baby. You have to stop."

She ignored me as her mouth and tongue worked the underside of my length down to that little space beneath my balls, her small hands massaging my sac in the process. I didn't know how long I was going to be able to hold on, but I knew I wanted to get up in her guts before I lost it.

I couldn't take it anymore, and with what felt like super-human strength I lifted her naked body up and positioned her over me in a backward riding position. She took the cue immediately and slid down on my pole, milking me with her tight walls. It was agonizingly delicious as she worked me, and I held tight to her hips just above her plump ass as I met her thrust.

Leaning up a little, I wrapped my arm around her hips and found her clit. Using the pads of my fingers, I stroked her slowly at first, building up a rhythm as it stiffened under my touch, indicating that she was about to blow. We moaned in unison as my cream began to rise to the top as well. I knew I should probably pull out, but it felt so good I just couldn't do it. In fact, I dug in deeper attempting to knock the bottom out of her pussy. It was so juicy and tight, and her warm body felt so good pressed against me that I felt a tear slide down the side of my face. I was glad it was dark in the room because I was in straight-up bitch mode.

She dug her nails into my thighs as my fingertips played a wicked song across her clit and I could feel her pulsate as her walls clinched and unclenched around me. We both went into convulsions as she bore down on me and we both shot off at the same time. That shit took the life from me, and I wondered immediately if the kids had heard us. That was confirmed when a tiny knock was heard on the door. Guilt spread across both of our faces, and as we unwrapped ourselves from around one another. I slipped into my boxers and a T-shirt to answer the door.

"Daddy, are you okay? I heard you crying," my little Janice said as she looked up at me from the door. That definitely made me feel like shit. My baby girl mistook my moans of passion for cries of sorrow. A hot damn mess.

"Yes, baby, Daddy is fine," was my response as I picked up her little body and carried her back to her bed. All of the other kids were asleep, thank God.

"Is Aunt Monica gone?" she asked as she rubbed her sleepy little eyes. This made me rethink for the hundredth time today if it was a good idea bringing her around the kids. Jasmine would have had a fit if she knew Monica was here like that around the kids. The only leg I had to stand on was that Jazz's mom thought it was a good idea also.

"Yes, she's gone."

"Will she be back to visit before she goes to Atlanta?" she quizzed in her little tiny voice.

"I think she will. She likes you and your brothers and sister."

"I like her too, Daddy."

Kissing her on the forehead, I tucked her back in, and before long she was asleep. When I crept out and closed the door Monica was standing at the front door in her coat with her car keys in her hand. Meeting her at the door I opened my mouth to say something, but she placed her finger up to my lips, silencing me. Leaning in, she kissed me once more then left. I locked the door behind her, this time not waiting to see if she pulled off. *What did I do? Again?*

Hopping in the shower, I did my best to wash her scent off of me, but my hardness betrayed me until I stroked one last one out. This shit was dead wrong, and I felt guilty as hell. Yet, I wanted some more. This was exactly how she got me in the beginning. For now on I knew I could not have her here without another adult being around, or I would be right back to where I was back in 2004.

Finally out of the shower, I laid my moist body across the bed, lost in her smell, which was still lingering in the air and on the bedding.

I had a wife.

In the hospital.

Possibly on her deathbed.

What did I do?

Rolling over, I jumped a little when the phone rang. I was going to ignore it because I thought it was Monica letting me know she had gotten home. When I looked at the screen I saw that the number was from the University of Penn Hospital.

"Hello?" I answered the phone hoping not to hear any bad news. Hell, I already felt like shit for what I did.

"Mr. Cinque, this is Nurse Samuels calling from U of P. I just wanted you to know that your wife is awake. The doctor is on his way here."

"Really? When?" I asked in astonishment.

"About an hour ago. When can you be on your way?"

"I'll be there within the hour."

Disconnecting the call, I immediately dialed up my mother-in-law to give her the news. After deciding that she would come here so that I wouldn't have to wake the kids, I got myself dressed, and waited downstairs for her arrival. Jazz's father was in the car, and he drove us over to the hospital. I was quiet the entire time. My wife was awake, and my mistress was back in town. What was I going to do?

At any rate, she was up and it was showtime. Whatever was going to happen from here on out determined the tone that our lives would be revolved around. I was scared, nervous, excited, feeling crazy . . . Like a million emotions flooded my senses all at once. There was no turning back, and no time to second-guess anything. My wife was awake. I had no idea what was coming next.

Jasmine

A Rude Awakening

Damn my head hurts.
Bad.
Like I got hit in my dome with a sledgehammer.
I started to panic at first because I didn't know where I was.
The last thing I remembered I was careening out of control on
an icy street before hitting a utility pole. I was glad that I made
it because as tight as that steering wheel was pressed against
my chest I knew I was a goner.

And the kids . . . *Oh my God! What happened to the kids?*
Did any of them get hurt or, even worse, die? I wouldn't be
able to live with myself because I knew I had no business
trying to drive and text under those conditions. Lord, I just
wanted to go back to sleep and rewind my life to the day before
all of this mess happened. *Things must be horrible because*
from the looks of things I'm in the hospital, and that can't be
good. I've probably only been out for a day or so, so I'm not
going to panic, but I need answers.

I tried to open my mouth, but an excruciating pain kept me
from doing so as I grabbed my face in reflex. My jaw appeared
to be wired shut. *Wow. Shit must be worse than I thought.*
Reaching up I felt that a patch of my hair was missing from
the side near my temple, and I almost couldn't breathe. *What*
happened? The tubes coming out of my mouth and nose, and
the swishing sound from one of the machines near my bed put
me on edge. *Did I die?*

My moving around caused an alarm to go off and I lay as
still as possible waiting for a nurse to show up. It's not like I
had that much mobility anyway considering that every inch of
my body hurt like hell, and I had a million tubes running in

and out of me. I tried to control my emotions, but by the time the nurse got to me I was in tears. *How long was I out for, and has my family been here? What's going on? Did anyone get in contact with James?* My head was spinning and I wanted it to stop.

"Mrs. Cinque, I'm glad you are awake," the nurse began as she stopped the machines from beeping and began to check my vitals. "I'll get you something to manage your pain as soon as I get all of your vital signs. You won't be able to talk due to the wiring of your jaw, but if you need to say something I can provide you with a pen and a pad. Not sure how much you will be able to write, but I'll do my best to help you."

I simply nodded as I felt her run an ink pen up the bottom of my foot, making my toes curl because I was ticklish there. The blood pressure cuff began to squeeze my arm, and the compressions on my legs began to squeeze me as well. I had so many questions, but I was so sleepy I couldn't keep my eyes open. The nurse must have given me something good because my body began to feel more relaxed, and I felt less anxious. As my eyelids got heavier I made a mental note to curse James out the first chance I got because if he wasn't out acting a fool we wouldn't even be here right now. I had a bone to pick with Mr. Cinque, but right now all I could do was sleep. . . .

Monica

Let the Games Begin

Wow. I can't believe we took it there. My trip to Philly was not to disrupt anything if I didn't have to. I came to check on my son, and things were cool with him. *Why can't I just leave? James just had to be nice to me, didn't he?* Making my way back through the city I took the time to get my thoughts together. It was definitely time for me to leave. I would see what was up with the judge, and in the meantime I would be looking for a flight out. I would just see the kids once more the day before it was time for me to go or something like that. I felt like if I didn't roll now I would miss my opportunity, and I just didn't feel safe here anymore.

I paid attention to my surroundings as I drove because I didn't know when Rico's team would strike again. It was obvious that Carlos had a hit out on me just going by the stuff that had happened thus far, and with these goons you just never knew when one of them would run up on you. I had the information for the judge to handle whenever he got better, but I was hoping to be gone before anything serious popped off. This was just too much, and sleeping with James threw my entire thought process off. That was definitely not a good thing, and I knew it, but why was my body aching to feel him inside of me again? Shaking my head back and forth in an effort to clear the naughty visions of us from my head, I gripped the steering wheel and focused on the road ahead. I just needed to make it back to the judge's house in one piece, and then I could lie down and think.

Jaydah was an entirely different issue. She called me a few times the other day when I had visited the Cinque household, but I just didn't feel like being bothered. Maybe I would call her before I pulled out as well. I mean at the airport right before takeoff.

Thinking twice about it I decided to just call her and get it over with. That way when it was time to jet out I wouldn't have to even deal with her. Peeping at the rearview for followers first, once I determined the coast was clear I dialed her number. I knew once I got back "butler security" would be on my heels. To my surprise she answered on the first ring.

"I called you days ago, Monica," she answered with a ton of attitude, not even bothering to say hello. I was still zoning and pulsating from the feeling of James being inside of me so I wasn't fazed in the least.

"I know . . . ummm . . . sorry about that. Where are you now? We need to talk."

"We sure do. I'm at home. How fast can you get here?"

"I'll be there in like fifteen."

She was saying something afterward but I had already hung up. I planned to just dip in right quick, and then I would be on my way. I needed a good night's sleep, and that wine I had back at the Cinques' had my head feeling a little fuzzy. Stepping on the gas, I zoomed across the city to get this done and over with. By the time I arrived she had the door cracked open for me to come in. I left the door cracked and didn't even bother to take a seat. It ain't like I was staying long anyway.

"So, what did you want to talk about?" I asked, really not even interested. This girl was surely a pain in my ass.

She sat down on the couch across from me after closing the door, and she looked like she was about to get into something I didn't even feel like exploring. I was so not in the mood for the nonsense this evening, so I gave her the game face right back. I was not easily intimidated, and I thought she was going to find out the hard way.

"We need to talk about us," she spat out like she meant business, and I knew instantly that I should have taken my ass to the judge's spot. Figuring I should just go end it, I let her make her point so that she could be done with it. That way I could just wrap up the situation with her as well as the mess with James and the kids, and once I left here that would be the end of it. *Philly has seen the last of me around these parts, and I just can't get out of here fast enough.*

Jaydah B

The Lion's Den

"What about us?" she replied like she was already bored. I swear I could tell that Monica was a bitch. She was wearing me out because she acted like she was a gift to all women or something. I was slowly beginning to see what my sister was talking about regarding her nonchalant attitude, and it was beginning to piss me off.

"We're going to be together so I need you to decide what we're going to do about your living situation. Am I moving to Atlanta with you, or are you coming back here to live with me?" I gave it to her straight, no chaser.

She sat there motionless for a second, just staring at me. I was confused because she was still like a mannequin almost. I looked at her, puzzled, waiting for a response. She blinked a few times like she was thinking, and then the next thing I knew she busted out laughing. I mean, homegirl was holding her gut and cracking up like she was about to pass out. That just pissed me the hell off, but I kept my cool. *Never let them see you sweat.* This entire scenario played out differently in my head for some odd reason. It definitely wasn't supposed to be going like this. She was supposed to be happy about us being together, and offer me a spot in her house for a while. We would commute back and forth until the commitment was made, and within a few months we would make it official. *What's happening right now is the exact opposite. Irked!*

"What's so funny?"

"You . . . This! We're not in a relationship, Jaydah. I mean, you're cool and all that, but this is just a fun thing. You know . . . no strings attached and all that."

Heart hurt and crushed at the same damn time. Was she telling me that we had nothing? At all? Like the time we shared in Atlanta and the love we made just days before was a "fun thing"? It didn't mean anything to her? I closed my eyes and counted to ten as I thought about my next move. Sheneka said that she was known for fucking over people's feelings. Monica didn't know who she was dealing with, and I was just the right one to show her.

I reached into my pocket, pulling the phone out a little so that I could see, and sent a simple message with two words: she's here! I had the message already typed so when I slid my thumb to unlock the screen all I had to do was hit the SEND button. That way I wouldn't have to pull the phone all the way out of my shirt pocket right in front of her. Once the message was sent I then pulled the phone all the way out, and pretended like there was something interesting going on.

My damn blood was boiling, and at this point I didn't give a damn if Sheneka and Carlos strung her simple ass up like a Christmas tree. I hated bitches like her, and I wasn't about to let her keep doing me or anyone else this way. I flipped over to my Myspace page and pretended that I was reading posts as we talked. I was just wasting time because my mind was already made up. The bitch had to go.

"Jaydah, listen, I'm sorry if I led you on in any way. I'm almost certain that I made it clear what this was. To be totally honest with you, if I didn't have to come to Philly to check on my son we probably would have never seen each other again."

My head snapped up from looking at the phone screen, and my eyes bore into her like looks could really kill. Was this chick serious? It took everything in me not to run across the room and drop kick her in the chest. She couldn't be serious. Could she? I mean, I didn't think we were head over heels in love, but I thought we at least connected in Atlanta. The way she was all up on me and sweating me all hard . . . I had to take a breather.

My sister texted me back to tell me she was on her way here with a crew and it would only take about ten minutes. I needed a damn drink in the meantime, but I didn't want her to try to leave just yet. I was busy counting backward from one hundred, trying to keep my composure. Tears were threatening to spill from my eyes, and I just wasn't having that. Not at least until I was by myself again. She was not about to see me weak and upset.

"Jaydah, I'm really sorry. It's just that this thing with my son and my having to run a business is a lot on my plate right now. Besides, you live here, and I live in Atlanta. It could get costly commuting back and forth you know."

"Would you like a drink?" I asked as I finally got up to get something. I couldn't take another minute of just staring at her, and listening to this bullshit she was trying to feed me. I really needed my sister to hurry up.

"No, I'm okay. I had a little wine earlier, and I'm already feeling a little fuzzy."

I didn't bother to respond, and simply poured myself a full glass of Moscato. I usually only did half, but I would need all of it tonight. I was itching to get at my laptop because that Monica character would be going in an entirely different direction now. I might just kill her off just because. I was so pissed I could spit nails! She just had this stupid-ass look on her face that I wanted to knock clean off, but it was cool. She was about to get what was coming to her simple ass.

There was an uncomfortable silence between us, and I couldn't help but feel like she played me. Okay, so we never actually talked about being in a relationship, and she never really said that she was interested in me. All we really had was amazing sex . . . over and over and over again. Maybe I should have given it more time to build. I was sure that if we spent a little more time together she would have been on board with my plan. *Damn, I think I just fucked up again.*

"Okay, this entire night just got kind of weird so I'm going to head out. Once again, sorry I misled you, and if you'd like I'll contact you before I head back down South."

As she was getting up to leave a knock came from the door and the knob turned. I didn't even have a chance to hide her. Before I could do anything, Sheneka and Carlos walked in along with two other people. I wanted to protect Monica, but I knew I couldn't do a damn thing. This was about to be a mess and a half, and I couldn't blame anyone but myself.

The look on Monica's face went from confusion to rage as she recognized the visitors to my house. I knew she and Sheneka had beef, but I wasn't sure I believed all of the stories that my sister told me, and how often they saw each other. I didn't know if she had ever seen Carlos at all. She looked from them, and back to me, and I could tell that she was trying to figure out her next move.

"I told you I would catch you slipping, bitch. You got my man killed; now it's your turn." Sheneka spat venom as she approached Monica. Not an ounce of fear showed in Monica's eyes though, and I wondered briefly who would win the battle.

"You set me up?" Monica asked me, but she kept her eyes trained on Sheneka and her crew. I could see her balling up her car keys in her fist with the key poking out between her fingers. She definitely wasn't going down without a fight, and that just made me love her even more.

I didn't get a word in edgewise before Sheneka charged across the room. The two women collided with such force, and before I could react they were both on the floor throwing wild blows that thudded upon connection. Sheneka was going ham, but Monica wasn't a chump, to say the least. The two women went at it, and my feet felt like they were stuck in dried cement so I couldn't even move to stop it.

In a desperate attempt to gain control, Sheneka reached up and grabbed my lamp from the end table, busting Monica in her head and face with it over and over. When a gush of blood flew from Monica's mouth, I knew I had to step in. My feet felt heavy, but I managed to get over to the women, and grab Sheneka off of her, afterward grabbing the lamp. She put up a hell of a fight, but finally let it go. Carlos pulled Sheneka up from the floor, and still had to hold her back. When I looked down, there was blood everywhere, and Monica's eyes were swollen shut. *Did she kill this bitch?* I stood there holding my breath, wondering what to do next, and suddenly Monica began to breathe.

The men who were with Carlos and Sheneka pushed me out of the way and began to bind Monica's feet and hands together with duct tape. A painful moan slipped from her bloody lips as the biggest guy scooped her up and threw her bruised body over his shoulder like a rag doll. A dark crimson circle was left on the floor where she was just lying, and I thought I might have seen a tooth in the midst of the carnage. *What have I done?*

Taking the car keys from the floor, Carlos tossed them to the smaller guy, and said something to him in Spanish that I didn't understand. I was sure he told him to get rid of the car, and the guy would probably be taking it to one of Carlos's garages. Sheneka was nursing her bruised hand and busted lip, but I didn't feel sorry for her. I just wanted them all to go.

"Good looking out, sis," she replied as she walked toward the door. Carlos didn't bother to say a word, and the ignorant bastard left the door open on his way out. After locking the door I ran to the bathroom and vomited for what felt like forever. How could I get her out of this situation before it was too late? I paced back and forth from the kitchen to the bedroom, past the blood on the floor. I was racking my brains for what felt like a lifetime when an idea hit me.

Sprinting into the bathroom, I grabbed a bucket and some peroxide, and got the blood up so that it wouldn't stain my hardwood floors. Afterward, I looked through Monica's pocketbook that was left here for a picture. I found her phone, but I didn't know who exactly I would call in it so I just tucked it away. I was hesitant at first, but I knew I was doing the right thing. As I pulled my cell phone from my pocket I dialed 911, and prepared myself for the ride that was sure to come.

"Nine-one-one emergency, how may I help you?"

"I would like to report a missing person," I spoke tearfully into the phone as my tears ran down my face and soaked the collar of my top. I needed them to act fast before it was too late. Sheneka would be mad, but I would just have to deal with that when the time came. For right now, I had to save my baby.

James

Back at Scratch

My wife was fully out of her coma. I didn't know if I was happy or sad about it, to be honest with you. Monica had my head boggled, and I was so pissed at myself for letting her get to me like that again. On the way to the hospital I found it weird that she didn't call me to let me know that she was home, but at the same time I was glad she didn't because I didn't feel like having to explain to my father-in-law why my phone was ringing this time of night and the woman on the other line wasn't a family member. I wasn't sure how much Jazz's mom had filled him in on the Monica situation, and I wasn't about to bring it up to find out. I didn't feel like being busted in my face about some bullshit again, so it was best to just let it go.

I was in a fog the entire ride, and I could not get Monica off my mind. So many thoughts were going through my head I was starting to feel sick.

When we got to the hospital, I was a mess. I was so nervous about seeing Jazz up and alert. Every time I'd been in her presence she was down for the count, and not able to talk. Her mouth was wired shut so she still wouldn't be able to say much, but I was sure that her attitude would do all of the talking if she could remember anything. Lagging behind a little, I followed her dad through the hospital and up to the intensive care unit where Jazz was being held. My palms were sweaty, and my heart was pounding in my chest. I was not ready for this, and I didn't know what to expect or how I would react.

When we got up to the room I could see the doctor attending to her. She shook her head either yes or no to whatever the doctor was asking her, and when he ran an ink pen up the bottom of her foot and her toes curled, I was suddenly relieved.

She might just be okay. I entered the room hesitantly, and when we made eye contact I busted into tears. My wife was alive. This all could have turned out so differently.

I sat in the chair next to her, and placed my head in her lap. The tears flowed like a faucet, and when her hand caressed the back of my head I completely lost it. Would my kids have been able to keep going without her? Yes, Monica was a nice distraction for them, but she wasn't their mother. I was crazy to ever think another woman could raise our kids.

I looked up into her face, and she had tears in her eyes as well. I could tell she wanted to say something, but the wire was preventing her from talking. I started to get her a pen or something to write with, but I decided that we would have plenty of time to catch up. For now, she just needed to rest, and I would take advantage of her being quiet while I had the chance.

"Jazz, I'm so glad you made it through. The kids missed you so much, and we were all hoping that you would make it out okay."

She looked at me with a puzzled look, and I knew that I had to at least fill her in on the basics. So much happened since she'd been gone, and I didn't know where to start. Did I let her know that I knew about the twin she got pregnant by? Although Monica gave me the number on her first visit I had yet to use it. I already decided that I would be calling them, but when would the time ever be right? *Do I hit her with the news that Monica is back in town? Do I inform her of Jordan's condition, because I'm sure that she would want to know that the kids are okay?* I just needed to say something to clear the air.

"You've been in a coma for about five weeks, but it was medically induced so that your brain would heal. You hit your head on the steering wheel pretty hard," I told her as I held her hand. The tears flowed from her eyes and I could tell she was shocked. I felt bad even telling her, but I knew she would want to hear it.

"You look great though, and the kids are all okay," I told her, trying to clear the air. I could see the relief on her face after hearing that.

I caught her up on the minute stuff that was going on, leaving out the incriminating details about Monica being back in the picture, and the sex we slipped up and had just hours ago. Jazz's father looked misty-eyed as well, and I just hoped that he would not tell her anything that would upset her right now. We still hadn't talked about how much he knew about Monica, but I was certain his wife gave him some details about her and why she was here. There was no doubt on my mind that once it all came down to it she would be pissed, but today we would have some peace.

I stayed up at the hospital well into the morning. Jazz's dad had left hours ago, and I didn't want to leave Jazz by herself. She was sleeping on and off, but I made sure that I didn't budge because I wanted to be there every time she woke up. The nurse gave me coffee and crackers to snack on, and that was pretty much what I survived on for the hours that I was there. All the hours in between I was in my head heavy and sleeping on and off.

I couldn't believe I slipped up and ran up in her without a condom again. What was I going to do if Monica turned up pregnant? I could check her getting rid of it off the list because she wasn't even about to do that. *Who knows? Maybe she changed over the years, and just might be up for an abortion this time around. Or if that isn't an option, at least keep it with her. The responsible thing to do would be for her to just flush it and keep moving.* I didn't even have to know all the details. As long as she wasn't bringing another child into the world at my expense we would be good.

What was I going to do about these kids? They'd already gotten a taste of Monica, especially the girls, and I knew they were going to want to know what happened to her. Kids can't even hold water without pissing the bed, so I knew they would tell their mom that she had been around. My dilemma was, *do I tell her beforehand, or do we discuss it once the cat is out of the bag? Jazz is off the chain, and I just don't feel like the bullshit that's surely going to come with it. Maybe with her mom present at the time of reasoning it will soften the blow.*

Besides, her mom thinks that Monica was just there to see her son, and that part is true. She doesn't know that I got up in her guts and it was the best thing since sliced bread. I'm chalking it up to being a freak accident, because I'm sure that wasn't her motive this time around. It was something that just . . . well, happened! Neither of us was really at fault, we just fucked up and gave into our urges. My heart was definitely heavy, and I had a lot on my plate right now. I just needed to figure out what to do next so that we could be moving along. The sooner Monica got back to Atlanta the better we would all be.

I dozed off sometime around seven in the morning, and the next time I opened my eyes I was looking at the doctor. I wondered how long he had been standing there as he made notations in Jazz's chart. I sat up, wiping the crust out of my eyes, waiting for the verdict.

"Good morning, Mr. Cinque. Glad you could make it over here last night. I'm sure your wife is happy you are here. Sorry we didn't get a chance to really discuss all of the goings-on with your wife when you first arrived."

"I'm glad she's awake."

"Well, she's pretty much right on schedule. We began weaning her off of the drugs that were keeping her asleep a few weeks ago so that she could slowly wake up with the least amount of pain. She may be out of it for a few days because of the dosage of pain medicine she will be given. Her jaw wire is scheduled to be removed by noon, and then we will take it from there. Your wife should be home within a matter of a few days."

That was a lot to take in, but I was ready for whatever came next. Jazz was gone from the kids long enough, and the sooner we got into our new routine the better off we would be. She didn't appear to have any memory issues, and knew who I was. She had yet to talk though, so that would really be the determining factor. Things were looking up for the most part, and I was ready to tackle what was to come in the future. Whatever it was, and with the help of God and family, I was ready for it.

After the doctor finished up his progress report he gave me all the ins and outs of the quick surgery that would allow

Jazz to talk again; then he was on his way. I called and gave the family the 411 on Jazz's situation, and I told Jazz's mom that I would take a cab back to the house once Jazz was out of surgery and stable. That way I could be home by the time the kids got in from school, and maybe by then Jazz would be up to seeing them. I knew they were missing her as well.

I was determined to get my life back on track, and move my family forward. I had to get Monica gone, and I had to make this work. It had to because if this didn't work I had no more options.

Jasmine

Back in the Swing
of Things, Kind Of

I lay there like I was asleep, but I heard every word that was said. The pain medicine that was being administered made me sleepy, so I was waking up for intervals, but I so had a bone to pick with him. He probably thought I was crying because I was happy to see him, but I was really just pissed that I couldn't get out of this bed and beat his ass. *He did this shit to us! Now I'm banged and bruised for no damn logical reason. Okay, maybe my texting and driving played a small part in it, but had he been on his game none of this shit would have happened. Point. Blank. Period.*

I was in a coma for five weeks. *Five weeks! Like, for real?* I breathed a sigh of relief when he told me the kids were okay, and I was happy to be alive so I wasn't going to complain. I was, however, going to knock his ass clean out the first chance I got. He thought that my brothers got with his ass back in the day. *He ain't seen nothing yet.* I would make sure of it; he would definitely pay for this.

A few times during the night I woke up briefly, and stared at James while he was sleeping. It was a restless sleep nonetheless, and I wondered what else had this man troubled besides this horrible accident. *What happened while I was lying up in this hospital all this time?* I knew James well enough to know that he was leaving shit out, and he wasn't giving me the full story on what was going on with everybody. I was certain something went down while I was asleep, and I would definitely get to the bottom of it. As for right now, I just needed to get through today so that I could get the heck out of here.

There was a lot on my mind, and I didn't even really know how to bring it up. By the time I dozed off a few times and woke back up I was being wheeled down to surgery. To be honest with you, every time James would wake up I would close my eyes real quick and pretend like I was asleep until I actually fell back to sleep. I wasn't really ready to face him just yet, even though I was so mad I could spit fire. I didn't have the capability to curse his ass out just yet, and if he said something crazy I didn't want to miss out on the opportunity to read him his damn rights. Nope, he wouldn't get off that easy, so I would just wait. Hell, I'd been out all this damn time and didn't even know it, so waiting a few more days or so wouldn't make that much difference.

I had the weirdest dream while I was in surgery, and I was certain that my blood pressure had to have been sky high. It felt like it was so real, and it had me nervous. I was still shaken when I woke up, but I played it cool like it was just from the surgery. I wasn't in recovery for long at all, and pretty soon I was back in my room. It felt like I was asleep for days, but once I heard the voices in my room I was pretty sure that it had only been a few hours. It still hurt to move my facial muscles, and I tried to be as still as possible when I opened my eyes.

Shutting them quickly, I was sure I was maybe still in a dream because there was no way I was seeing what I just saw. Yep, that good old anesthesia still had me in a zone because there was no way this was happening to me so soon. I chanced a peek out of one eye and then the other, trying to focus either way. A sheen of sweat quickly appeared all over my body. I wanted to get out of the bed and run but I couldn't move. I closed my eyes and counted to ten only to open them and still see a nightmare. My husband was conversing with the twins, one of whom was my kids father. I still didn't know which one had actually gotten me pregnant, and had successfully avoided them up until now. What were they doing here, and did James know how we were connected?

I could have gotten run over by a bus at this very moment and wouldn't have cared. This was just too damn much at one time, and Lord knows I wasn't in the mood. I closed my eyes again, and zoned in on their conversation, and sure enough the cat had been let out of the bag. James found out that the twins weren't his. That wasn't even what intrigued me the most though. *Did he just say that Monica was in town and had come by?* Yeah, I had to have been hearing things, because there was no way God would allow both of my pains in the ass to visit all at once.

I chanced a peek again, but this time James saw me and immediately ceased the conversation, walking over to my bed with a straight face. Gone were the relief and the happiness to see me alive. Although he didn't have a look of death on his handsome face, he definitely didn't look happy. I looked him in the eyes with worry on my face, for the first time happy that I couldn't talk just yet because he would undoubtedly want answers that I couldn't give right now. The twins came to the foot of the bed as well, and they all had the same semi-pissed look on their faces. I could clearly see my twins in their identical faces, and it was weird that all three men favored so much, like they could be related. *How did he get in contact with them?*

"Jasmine, I'm certain you know who these gentlemen are," James spoke in a strained voice, like he was trying to control his anger. "We have a lot to discuss, but it won't happen today. We do have each other's contact information and once the time is right we will all sit down and hash things out. Okay?"

I slightly nodded my head up and down as best I could as tears streamed down the side of my face. Things were not good, and more secrets were flying out of the closet. James bid the men farewell, and sat by me on the side of the bed. It wasn't a loving sense of comfort I felt this time around, and all of the shade I planned to throw him was retracted. *Seems like I'll be kissing ass for a while.*

I wanted to talk to my mom and dad, and I knew they would be here eventually. I was scared to stretch my jaw because it was still painful, and I wished I could go back to the day before I met Monica so that we could do things differently. I should have never agreed to that threesome. Things probably would have been way different and better between me and James now. My head hurt, and I just wanted to ball up under the covers and go to sleep.

Anna J.

Pressing the button to administer more medicine, I allowed the drugs to rock me into a fitful sleep. I was so not ready to deal with all of this, and I hoped by the time I woke up my family would be here. I would just avoid this situation with James for as long as I could, but I did have questions. Lots of them. I needed to know all the details, and, furthermore, where was Monica?

Monica

Fit to Be Tied

My head was pounding when I came to. I shook my head a few times to clear the fog only to be met by an overwhelming smell of piss. I was lying on my side on something kind of soft like a mattress, and my mouth was covered. My hands and legs were also bound tight, and I could barely move. I saw enough movies in my time to know that this wasn't a good thing. The room was pitch black, and the only sound I could hear were the muffled voices coming from the next room. There were no windows in the room I was in, so I assumed they took me to some location where my body would probably never be found. Laying my head back down on the surface I was lying on, I could only breathe and think. I knew one day it would come to this. Well, maybe not this exactly, but I had done so much dirt to people over the years that it was bound to come back to me eventually.

Jaydah definitely had me fooled! Out of all the people in line to get payback, I never thought that she would be the one smart enough to set me up. It's a small world, and you'd be surprised how many people know each other. *She and Sheneka know each other? Wow, I would have never put that together in a million years.* Shit, they were both crazy as hell, and they always say birds of a feather flock together.

I was trying to ear hustle on the conversation, but I couldn't really make out anything they were saying. I just knew that this might be the last of me that Philly, or anyone for that matter, may see. I wished I had done so many things differently in my life. At the same time so much horrible shit happened to me that revenge and payback was all I really knew. It started with my uncle molesting me when I was young, and from the

time I tried to kill his ass up to now I had always been in survival mode. Shit, if family doesn't give a damn about you, you
can't expect anyone else to. My mother taught me that early on.

Out of all of the horrible things that happened in my life I
couldn't really say that I regretted everything. I managed to
open up a refuge for young girls who had been molested just
like I was at their age. I remembered feeling like there was no
one in the world who could understand the pain I was going
through at home, and I had nowhere to turn. At least I made
a way to give back to the community and help people. I also
got to live out my dream by opening my art gallery. I spent so
many nights up painting my pain away, and the pieces that I
created and sold helped to fund the Safe Haven that these girls
called home. That definitely made me feel good on the inside.
These young ladies went from battered and bruised victims of
abuse to college students, and other forms of furthering their
education. Of course there were a few who got away, and we
couldn't undo the damage, but the good outweighed the bad
and the refuge helped.

When it came to my little sister, I did all I could do to help
her. I figured taking her out of Philly would help, but there
were drugs and dealers everywhere, and the girl had a habit
she couldn't control. My mom always told me to look out for
my siblings, but there wasn't much I could do for someone
who wasn't ready for help. All I could do was be there when
she needed me, and ready to go when she was willing to get
help. I knew once I was dead she would be gone soon after.
The money that she would inherit from me would no doubt be
used to support her habit until she overdosed. It was a crazy
demise, but that was probably how it would all go down if I
knew Yolanda like I thought I did.

I got to see my son. The thought brought a huge smile to
my face and tears to my eyes. After all of these years I never
thought I would step back into Philly for anything. Coming
back here put me in the situation I was in now, but I accom-
plished what I came for, and I was okay with that. At least he
got to see me face to face, even though it was a lie how we were
introduced. He would forever think I was his aunt, but I felt
great knowing he was in good hands. The Cinques were good

people, and I was glad that my son would be okay. Maybe they would tell him all about me one day.

As the tears flowed I thought about James. I regretted sleeping with him, but I wished I could do it again once more before these goons killed me. He was so gentle with me, and I briefly wondered how life would have been if I were his wife instead of Jasmine. I would have made sure he never looked outside of the marriage for sex and support. That's what they were lacking, and that's how I was able to get in. That's not to say that he wouldn't have done the same thing to me, because men are never satisfied.

I had been nothing but a huge burden for the Cinque's since I came on the scene, and it was all just pure selfishness. I could have just had the threesome and kept it moving, but I had to be greedy and mess up a good thing. I probably could have kept getting it if I had played my cards right. It was like I fucked up everything and everyone I came in contact with. Maybe it was better that I did go now. My son didn't need me coming back messing up what he had, and no one else really needed me around for that matter. The Safe Haven and my art gallery were left to a trusted business partner, so everything would be run as planned. I was at peace with leaving this earth knowing that.

Closing my eyes, I lay there and listened to the incessant muffled conversation on the other side of the door, wishing that they would just come and get it over with. Would they torture me or would it be over before I knew it with a quick shot to the head? All of this was because they thought I got Rico killed. I could tell them until I was blue in the face that I didn't have anything to do with it, but I learned a long time ago that when a person's mind is made up there was no changing it. I wasn't even about to waste my time or breath trying to convince them otherwise.

It felt like I was still clothed, and my body didn't feel sore in any other places but my head, so at least they hadn't raped me. Hell, I probably deserved it after all the shit I'd done. Sheneka looked crazy and deranged when we got into that fight, and I remember the day I met her up at the prison when the guard was giving me a hard way to go. I didn't know that I was there seeing her man at the time, and she even helped me mess up the guard's car afterward. It just goes to show you never know people. Not that I knew her like that before, but came to find out she was more of a lunatic than I was.

The sound of footsteps nearing the door snapped me out of my trip down memory lane. I wished I could wipe my tears from my face before they came into the room, because although I was scared to death, I didn't want these fools to think they had me that easily. This was some fucked-up shit, but everybody had to go somehow, and this was the way it was written for me.

The door opened up and it took a moment for my eyes to adjust to the light that was streaming in from the space behind them. I couldn't make out any faces in the semi-dark room, so they just looked like big black shadows looming in the doorway. I was holding my breath, trying to pretend like I was still out. I didn't know what to expect, and I wanted whatever was going to happen to be done quick so that I could meet my Maker. Wasn't any use in dragging out the inevitable, right? Closing my eyes tight I started to pray in a low whisper, and that was my plan for up until they shut my lights out.

I heard the footsteps of one of them come closer, and my body tensed up as I forced myself to keep my eyes closed and to stay in prayer. I asked God over and over again—in my mind, because I didn't want them to see my lips moving—to forgive me of my sins. My heart was pounding in my chest so hard that I thought a heart attack would take me out before they could. This was some bullshit, and I just couldn't believe I got caught slipping like this.

"Is she still out?" asked the guy who sounded farthest away. My palms became sweaty instantly, and my head pounded harder than before.

"I don't know, she's not moving still," another answered as he gripped me by my hair and pulled me up on the bed. I wanted to scream, but I managed somehow to stay quiet with a limp body. I knew there was a possibility that they were going to beat the shit out of me, or at least Sheneka would. They were definitely going to let her get her shit off since she had waited so many years for revenge.

"Well, it's time for that bitch to wake up then. Flip the switch and bring a chair in here. We need to get this done and over with." The guy near the door barked out orders. I heard several pairs of feet shuffling to fulfill the command, and when he tossed me back to the bed I blinked my eyes and pretended like I was just waking up. The light was definitely blinding, and my face ached from the earlier attack from Sheneka, but I still played it cool.

I was dead weight as my body was hoisted roughly from the bed and up to a sitting position in a hard chair. My head rocked back on my neck as I performed like I was really out of it. A painful moan escaped my lips as they cut the bind from my hands and secured them roughly with rope to the back of the chair, afterward doing the same to my legs on the sides.

"You sure your sister won't say anything?" I heard one of the men ask.

"If she does we'll just get her ass next. Both them bitches can go as far as I'm concerned."

Just as I was preparing to open my eyes, a hard slap jarred my eyes open, making blood gush from the side of my mouth. A scream rang out only to be quieted by a slap from the other side. I was seeing stars as a blow to my chest knocked the wind out of me, and vomit rushed up my throat, splattering all over my legs and on the floor. I could feel my eyes start to swell as blows rained down on me, and I could no longer hold in the screams. Just as quickly as it began it was over, and I cried as bloody saliva dripped from my busted lips. I wanted God to take me now, but it wasn't going down like that. I would have to suffer this one out until they were ready to take me out of my misery.

"You had my man killed, bitch," I heard Sheneka say close to my ear as she circled my chair. I kept the prayer going in my mind because trying to reason with Sheneka at this point would be useless.

"I knew you would slip up and come back here eventually. When Carlos got the call from Yolanda that you were touching down here I didn't believe that your very own sister was still that scandalous after all these years. I thought she was pulling my leg up until I saw you at the airport. I knew I wasn't letting you leave without an ass whipping. This is for Rico."

Anna J.

The punch that landed on my forehead was so hard it knocked the chair backward, sending me crashing to the ground. It wasn't lost on me that she said my sister set me up. Now it all made sense. No one in Philly knew I was coming here; that's why it was so weird that I was being followed after only being here for a few days. I was hurt, but I wasn't surprised. This wasn't the first time Yolanda put me in harm's way, but I vowed that if I didn't die out here and I made it back home she would definitely get what was coming to her. Keeping up with the prayer, I did my best to brace myself as Sheneka kicked and pounded on my body. I could feel myself losing consciousness and I hoped that the next time I opened my eyes I would be out of this world and on my way. I had no regrets at this point and was ready to go.

"Cancel this bitch," I heard Sheneka say as she got one last kick in before leaving the room. Her crying could be heard from the hall, and it rocked me to sleep like a lullaby as I slipped away. I felt my body being scooped from the floor as they lifted the chair up, and just as they were cutting me out of the binds and picking my bloodied and battered body up I surrendered to my will.

I was hoping to be out completely by the time we got to wherever they were taking me, and by the time they slammed my body into the trunk of a car and pulled off I just prayed that this was the end of it and I could just go. I had already made my peace with God, so there was nothing left to do but get in line and head toward the Pearly Gates.

Jaydah

Second Thoughts,
Last Regrets

What the fuck did I do? I was pacing the floor as the cops questioned me about Monica's whereabouts, and I felt like shit about what I was getting ready to do. I couldn't let them do my baby like this, and if they acted fast maybe they could catch them before too much damage was done.

"So you're saying that she got into a fight with your sister outside, and some men came and snatched her. Do you know who the men where?" the detective asked, looking at me skeptically. It dawned on me that they might take me down with the rest of them, but I didn't touch her and was at least trying to help her. Maybe that would work in my favor.

"Yes, well only one of the men. His name was Carlos. He runs an auto body shop in the city, and I can give you the address. My sister's name is Sheneka, and she's certifiably crazy. I really hope you act fast because I think they are going to kill her," I responded as I pulled out a pen and pad to write down all of the information I had on both of them. I could feel myself hyperventilating and feeling lightheaded, and I had to take a seat before I hit the floor.

"Ma'am, are you okay?" one of the officers asked.

"Yes, here is the information. Please hurry," I said to them as tears stained my face. *I fucked up royally this time, and I don't know what I will do if they killed Monica. I wouldn't be able to live with myself.*

They took down my contact information as well, and after they left I collapsed on the couch in a heap of tears. Monica was going to die if something wasn't done, and I just couldn't stand by and let it happen. Hopping up from the couch, I grabbed my wallet along with Monica's belongings. I had to get over there and try to stop them. Once I got to my car I called my sister's phone, only for it to ring out to the voice mail. Deciding against leaving her a message, I started my car and typed into the GPS the address I obtained to the auto shop. It was only about a half hour away, from what the screen read, and I figured maybe if I took the back roads I could shave off some minutes.

Once on the road, I called my sister's phone a few more times, and decided I would keep calling until she answered. I was getting angrier as the minutes passed, and I was losing hope. What if I was too late? What if they had already gotten rid of her? I called my sister at least fifty times before she answered and I was pissed. *They better not hurt Monica too bad, or it will be on.*

"Why are you blowing up my damn phone?" Sheneka answered in an angry voice laced with tears. She was still hung up on this Rico shit after all these years, and it irked me that she never got past it at least a little bit.

"Did you hurt her, Sheneka? Tell me she's okay," I pleaded into the phone as I rushed through the streets.

"That bitch is canceled, and if you keep up with the dumb shit you will be next. Don't call my phone no more!"

"Sheneka, wait," I screamed into the phone. I was met by dead air, and when I looked at my phone the call was dismissed. I was so super irked, and couldn't stop crying.

As I pulled up to a stop sign I noticed Carlos and his boys riding past in the opposite direction. After they got past me I made a U-turn and quickly followed them. Reaching for my phone again, I called the cops. They needed to come now.

"You've reached nine-one-one emergency. How may I assist you?"

"There is a body in the trunk of the car I am following. I need someone to come now!" I yelled into the phone, hoping that would get someone to come out quickly. I didn't know where they had Monica at, but at least if they pulled the car over and searched it or something, they may get arrested and tied into Monica's missing person's case.

"Ma'am, how do you know that? Did you see them put the body in there?" the officer questioned. I was getting pissed that there wasn't a squad chasing us down by now. Every minute that went by was wasted time on saving Monica.

"Yes! The license plate number on the car is C-B-O-4-Z! Please hurry!"

I stayed close behind as I waited for the cops to show up after giving them my location on the block that we were driving down, and we went for about a good six blocks before I started to hear sirens from police cars. A part of me hoped Monica was in the trunk so that she could be saved. I was so stupid for setting her up, and once again acting on my emotions. At the next light the cops began to swarm in, and I slowed my car down a little to lag behind. When the cops pulled them over I parked my car a few spaces back to see what would happen.

They were first ordered out of the car, and were lined up against the wall as the car was searched. I was starting to lose hope, and was hoping they would open the trunk up to be sure. The cops began to search the vehicle, and discovered several guns in the back seat. There were at least five of them, and they probably used them to kill Monica if she was already dead. I wanted to scream out the window for them to pop the damn trunk already, but before I could say a word the lid of the trunk went up and a few of the cops rushed over to it. Before I knew it I was out the car and over there too.

"Ma'am, you have to step back." One of the officers grabbed at me. I was still trying to push through to see the inside of the trunk, but the cops had me gripped tight.

When the cops dispersed there was nothing but guns inside of the car. There was no body in the trunk like I had hoped. Just more guns and a suitcase that had yet to be opened. Where was Monica's body, and where was my sister?

"What did y'all do with her? Where is she?" I screamed as I cried and collapsed into the officer who was holding me up.

"Ma'am, you need to calm down."

"These guys killed my friend. Where is the body?" I was feeling delirious, like I was going to faint. It was too late, and there was nothing I could do about it.

Anna J.

I heard one of the cops calling for an ambulance, but all I could do was ball up in a fetal position on the ground and cry. It was too late. My baby was gone, and it was all my fault! All I remembered was the EMT scooping me from the ground as I watched the officers handcuff Carlos and his crew. I couldn't let it end like this. I had to find out what happened to her. As I was stretched out and checked out in the ambulance I began to formulate another plan. I had to make sure that they stayed in jail until I at least figured out where the body could be. They wouldn't get away with this, and for Monica I had to find out what went down.

Jasmine

Home Sweet Home Going

I was pretty quiet for the days remaining after I came out of surgery to have my jaw wire removed. James ran it all down on how he found out that the kids weren't his because Jordan needed a blood transfusion for his injuries from the car accident. When they ran his blood for a match it came about that he wasn't the dad, and wasn't even the same blood type to be able to donate. I felt like shit when he revealed that information to me. A lot of stuff happened in our past, but that type of secret was unforgivable. I couldn't blame him for being upset, and I allowed him to get his feelings off his chest without interruption. He deserved at least that much.

I was shocked when he told me that my mom knew everything. I mean everything! She was there when the doctor revealed that the kids weren't his, and he even told her Monica's role in all of it. They both knew about the twins, and came to find out my dad was the one who called the twins up to the hospital to talk to James. They had been trying to be included in the kids' lives for years, but I never allowed it. James didn't know that when we moved from our old house I was not only running from Monica, but from them as well. I didn't need them just popping up one random day, especially considering I cheated right in our very bed that James and I shared every night. Everything was a mess, and I deserved whatever happened to us and this marriage.

None of that took away from the fact that the accident happened, and because he wasn't holding up his end of the responsibilities I had to come out of work that day and almost killed all of us. Just thinking about it pissed me off, but I knew arguing the point was pointless. *The main thing is both me and the kids made it through, and hopefully we can pick up the pieces and move on with our lives.*

I was released a few days later from the hospital in a whole lot of pain. It felt like every inch of my body was falling apart, but I was alive at the end of the day, and that was all that mattered. I got a prescription for some painkillers, and was also set up with appointments to manage my back pain because I had developed herniated disks from the accident, and it was hard for me to bend. I would be in therapy a few days a week to get my body back in working order.

On the day that I arrived home I was surprised with a welcome home party. People from my and James's jobs, as well as family and a few friends were there to greet me. I stayed downstairs with them for a while, but the level of pain that I was experiencing made me turn in early, and once James was done with assisting me up the steps and helping me get ready for bed he went back down to the party. I was out quickly, and didn't even realize James was in the room until a sharp pain woke me up. I tapped James, and he jumped up immediately to help me. I wanted to smile but it hurt too bad. Even after all of the mess that had come out and gone on, he still loved me enough to take care of me.

It didn't take long for me to start slowly moving around the house by myself, and I had to tell James to let me be sometimes so that I could do things myself. We had yet to talk, but I knew we had to clear the air. Things were different around the house. I could still feel the tension between us. When, during dinner one night, the kids asked him when their Aunt Monica was coming back to visit, I was surprisingly able to keep my cool. She was here to see her son I was sure. We did just up and move out of the blue, and she had no way to contact us. I wasn't sure what she did to find us, but any mother who loved her child would have gone through the same measures that she did. It was just sad that I didn't get a chance to talk to her about her son, and I wondered how much she knew.

Junior got on my nerves, but lately he seemed like a different child. He was a lot calmer, and got along better with the kids. James even said that the people at his afterschool program said that he was doing a lot better. I was happy to hear that, and I knew my behavior toward him had to change. That was probably the biggest part of the reason why he was acting the way he was in the first place.

"So, the twins want visitation rights. I think it's only right. They are willing to be in the kids' lives under the guise that they are their uncles so as not to mess up the flow of how we have things going. Monica did the same thing when I introduced her to the kids, and I think it's the best thing for everyone," James said to me before bed about a week after I got home.

"I don't have a problem with that. What's up with Monica anyway? Why hasn't she been back?"

"I'm not sure. Her phone has been going straight to voice mail for the last week or so. Maybe she lost the phone, or got caught up in something. I don't think she will just go back home without at least seeing her son one more time. She'll pop up. I'm sure of it."

I didn't say anything more about the twins or Monica, and decided to cuddle up with my husband and enjoy right now. We had so much damage to get through and undo, and work through. Years and years of damage and dumb shit that almost crumbled us. I would have never thought that years down the line this was where we would be. *I'm just glad that we are at a point where we are willing to make it work.*

As I snaked my arm around his back in the bed, my hand got caught a little between the headboard and the mattress. I felt something silky on my fingertips, and yanked at it to see what it was. The looks on both of our faces were of pure shock as I revealed a hot pink thong with a gold "M" monogram sewn into the top part of the thong right where it would sit at the top of her ass if she had them on.

"What the fuck is this? James, was Monica in my room?"

"Babe, let me explain . . ."

I didn't know where I got the energy from, but before I knew it I was up out of the bed and pounding on his chest. This bitch was still causing havoc in my household, and James's simple ass had fallen for her again. He got me back down on the bed, and was trying to restrain me without reinjuring me, and all I saw was red through the tears. I knew I hated her for a reason, and I was so pissed that she was able to sneak back in again. I couldn't do this with her, and she had to go. She could never show her face around here again.

"Jasmine, it's not what you think. She came up here to use the bathroom while she was here with the kids. Your mom was here with us, and so were the kids. She must have snuck them in here then. Baby, I love you. You have to believe me."

The look on his face was one of desperation, and I wanted to believe him so bad. He held me in his arms and we just cried. Every time we thought we had gotten away, Monica found a way to throw a monkey wrench in the program. I knew we had to stay strong, and we had to keep moving forward.

Turning the television up a little louder so that the kids wouldn't hear us, we both were silenced by what flashed across the screen. A split screen with pictures of Monica, one with a made-up face and one of her badly beaten, was shown before the newscaster started her story.

"Early this morning, the woman that was just shown was found badly beaten and raped in Fairmount Park along the joggers' trail. A female jogger saw her crawling from the side of the hill near Lemon Hill, barely able to move her left side. She was naked from the waist down and there was blood everywhere. It is said that when she got to the hospital she could not tell the cops who beat her, and that she was from out of town visiting a family friend.

"It wasn't until this woman, famous erotica writer Jaydah B from right here in Philadelphia, came up to the hospital and identified the guys to the police. Apparently, just over a week ago, the very men she identified were pulled over for supposedly having a body in their trunk, but the cops only found guns and drugs. What was even more interesting is the writer's sister was involved with the beating as well, and all of them are in custody of the police and are being charged with rape and attempted murder. More of the story to come after this commercial break. . . ."

Both James and I were sitting with our mouths wide open. *What the hell is going on in the world?* No wonder James hadn't heard from her in over a week, and she was lucky even to be alive after all this time. I felt horrible about what happened to her, and I wondered how I could find out what hospital she was in. *She must have fucked up someone else's life for that to have happened to her, but damn. Was it that serious?* They flashed the photos of the guys who beat and raped Monica, and of the girl who set her up. This was some crazy shit, and I knew at that moment that we had to get our household and our lives right for these kids. We weren't perfect, but we were all they had. When they say what goes around comes around, it definitely does. Karma is a bitch who isn't playing any games. I was content with not running into her anytime soon.

Later that night after we checked on the kids, James and I decided that we had to make this work. We had a lot of pain and secrets in our lives, but we had to start living for today. We were starting from scratch. As I lay in his arms and inhaled his scent I knew this was where I belonged and there was no looking back. We would get things straight to find out which twin fathered our twins, and we would deal with Monica when the time came. All of this was scary for both of us, but we had to make it work. We just had to.

Monica

On a Wing and a Prayer

Raped and beaten to damn near nothing. Is this what my life is going to be like from here on out? It's like, I know I've done some shit, but why couldn't I have just died? Why did God allow me to live through all of that, and what was I supposed to do now? I wanted to get out of here on the first thing smoking back to the ATL. I had plans to see my son once more before I went, but I just needed to get gone. Philly was not the place for me.

I really thought my time was up though. Those guys raped me for what felt like hours, and the beatings that took place in between were unbearable. My eyes were swollen up to mere slits, and I was missing at least ten teeth. There were patches ripped out of my hair, and everything was so sore. I had cracked ribs, and my clavicle bone was fractured on the left side. Both of my arms were broken, and several of my fingers. My wrist was fractured on my left hand, and my right ankle was sprained something horrible. The doctor said that I was lucky to even have been able to crawl out of the space I was in and up the hill with all of the broken bones I had. I was surprised at the amount of damage as well.

What I did know was that I didn't want to spend any more time here than I had to, and I didn't even get into who did what when the cops came. I told them I was kidnapped and didn't know who did it. Jaydah was the one who ran everything down to the cops, and luckily the guys were already in custody from being caught up earlier in the week. Sheneka was found in a crack house out of her mind, and on the brink of overdosing. Everything was a mess, and I was just glad that they would be served.

I denied all visits to Jaydah, and when she came up here the nurse had to call hospital security to have her escorted out because she went off in the hallway. As far as I was concerned we didn't have anything to talk about. I was grateful that she told the cops what happened, and even more glad that she turned in my pocketbook with all of my stuff in it, but I still didn't have any rap for that simple bitch. She was just as crazy as her sister, and I could do without the drama.

My sister would be cut off as well. The nurse was kind enough to charge my phone for me once I was able to talk, and she even put my earpiece in so that I could make calls. I loved that all I had to do was say a name, and my phone would call it without me having to dial. I spoke with the judge first, and he was hysterical on the phone.

"Why didn't you stay in the house, Monica? They could have killed you! What hospital are you in? I'll have security outside of the door twenty-four/seven. Are you trying to give me another heart attack? What the fuck where you thinking?"

I let him ramble on for a while before cutting him off to give him the information he needed. He was coming up here regardless of the bed rest restriction that he was on. There was no use in trying to stop him. Once he made up his mind there was no changing it. I called the Cinques next, and spoke with James. I wasn't ready to talk with Jasmine yet, and I simply thanked him for the opportunity to meet my son, and I apologized for everything else. I had their address, so I informed him that I would resume the payments as scheduled, and that I would only keep in contact when he reached out to me. I knew that he and Jazz were probably trying to pick up the pieces and put their lives back together, and I didn't want to be a distraction. He offered to escort me to the airport when I was ready to go, but I declined. The judge had me covered.

As I settled into my bed and got as comfortable as I could, I thought about the direction my life was going in, and I knew that it was time for a change. I needed to settle down, and maybe find someone of my own. I thought I was on my way out of here, but since I was given another chance at life I decided to do things right. No more messing with other people's wives or husbands. No more blackmail and conniving situations, and no more holding grudges and lying. I wasn't getting any younger, and it was time for me to start living my life . . . whatever that was.

The doctor told me that I would be here for a while, and he wouldn't recommend me flying back home right away. I decided that I would stay at a hotel even though I was certain the judge would insist that I stay with him. I just wanted to be by myself so that I could put my life in order. A new Monica was emerging, and it was better late than never. My new life was starting now, and as soon as I could I would start by clearing out my phone of numbers that I wouldn't need anymore, and my sister was at the top of the list. She was poison, and I just couldn't do it with her anymore.

I also decided that I needed to move, and I would contact my Realtor in the morning to start looking. I didn't want anyone I didn't want in my life anymore to know where I was. It was time for a new beginning, and I was taking my life back. *Maybe I'll move out of Atlanta, and go to Cali. I always wanted to live among the stars.* The more I thought about it the more I loved the idea. Smiling, I imagined my new life, and the new potential businesses that I could open up out there. Oh, yeah, I was ready to go. *Good-bye, Philly and Atlanta . . . Hollywood, here I come!*

James

Getting Back to the Basics

I was surprised to hear from Monica. Those dudes really did a number on her, and it was the running top story for about a week on the news. Jazz and I still couldn't believe that she got handled like that. *I hope that never happens to any of us, and I hope Monica has learned whatever lesson she was intended to learn from this.* I offered to escort her to the airport when she was ready, but she said that she was cool. She just wanted to let me know that she was okay, and that she would call soon.

As for my family, Jazz and I are in marriage counseling. It was for the best. Although we tried to move past our issues, there were too many to try to push to the side. We had a lot on our plates, but we loved each other and we wanted to make it work. Therapy was hard, but it was necessary if we ever wanted to get over that hump and live life happily. The kids deserved that much.

As I sat in the sunroom and watched the snow fall I took in everything that had gone on in my life for the last few years. The kids were out back building snowmen, and making snow angles. A cute little snowball fight took place, and all of the kids were in their element and getting along. This was how it was supposed to be. I peeked over at my wife curled up on the chaise enjoying a novel as we both took periodic sips of hot chocolate from our mugs. This was what life was really about: meeting your soul mate and building a family, growing old together, and instilling family values in your kids so that they could pass it along to theirs. These were the moments that made it all worthwhile.

Sometimes we think what we have at home isn't enough when in reality it's exactly what we need. It's crazy that it oftentimes takes a tragedy for us to see it. Getting up from my spot, I went out and joined the kids in a quick snowball fight before running back in the house to start dinner, since Jazz still couldn't really stand that long to maneuver around the kitchen without being in a lot of pain. I whipped up their favorite meal: spaghetti.

I called out for Jazz to have the kids get ready for dinner, and they all showed up just as I was putting out the place settings. Once we were all seated we joined hands, and it was Jalil's turn tonight to pray over the food. I smiled as I looked around at my family, and it saddened me that all of this was almost destroyed. Giving Jazz a wink, I began to serve the kids as they all told us about their day in school. I loved my life, and now that I had another chance at making it right I was determined that it was going to work. *I wouldn't give up this moment for anything in the world.*

Jaydah B

Not That Easily Broken

How pissed was I that this bitch had the nerve to deny my visits after I helped her? I mean, for real? I loved her. Didn't she know that? I didn't even get the chance to apologize to her for what I did, and I was just so happy that she made it out alive. I was going through it, not knowing where she was at or if she had even survived the ordeal. Sheneka and I got into the biggest falling out behind this, and then she fell off the face of the earth. I didn't know what happened to her until the cops had informed me that she almost died in a drug house, and one of the fiends was kind enough to alert the authorities to come get her because she was crashing everyone's high. A damn mess.

Monica hasn't seen the last of me though. I still had her address, and since she wouldn't talk to me here, I would just wait for her to go back home. I was already looking into hotels and airfare so that I could get down there. The nurse wouldn't give me any information on her, but the cute little receptionist kindly informed me that Monica had been discharged when I called the hospital two weeks later. Monica loved me, she just didn't know it yet.

Once my travel arrangements were made I curled up on the couch with my laptop, eager to start my next novel. Monica would be the star, and I had a scandalous story that I was ready to tell.

As my fingers flew across the keys I knew this one would be a bestseller, and I may even write a sequel to it. Either way, once I moved to Atlanta with my baby everything would be all good. *While she's painting her pictures I'll be writing my novels, and we will be like a power couple or something. My*

books will eventually be movies, and maybe we could even-
tually move to Hollywood to set that into motion. I smiled at
how bright my future was looking, and I couldn't wait to share
the great news with Monica. Time waited for no one, and like
it's been said in the past . . . don't put off tomorrow what can
be done today. Let the games begin!